PHASE OUT

"The Liar's Moon"

By

D. J. Wallace

Phase Out – The Liar's Moon"

Copyright © 2013 by Douglas Wallace

Printed in the United States of America
ISBN – 13: 978-0615929545 (Fabfables Publishing)
ISBN – 10: 0615929540

Acknowledgements

"For Kitty and Shawnee"

"Three things cannot be long hidden, the sun, the moon, and the truth."

The Buddha

PROLOGUE

Forty-seven years into the new millennium, the U.S. Government had been downsized to a tenth of what it was at the turn of the century. No program had been spared and most had been cut to levels lower than memory could recall. Even the defense budget, once the largest in the history of the world, had been reduced to a point of operational absurdity. The military, as it was known, was no more. Private Armies financed by large corporations had come to be the keepers of the flame, an incendiary and avaricious Force that had spread across the globe to become the custodian of perpetual war. But the might of arms was no longer limited to the terra firma of earth, but had extended its dark prowess beyond all boundaries and was now threatening to destroy other worlds. A war was currently being fought on lunar terrain, a conflict, as it was called, between Namacal, a powerful mining conglomerate and weapons manufacturer, and Amerex, a Globo-Tech-Corporation heavily invested in power and defense systems. The conflict, which had been underway for more than a year, was over the disputed lunar mining rights, which Namacal claimed and controlled, to the recently discovered and most powerful fuel of the future, HELIUM 3. As a result of massive global misuse and illicit profiteering, nearly all of the earth's fossil fuels had been depleted, and Helium 3 now represented the world's greatest new resource for energy. Whoever controlled Helium 3 controlled the future of the world.

CHAPTER ONE

The night had no known names, and the moon, as myth had often suggested, spoke only in crescent whispers. There was mystery in its undulating silence and intrigue in everything that it shed its light upon. It had been a sweltering summer day in Tilapia Springs, but the evening, though still infernally humid, was welcoming the cool light of the moon like a lover. Tilapia Springs was a "play your morals loose" town on the Gulf Coast of Southern Florida, a place that had once been known only to fishermen, dreamers, drunkards, pocket whores, and small time drug dealers. But at the turn of the new century when the Military arrived, the old school atmosphere changed from that of a good ole boy, roll your own enclave to one of a high grind strip of bars and clip joints. The town retained some of its original salty dog charm, in that it still had its Marina and a handful of old time hang outs, but most of what were once its mom and pop shops with their homey nautical themes had long ago been replaced by the shimmering neon glaze of a new world order. The Chamber of Commerce knew well whom they were appealing to when they opened their arms to the new investors and opportunists. And the biggest and most opportunistic investor of them all was the Namacal Corporation.

The Namacal Military Training Facility was less than a mile out of town, and the city fathers would have been remiss not to cater to their every whim. Tax revenue had quadrupled in recent years, not to mention the kick back funds that had flooded their coffers in surplus. Namacal was a Global Energy Conglomerate and Weapons Manufacturer who were, militarily speaking, as powerful as any government the world had ever known. Their armies numbered in the millions and they had facilities in every country around the globe. The Tilapia Springs Division housed over two thousand troops on any given day, and at night, any number of those young warriors would descend upon the town hungry for pleasure. With so many inexperienced and developing minds wielding new money anxious to be spent, the town also attracted its share of shysters, whores and sharks of every ilk. This was a city where Sunday had once been reserved for Jesus, and the Bible belt had been a tight fit around the town's beer bloated waist. But now there was only one church left, and it was mostly just a refuge for bad drunks in need of repentance and shot of hair of the dog. The Sabbath was no longer a holy day, but a party day where salvation was played out in terms of fast cash and quick scores. For the shrewd and the slight of hand, the pickings were there for the taking.

The Gambling dens were full of gifted players, who had moved in to take advantage of the feeding frenzy, and it wasn't always easy to tell who was who until the damage had been done and the cash was gone. At a glance, Benjamin Denning could fit into either category, giver or taker, but he worked hard not to be categorized. He was young, and didn't look that different from the soldiers he played cards with, but he was nobody's grunt. The military had zero appeal to him, and in spite of all the hype about being the best that you could be, his position was simple – the armed forces were spirit robbers who created a sense of false bravado, and ultimately reduced a man to the lowest denominator, not the highest. Even before the Army was privatized, he found it impossible to imagine himself as a soldier, but being exposed to so many of these young men in recent days, his cynicism had softened, and he had come to sympathize with them. The levels of propaganda they were subjected to were heavy, and the majority of these boys were clueless about the wry machinations of the world, and just wanted a place to be. Ben understood that need all to well because growing up with heavy drinking, errant parents, he felt that he had never had a real home. But it wasn't only the army that he had a distaste for, he hated organized groups of all make and measure. A joiner he wasn't. Even when he had played sports in high school, and enjoyed the camaraderie and challenges of the game, he was never wholly a team player. It wasn't that he was ego bound, or anti-social, he just didn't like being part of the groupthink mob. There was obviously strength in numbers, but he felt those numbers robbed you of your own personal identity, which in turn was your greatest strength. He also found the world inside his head more fascinating than the one outside. It had been that way ever since he was a boy, at least since the time of the accident. That's when he first became aware that he was different, when he first saw the world through a different set of eyes.

Ben had been on his own since he was seventeen, and in that time had proven himself capable of living outside the social strata. It wasn't that he relished the idea of being an outsider, he just felt compelled to be a better player in the game of life. Outsiderness, in that sense, went with the territory. Games of every type had intrigued him as far back as he could remember, and whether the game was mental or physical, he found he had a natural knack for the world of games. It was the adrenalin rush that came with the risk of losing that excited him. Facing the unknown was a definite high, and he had discovered that secret place that all thrill junkies come to love, that place deep inside that's willing to risk every thing for a small thing. Early on he had challenged himself in physical games, but as he grew older, the psychological challenge, became the only challenge. It was the head game that he loved most of all. Intellectually, he had an affinity for the game of chess, but it was the more pedestrian card games where he felt most at home. There was something about their raw energy and circus-like playfulness that struck the right chord with him. He loved mining hands, reading tells, staking bets, and of course, raking in the cash. Poker had become his game of choice, and he was fast on his way to establishing himself as something of a master. But it was also important to keep this mastery cloaked in secrecy. If people knew the degree of his skill, then he was a dead player. In that regard, he remained a stranger to all but the few.

****

The Tilapia workweek had ended, and the clubs were filled with soldiers wanting to kick out the proverbial jams. The Apocalypse Saloon was one of those clubs, and was considered by many to be jam-down central. Not only was it a fine bearer of distilled spirits and fiery brews, but also a lush card parlor and one of the favorite hangs for card wranglers of all creed and color. Like many others, Ben was no exception in his affection for the Apocalypse; he liked its smell, the smell of whisky and cigars, and the plastic wrappings off new playing cards. He liked its wood hewn floors and Neo-Gothic Space Rage decor. It made him feel like he had been transported into a different century, forward and backward all at once. But its most appealing characteristic was its high stakes Poker parlor where the limits were not regulated and policy was, simply, unbridled WFO. Fortunes had been made and lost there, and Ben had walked away a winner more than once, albeit a quiet one. The idea was to win, but pocketing too many large pots drew unwanted attention, and that kind of attention was poison to a player like himself. His modus operandi was to get his healthy share, but not gouge. Sometimes he would fold even when he knew he had the winning hand, just to keep the spotlight off himself. Sometimes he would let a player win just because he liked him, or had mercy on him. But when the stakes were high and the cash stacks higher, he didn't hesitate to pull the big guns. It was all about timing, and he was a damn good timekeeper.

On one particular Saturday night, the game had gone on for some time, and Ben's winnings were meager, more by intention than the fall of the cards. His fellow players were mostly young soldiers, but a few pros, some of whom he recognized, were also at the table. He watched them with the studied eye of a scholar as they watched him in turn. Each knew the unknown, although no one let on to the better. But the players at the table weren't the only ones focused on Ben. Someone else was watching him even more closely, not just the way he played the game, but the way he saw it. The watcher was a tall, broad shouldered black man dressed in a set of crisp pressed Military Fatigues. He sat at the bar to Ben's right, nursing a whiskey, and murmuring a blues riff just beneath his breath. His eyes were intense, but lightly softened by the gleam of his pearly white smile. There was a definite aura of intelligence about him, not the academic type, but something of a more worldly nature. And yet, he had an almost otherworldly air about him also, something ineffable and difficult to define. His name was Ivory Keyes, and the clusters of silver on his chest and collar indicated that he was an Officer in Namacal's Corporate Army. His interest in Ben was keen, but circumspect and beyond the periphery of Ben's immediate awareness. At the point of any potential eye contact, he always looked away, but only for a moment before returning his gaze to Ben. As he watched him reshuffle the deck, he noted a subtle glow around his hands, a glow similar to the light typically seen in Kirlian photography. That same subtle glow was also visible around Ben's head. The light in the room was dim and smoky, but this was not smoke. And it wasn't something Ivory hadn't seen before; he knew exactly what it was. But not everyone could see this. Like Ben, Ivory saw the world differently than most people, and yet it wasn't Ben's aura that interested him either; it was his technique. He could see that he was reading tells, behavioral modes and quirks that keyed him off to the way other players played their cards. But Ben's readings were not done in the ordinary way, nor did he rely on the normal physical indicators. What Ivory saw was a more internal methodology. As Ben dealt the cards they appeared as mental triangles of prism light, illumined by numbered symbols, a type of code not visible to the normal eye. Ben could see diffuse images of the cards as they appeared in the other player's minds. It was like a psychic bar code that only he could translate. What he didn't know was that Ivory could see it too. And what Ivory didn't know was that someone was also watching him watching Ben. Across the room, a man with a templed grey crew cut and tinted glasses was smoking a cigar and blowing smoke rings off the tip of his nose. Through those rings, Ivory became his center of focus.

As the card game continued, one of the players, a brash, young soldier holding what he believed to be a winning combination, bet hard and heavy in an attempt to drive the other players to the banks. It was a successful strategy in that everyone folded, everyone but Ben. The table grew quiet and the eyes around it became more intense. Bets and raises went back and forth and the cash stacks rose higher. Finally, when the pot was fitfully rich, Ben made the call. The young Solider, unable to withhold a foolish grin, laid down his hand, a beautiful ten high straight. All eyes went to Ben, who showing no emotion; simply placed his cards on top of the Straight. The Solider was, at first, incredulous at seeing the four Jacks, but his incredulity quickly changed to an uncontrollable rage.

"Motherfucker!" He screamed out, his voice cutting the air like a gunshot. Ben did not flinch, but kept his eyes trained on the soldier as he reached across the table to rake in the pot.

"You Motherfucker, you tripped those Jacks off the bottom."
Ben's eyes were locked on the man like magnets, yet he remained silent. But another player sensing trouble evolving opted to intervene.

"Did you see him trip?"

"I've been watching his ass all night. He's a method player and a card cutter."

"I didn't ask you if you'd been watching him, I ask you if you saw him cheat."

"I saw him."

"That's a lie." Ben finally said, a forceful change in his manner. "Cheating a player like you would be like cheating a chubby boy out of a cookie. You're too stupid to cheat."

The Soldier rose up and leapt across the table. Cards, drinks, and money went flying. Chairs toppled and players scattered. Ben, reacting with bullet speed, snagged the Soldier by the pits and smashed him to the floor. But no more had the man gone down than three of his buddies, who'd been watching the game, jumped into the fray. They came at

Ben like bulls, but Ben, with Matador finesse, sidestepped the first, and with a rapid succession of blows, leveled the second and third. But as one went down, another jumped up; and even though Ben was quick and spider agile, he was not quick enough to avoid taking a few primary shots. He held his own for a while, but four against one was a tough go and the tide eventually shifted. To add madness to mayhem, the offended soldier pulled a laser-knife and began to slash. Ben grabbed his arm, snapped it, and sent the knife flying. It was a battle short won because the other three men moved in and quickly pinned him to the wall. Digital knuck-chucks came out and cut the air with diamond precision. But just as Ben was at the point of being pummeled senseless, Ivory, who had been watching the entire encounter, stepped in to even the odds. Coming from behind, he ripped the knuck-chucks from the soldier's hand, and with a jab to the kidneys brought him to his knees. Spinning the chucks in the opposite direction, he took out the solider beside him and set Ben free. With Ben back in the fight, they readily regained the upper hand and were backing the soldiers to the wall. But as they were handily reducing them to flesh pulp, a group of the club's bouncers descended upon them with whipping jacks and stun guns. Realizing that the fight was too heavily weighted against them, they decided it best to take the winnings and make a hasty retreat. Slamming out a few more punches, they fought their way to the door and out into the parking lot. The bouncers and the soldiers were still in pursuit, but they were able to make it to Ben's car, a vintage jet fueled Porsche, and with demon swiftness, scorched a black streak of rubber out of the lot into the street. The crew cut man was outside at the curb watching them as they sped away. His observations were studied and acute, but he was unaware that across the street in a black van, another group of men were watching him. They were also watching Ben's car on an internal monitor. The car was no longer visible, but they were following it via a tracking signal. Henry Soledad, a chiseled Latino with lucid dark eyes and braided hair, shifted his focus back to the crew cut man who was walking away. He obviously knew who he was, and the fact that he was there attentive to Ben's exit, was just what he was hoping for, and that small fact brought a satisfied gleam to his eyes.

****

The sea air of Tilapia hummed with kinetic energy as the roar of the Porsche's engine whirred through the night streets. But even the power of excessive RPM's was subdued in comparison to the resonating laughter pouring out of Ben and Ivory. They had garnered a few war wounds, but wore their battle scars like two cackling schoolboys who had just pulled a fast one.

"You pack a helluv' a punch." Ben said. "Timing's not bad either."

"Didn't like the odds." Ivory replied with a glowing grin.

"Boy scouts get frisky sometimes."

"And stupid. It's the sad story of the world."

"Too often told."

Again both men laughed, mischievous glints in their eyes.

"Ben Denning." Ben said, offering his hand to Ivory who took it with a hearty squeeze.

"Ivory Keyes. I appreciate the ride, but you're going in the wrong direction. I need to go back that way."

"You need to let me buy you a drink."

"Not necessary. "

"In your universe. In mine, it's necessary."

CHAPTER TWO

The Katana Club was a sleek, roustabout beach bar, miles away from the hardcore watering holes of the strip. It was a place where the hook up junket for the touchy-feely crowd was renowned and sanctified. Ben and Ivory entered the club and made their way to the soft pallet seats of the chrome-gilded bar. With the robust joy of old friends reacquainted, they toasted themselves with good-humored bravado, savored cups of honeyed whisky, and checked out the spark and flow of feminine fare. The hour was late and the crowd had thinned, but those that remained were hungry for the touch of flesh. Eyes spoke in glances and Ben had a very good eye for the subtext of a glance. He had marked his territory from the time he entered the bar, and had been charting the movements of two sweeties who were doing the same with him. It was an eye game of flash and fold, none of it lost on the girls who were eager participants. There was always a hint of the bad boy in Ben, something dangerous, yet not without sensitivity. His pale blue eyes had an ethereal glow that intrigued both men and women, but for many women he was a magnetic draw. With his eclectic charm and Ivory's charismatic smile, it would have been hard for the pair not to find a well-matched love junket.

"Place is like a holy temple to the gods of flesh." Ivory said.

"This is my body, which is given for you: do this in remembrance of me." Ben quipped while indicating the red headed beauty across from them.

"No Corinthian ever said it better."

"Nor in a holier place."

"A lot holier than the one we just left."

"Boys will be boys."

"And men will be men. You've got a knack, you know."

"For what, trouble?"

"For the game."

"And what game is that?"

"For lack of a better term, let's call it life."

"Let's call it love." He said nodding to the two women he'd been playing eye tennis with, the well assetted ruby red Creole, and the beautiful dreadlocked brunette.

"What's your pref, man? Mango-Coconut, or Rio Creole?"

The drift was clear, and after a long night of fisty-cuffs, Ivory was up for the play.

"I've had some good times down on the bayou, but I'm feeling a little more tropical tonight."

"Then hot in the tropics it is."

Ben approached the girls, lofted them up with a lashing of silver tongue, and then brought them back down for a round of drinks. This was more ritual than necessity, because Ben already knew where they were all going. He always knew. The same gift he had for reading poker faces, applied similarly to the sweet eyes of the fairer sex. Ivory saw this talent too and happily joined the mix. The couples paired off, each giving knowing nods to the other and to the portent pleasures of the flesh. They chatted playfully for a while, downed several more toddies, and then left the bar for a more intimate setting.

By the time they arrived at their top floor, Neo-Cartesian hotel suite, the quartet was already deep into the wet seas of sensuality. With smoke and whiskey swirling through their brains, it wasn't long before clothes came off and fevered groping took over. Bouncing off couches and trouncing naked like mischievous children, theirs was a dance of midnight teasings and mercurial titillations. In a roundhouse of touch and taste, the foreplay soon gave way to the more serious nature of sexual engagement. Each couple slipped away into the shadows, where they, under the soft veil of darkness, sought the fulfillment of their desires.

The lovemaking was pure animal, but had its moments of tenderness. From rough and ready to slow and sensitive, Ben reveled in the sensations of Red's scintillating body. Her thoughts sung to him from the glow that surrounded her and he responded to every nuance accordingly. It was a curious thing, he thought, the magic of the mind and how he could actually hear the whisper of her libido tickling his in turn. It was a secret melody that entranced his body and elevated his euphoria to near sacred heights. Ivory, knew this music too, and heard similar whispers, but abandoned them for the pure, tactile sensation at the ends of his fingertips. After he and his island beauty had reached the pinnacle of their love making, he turned an observant eye back to Ben. Without Ben knowing, he watched him absorb thought crystals from the Creole's mind. Ben was oblivious to his psychic pryings, but not the curiosity of his eyes. He knew Ivory had been watching him, but wrote it off to manly camaraderie, and nothing more.

****

The curtains in the hotel room were drawn tightly, but a thread of sunlight was able to break through like a flame off the edge of a sharp knife. Ben lazily opened his eyes onto the naked red head sleeping peacefully beside him. She and her friend looked beautiful and almost innocent in the morning light - quite a change from the writhing wildcats of the night before. While pondering the sleeping girls, he noticed that Ivory was no longer in the other bed where he had last seen him. Curious, Ben got up, slipped on his pants, and stumbled into the main room of the suite where he found Ivory at the coffee klatch brewing a double espresso.

"You're up early." Ben said yawning.

"It's an old habit." Ivory replied in a deep, whiskey voice. "I love the party, but I love the game more." He smiled as he spoke, an enigmatic smile that washed over Ben like warm water. Even though they had only known each other for a few short hours, Ben felt completely at home with this man. Curiously though, Ivory's thoughts weren't easy to read, and Ben wasn't sure why. On occasion he had come across people whose mental fields were opaque, but they were the exception, not the rule.

"And what game is that." Ben asked.

"The biggest and badest game going...at least for them's got the balls for it."

It was a playful, but evasive answer, almost like a tease, indicative of something unsaid, but reflected as a mysterious glint in Ivory's eyes. Ben wondered if he'd been numbed by too much whiskey, but he had partied hard many times without the indulgences dulling his psychic senses. No, it wasn't clouded thoughts shading his perception; it was Ivory who was projecting that shade. He was obviously an exceptional man, but Ben wasn't thinking in terms of character, or street smarts, he was thinking of psychic power. Ivory had power, he sensed that unequivocally.

"You're being indirect." He said, continuing to probe Ivory's thoughts.

"Indirectness is only the long way around to directness, the central pathway in the game of ultimate destiny."

Ben laughed at the loftiness of the expression.

"And the more you talk, the more abstract you get."

"Abstraction is only light refracted in a different way."

"Then I'm obviously not seeing the light."

"But you could be...if you were interested?"

"I'm not sure what it is I'm suppose to be interested in."

"As designed. But if you'd like to get some breakfast, I'd be happy to shed some light on it for you.

****

They left the two girls snuggled beneath the sheets and went down to the hotel coffee shop where they ordered a plate of chops and chatted conversationally. It was a pleasant enough conversation, but it quickly became obvious to Ben that Ivory was taking his own sweet time getting round to the so-called game of games.

"So why don't you deconstruct this game of ultimate destiny for me." Ben said eager to play out Ivory's tease.

"To start, that's not really the best description for it. The better phrasing would be the game of ultimate minds. But in reality, if one could adhere to such a concept, it's more like a chess match composed of the best players in the world, and out of the world too."

Ivory had a marvelously enigmatic and illusive way of describing things, and though he definitely had Ben's attention, there was also a hint of divisiveness in his voice.

"Your uniform speaks for itself, but you don't seem like a military man to me." Ben said. "You don't talk like a military man either."

"In my division, it's better not to talk at all. But that's not to suggest that it's not military."

"Your division?"

"N-Sight. Post military. Essentially a Psy-Ops division; although that may be putting it a bit too simply."

"Sounds a little spooky."

"There are more than enough spooks out there to go around, but N-Sight is a breed apart."

"Not that up on my breeds, or how far apart they stand up or down."

"I'm talking about people with a gift.

"Beware of the Greeks."

"Look in the mirror. You know exactly what I mean."

"You're playing games with me, man."

"Like I said, there's only one game, the one reserved for special people like yourself."

"Sorry to burst your bubble, but I'm just an ordinary schmuck."

"Yea, so was Edgar Cayce. Don't feign modesty, Ben, it doesn't become you. But let's put this in easy terms. You're a fucking good poker player, maybe great, but it's not just because you've learned the various mechanics of the game and how to profit by them. It's because you've got a knack...and not just a knack for that particular game, but for all kinds of games, right? The knack is you can read people. You read those shitheads you were bouncing knuckles off last night. You read those lil ho's we traded joy juice with in the rap sack last night. And you've been trying' to read me since we first met, but it ain't been that easy has it? And you're not sure why? So let me tell you why. I know about readers, because I read the book long before you did."

"Maybe you didn't read the same book."

"Oh, it's the same all right. Seeing is believing; excuse the cliché. I saw you a long time before you saw me."

Ben was all too aware that the subtext of their conversation had a strong and undeniable psychic component to it, one that he was unable to nail down precisely.

"You didn't just stumble on me by chance, did you?"

"Fortune favors the prepared, and I like to be prepared. N-Sight is always on the lookout for potential candidates. One of our scouts spotted you and your skill several weeks ago. That's when they called me."

"And?"

"You have a gift, a great gift, but you're not using it in the most optimal or profitable way. Sure, you can haul down some heavy green gambling, and you can finagle a sweet treat right out of her cute little panties. I'm sure you've got a full bag of tricks to help you get whatever you want, but you're still selling yourself short. There's so much more you can do with your gift, and that's why I'm here. I'd like to make you an offer you can't refuse."

"Didn't realize there was such a thing."

"Then realize this – imagine more money and prestige than you've ever thought possible. Plus the adventure of a life time."

"I'm listening."

"N-Sight is an elite and clandestine arm of Namacal's Global Military Force."

"Grunts."

"Warriors."

"Corporate Warriors."

"Psychic."

"I'm sure you're good at what you do, Ivory, but I'm not into war, or corporations."

"That's because you don't know how they really function. The corporate army is a far better trained and paid force than the one that our old Governmental system had in place. But forget the politics for a moment; we can discuss all that in good time. What you're looking at here is a very special opportunity; one that few people get, or even know exists. I would call it the opportunity of a life time...the chance to advance your powers and to make more money than you've ever dreamed of...and to connect with people like yourself, some of the smartest and most powerful people in the world...plus the opportunity to go on one of the greatest adventures that man has never known, and to do things that ordinary men never dream of much less get the chance to do. I can make that happen."

"And who do I have to kill?"

"If I wanted killers, I wouldn't be talking to you. Killers are a dime a dozen."

"Then what's the catch?"

"No catch, no trick, no subterfuge. But there is a call to duty."

"Duty sounds like a catch. I'm not the military type."

"Neither was I, but N-Sight isn't real military, it's a special division, with special privileges. Think of it as a non-military organization within a military framework. The Military is just the umbrella that we work under, part of the corporate structure we perform a service for."

"And what exactly is that service?"

"Intelligence – intelligence that takes on many forms and facets, but utilizes the powers of the mind in unconventional ways."

"Unconventional is always tasty, but not in the mouth of Corporate America. I'm not looking for a job, no matter how elite the group, or fat the paycheck. I'm not a "group" kinda' guy."

"That's a group in itself. And I'm a member of that same club. But you have to look beyond your own prejudices and see this for something more than what you think. Forget what you think you know about politics, corporate armies, corporate greed, and all the rest of that horseshit. This is a different paradigm, a way to enhance the gifts that you already have without being a pawn in the game. With our team you have the chance to actually create the game itself.

And creativity is what it's all about, isn't it. Creating the coolest existence that you can dream, or imagine."

"You're good pitchman, Ivory, but I'm not a good catcher. You've wrapped your package in pretty paper and ribbons, but when you tear all that away, it's still military. You want to train me to be a spy."

"Spy is an interesting term, but too limited a job description. I'm talking about something much broader here. With you I see the potential for greatness; but I can honestly tell you; you won't find it in these little bars and whorehouses. Your destiny begins up there." Ivory nodded out the window to the pale crescent moon that was still visible in the morning sky.

"Space?"

"Hey diddle, diddle."

"I don't play."

"But you still know the tune...and you know about the conflict."

"You mean the war?"

"Semantics. It's more than a war; it's a battle for the future of the world. And that's where your destiny lies. That's where your journey begins."

"You want to send me to the moon?"

"The moon today, the far reaches of space tomorrow. Look, it's obviously much more complex and expansive than what I can sketch out for you here over jam and coffee, but you'll be thoroughly briefed and trained on all the specifics once you've come on board."

Ben chuckled at what he perceived to be the absolute absurdity of Ivory's offer."

"A trip to the moon, for a war on the moon, to be a spy on the moon...that's an insane and yet enticing carrot on a stick...for someone, but not me. I like making money and spending it. It's going to take more than a trip to the moon to win me over."

"Of course, and I wouldn't expect anything less." Ivory slid a slip of paper across to him. Ben glanced at the numbers on the paper, his eyes widening slightly.

"That's a lot of dough."

"Call it a signing bonus. And that's only the beginning."

"How about the ending? What time frame are we talking about?"

"One year mandatory, with an option for another two."

"Guarantees?"

"There are contracts, of course…to protect both your interests and ours. We're giving you lot, but we expect a lot in return. You would be large investment for us in both time and money."

"Yea, but I would be investing my life."

"You could do worse."

"And maybe better."

"Everything is negotiable."

"When would this moon madness begin?"

Ivory glanced out the window, this time nodding toward a sphere shaped C 77 Nuclear Helicopter that was landing in the street at that exact moment."

"Your carriage awaits you."

"You gotta be kidding."

"I never kid." He looked at his watch, and then threw some cash down on the table to cover breakfast. "I'm stepping onto that Chopper in ninety seconds. If you're interested, there's a seat on board for you too. Choice is yours."

This was all happening a little too fast for Ben's taste, but looking back out at the idling Chopper, his mind began to dance around the fantasy of what Ivory had presented.

"How did they know we were here?"

"Maybe they read my mind."

"Or not."

"Then maybe I read yours."

Ivory smiled and got up from the table.

"Coming?"

Ben didn't answer, and Ivory kept walking. When he reached the door, he stopped and looked back. Ben remained reticent, skeptical, yet intrigued. Ivory smiled one last time and stepped outside.

"Wait!" Ben cried out, and hurried to catch up.

"What about my stuff, my belongings?"

"You won't need your stuff on the moon. Stuff has a tendency to float away."

"And the contract?"

"I have a copy in the chopper."

"You're pretty goddamn sure of yourself, aren't you?"

"No, but I'm sure of you."

As the big Chopper lifted off the ground, the town of Tilapia Springs and everything that Ben had known disappeared beneath a thick layer of clouds. The future was indeed uncertain, but the call to destiny was not. The crescent moon lay straight ahead.

CHAPTER THREE

Night had once again descended upon the Florida Coast. Spectral glitter from streaming shafts of moonlight fell softly over the ocean currents that surrounded it. A sense of mystery could be felt in the way the light cast its glow upon the sea, something easily seen, but not easily defined. The moon spoke its own language, symbolic whisperings that could only be understood when equated with the sounds of silence. The shoreline of the cape was quiet, but the hum of bustling energy lay just beyond its wet grasslands. Streams of rocket fuel laced the horizon and clouded the Namacal launch site where the Aragon Space Shuttle was being prepped for take off. But just beyond the launch pad, on the far side of the gated compound, a crowd of noisy protesters had gathered. They were chanting and carrying anti-war signs that attacked Namacal policy and the on-going conflict that was being waged on the moon. The protests were peaceful and far enough away from the site as to be essentially meaningless, yet still necessary. The so-called, but not so liberal media, had been bought and paid for and were no longer even covering the demonstration. But that didn't mean it wasn't being watched, or broadcast. The same van that had been monitoring Ben at the bar was parked at the edge of the protest zone with cameras rolling. Soledad and his team were there to record the event and to offer assistance to the protesters. But the protest was not Soledad's only reason for being. On a separate monitor from the others, pictures and data regarding Benjamin Denning were ostensibly on display.

****

The passengers and crew had boarded the shuttle and the countdown had begun. As the seconds ticked away, the powerful rocket boosters began to rumble. Ignition took place and sent a fiery combustion of billowy plumes into the surrounding sky. The huge Shuttle lifted off the pad and rapidly gained altitude as its rocket thrusters propelled it into the earth's upper atmosphere. It crossed the sky like an embered phallus and cut a diagonal path through the heavens. As the rocket fumes diminished into a dappled arabesque of cirrus forms, the lunar orb revealed its face in tones of smoky red. The color was due to the gaseous haze of the upper atmosphere, but could also be interpreted as symbolic of the blood that had been shed there over the last year. Helium 3, as it had been stated in the media time again, was the fuel of the future, but there was a price for it, one unaccounted for in terms of blood and death.

****

The Shuttle soared across the Space continuum at speeds that made the flight seem like a motionless ride on cushioned air. In addition to the flight crew, a dozen other military passengers were on board, including Ben and Ivory. Idle chat was bandied about, but for the most part everyone was quiet, eyes watching the earth get smaller in the receding distance. Ben had flown in many types of aircraft, but nothing like the shuttle, and nothing beyond the atmosphere of the earth. He was awe struck by the amazing beauty and vastness of space all around him. For Ivory, who had made the trip dozens of times, it was just another day at the office.

"Incredible." Ben said, feeling a strong sense of unreality.

"Always is the first time." Ivory replied, understanding exactly how he felt. "But this is only the beginning of incredible. What you'll experience from here on out will take you to places far beyond what you think of as incredible today."

" Functioning in zero gravity should be a good start."

"You get used to that. Curiously enough, we don't spend that much time in zero G's. The Colonies and bases are all gravity controlled - a vast network of pressurized bubble pods connected by a massive tubular network. I'm sure you've seen pictures."

"Some. But I haven't seen much on the war."

"It's important not to cause the public unnecessary angst. Plus war is an archaic term with too many negative connotations. We prefer conflict."

"We?"

"Namacal. You, me, us."

"And the enemy?"

"The competition."

"You make it sound like a game."

"It is a game...the biggest game going, but still a game. A battle for the future of the earth."

"Not to mention outrageous profits and corporate control of the world's populations."

"The world is a business, Ben, and everyone wants to make a profit. Namacal is no different. But our intentions are honorable, we're just charting new territory, and why not? Namacal is the most successful company in the history of the world. And we didn't arrive there by letting things get out of control. Controlling the market and the populace, if you want to phrase it that way, is essential. Order has to be maintained otherwise we would resort to a caveman society. You can't leave people to their own devices, for those devices would soon become divisive. I can assure you that our competitor, Amerex, wants nothing less than complete control, heart, soul, and mind, of all the people. We've never gone so far as to take that position, it's too totalitarian, but we are willing to fight for our market share. But politics aside, and whether you agree with that or not, at the end of the day, we all have to work for a better world, and in that, I believe Namacal is providing a great service. The world needs energy and with the depletion of fossil fuels, Helium 3 has become the most important fuel of the future. Believe me when I tell you it's worth fighting for."

"What about the Helium 3 on earth?"

"Limited quantities on earth, but not so for the moon. Exploration is ongoing, but enough has already been discovered to fuel the earth for many years to come, and at a cost effective price."

"What about the price of human life?"

"It's ugly. I don't like it, you don't like it, but collateral damage is part of the equation."

"Collateral damage, what a fucking euphemism. Same old same old. Same game, same justifications, all just played out in a new time and place, the new world order."

"We make the order, Ben. If you're looking for fairness, you'll have to keep looking. The world has never been fair, never will be. You don't have to like it, but if you want to get on in it, you have to pick a side."

"Seems like the side has picked me."

"We want the best people."

"And Amerex doesn't?"

"Amerex has many divisions, they don't need to control Helium 3."

"But Namacal has divisions too. Aren't you also in the weapons business?"

"We have subsidiaries, yes. When you're engaged in conflicts such as this, it only makes sense to help cut cost.

"It also creates a market for weapons sales."

"The market has always been there. Look, I understand your doubts and abrogations. The powerful have always been looked upon with hate and suspicion by the less powerful. But keep this in mind, we're the largest and highest paying corporate army in the world...and beyond. Like the space continuum itself, we offer limitless possibilities. This is an opportunity you'll never find anywhere else. A door has opened for you that only open's to a few. Don't lose sight of that."

Ben leaned back pensively in his seat and took another look out the portal window. The earth was growing smaller and dimmer in the background, but up ahead, the moon filled the dark night sky like a grey disc of undying mystery.

CHAPTER FOUR

The Shuttle entered into the moon's force field, its grey-cratered lunarscape highlighted by the streaming spectral flares of the sun. Descending to a lower altitude, small colonies of bubble domes linked by serpentine causeways were scattered across the vast pock marked surface. Ben took it all in with increasing excitement as they glided over the great lunar plains toward Namacal's Central Base and Operational Modular Network. The facility was more massive than he had imagined and composed of hundreds of cell-like clusters of bubble vestibules linked by a Gordian knot of see through polyplex traversing tubes. The Spaceport and Military Facilities were all ensconced in a cratered valley between two looming lunar mountain ranges. The location was strategic, as the base was enclosed in a niche at the far end of a long, winding canyon. Ben, with an attentive eye, made out several open passages in the mountains that looked more like turrets than natural formations. He was no war strategist, but he could see the thinking that had gone into development of this colony. But as well planned as it was, it wasn't impervious to attack. The rifts in the mountain were narrow, but large enough for an enemy Fighter to fly through. Ironically, no more had that prescient thought come to him, than a blast of brilliant light flashed before his eyes. The lunarscape suddenly lit up with more light as a series of explosions spotted the dark sky. An Amerex Suduki Sling Shot Style Fighter Craft zoomed out of one of the very passes that Ben had been focused on, and was moving at a high rate of speed, spitting rocket fire at the Namacal cubicles below. One cubicle exploded and fire and debris splattered the canyon with gravity-less metal and burning debris. As the attack continued, Ben suddenly found himself face to face with the hardcore reality of war. Before that moment, it had all been a fantasy, but no longer. The sky around them was alive with the heavy vibratory pulses of exploding laser rockets. It appeared to Ben's unseasoned eye that they would surely be blown to pieces at any moment, but Ivory, sensing his apprehension, moved to calm him.

"Only battle jabber and saber rattling, it'll all be over shortly."

With the echo of those words still in Ben's ears, the Pilot switched the Shuttle to evasive mode. The entire craft flipped on its side and shifted into a sonic stealth spin. Enemy rockets zipped past and hit the landing field, leaving forty-foot long craters at its center. The attack was quick and precise, but so were the Namacal forces in response. Before another rocket could be ignited, the antiaircraft system filled the sky with dozens of cluster bombs. It was a statement of pure overkill because the first bomb hit the Amerex Fighter and erased it from the sky. The other bombs only punctuated that destruction. But as the Craft crashed to the ground, another Fighter soared through the pass at high speed and zeroed its rockets in on the Shuttle. The sizable Shuttle appeared an easy target, Ben thought, but before the Fighter could maneuver into position, Ground Defenses shot it down with equal promptness. As the smoke settled, the Pilot calmly looped the Shuttle back around and descended toward the landing port. Debris was still lofting in the zero G's, but the fires had been extinguished because there was no oxygen to feed them.

"Welcoming committee." Ben said, trying to make light of a frightening situation.

"Amerex knows when a Shuttle is coming in and likes to take pot shots. One of these babies cost around a billion dollars, so bringing one down would be a major coup."

"A financial coup."

"War is money."

"Has it happened?"

"No, and not likely to, but they still try."

"A little unnerving."

"Nothing compared to what goes down in the zone. We're fifty kilometers away, but if you want hairy; that's where hairy lives."

The Shuttle continued its descent to the Spaceport where it finally touched down on lunar turf and was guided into a pressurized bubble hangar.

****

Ben deboarded the Shuttle, and after a brief indoctrination, was taken to his living quarters, a small bubble pod at the snake end of a polyplex tube.

"This will be home while you're in training." Ivory explained showing Ben the no frills room. "Quaint I know, but it does have one spectacular feature." He was referring to the large bubble window that looked out onto the lunarscape and the vast reaches of space beyond. A quarter profile of the earth could also be seen from that vantage point, a phenomenal view, Ben thought, larger and more intensely blue than he had imagined.

"Beautiful, isn't it. Always makes me feel just a little homesick." Ivory said. "You'd think you'd get used to it, but you never do."

****

Ivory escorted Ben through a labyrinthine series of poly-plex tubes and serpentine structures that looked like glass skeletons, but had been created by 3-D printing from ground lunar rock and were ultimately stronger than steel. After undergoing a saliva scan and DNA recognition, they were granted entry to the headquarters of N-Sight Commander, Terrence Salt. Salt's Attaché, Corporal Vidov Ludovic, a steely-eyed palace dog with street cop sensibilities, led them into the sprawling office. It was a sleek, faux chrome enclave with a dozen orb shaped floating computers, a raised micro-tech center, giant bubble windows, and a revolving desk where Salt did business. What was ostensibly missing was Salt himself.

"The Commander will be with you in a moment." Ludovic said, and exited the room without further explanation. Ben and Ivory traded glances, but neither spoke. After a long, silent minute, the Commander stepped through the looking glass of what appeared to be a window portal, but was actually an alternate door. He said nothing as he locked eyes with Ben in an intensely engaging manner. Ben could feel the force of his gaze and immediately sensed that this was no ordinary man. In fact, Ben had never seen such radiant and penetrating eyes. They were like painted prisms that shone in different colors that seemed to shift with the movement of his body. He was well chiseled, a relatively handsome man in his late forties, and in spite of a lengthy tenure on the moon, he was tan like a seaman who had spent weeks in the sun. A curious contradiction, Ben thought, given the moon's gloomy environment. Additionally, his closely cropped beard gave him something of an academic look, but with an old school flare that was somewhat counter to his military position. But it wasn't his physical appearance that captivated Ben; it was something more ethereal. Salt had an aura of psychic energy that draped around him like a numinous shroud. Ben was not easily impressed, but this man was impressive – so much so that it made Ben feel instantly uneasy – not because of the strength of his presence, but because Ben felt vulnerable to the extent that Salt was looking through him and could read his every thought. In turn, Ben was finding Salt difficult to read, but wasn't sure why. He picked up a thought here and there, but what little he could decipher came to him in jumbled patterns and broken prism visuals.

"Ben, I'd like you to meet Commander Terrence Salt." Ivory said watching the silent interaction between them. Salt extended his hand and gripped Ben's with a deceptive lightness, as if the hand were moving through his sans any molecular interference.

"I've been looking forward to meeting you for some time."

"Some time?" Ben asked as if the words didn't fit right in his mouth.

"Since I first read the scouting report on you. Looks like you had a bit of excitement on the way in."

"Don't know if excitement is the right word, but it was different. Up until yesterday, I never pictured myself in the military."

"That's because it wasn't a picture to be pictured; it was a vision. And you hadn't recognized that vision yet."

"You seem to know more about it than I do."

"I only know what I sense."

"Then you probably sense that I don't think of myself as a visionary, and I can't really see into the future."

"Perhaps you haven't looked far enough, or gone that deeply into your own psyche. Sometimes the mind has to be made aware of its own propensities. I certainly believe you already have those propensities."

"Based on what?"

"Intuition for one, your dossier for two."

"I never filled out a dossier."

"No, we did it for you. It's imperative that we look very closely at our candidates. Keep in mind; this is a highly specialized unit, an elite group of extraordinary people. And when we open that door to someone, it's essential to know who they are."

Ben watched him closely, still trying to penetrate his mental stronghold, but felt like his psychic perceptions were somehow being blocked.

"But you can't really know anyone completely, can you? Everyone lies; even to themselves."

"So true. But it's also possible to look beyond the lie and the limitations it imposes. Our intelligence network is the largest and most comprehensive ever created. We can find out anything about anybody at anytime from the day you were born until the day you die, lies and all. So the fact that you've made it this far, says a great deal on your behalf. In short, we believe in you, perhaps more than you believe in yourself, and we're willing to back that belief up. We're willing to train you at our expense and pay you a phenomenal sum of money just to show up. Where else can you make the starting salary we've agreed to pay you?"

"I was doing all right before I came on board."

"But now you have the opportunity to do better than all right. You have the opportunity to expand your mind and rise to heights you never imagined."

"I have a pretty fertile imagination."

"But have you imagined yourself as a universal hero?"

"I've never really wanted to be a hero."

"Everyone wants to be a hero whether they admit it or not. But we don't choose heroes, we create them, it comes with the territory. We take what you have, your special talents, and make them even more special. The people that work for us are the best in the world. They come from all walks of life and backgrounds, some not so different from your own."

"And what would you know about my own?"

"As I said before, it's important for us to know all about you....your beginnings, endings, and everything in-between...like how you grew up on the streets of L.A....how you were raised by an alcoholic father and a part time mother...your early troubles in school...and more specifically the incident that changed your life...that of being struck by lightning when you were eleven. Everything changed after that, didn't it? Your way of seeing, your way of being, it all changed. And what started as a negative quickly became a positive. We know about your initial learning disabilities, your rebellion, acting out, too much drinking, too many drugs, always hustling for a buck, scamming pigeons and whores. Your life reads like pulp fiction, but it's all been part of a learning process, hasn't it? You've done better in recent years; you've learned how to use your gift in a more relevant and productive way, but in the final analysis, you're still just a two-bit hustler. I don't mean that as a derogatory slam; I just want to emphasize the fact that you've been squandering the greater part of your talents and abilities on boyhood games. We've now taken it upon ourselves to bring you into the adult world, and to see that you make the most of those abilities."

"It may be the adult world to you, but it feels like an invasion of privacy to me."

"Privacy is a thing of the past. Nothing is private. But our intention is not to invade, but to enlighten, to offer insight, knowledge, and ways to enhance the miraculous powers that you already possess."

"And how is that?"

"You've taken the first step by being here. The next step is behind that door." He pointed to a spot in the center of Ben's forehead. Ben got the inference, but was still trying to unlock Salt's thoughts, albeit, making little headway.

"Well, you've certainly captured my interest."

"Your interests are our interests. You see well, but the world you're about to enter will open up an entirely new way of seeing. And that's exactly what our training program is designed to do."

CHAPTER FIVE

Two Namacal soldiers escorted Aden Calder out of the N-Sight cubicle where he had spent the night. There was a cockiness to his walk that hinted at artificiality, but there was also an unusual luminescence in his eyes that referenced a depth beyond the appearance of a shallow exterior. He was in his twenties, about the same age as Ben, but beefier and with more swagger. He could see the thoughts of his two escorts forming, and hear their words before they spoke. Their voices to him were like echoes in reverse. Their lips moved, but only after he had already heard what they were thinking. It was similar to watching a film that was out of sync. Like Ben, he was gifted, the result of an injury sustained when he was a boy hit in the head by a baseball. His doctors and parents initially feared brain damage, but what developed instead was a unique type of extra sensory perception. This life altering accident ultimately became an asset as opposed to a disability. It helped him get through school, which he hated, and to win football games, which he loved. He had always been a sports junkie, and loved to push himself to the limit in games of physical contact. As for reading psychic tells, he found that to be more of an annoying side effect than a benefit, but when it came to winning pretty skirts and ball games, he used his gift to the fullest. He knew he was different, but that difference only served to feed his ego and strengthen his physicality. What he liked and savored above all else was to be the top dog. And seeing into other people's minds increased both his confidence and bravado to a frightening degree. Unlike Ben, he more than often wore his gift like a badge and lauded it over the uninitiated. Humbleness wasn't in his character, but the idea of enhancing his abilities was. So when he was approached by Namacal, in a seemingly chance meeting, he leapt at the opportunity. For him it was a simple decision, an opportunity to not only go to the moon, but to become more god-like.

Calder and his escorts traversed the interconnecting tubes finally arriving at a large geodesic bubble vector on the far side of the base. Given that there was a war going on, security gates were in place, equipped with DNA scanners and other ID devices. Passing the scans, Calder left his escorts behind and entered the great geodesic room alone.

Stepping through the security door, he was met by two men in spider-web style lunar fatigues. He already knew Ivory, but it was the first time he had seen Ben. He could hear the murmur of their thoughts as he walked toward them, but their minds were tuned to his thoughts too. A conversation between the three took place without anyone actually speaking aloud.

"Who are these fucking donkeys?" Calder thought, but a thought that came out like a shout that blew right through Ivory's mind.

"The only donkey showing his ass around here is you, Calder." Ivory fired back, though the response didn't come from his mouth.

"I was just bullshitting, man." Calder said laughing out loud. "I figured you were listening."

"We're always listening."

"We? You and your pet cockroach?"

"A spitting cobra. But in this case, I think I can speak for we. This is Ben Denning, Calder, and just so you know, he heard you before he saw you."

"Well then turn up the goddamn volume and let's party."

Calder laughed again and hardily shook Ben's hand. "Welcome to Strawberry Fields."

"Where nothing is real, and nothing to get hung about?" Ben volleyed back.

"Only looney tunes."

The old school subtext evoked a laugh, as their minds entwined in a brief, but friendly play of show and tell. They were completely different personality types, but there was an instant and undeniable simpatico between them.

"We're waiting for two others." Ivory said. "Taylor and Lasgow, good heads we brought up from the ranks; they'll be going through training with you."

"You've been talking about training since day one, but I still don't know what it means?" Ben said, trying to read between the relevant lines of Ivory's mind.

"A little mystery in life is good, Ben. To know too much too soon is to not know enough. But if you need a snap shot, the training is more mental than physical, and usually lasts for three to five days depending on the individuals involved. Essentially, you'll be exposed to various mind enhancement programs, some you're familiar with, some not. And overview would include telepathy, bio-feedback, synergistic reprogramming, remote seeing, telemetric reading, mind games, voodoo, magic, hallucinogenic viewing, Akama remote hearing, psychometry, technological brain/image thought transference, and more."

"A goddamn psychic smorgasbord." Calder interjected.

"Hallucinogenic viewing?" Ben said probing deeper.

"A drug enhancement and vision guidance program."

"Moon tripping." Calder added.

"That's putting it in a soup can, Calder, but --"

"You're talking about the use of drugs." Ben confirmed.

"Man made and psychotropic. But this is no day trip into the psychedelic ethers; these chemicals are specifically designed to open wider psychic channels in your mind and guide you into realms of higher thought."

"The military has a bad rep for dosing soldiers and using them as guinea pigs." Ben pointed out. "The idea of someone fucking with my mind is..."

"It's not a mind fuck, Ben. It's not even mandatory that you take them, but we highly encourage it. Stay tuned to the fact that we're looking for higher levels of mental proficiency. These drugs are only aides, channel shapers, virtual stepping stones to a higher reality and a higher type of proficiency."

Ivory was both sincere and convincing in what he said, but Ben remained skeptical. While the pros and cons were left floating in air, thoughts and images of the two other trainees were already forming in Ben's consciousness. A moment later, Taylor and Lasgow stepped through the door of the dome and joined them. They were strong and mentally agile young soldiers, but Ben didn't pick up the same psychic vibe from them that he had from Calder. He looked to Ivory for a read, but Ivory blocked him. It was an evasive move, but Ben didn't need Ivory to tell him that the other two men were different; he was already picking up strong levels of fear and low levels of mental energy from both. Calder was picking up on it too, although neither voiced their concerns outwardly. Nevertheless, they realized that the psychic energy in the room was skewed and could have an adverse effect on the training. Calder didn't care one way or another, but the mental curvature made Ben uneasy. The program was purported to be for the gifted, but Ben had not detected the gift in these men beyond the rudimentary level. Ivory was quick to sense his uneasiness and placed a reassuring hand on his shoulder.

"Everything is as it should be, Benjamin. Let's begin."

••••

The trainees were taken into a Prepatory Room where they were introduced to a pair of Namacal Neurologists. After a few questions regarding medical history and the undertaking of body scans relating to physical condition, the Doctors readied a powerful adrenalin solution. Ivory explained that they would need to be awake for the next forty-eight hours straight and the adrenalin would help sustain their energy resources. Again, Ben raised objections to the application of pharmaceuticals, but Ivory, in his always, forthright manner, assured him of the importance of keeping his mind alert during the exhausting program. The tasks ahead demanded that no one sleep, and that the risk of mental and emotional breakdown was a very real possibility. Additionally, the adrenalin boost had been used many times and was found to be both safe and effective in aiding mental stability. He reminded everyone that psychotic breaks and temporary insanity were always possible components to any transcendental experience. Ben didn't argue the point, but couldn't help but wonder what he'd gotten himself into. Had he sold himself out to the lure of money and adventure? He had definitely taken a big bite of the proverbial carrot, but was it a mistake? Ivory could hear and feel those doubts and kept reassuring him that the doubting was natural, but the benefits in the end would far outweigh any negatives. He himself had been through the same program and knew its values. It was, as ever, a good sales pitch, but Ben wasn't completely sold.

****

As the adrenalin kicked in, the trainees loosened up physically via calisthenics, and a long run through the veinular tubes that composed the base's internal structure. The mixture of adrenalin and piped in oxygen flowing to their brains left them light-headed and giddy. Although Ben felt extremely alert, it was more of an artificial clarity that came with an edge, a hyper-zeal similar to that of taking a large dose of clinical cocaine.

When they returned from the run, floating electrodes were attached to their bodies and each was put into a separate isolation booth for brain wave testing. In spite of their pulsing heart rates, their mind states fluctuated from high beta, to Alpha, and in some cases, specifically those of Ben and Calder, registered deep in the Delta zone. Once these tests were completed, the trainees were taken into a biofeedback lab where they were tested on using their brain waves to move small objects. Taylor and Lasgow's scores were relatively low, but Ben and Calder both excelled, and went on to the more advanced tests, those of moving lunar modules by the power of their minds alone. It was clear at this point that Ben possessed the strongest abilities of the group, but Calder, a tireless competitor, was not far behind.

When the Biofeedback tests were complete, the men were taken to an enclosed firing range where they were schooled in the use of Telemetric Armaments. There were many variations on these unconventional weapons, but all were designed to disrupt the thinking process, to create mental confusion, disorientation, and in some cases, to implant suggestion and hallucination in the minds of the enemy. As the weapons were demonstrated, the men were also tutored on EMF shielding techniques, or how to block Electro-magnetic frequency signals from reprogramming or inducing automatic suggestion in their own minds. To illustrate how this worked, they were subjected to small doses of microwaves and other sonic frequencies that attacked neurological cells and altered brain waves. The learning curve was steep because, like any powerful drug, the mind was susceptible to chemical changes, and the frequencies made the changes happen almost instantaneously. Once a hallucination began, chemically, or telemetrically, it was hard to stop. Putting up strong mental blocks had to be learned, and each trainee was guided through various defensive maneuvers. Thought had to be reshaped and reorganized, and even Ben found the defense strategies difficult to implement. Many hours were spent inducing the proper mind states that could defend against the powerful mind control weapons.

After the telemetric training, the weary trainees were taken to a quiet lounge where they were allowed to relax before being introduced to the next cycle, a series of trance states, meditation techniques, and various ancient disciplines such as tantra, yoga, voodoo, Sufi gyrations, and auto-genics, among others. Once they were centered and energy focused in the deeper realms of the brain, each trainee was again placed in an isolation cube. Audio signals of both high and low frequency were fed into the cubes each designed to alter brain chemistry. Once the alterations were in place, electronic hallucinations were induced. Ben had only been in his cube for less than a minute when it began to swirl with kaleidoscopic patterns of color. At first he wasn't sure what was happening, but as the light began to crystallize into visual images, he knew that he was under the influence of a hallucination. Plasmic forms, fetal, wet, and coated with lava-like diamonds filtered into his consciousness. Suddenly, he saw himself on the back of a cubist Chimera racing down a sky artery at high speed. Slivers of lightning cracked in the air around him, one bolt shattering the image into dozens of shards that splintered off into hundreds of fiber-optic micro-serpents. The serpents wiggled away through a hypnagogic door and left him in an immense darkness. Memories rushed in and flooded his mind like water from an open spicket. They flicked past him, like cards going down at a gambling table. One of those cards was captured in his mind's eye and exploded into a full-blown memory. It took him back to a day when he was a boy riding his bike home in an unrelenting downpour. Voluminous thunder rattled the heavens, and lightning crackled furiously all around him. He had never been afraid of lightening, but he had never seen lightning of this magnitude, so brilliant and with such intensity. And then he was hit. His bike literally melted out from under him and he crashed to the ground with such force that the earth itself disappeared. The memory was so real that it jarred his psyche and broke the reverie apart into smaller, pebbled thoughts. He felt the impact as if the event had happened that very second. Rising upward, he saw himself lying on the ground, motionless and near death. But instead of dying, a flush of new breath filled his lungs and spirits began to gather around him. They were whispering to him in an inconceivable language, their words wafting down on him like geometric bubbles. As each bubble popped he felt a telepathic surge, like an electrical current moving through his mind and tripping his synapses. Suddenly, he drew a deep breath and his eyes sprang open. He was no longer in the memory, but back in the isolation cube. The door opened and Ivory looked in.

"You OK?"

He nodded that he was and Ivory signaled for him to come out. Stepping into the light, he realized that he had lost all sense of time while in the cube. He didn't know if he'd been in for an hour, a day, a week, or an eternity.

After an electronic evaluation by one of the attending physicians, Ben joined the others in yet another cube this one complemented with soft couches and cushiony chairs. Each of the trainees had been put through a similar process as Ben, and all looked a touch dazed from the experience. Each sensed what the other had been through and they were left on their own to discuss their experiences and compare notes. Calder was the most excited and willing to talk about the journey, Taylor and Lasgow less so. They had all experienced visions and hallucinations, each unique unto his own, but each different in their reactions. Ben was more pensive than the rest, but was quick to notice that Taylor and Lasgow were obviously disoriented and becoming more so with each new exercise. Their faces were marked with fear and uncertainty, and when they spoke their words often came out jumbled and incohesive. Ivory monitored these conversations from an undisclosed location, and recorded all brain wave patterns for later evaluation.

****

After more than forty hours of testing and training exercises, the mental and physical strain on the men was beginning to show. The adrenalin had diminished and an acute edginess was evident in all. Ben questioned Ivory as to how much more was involved, but he answered unspecifically, stating only that a few more tests would be necessary.

For the next exercise, they were taken to a large, metal tank connected to a small tube tunnel that led into a cold and dismal darkness. There was a table at the center of the tank that held four crescent shaped sugar cubes. Ivory offered no details, only that each man was to take one under his tongue for psychic enhancement.

"One pill makes you larger?" Ben said, indicating the obvious.

"And one allows you to see within the substructure of all things." Ivory replied with a skewed wink.

"You've been there?" Ben asked.

"Everywhere you've been, I've been. Everywhere you're going, I've gone. This door opens in only one direction, toward an expanded consciousness - nothing to fear but the broadening of your own mind."

"Then let's rip some synapses and get on with it." Calder growled. "I'm ready to kick some psychic ass." He laughed boisterously at his own bombast, but no one laughed with him. Taylor and Lasgow looked pale and weary of the entire affair. Ben, as usual, was more reserved, yet wary of yet another head-trip sold under the guise of psychic training. No matter what was being presented, he felt he was being mentally manipulated and psychically eavesdropped on. Ivory assured him that his fears were unwarranted and that any perceived manipulations were just imagined. Ben didn't buy the explanation, but was confident enough in himself to accept the crescent. Placing the cube under his tongue, he pressed his lips together and looked to the others who were already following suit. Calder put on a bold face, but there was a creeping uncertainty in his eyes. Ben could also see the near unbearable angst that Taylor and Lasgow were suffering through. They were obviously in over their heads, burning out, and it was only a matter of time before someone snapped. But as he was considering these things, the tank lit up like a neon arabesque coiled within a swirling helix of lavender light. Ivory stepped out of the helix and instructed the four men to follow him down an auxiliary tube that lead to a small, dark room no larger than a closet. There, they dressed in pressurized suits and helmets, and were taken outside the cubicle and onto the cold, grey regolith of the moon's cratered surface. In the zero gravity they suddenly found themselves floating above the ground. The sensation, as each experienced it, was one of surreal amazement. In the rarefied atmosphere, their angst diminished and a sense of play returned. They began to jump, bounce, and flip upside down like carefree children. Ben did a triple somersault that lofted him twelve feet into the airless space. It was a feeling of extraordinary exhilaration and the others joined in to perform similar acts of zero g acrobatics. But as each returned to the terra firma, they suddenly realized they were not outside at all, but still at the table where they had just taken the crescent.

"Fuck." Ben muttered as he became aware that what he was experiencing was a hallucination within a hallucination. He glanced at others, their proportions distorted, and their heads expanding like elastic bubbles. Their eyes popped from the sockets like the snap of a rubber band, and Ben watched incredulously as Lasgow's brain literally oozed out and plopped on the floor. The disembodied brain turned into a glowing mound of psychic mush that streamed off into a luminous puddle that stopped at Ben's feet. Reflections holding myriad images quavered in the substrata that composed the flucuating brain mud. Ben fired a glance at Calder wondering if he was seeing the same thing, and apparently he was, because his focus was locked on the same reflective pool. Taylor, also, saw what they saw, but the sight of it frightened him to such degree, that he began to panic. He tried to break the force of the hallucination, but its grip on his consciousness was too powerful to escape from. Ivory saw what was happening and suggested transcendentally for Taylor to quit resisting the vision and just let go. If he continued to resist, he could find himself drawn into a nightmare more difficult to escape from than the current illusion. Just the word "nightmare" struck like a thunderbolt and went straight through Ben's head. He reeled backward and fell against the wall momentarily dazed. Regaining focus, he saw Ivory melting into a waxy pool of fulgent color and Lasgow trying to retrieve his mind by sucking it up into his body like a vacuum. Calder was in his own private world shaping his body into strange contortionistic poses as if trying to feel and deepen the experience of elasticity. While this carousel of illusion was spinning all around them, Ben reached inside his chest and pulled out several strands of stringy membrane that had become attached to his heart. He plucked each strand like the string of Viola, creating a private pizzicato concerto that resonated through his cells and made his eyes bounce like rubber balls. As he watched his heart beat in syncopated rhythm, a geyser of blood suddenly shot out of his chest and splattered the ceiling. The blood drops dripped back down in long sinewy strands like a shower of taffy and formed a sticky hieroglyph on the wall in front of him. The hieroglyph suddenly came to life, and with it the sound of gunfire. Ben and the others were instantly transported to the war zone and into the heat of battle. The violence was incendiary, and yet curiously abstract. Bodies were everywhere and explosions were leaving pocked open graves at their feet. Bullets were pinging, but they weren't normal bullets, they were thought waves, full of thought shrapnel. Everyone was ducking, rolling, and trying to evade the brain-altering onslaught. As Ben sidestepped the thought bullets, he watched them explode into the wall behind him. Each explosion burst into a full blown illusion and dissolved into a series of dying images, each image a sliver of potential life. As he dodged yet another shot and watched it explode, Ivory stepped out of the wall where the thought bullet had hit and the war zone disappeared inside his head. While the trainees were still spinning in the mental dust, Ivory calmly instructed them to take a seat in the four flight chairs that had been suspended from the alloyed rafters. Each man followed the order, took a seat, and strapped himself in. They were then lifted out of the tube, and trammed toward a crater just beyond the outer walls of the tank. From there, they were lowered to the bottom where their harnesses were automatically unsnapped and they were free to walk around. It was a strange place to find oneself by any leap of the imagination, Ben thought, but to be in a crater on the moon under the influence of an unknown mind altering substance was absolutely insane. Everything he saw and felt only confirmed that logic itself was mutable and without foundation. The world, both inside and out, was a flowing river of ever evolving thought energy. At once it was a panorama of abstraction, which then shifted into tentacled forms that appeared to have substance, but only tied themselves around his body and mind in an infinite series of mental knots. The knots quickly melted and took on a plasmic, lava-like quality that seeped into his pores. Everything was flowing, merging, attaching to everything else. In essence, everything that began in multiples was quickly reduced to singular form, and all the trainees were left floating above the ground, like flesh balloons with gummy tendrils linking them together. Ivory held the end strands of these tendrils in his hand and flew the men like kites. A blast of blue steam burst from Lasgow's head and swept him off course away from the others. As Ivory tried to reel him back in; his body strands got tangled with those of Calder's. He kept trying, but was unable to separate them. Ben saw what was going on and that Lasgow's mental energies were being extracted and drawn into Calder's mind. Lasgow began to pull at the tangled strands, but his resistance only knotted them more tightly. He was screaming for help, but no one could help him. His screams sent sharp pains through Calder's brain and made him yank back violently on the tangled flesh threads. Taylor also tried to help, but Calder exploded on him forcing him to back off. Simultaneously, their bodies began to spin and weave into a Celtic knot of twisted fates. Ben made another attempt to spool them in, but the psychic forces at play were too strong. As the strands continued to knot and tighten, Lasgow's blood began to seep from his veins. The lunar ground turned red and spears of red light shot up from the dead soil and pierced Ben 's body like needle pricks. Everyone was affected by this cataclysm of psychic entanglement, but Lasgow suffered worst of all. Trying to escape the increasing mental pain, he began to twist, turn, and tear at his pressure suit. Black globs of hardened mist formed in and around him. Suddenly the world shuddered with seismic force and Lasgow's skin fell away. Ben could see every bone, vein, and strand of tissue in his body. A gust of nausea shot through him and a hurl of rainbow vomit sprayed out of his mouth. The vomit streamed outward like a coif of ribbons in the wind and wrapped around the others adding additional tension to the already forming psychic knots. But just as the tangled scenario looked hopelessly inescapable, the black globs of nightmare mist began to disintegrate. Ivory clicked a laser remote that sent out a brilliant beam of light to encircle them. Once set, the light exploded and washed over their bodies removing every visual clue of their physicality. After several minutes, the last vapor of luminescence evaporated leaving only a dim cloud of fine mist.

As the mist dissolved, the men found themselves back in their harnessed seats where they had originally started. All were quiet and no one was moving. Lasgow opened his eyes and immediately began to scream. His body went into muscle spasms so violent that Ivory and two technicians immediately rushed in to help him. Unable to stop the spasms, they were forced to take him from his seat and remove him from the room. With his screams still echoing, Taylor unhooked himself and charged out after them. As soon as they were gone, the energy in the space settled and returned to normal. The calmness was acute, a reflection of the minds that remained. Ben stood up and opened his palm. The crescent was still there – the same for Calder. Both were surprised to find that they had not actually taken it, but at the same moment watched as it absorbed into their open palms and spirited them away in a hurricane of interwoven thought threads. As they reached the center point of that cyclonic mental weave, their minds exploded into a million glistening particles, each containing a micro-image of themselves being torpedoed into the vastness of an undefined yet luminous universal sea. As the waves of that sea crashed upon the beaches of their minds, they were washed ashore and brought back to waking consciousness. With dazzling abruptness, they found themselves in the lounge on the couch where they had been earlier. Ivory was sitting across from them, lacing his tongue around a Cheshire-Cat grin.

"Well done."

Ben's eyes were glassed over and his own tongue was still tied to his diffusing brain. And yet, there was a startling alacrity to his overall being.

"What about Taylor and Lasgow?"

"The program is not only about enhancement, but also endurance - psychological war games geared to prepare you for the real war. We often use a control group for statistical purposes and the results are almost always the same. Simply put, their psyches weren't up to the task."

"You mean simply put, they were driven mad."

"Madness is relative and subjective. We're all mad on some level...some more than others. Welcome to N-Sight."

CHAPTER SIX

Ben and Calder were taken to new quarters where they collapsed in utter exhaustion. With the glow of the earth glimmering through the large portal windows, they fell into a deep sleep and an even deeper dream. The room sparkled with hypnagogic energy that appeared to the inner eye as tiny luminous drops of rainbow dust. Undefined images within the drops continually shifted and reanimated. As this dream interlude was taking place, Salt's voice came in over the intercom congratulating the two young men on their success. He spoke in a soft, almost soundless voice that got lower in pitch with each word. Finally, there were no words at all, only silence. But from that silence, a shadow appeared and moved toward the two sleeping men – a figure, militarily dressed, but undeniably female, stopped beside them. She leaned in and put her hand on Ben's shoulder, but before she could speak, he grabbed her wrist and flipped her sideways onto the bed. She was startled by his bullet reaction, but not completely caught off guard.

"Who the hell are you?" He snarled at her.

"Chief Warrant Officer Eribisu. I work for Commander Salt."

He studied her for a moment, reading her thoughts and the truth that lay within them. Satisfied with her response, he let her go.

"What do you want?"

"I'm not the wanter, only the messenger. I brought you some clean clothes, not to mention that you smell like hell. The Commander wants to see you."

Ben looked over at Calder who was still basking in REM's.

"Hell has many variations." Ben quipped.

"But they're all still hell." She vamped. "I'll wake him: you get yourself together."

****

45

With bloodshot eyes dry and burning, Ben and Calder reported to Salt as ordered. Arriving at his Cubicle, they found him going over holographic videos of their training exercises, and examining the electronic analysis sheets that had recorded all of their brain data. They stood in front of him, trying to detect what he was thinking, but were unable to penetrate the psychic wall that seemed to always be around him. Ben had never met anyone who was so competently difficult to read. Calder was drawing the same blanks, but less curious as to why. Ivory entered the cube, nodded with a knowing wink, but said nothing. After a few more moments of silence, Salt finally met their eyes.

"Impressive. Some of the best scores ever. Not perfect, but with potential that we rarely see. Quite frankly, you've both exceeded my expectations, and I fully expect that you will continue to exceed them.

"Excuse me sir, if I may." Ben said. "But I'm still not clear as to what those expectations are."

"If you were reading the mental fabric properly, Mr. Denning, then you would be. Growth comes gradually, but I have no doubt that you will grow to be giants. But before we throw you in at the deep end of the pool, I think you both deserve a well-earned respite from the brain drain. I want you to take some down time, get to know the base and the surrounding areas. Let your minds relax. The war is not going anywhere. Captain Keyes will brief you on the next stage of endeavor, but for now I want you to know how very proud I am of you both, and that I look forward to working with you." He spoke with authority, but tendered his tone with earnest sincerity. His voice carried a stronger emotional component than before and that made Ben feel more comfortable, although not completely at ease.

Ivory escorted Ben and Calder out of the office and back to the main sector. As they walked from tube to tube, he took time to praise them yet again. Ben felt that this ongoing plethora of strokes was too heavy handed. He also felt that Ivory was holding something back. It wasn't so much what he said, but what he didn't say. Ben liked Ivory and had since they first met, but he hadn't lost sight of the fact that Ivory was also a dutiful soldier in the service of Namacal. And to date, in his dealings with Namacal, he maintained a strong sense that everything wasn't as purported, and that something was always hidden just beneath the surface. He could tell that Calder was suspicious too, but not to the same degree. Calder appeared to know that they were going to use him, but he seemed more willing to be used than Ben. For him, it was all just a big game. Ben recognized the game element too, and liked Calder in spite of their differences, but still didn't completely trust him. Calder was a wild card and much more unpredictable than Ivory. In this strange world that he'd now come to occupy, he realized that making friends, true friends, was going to be difficult. But just as he was considering all this, he caught both Ivory and Calder trying to read him. He quickly laughed off his mental wanderings with a shrug and slapped them on the shoulders.

"Fuck it." He said. "We're on the moon."

****

Ben and Calder had climbed to the top of a bulbous-domed observation tower where they could look out across the vast lunar land mass. Red embered skies could be seen in the distance, along with left over vapor trails from Fighter Craft returning from the war zone. The jarring booms of laser rockets and sonar bombs could be heard and felt, but not seen. Through that thin veil of death, the earth hung in space like an all-seeing eye. It was at once beautiful and overpoweringly surreal. But for Ben and Calder, the war was temporarily on hold. They had not climbed the tower merely for the view; they were there for the thrill of a leap into zero gravity, a function for which the tower was commonly used. Embracing each other's thoughts, they latched the faceplates on their pressurized helmets and stepped through the air lock to the outer edge of the tower. Drawing deep breaths and bellowing Comanche-like war cries, they leapt from the platform into the vast vacuum of space. The exhilaration was instantaneous and the joy of the descent prolonged. They floated to the lunar surface like ravens playfully wafting on the wind. Along the way, they flipped, spiraled, and executed a variety of flying tricks and maneuvers enjoying the freedom from gravity. It was a Peter Pan moment that both reveled in sharing.

Returning to the ground, they continued to run, bounce, and find new ways to enjoy the gravity-less world. With the psychological pressures temporarily suspended, it was a time of playful bonding, a time when the two of them were like boys again, innocently enjoying the rare atmosphere and the pleasure of each other's company. This mood of levity continued throughout the day as they explored the base, shared stories, and got to know one another better. There was a sense of freedom and camaraderie in their wanderings, but they never completely let down their guards.

Later that evening, they were joined by, Warrant Officer Eribisu and another Female Officer for drinks at the one of the Base Canteens. These small rec centers, composed of foamy 3-D materials, were skeletal sleek in design, and not that different from bars back home. Although one glance at the earth poised in the distant sky quickly reminded one how very far away they actually were. It was a well needed moment of relaxation, but one where the thought of war and the execution of duty never left their minds for long.

As the day ended, Ben and Calder returned to their quarters physically tired, but mentally refreshed.

"Quite a ride, huh?" Calder said as he dropped down on his bed. " And we're getting paid for it too."

"Calm before the storm." Ben said, collapsing into a chair.

"I know it probably sounds fucked up, but I'm actually looking forward to it. War mongering psycho-freaks juggling hi-jinks on moon, man, who would have thunk it. And not just as grunts either; we're kings, brother, they love us."

"But do they love us as much as they say? Too many strokes only sets you up for blows."

"Gotta take a few shots here and there, man. But you worry too much; they'll take care of us. Not to worry." He held his fingers up crossed like an "X". "No paranoia."

"There's a very thin line between paranoia and reality. They didn't bring us up here for the party, you know. Right now, you probably feel like your going a hundred miles an hour, but that's an illusion. The corporation is going a hundred miles an hour; you're standing still."

****

The next morning, Ivory met with Ben and Calder to brief them on the up and coming. Their R & R had been cut short and both had been ordered to prep themselves for special missions. Calder was to report to a Psy-Weapons Unit, and Ben was to go straight to Salt. As they parted, Ben gave Calder his hand, but caught a hint of jealousy in his eyes. He wasn't sure why at first, but after doing the math, realized that it was because he had been called to Salt and not Calder. Calder was a fierce competitor, and that Ben had been favored over him did not go down easy.

****

Ben reported to Salt and was again greeted with warm praising for his recent performance.

"Thank you, sir, but I can assure you, I haven't done anything special."

"And I can assure you have."

"Then Calder too. I believe he's much more suited for this program than I am."

"Very considerate of you, Mr. Denning. But given your lack of experience in the program, I don't feel you're qualified to make those types of judgments. As for Mr. Calder, you're right, he is good, a wonder in his own right, but not as good as you."

Ben watched him closely, and could feel that he was sincere in everything he was saying.

"Good is always good to hear, but being here on the moon, I'm no longer sure what that means."

"It means you're in a very unique position right now, a position of honor and respect. This is not the old army, Mr.

Denning; in the old army you were just a slave, cannon fodder. In the new army we know that money matters, therefore we make it matter. We put our money where our mouths are. The old way of training soldiers was to crush the individual spirit. The new way is to nurture it. Your resistance to structure and group think is actually what we're looking for, an asset in the type of work we do. But talking about it is just a waste of time. What we need to do is to start putting those amazing abilities of yours to work."

Ben tried to read his thoughts again, but Salt's psyche remained an impenetrable fortress. What did come through, and what Ben was able to decipher, was a positive emotional component. Salt was a genuine nurturer, and Ben already felt something of a kinship with him, something that went deeper than what he had experienced with either Ivory, or Calder. They were his peers, and he liked them, but Salt was more like a father figure. He had a compassionate quality that eased Ben's doubts and made him want to get closer to the Commander. Ben had never had a strong father figure in his life, so Salt, to some degree, was filling an old emotional need. But maybe that was just what he had intended, Ben thought. After all, Salt did know about Ben's father, the drinking, the absenteeism, and the abandonment. Maybe he was just playing the father card to win Ben's favor? Salt, sensing Ben's doubts, walked over and placed his hands on his shoulders.

"You've got the seed of greatness in you, Ben, and I don't say that lightly. You have more potential than anyone I've seen in this program. I'm absolutely certain you will do extraordinary things."

"I appreciate your vote of confidence, and hope that I can live up to it."

"You will?"

Salt smiled and clicked the star button on a remote that appeared in his hand as if by magic. A holographic orb opened above Ben's head like a caption cloud for a comic book character. Within the orb, a large lunar colony could be seen set against a vast landscape of plains, craters, and distant mountains.

"Junoko." Salt said. "I'm sure you've heard of it; it's the largest, one of the original six lunar colonies. It's a no fire zone, initially built to house technicians and Miners, but in recent years, particularly since the arrival of combat forces, it has grown into something of an R&R getaway. "What happens in Junoko stays in Junoko, get my drift?"

"I believe so."

"No weapons are allowed, which is a good thing, but it hasn't slowed down the flow of contraband and the trading of secrets. The pleasure sector is one of eight sectors that compose the Colony, a lunar sprawl of bars, dope dens, tat parlors, and whore stores of a wide variety. You'll see what I mean when you get there."

"Am I going on vacation?"

" No, but I want you to make it a vacation, at least by appearance. Your real mission is one of search and destroy...keeping in mind that information is always our most valuable commodity. Even though the battle zone is fifty kilometers away, Junoko is filled with spies, siphoning data wherever it falls. Loose lips tend to get looser with the vast array of mind-altering chemicals available there. Our soldiers go to blow off steam, but that steam often contains intelligence that falls into enemy hands. We want to handcuff those hands, or even better, take them out of the picture all together. That's where you come in."

He clicked the remote again and another holograph appeared, this one exhibiting a slow spinning carousel of faces.

"Potential suspects, spies, and Amerex operatives. We have reason to believe that some, or all of these individuals have or have had some connection with Amerex, past, present, or future. We also believe these people may be operating in Junoko. If they are, we'd like to know, and in what capacity they are functioning. But be aware, the air there is full of fabrications. What you see is not always what you get. But what we'd like for you to see and confirm is any intelligence regarding recent Amerex activity that could feasibly change the complexion of the war. Certain elements have been sniffed out that indicate potential missions, but nothing concrete. Given that Namacal is in the process of shuttling troops to an undisclosed location in preparation for an attack on one of Amerex's main Helium 3 processing facilities, it's imperative to uncover even the most seemingly insignificant innuendo. This operation is highly classified and we'd prefer not to see it jeopardized. Do I make myself clear?"

"I'm on a fact finding mission."

"Essentially, yes, but not exclusively. Amerex has their own team of mind operatives at work, and some very good ones too, I might add."

He clicked the remote and the singular image of a beautiful woman with dark, penetrating eyes filled the hologram.

"Her name is Eliana Ruiz, a known Amerex Intelligence Agent. We believe that she may be somewhere in Junoko. We also believe she may be in possession of valuable intelligence, but be advised she's an extremely dangerous woman, highly trained in psychic warfare. It would be better to kill her, than to let her into your psyche. In that, you must be explicitly clear."

"Death is about as clear as it gets. Would she or anyone else in Junoko know who I am?"

"No. You'll be given a cover, a false identity as a structural engineer here to study the technical viability of lunar structures. We'll give you enough details to pass the real thing test, but no one will question your identity unless they have other motives."

Salt clicked the remote again and the holograms were decentralized and withdrawn into a wrist computer. Salt then handed the computer over to Ben.

"Captain Ivory will give you additional specifics and introduce you to your escort team."

"Escorts?"

"Hard tenured muscle, in case you run into trouble."

"What kind of trouble?"

"It's a war, Ben. You may not be in the trenches, but blood runs red far beyond the trench. Make me proud, son, make me proud."

CHAPTER SEVEN

Ben was given civilian clothes and introduced to his escorts, Decker and Blalock, two Special Forces Rangers with high grade fighting skills. They weren't bubbling over with personality, and their humor was all but non-existent, but what they lacked in social graces they made up for with hard sinew. The term lean and mean was no misnomer. Nevertheless they were cordial and happy to be joining Ben, not because he was in command of the mission, which he was, but because it was easy duty, the type of assignment that didn't come everyday, and one in which they weren't being constantly shot at. Any mission outside the war zone was a welcome relief. Ben got all this information from simply reading their thoughts. In turn, they knew he was a reader and that they were on an intelligence mission, but that was the extent of their information. Everything else was on a need to know basis.

****

The Lunar Flight Module carrying Ben and the Rangers landed at the Junoko Spaceport late in the afternoon of that same day. The blue glow of earth seen in the distance was a constant reminder just how far away Ben was from the real world and everything he had ever known. A sense of the surreal permeated his thoughts and left him longing for home.

As he and his escorts entered the Colony's Pleasure Sector, his first impression was that of a carnival. The Sector was a bustling honeycomb made up of endless cubicles with circus-like thematics that seemed surprisingly out of place in the dark lunar glom. Music filled the tubular streets, and the smell of synthetic alcohol was fulgent in the piped air. A vast series of polyplex tubes wound off in different directions and linked the extensive network of sectors and cubicles together. It would be easy to get lost or to hide in such a maze, Ben thought, and he was already feeling at something of a disadvantage in its myriad passageways.

Decker and Blalock had been to Junoko before, but on their own time, not as agents of Namacal. Command had provided them with an itinerary, but the parameters were broad.

Moving from cube to cube, Ben picked up more than just the flow of mood and traffic; he picked up the aural and visual thoughts of those around him. Much of the mind chatter was drug addled, overcharged with lust, and mostly meaningless, but there were kernels of potentially relevant information to be found here and there. But as he familiarized himself with the sector, and after filtering through a massive amount of brain data, it ultimately all added up to nothing.

Trawling the network of tubes, the trio entered several designated bars, one of which had great open views of the surrounding lunar cliffs and the massive crescent walls of an adjacent crater. A dream-like quality was pervasive throughout. Ordering up a round of Grog, the locally brewed synthetic beer, and a freeze-dried snack of space jerky, which Decker described as cardboard gourmet, they took their time and enjoyed just lounging about. It was easy work, perhaps too easy, Ben thought, because he could not rid himself of a strong gut level sense that something of a darker nature was about to happen.

He tried to keep his mind focused on the business at hand, but there were distractions at every turn. Everywhere they went, they were met with offers for gravity-less sex, one of Junoko's bigger pleasure attractions, and a must do, as Blalock explained eager to escort Ben into the experience. And though the appeal had obvious attractions, and the whores in Junoko were imported and much better than the average street trade, Ben stayed committed to the mission.

Sticking to the loose itinerary, Decker guided them to Sungu's Galaxy, a bar renowned as one of the wildest places in the complex, and one thought to be frequented by Amerex operatives. Upon entering the club, they were bombarded by digital music, electronic flying games, and semi-nude girls suspended in floating laser bubbles that bobbed from the ceiling like the accoutrement of a pre-century disco. The place was exploding with discordant energy, extremely distracting for Ben's purposes. The circular bar at the center of the club was stocked with every form of alcohol and chemical substance imaginable, and some that weren't. Poppy Drops, drug infused sugar cubes, floated down from the ceiling like snowflakes, and papyrus rolled opiated herbs were traded like seeds at a farmer's market. The smoky fumes of designer drugs raped the nostrils and filled the air with intoxicating perfumes. This was the quintessential den of iniquity, Ben thought, and equal to any counterparts back on earth. A few scuffles broke out on occasion between the over amped, inebriated workers, but for the most part everyone was just slaphappyily stoned, and civility was in surprisingly good form.

Ben and his men ordered drinks and moved through the bar watching the crowd. He was discreet in his mental maneuvers, purposefully not wanting to draw attention to himself. Retreating to a darkened corner, he used a RS47 scanner to eavesdrop on miscellaneous thought forms too far away to read mentally. The scanner, which was easily concealed on his thumbnail, was capable of measuring brain waves and converting them into language. As he randomly directed the scanner's energy beam, he picked up plenty of chat about sex and drugs, tid-bits of tech talk laced with standard moon jargon, but essentially nothing subversive. In that same regard, he was very careful to keep his own thoughts bridled and blurred from invasive minds or telepathic equipment.

As the night wore on, he continued to use this same method of eavesdropping as they followed Decker's itinerary from bar to bar and club to club. Along the way, they passed a group of U.S. Dignitaries who were being given a tour of Junoko by members of the Colony's Council. One of the dignitaries was a key member of the International Peace Organization, a group committed to both World and Interstellar Peace. His name was, Alazar Soledad, and he was the same man who had been monitoring Ben before he had left earth on the Shuttle. The two men's eyes met briefly, and though neither of them spoke or gave any indication of knowing the other, there was a passing hint of recognition, though too subtle to be anything but inconclusive.

Ben and his team continued hitting bars, and the cumulative effects of alcohol were beginning to show. Ben had been backing off, not finishing drinks, and advised Decker and Blalock to do the same They insisted they had it under control, given that they had taken a couple of "Super Blacks", a type of designer speed which was capable of defeating alcohol levels faster than it could be ingested. Even so, as Ben monitored their thoughts, he could see a definite shift in alertness. There was also more lust and aggression in their actions. Given the environment, a little of this was to be expected, but he feared these aggressions would draw unwanted attention. Desiring to keep a lower profile, he sought a quieter climate in which to do business.

****

Sonar bombs exploded across the vast Maria, and huge hunks of lunar earth floated in open space along with the dismembered limbs of Soldiers slaughtered in the heat of battle. Fire streams from laser rockets streaked the dark sky where Fighter Craft had recently engaged in lunar dogfights.

Calder and a Platoon of Namacal Rangers moved stealthily through a regolith trench trying to reach a Namacal Controlled Mining Outpost that had recently come under siege. They were tracking a rogue Colonel who was reported to have sold information to Amerex that had ultimately led to the attack. It was Calder's first taste of the real war, but in spite of the carnage and horror that was all around him, he felt more at home than the men who accompanied him. He seemed to feed on danger and thrive on the possibility of death. He wielded a semi-automatic Microwave rifle, and used it proficiently to project disorienting thought waves at the enemy. Subsequently, confused Amerex soldiers were easily picked off, never knowing what hit them. But Calder didn't limit his actions to the ground; he was also able to take out an enemy Fighter Craft with a laser rocket launched from his shoulder. He had yet to apply is psychic power to the battlefront, but his amazing prowess with weaponry had his platoon cheering him on.

****

In Junoko's Lagoon Club, the fever of chemicals and lust were still evident, but the tone of play was less manic than the other watering holes Ben and his team had been to. It was a fluid, sexy place with a wraparound bar circling a waist deep faux crater at its center. The crater was actually a dipping pool that served as a cooling off place for hot bodies and weary dancers. A stage was set up at the rear of the room where a Techno-fusion band pumped out a slow grind of electronic space jazz. The sexual vibe was strong in the club and Ben quickly found himself playing eye games with several women. The hour was late and the thought of lying down somewhere next to a warm body began to impose itself upon both his body and his mind.

After ordering a round of drinks, he used the scanner to eavesdrop on thoughts around the room, and for the first time since arriving in the Colony, the name of Amerex popped up more than once. Ben stayed with each thought line for a short turn, but ultimately the results were disappointing. Conversations rolled over him like luminous waves that filtered in and out of his brain. His eyes wandered over the endless array of faces, all cast in the light of the lunar night that drifted in through the bubbled dome cupola. He scanned dozens of faces and sifted through as many minds, but results were endlessly lacking, and he was beginning to feel the pure futility of his efforts. It was the search for the proverbial needle in a haystack, and he was just about ready to call it a night when a beautiful saloon singer stepped on stage to join the band.

"Sweet babies, welcome." She said breathily into the microphone; her voice reverberating in a sultry tone that entered Ben's ears and coursed through his body like a wave of heat. "I know the moon is rising, and the tides are high, so why not fly with me for just a little while and let my song kiss your worries away."

Decker and Blalock gave her a hungry look, but were more interested in two bar girls who were walking past. But Ben never flinched; he kept watching her as the words dripped off her lips like warm honey. The effect she had on him was instantaneous, and he could literally feel the force of her presence and the electric surge of her libido passing through him.

"My name is Eliana." She whispered, stroking the microphone with her fingers. "And if you love to dream, then pull down the shades on your mind, and join me in a dream."

It was pure theater, but enticing enough to make Ben feel like he was slipping into a dream. But the echo of her name suddenly came back and snapped him out of his reverie. He knew the name and now remembered the face. For a moment, he'd almost forgotten what he was doing and why he was doing it. But while he was clearing his head, Eliana began to sing and the melody floated off her tongue like a delicate piece of lace that wrapped around him and stole his thoughts once again. Her voice was ethereal and the song one of longing and unrequited love. Ben watched the gentle heaving of her breasts as she poured herself into the music. With each new breath, she drew him out of himself and into the twisting vectors of her mind. It was a strange sensation, he thought, because it felt like she was singing to him and him alone. He checked other people's reactions, but most of the audience had turned away, back to their drinks and the sweet dreams at their elbows. But Ben stayed with her, word for word, nuance for nuance. He had been knocked off his feet by women before, and had even encountered love at first sight, but one heartbreak had been more than enough to make him cautious. In love as in gambling, he had learned to play his cards close to the vest. But there was something different, almost magical about this woman, something that spoke to him in a different way. Each word she sang penetrated his body all the way down to the cellular level. Her effect on him was hypnotic, but remembering the mission at hand, he broke the spell, and re-checking his computer, scrolled through the images that Salt had provided for him. Yes, she was there, different makeup, different hairstyle, but the very same woman that Salt had designated as a dangerous Amerex Agent. Ben wondered why he hadn't recognized her immediately, and why she was having such a powerful effect on him. Maybe she was projecting thought illusions, or mind manipulations. Her long, dangling earrings could be transmitters he thought. Ultimately, it seemed impossible, because she had no idea who he was or why he was there. And the curious, almost instantaneous attraction he had for her felt completely real. He tried hard to read her thoughts, but her focus on the music was so concentrated, there was no room for anything else. Still, he was completely intrigued by her and knew he had to find out more.

He didn't say anything to Decker or Blalock, but left them at the bar and took a table closer to the stage. From that vantage point, he could see her eyes, dark, cobalt blue, almost black. They were focused directly on him, and seemingly looking right through him. His heart had begun to race and his pulse was pounding. She was even more beautiful up close than from afar, and her olive skin was glowing as if luminescent blood flowed through her veins. Perhaps it was only the thin air and heady alcohol rushing through his brain that had skewed his thoughts and stirred his emotions, but no one else in the room seemed to be effected in the same way. It wasn't the lyrics or the music that touched him, but the way she sang them, so personal, so lovingly. He was beginning to see and hear her internal dialogue, coming directly at him and telling him how beautiful she thought he was. The veracity and seductiveness of those thoughts drew him even deeper into her emotional circle.

Decker and Blalock kept a periodic eye on him, but were becoming more distracted by the bar girls who had joined them for a drink. The night had heated up to the point where the pull of the flesh was getting harder to resist. But it wasn't only the flesh that was affected; Eliana's song had swept the entire room into a swoon, a strange and subtle hypnotic heat. The crowd was sweating and getting curiously fidgety. Foreplay was evident in every glance and touch. Ben was aware that something odd was going on, but it was a new and pleasant sensation that he did not want to abandon, much less try to explain. By this time, Decker and Blalock looked like docile little doughboys in the hands of the fleshy women at their sides. The room seemed to be moving, swirling, tables and chairs floating just above the floor. Was he hallucinating, or was it just the reflection in the bubble glass surrounding him that revealed the gravity-less flow of the lunar world outside? Ben was questioning everything, but determinations were illusive. Eliana was bringing her song to an end and the emotions that rose with the melody were touching the very fiber of his being. He could feel the music in his bones and in the blood coursing through his veins. It was like a drug, a strange siren's song, that no matter how hard he tried to elude its effects, they proved irresistible. Her voice rose to a fever pitch, finally hitting a climatic high C. The note shot through him like a jolt of electricity and held him in total limbo. When the note finally faded and the band brought the phrasing to and end, a dead silence fell over the room.

"Eliana." The Electric Kyoto Player shouted, offering his enthusiastic approval. The audience followed suit and broke into a boisterous round of applause. Ben found himself clapping perhaps a bit too forcefully, and in a manner that made him stand out from the crowd. He softened the verve of his applause, but Eliana had already recognized his hearty appreciation, and much to his surprise, was walking toward him. Her smile was warm and disarming, and it looked as if she were about to speak, but when she was only a step away, she walked past him without a word. He was certain she had been looking directly at him, but had passed as if he were invisible.

"Hey." He blurted out, wishing he could pull the word back, but it was already too late. She turned, locked eyes with him, but said nothing. Words weren't necessary as her thoughts were already pulsing out of her forehead and into his. What she thought, he saw, and what he saw was mesmerizing.

"You're so beautiful." She spoke without moving her lips. "Why don't you ask me to sit down for a drink instead of staring at me?"

"Loved your set." he said, "Could I buy you a drink?" She studied him for a moment longer, sensing that he had stolen her thought, but not letting him know that.

"Thought you'd never ask." She said smiling and taking a seat beside him. He signaled a waitress over and --

"Your pleasure?"

"Moonshine."

"Moonshine?"

"It's actually synthetic bourbon. Fitting name though. Not as good as the real thing, but sweet and smooth. My father was from the south and he always drank bourbon."

"I've spent some time down south and sipped my share of bourbon. Love the food and drink, not so much the mind set."

"The people have a tendency to hold on to the past, but people are people wherever you go, right...the good, the bad, and the ugly."

"And the beautiful." She knew he was referring to her, but she played the compliment demurely.

"True beauty is in the heart, not the eye."

"But recognizable either way. And often the subtext speaks louder than the text itself."

"But only if it has something true to say."

"Truth is mutable."

"But comes in many shades."

"Like the shades in your song, so passionately expressed. When something like that touches you, it goes beyond thought straight to the soul."

"You're a philosopher."

"Not at all, but I was moved.

"By me, or the song?"

"Without you the song wouldn't matter. You gave the song breath, made it come to life."

"Then I did my job."

"I doubt anybody would argue that."

Ben looked past her to Decker and Blalock who were still chatting up the bar girls.

"Good, I hate to argue, don't you?"

"Sometimes it's necessary."

"Like evil.

"Is evil necessary?"

"Sounds trite, but without it we wouldn't truly appreciate the good. You look familiar to me." She said, steering the conversation in a different direction. "Have we met; have you been here before?"

"No, I just downloaded a few days back. I'm an engineer here doing a study on lunar structures and how we might develop more stabilized building components using lunar materials."

"It would certainly be cheaper than transporting them from earth."

"Exactly. We're already using regolith in many designs, but we need to find a way to strengthen those structures. 3 D printing has become a helpful tool."

"We'll be printing human beings the next thing you know."

"Maybe already."

"You think so?"

"The world is full of secrets."

""So it is. Who is backing your study?"

"Primary financing is through the International Scientific Committee. But this is all pretty boring stuff. Not like being a torch singer in a moon club."

"I'm just a moonlighter, not a real singer. The guys in the band are friends and are sweet enough to let me sit in now and then."

"They should let you sit in more, you steal the show."

"You're too kind."

"No, you're just that good. I didn't just hear that music; I felt it."

As their conversation continued, Ben kept trying to read her thoughts, but received a lot of blurred interference. Maybe it was the music that was still in her, repeating its phrases, but whatever it was, it was powerful.

"So if you're just moonlighting here, what do you do in the daylight?"

"Daylight? There isn't any daylight on the moon. " She smiled as she spoke, so seductively that he felt his pores expand as if he were melting. "I'm actually a nurse at the Medical Facility...four on three off. This is my three."

"Lucky for me."

She watched his eyes drop and take in the lines of her body. It was a tactful glance, but one that didn't get past her.

"So you're interested in other structures, not just the purely lunar."

He heard her speak, but her lips didn't move.

"I'm sorry, what?"

"Didn't say anything, but...structurally speaking, you don't really look like an engineer."

"Didn't know there was a look. What do I look like?"

"A guitar slinger."

"Never heard that one before."

"Do you play?"

"I've tinkered, but I'm not that good, although my father was a musician."

"I knew there was something there."

"Not much. I didn't really know him that well; he wasn't around a lot.

"And your mother?"

"Mom and Dad never won any awards for parenting."

"Sorry, didn't mean to pry."

"It's all ancient history. But tell me about your music. Where did you learn to sing like that?

"Mostly from my mother. She was Portuguese and was always singing around the house. She loved Fado. Do you know Fado?"

"I've heard of it, but..."

"It's an ancient style of music, been around for centuries, mournful, but beautiful. That was a Fado song I just sang."

"I'd love to hear more."

"I've had my moment in the spotlight for tonight, but there is a club in the next tube that has an amazing Fado singer. I could take you if you like."

The invitation came as something of a surprise, but one that made Ben pause.

"Unless, of course, you're doing something else."

"No, no, not at all, I just..."

He looked back to Decker and Blalock who were no longer watching him, but fully ensnared by the bar girls.

"Why not?"

"Perfect. And what was your name again, Ben?"

"I didn't tell you my name."

"But it is Ben, right?"

"That's right, but..."

"You look like a Ben. C'mon, it's not far."

                        ****

The Majog was a tube away, but in a separate vector that Ben had not been to before. It was a sultry bar with steamy walls and a liquid dance floor. Dancers were out in force, half clad and painted with sweat. Donna Carrado, the singer whom Eliana had praised, was already on stage, but recognized Eliana as she and Ben entered. Donna was a petite beauty with the voice of a lioness. Her song, in Portuguese, had a mournful melody, but she rendered in an oddly seductive tone. The effect was hypnotically sensual, and Ben was drawn into the music in the most immediate way.

"Spectacular, isn't she?" Eliana said. "And so fuckable too."

He shot her a questioning glance, but realized her lips had not moved.

"I said she's spectacular."

"Yes, amazing."

He had only heard the thought, but it was a thought that laced around him like a barbed tease. Was she playing him, he wondered? Playfulness was in her eyes, but so was earnestness. The problem was that she shifted from one to the other so quickly that he could barely keep up.

"So how long have you been here?" He asked.

"On the moon? About six months."

"And is it what you expected?"

"I don't think one can predetermine war and the effect it will have on you. I have good and bad days, like everybody. Sometimes it feels absolutely surreal. You'll know what I mean after you've been here a while."

"It feels that way already. The light, the claustrophobia, the lack of gravity, the people."

"The people?"

"I'm not sure what it is, but people don't seem quite real here, or at least a step removed from real. It's like watching people in a movie, only you're in the movie with them. Even you; I look at you, and I know you're real, but at the same time you're like an enigma, someone from a dream."

"It's the canned air; it makes you dizzy."

"Maybe, but...from the time I first saw you...I don't think it's just the air."

"Am I making you nauseous?"

"No." He said laughing. "It's just...you're such a beautiful woman...what can I say."

"It's the moonlight. It plays tricks on you."

"If that were the case, I'd be falling in love every second."

"Woo, love....love is a big word."

"Enchantment is probably a better one."

"I like enchantment. And I love to be enchanted."

The subtext of her words ran deep and he could feel her eyes penetrating him, working their way into his mind and heart. But she could feel him too, not just the attraction they were sharing, but the power of his psychic presence.

"Are you reading my mind?"

"Reading your mind?" He said, feigning surprise. "I'm an engineer, remember."

"And I'm a nurse."

"Do you heal the sick?"

"Are you sick?"

"I could be."

"You're not sick. I see the sick day in and day out. I see the wounded, the mutilated, the dying, the horrible underbelly of this war. I see young men maimed and destroyed for the prosperity of old rich men. And I hate it. I hate every bit of it, every drop of spilled blood."

"But you're still taking part in it."

"No, I'm trying to do my part; there's a difference. "

"With such strong anti-war feelings, I'm surprised that you have a part at all."

"One doesn't have to agree with a thing to do a thing. I do what I have to do."

"And I'm sure you do it well."

"Obviously not well enough. Say what I will, do what I will, I'm still working for the corporation."

"We all work for the corporation."

"Not you."

"Indirectly."

"But not as a warrior or a profiteer."

"I've made my own deals with the devil, believe me."

He looked past her to the door where Decker and Blalock we're just entering.

"Someone you know?" She asked, watching the movement of his eyes.

"No, I...not really."

"You're lying."

"What?"

"I didn't say anything."

He watched her closely trying to catch up with her thoughts, but all he could see was the allure in her eyes that kept drawing him back to her beauty.

"Are you okay?" She asked touching his hand.

"I think I just had one of those surreal moments you were talking about."

"Then you're one of us."

"Human?"

"Did you doubt it?"

"I'm still learning to accept it. Being human carries with it certain responsibilities. I've been shirking those responsibilities for a long time."

"But that's part of being human too."

"I suppose, but...you have the most incredible eyes."

"They keep me from running into things."

"They didn't keep you from running into me."

"Things in the mirror look closer than they really are. "

"And reflections are sometimes more real than substance."

"Is that what you see in my eyes, a reflection?"

"A reflection of your inner being."

"So you are a philosopher. But if you can truly see my inner being, then you can probably see the wicked bitch that I really am."

"I doubt you're that wicked."

"Catch me on a bad day."

"I'm betting any day with you would be a good one."

"You're a dreamer, a romantic."

"A cynical romantic, I would think."

"And I think you've got more teddy bear in you than you'd like to admit."

"It's an illusion. I killed that teddy bear a long time ago."

"Maybe you just wounded him...and he's been waiting for an opportunity, the right moment to reappear."

"I think maybe you're the romantic."

"I love romance, and I'd love it more if it weren't an illusion...of course that doesn't mean I don't love the illusion." Every word she spoke touched him, charmed him, and turned his thoughts inside out. Whoever she was, she wasn't what he expected. Salt had described her as dangerous, and maybe she was, but she was also the most exciting woman he had ever met.

"Where do the nurses stay on base?"

"Do you mean where do I stay?"

"I guess that's what I mean"

"The nurses quarters are near the hospital, but when I come here I usually book a sleeper. Just in case."

"In case?"

"I drink too much, or... I meet someone."

She might as well have stuck a fire poker in his heart and set it aflame.

"And what happens then?"

"That's up to you."

"Are you trying to seduce me?"

"If you have to ask, I must not being doing a very good job."

He said nothing, just leaned in and gave her a soft kiss.

"If you did any better, you could wipe me off the floor. But you realize, of course, that we only met an hour ago.

"Seems like a life time. We are at war, you know. There's no guarantee of tomorrow, and I don't believe in wasting time. If I see something I like, I go for it."

"That can be dangerous."

"I'm not afraid, are you?"

She entwined her fingers in his and lifted his hand. With that touch, his body seemed to rise out of the chair floating on air. Donna Carrado was still singing, but she was also watching them, as were Decker and Blalock. No one knew what was going to happen next, but something was definitely going to happen.

****

Ben and Eliana left the club and made their way along the tube toward the Rikko Sleeper, a triple bubble structure at the far end of the sector. As they reached the entrance, Ben glanced back expecting to see Decker and Blalock shadowing them, but no one was there. It was nothing to cause him concern, because he could feel their energy and knew they were somewhere close.

As they passed through the Rikko lobby the rugged lunar terrain was visible through a large portal window. It was another surreal moment, Ben thought, walking hand in hand with an extraordinarily beautiful woman for a rendezvous on the moon. There was no longer any conversation between them, and no need for it, everything they thought and felt was expressed in their eyes and the sensual movement of their bodies.

Entering the small cozy sleep unit, they immediately fell into each other's arms. The temperature inside was warm, but the heat from their bodies was almost radiant and began to steam the bubble windows.

"Fuck me." She said, the words effortlessly clear, but not issued aloud. Hearing her thought, Ben pressed himself closer, so close that he felt he was sinking into her flesh. For a moment, he experienced a sensation of reconnection, an imaginary reflection of what it would be like to be a Siamese twin. It was only a passing thought, but the touch of warm flesh wasn't. Their clothes were already damp with sweat, and they pealed them off like shredded paper. Passions were running wide open, and Ben knew that he was quickly losing control. The woman he was with was a suspected enemy combatant, a woman he'd been advised to be cautious of and to kill if necessary. But how could he destroy such a beautiful creature, he wondered? The attraction between them was so magnetic, that he couldn't imagine himself laying one harmful finger on her, much less actually taking her life. Could it be, he wondered, that Salt was wrong, and that she wasn't what she was made out to be? Ben had been given an order, but that didn't mean he had to follow through with it. Plus, she may have information that warranted further investigation, and the closer he got to her allotted him the possibility of getting more from her. He was being deceptive, he knew, but on the heart to heart, body-to-body level; he wanted her in a way that he had wanted few women before.

He opened his eyes and saw that the room was turning in a carousel-like motion and shifting geometrically. Eliana was in his arms, but now completely naked and pulling him across the hexagon air-suspension bed in a horizontal dance. The bed floated several feet above the floor and rotated slowly while undulating up and down. Their bodies reallocated and he suddenly found her sliding across his chest, stretching her legs around him.

"I want your heart." She whispered, but only in thought. "Till death do us part," she continued, the words drawing his eyes into hers and turning them inside out like inverted whirlpools. Her thoughts kept coming at him in broken breaths. "Fuck me, fuck me." She kept repeating the phrase like a mantra that entangled his mind in heated supplication. Suddenly, her tongue flickered like that of a serpent. It was an image that startled him and drew him up and out of the sexual vortex with bullet-shot quickness. But as her tongue traced the shape of her heart on his body, he sunk back into the heat of her flesh and lost himself there.

Stirred by desire and driven by a fire he could no longer control; he kissed his way from her neck down to the soft mounds of her breasts. There, he circled her nipples, and continued his descent by doing tiny laps around her navel. The taste of her skin ignited his passion to even greater heights. With her legs coiled to her elbows, he entered her body and they began to make love. The sensation of merger was electric and sent veritable shock waves through every cell within them. Sex was not a new experience for either, but this was not ordinary sex. Ben felt as if he was melting inside of her and being transformed into a new being. It was no longer just a physical act, but the act of the soul in ecstasy. Their bodies were on fire, but more than that it was, curiously, an out of body experience. They were levitating, transcending the world together. But suddenly Eliana's eyes broke free of the dream and shifted to the door. It was shut and locked, but she sensed a presence just beyond.

Decker was on the other side of the door signaling to Blalock who was waiting at the end of the hall. He listened for a moment longer, and then backed away. Eliana felt his departure, but didn't react. Once again, she allowed the sensations of their love making to overtake her. Ripples of energy, like waves of atomic heat, rushed through her and opened the pores of her flesh. Fluids ran like raging rivers and an explosion of ecstatic force shook the room. Their bodies were lifted off the bed, and slammed back down again. The motion kept repeating over and over until they were at last drained of the fire that drove them. By the time reality filtered back into their consciousness, they were left trembling in each other's arms. Minutes passed before either of them was able to speak.

"Beautiful." She finally said, the words caressing his ears like the tickle of a feather. "If only you weren't such a liar." The phrase hit him like a slap in the face he didn't see coming. He opened his eyes only to find that hers were still closed. All he had heard was a thought, but if it were a true thought, what was behind it? As he pondered the question, she rolled over and snuggled up against him. He could feel the pulse of her heart and the warm stickiness of sweat that still clung to her body.

"Like a dream." He whispered to her.

"A dream within a dream." She said giving him a soft kiss. With her lips still on his, they closed their eyes again and the world around them disappeared.

CHAPTER EIGHT

The moon turned in the sky of Ben's mind like a glittering dance hall orb. It pulsed with a heartbeat rhythm, the blue glow of earth shining behind it in the distance. With each new pulse the image slowly began to dissolve until once again he could see and feel Eliana's breasts pressed against his chest. The warmth of her body was all around him and clung to him like a sensual cocoon. He was still naked, but no longer in bed. He was floating in a gravity-less void above the lunar surface. He was as relaxed as he had ever been in his life, but as he glanced up, he saw dark clouds forming on the horizon. Given that the moon had no true atmosphere, he wondered how there could be clouds at all? The question broke the spine of his dream and brought him back to consciousness. Suddenly, he was wide-awake, trying to remember where he was and how long he'd been there. Glancing around the room, it all began to come back to him: the club, the Fado, the night of lovemaking. It had been perfect in every way, but something was missing, and that something was Eliana. The covers were pulled back and he could still see the imprint of her body on the dampened sheets. He was about to call her name when he noticed something in the room that wasn't there before. The dark cloud he'd seen in dream was now hovering near the foot of the bed.

"Eliana," he called out, but to no response. And then something moved, but unclear as to what it was. And then the cloud vanished.

"You're awake." She said standing where the cloud had been a moment before. She was still naked and her skin was glistening and speckled gossamer red.

"What time is it?" He asked.

"Time to wake up." She said softly with her mind.
Suddenly his eyes sprang open with the realization that he had not been awake at all. He looked back to the end of the bed, but she was no longer there.

"Eliana?" He called out, but again to no answer. He threw the covers back and put one foot on the floor. Upon contact he immediately felt something sticky. A glance down revealed his foot resting in a pool of blood.

"Jesus." He exclaimed, lifting his leg, blood flicking from his heel onto the sheets. He wasn't sure where the blood had come from, but as his eyes became accustomed to the light, he spotted the silhouette of a body just visible in the shadows. His breath broke and froze in his throat. His muscles locked in a static position, and for a moment, he was unable to move. Finally, he climbed out of the bed, stepped over the blood pool, and moved cautiously toward the body. As he got closer, he saw the military boots – and more blood - on the carpet and walls. But it was something else that literally froze him in place – a second body. Panic ripped through him with a sharp thrust and set his eyes to darting. There was no one else in the room, but he snatched a small chrome vase from the dresser as a make-do weapon. He returned to the first body, which was turned away from him, and knelt down beside it. The shadows were deep, but there was just enough light to see the open chest wound. Touching the shoulder, he pulled the body toward him exposing the pale, white, and breathless face of Decker.

"Fuck." He muttered, fear pulsing through him and questions flooding his mind. Shaking off the initial shock, he stepped past Decker and identified the second body as that of Blalock. He had no idea what had happened, but one key question kept burning through his mind - where was Eliana? Dazed and confused, he stumbled back to the bed, grabbed his clothes, and hurried to dress. As he snapped the last button on his shirt, he noticed a slip of torn paper on the nightstand. He picked it up tentatively and read the scribbled writing.

"CONSIDER YOURSELF LUCKY"
****

Ben left the Rikko and returned to the Lagoon Club his mind burning with questions and bristling with rage. It was early and the club wasn't open yet, but he kept ringing the door buzzer until a Steward finally came.

"We're closed." He grumbled at being interrupted.

"I can see that." Ben snapped back. "But I'm not here for a drink, I'm looking for the girl who sang here last night."

"Get the fuck on." The Steward moved to close the door, but Ben wedged a foot inside.

"On is in. It's important."

"I don't know any girl singer."

"Eliana. She was here with the band last night."

"I wasn't here last night."

"Somebody was."

"Come back at five."

"I need to find her now. What about the manager?"

"Not here."

"You're lying."

The Steward was indignant, but Ben's intensity was forceful enough to make him reconsider.

"He's doesn't like to be interrupted."

"It will only take a minute."

He agreed reluctantly, and led Ben back to the Manager's office.

"Somebody here to see you."

The Manager, Leo Vasquez was a big man with a salt and pepper goatee and small beady eyes. He was parked behind a monochrome desk covered with laser documents, and not at all happy to see Ben at his door.

"He says it's important."

"Then it better be a matter of life and death." Vasquez barked back.

"I'm looking for Eliana."

"I don't know any Eliana, and that's not even close to life and death.

"She sang here last night."

"She may have sung somewhere, but not here. We don't have a girl singer."

"She sat in with the band. I bought her a drink and…"

"You could have bought her a diamond ring for all I know, but not here. We don't have a girl singer, and I don't have time for this bullshit."

Every word he spoke was a lie. Ben read him easily, but wasn't sure why he was lying. He could have forced the issue, but decided to hold off until he knew more.

"Yea, maybe it was somewhere else. Sorry to have bothered you."

****

Ben left the club and stopped in the street, his mind racing back over the events of the previous night. He relived every moment that he had spent with Eliana, but was still unable to connect the dots. How could he have been so blind as to have not seen any of this coming? Could his instincts have been that far off? He knew enough not to trust his head, reason was too often unreliable, but he trusted his gut unequivocally. But in this case, trusting his gut had only led to disaster. Decker and Blalock were dead, Eliana had disappeared, and the people who should know her were denying it. The fact that he'd been had was not a matter of question; the question was what to do about it. He couldn't just leave the bodies in the sleeper unit, and didn't want to alert the Junoko authorities, or try to explain to them what had happened when he couldn't explain it to himself. Going back to Salt would be an embarrassing admission of failure, which he wasn't ready to concede to yet. There was only one-person left that he felt he could turn to, and that was Ivory.

CHAPTER NINE

The Lunar Module carrying Ivory landed at the Junoko Spaceport less than an hour later. Ben met him at the gate as he deboarded, his face stern and serious.

"You okay?" Ivory asked.

"I'm okay, I just don't know what the hell went wrong."

"That's what we're going to find out."

Ben and Ivory returned to the Rikko where he had left the bodies of Decker and Blalock. But when they stepped inside the small sleep unit, there were no bodies. The room had been cleaned, the bed made, and no signs of blood remained.

"They were there, right there when I left. The floor was covered in blood. The bed was..."

"You sure this is the same room?"

"Of course I'm sure. They were there. Fucking dead."

Ivory's glare was penetrating, but Ben could see that he was only trying to understand what he couldn't explain.

"Stay cool, Ben, somebody is obviously running a game on you."

"Obviously, but that's what I don't understand. I came here a stranger; no one was suppose to have known me. "

"But someone did. What we need to do is find out who."

"I went back to the club, looking for the woman, but the staff claimed not to know her. They were lying through their teeth, but..."

"Show me her picture."

Ben clicked in her photo and projected it holographically.

"You know her?"

"I know of her - tricky, treacherous, and...but you should have known that too."

"I was trying to gain her trust, get inside her head."

"You got inside her head all right, but she was inside yours first. While you were busy fucking her, she was fucking you."

"But she didn't know me, she didn't know who I was."

"She knew."

"Then why am I still alive and Decker and Blalock dead."

"Good question. She's not known to be the charitable type."

Ben took the note from his pocket that Eliana had written and handed it to him.

"She left this on the nightstand."

"Then I'd say you are lucky."

"But that doesn't account for the missing bodies?"

"You don't have to worry about the bodies, it's unlikely we'll ever find them. Space is a big place and a big dumping ground for people who want to dispose of something. Those boys are gone, but she isn't, and she isn't working alone. We'll find her soon enough, but in the meantime you'll need to talk to Commander Salt."

"He knows?"

"He always knows."

CHAPTER TEN

Ben returned to the Namacal Base and was sent to N-Sight Headquarters to meet with Salt. He tried to present an image of calm, but inside his stomach was churning. He'd played his first game of mind control and lost badly. Salt would be disappointed, but it was more than failure that gnawed at Ben, it was the idea that he'd fallen for one of the oldest games going; he'd been suckered in by a pretty face. And with that face came the faces of Decker and Blalock. They appeared before him on an endless reel of memory, their dead eyes glaring accusingly.

Ludovic led Ben into the Commander's office where he was waiting, quietly gazing out the portal window. He didn't acknowledge Ben at first, and that gave Ben a chance to try to read his thoughts. It proved, as it had before, to be a futile effort. Ben had learned how to be thought evasive, but Salt seemed to be able to shatter thought itself, a mind trick that Ben did not know and had not mastered. A long moment of silence passed before Salt finally turned to him with a scrutinous and critical eye.

"Of all the candidates, of all the amazing minds that have been brought into this division over the years, you've shown more potential and ability than any other. I knew you were special when you came to us, a mental giant, in my opinion, and with only minimal training showed your talent to be the best of the best. Watching you was like watching my own son. You filled me with hope, pride, and expectations of greatness. The mission you were assigned was not a test per se, but it was an opportunity to secure a ranking position within the hierarchy of this force. But you blew it. You tripped over your own cock and fell for the oldest trick in the book. It was a fatal error that costs the lives of two good soldiers. "

"I can't argue that, sir, but what I don't understand is how she knew who I was. It's almost as if she knew I was coming and played me accordingly."

"It's her job to play you. You can't assume anything in this game, Lieutenant."

"I didn't assume anything; I was tricked."

"Of course you were tricked; it's her job to trick you. What we're paying you for is to be trickier than she is, and you failed the test. And by all accounts you should be dead right now."

"That's another thing I don't understand. She could have killed me easily, but she didn't. So maybe I did something right."

"The fact that you're alive does not meet the criteria of doing something right. You knew who she was and yet you fucked her anyway. You let your dick think for you. You forgot who you were and became who she wanted you to be - her fool."

Salt clicked on an image of Eliana and projected it holographically between them. The image rotated in place creating a three-dimensional form.

"Anna DiAngelo, that's her real name. But it may be the only real thing about her. We know she has powerful psychic abilities, and is proficient in the use telemetric weapons. In other words, she can make you see what she wants you to see. So I'm not completely surprised that you tripped and fell, but I am disappointed. You have tremendous potential, but compared to her you're a mere schoolboy."

"I recognized her right off, but instead of making a move on her, I thought I might be able play her for inside information. But while I was setting her up, she set me up and I never saw it coming."

"No one ever does. But if she trapped you in her web, then she most likely trapped your thoughts too. That means whatever you knew, she took that from you."

"But I didn't know anything, at least anything of value."

"You knew about our operations. You knew about troop movement and our plan for a surprise attack."

"Not in detail."

"But enough to tip them off and put them on alert. What we needed was what she knew, and all you delivered was two dead bodies."

"I didn't exactly deliver them; I don't even know how that happened."

"And you never will. That's the way business is done here. But next time out, if there is a next time, you may not be so lucky."

"The next time, I won't be relying on luck. Send me back to Junoko, and I'll finish what I started."

"On the contrary, it's more likely she'll finish you. Don't be offended, Ben, but she's smarter than you, more adept at her craft, and more refined in her abilities. Even if you could find her again, you're not ready to compete with her on the psychic plane."

"Then you underestimate me. All I'm asking is for you to give me another chance and I'll prove you wrong."

"Have you ever killed anyone?"

"No."

"The first time is not easy."

"But the right motivation makes it easier. She used me, and then killed Blalock and Decker. That will ease the pain of first-time uncertainty."

"Revenge is a powerful and functional emotion if used properly. But if she knows you're looking for her, and trust me, she will know, then this time she'll kill you. And as troubled as I am over your performance, I'm not ready to lose you. I wouldn't even consider sending you back out without you first undergoing additional training."

"What type of training?"

"Enhanced psychic warfare...an advanced program where we introduce you to newly developed technical weapons, and further expand your ability to use your mind as a weapon."

"The mind is always a weapon."

"A more lethal version. As gifted as you are, you're still functioning under a lot of old mental constructs and thought patterns. Those patterns need to be broken down and rebuilt."

"And how do you do that?"

"Via a blend of psychotropics and a guided tour through hell."

"I've been to hell before; it's not my favorite retreat."

"I'm sure Dante felt the same way, but there are benefits to be garnered. We need your talents now, not tomorrow. There are a number of ways to get to tomorrow, but the psychotropic path is the quickest."

The hologram of Eliana remained in front of Ben and served as an inspiring reminder of what he needed to do.

"And what blend are we talking about? Bath salts, LSD, Ayuhausca?"

"Old school. The world has changed since those drugs were discovered. We have synthetic hallucinogens now that are ten times more powerful."

"You're not serious?"

"I'm serious."

"That's a trip to the madhouse."

"The madhouse is just another name for a higher state of consciousness. But if you truly want to find Eliana; if you're sincere about wanting payback, and not afraid of expanding your own mind, then the madhouse is the only way."

****

At the Junoko Space Spa, a gym and rejuvenation center, Eliana was swimming out the anxieties of recent days in the synthetic waters of its serpentine lagoon. After doing a few laps, she swam to the edge of the pool where she found Vasquez waiting for her.

"Nice day for a dip." He said, his eyes dropping down to her breasts as he spoke.

"How did you know I was here?" She replied turning her body to occlude his glare.

"Better that I know where you are than someone else. People are asking about you."

"Who?"

"The man you left the club to play footsies with."

"It was business. What did you tell him?"

"That I didn't know you."

"Did he buy it?"

"No, but he didn't press it either. That's not to say that he won't be back. It's only a matter of time."

"Time is not the matter. I'll deal with him when and if the time comes."

"He should have been dealt with already? Dead men don't talk."

"He doesn't know anything to talk about."

"He knows that two bodies were left in that room."

"But he doesn't know what happened to them, nor will he ever know. But he might know enough to follow you. Coming here was not the smartest idea."

"I'll take care of my end, you take care of yours."

"Your end is my end. Next time you want to talk to me, do it behind closed doors. "

****

Ben was back in his quarters pensively trying to understand the strange effect that Eliana had on him, and to some degree still held on him. The rage he felt against her was undeniable, but so was his attraction for her. He kept seeing her in his mind's eye, picturing them in bed together, touching, talking, and exchanging intimacies. There was no subterfuge in those moments, he thought, or was it all subterfuge from the beginning? Her image stayed with him, but little by little a tidal wave of blood rose and washed over her face. He heard someone walking toward him and opened his eyes to find two N-Sight Technicians standing in front of him.

"They're ready for you."

****

The Technicians escorted him to a small bubble cube where he was met by a Special-Ops-Medic. The Medic checked Ben's vitals, but was aloof and conversationally aversionent.

"Are you ready, Ben?" Salt said as he stepped out from the shadows. The paternal kindness in his voice had a curious and comforting effect on Ben.

"Let's do it."

Ben was instructed to strip down and a series of wireless electrodes were attached to strategic pressure points on his body. When all the sensors were in place, he was guided into a small lunar module, essentially a pressurized isolation tank just large enough to accommodate his full frame. He was placed in a reclining seat and the tank's canopy was closed and sealed. There was virtually no light inside the module and the feeling was one of solemn claustrophobia. The recliner tilted back and the shoulder rests came to place fitting snuggly against his arms. Four electronic syringes clicked on and injected four psychochemical solutions into his blood stream. He did not react to the injections, just waited in silence for Salt's voice to come over the intercom.

"I'll be able to talk to you at any point in the journey. You can talk to me too, if you like, the choice is always yours. We'll also be monitoring your brain activity every step of the way, so we'll know exactly what's going on. We don't anticipate any problems, but if for some reason something unexpected should happen, we can pull you out in an instant. Any questions?"

Ben had been trying once again to read Salt's thoughts, but his perceptions were still blocked.

"No."

The deep silence returned, but was broken as the tank began to rise. Ben sensed the motion, but had no idea where he was going. What he couldn't see was that he was being lifted out of the lab and transported outside where he was set down on the lunar surface. The arm of the Crane that held the module detached itself and left him there alone in total isolation.

"Ben, can you hear me?" Salt's voice echoed through the tank like the ripple of wind through a dream. Ben could actually see the voltage spiral of his voice coiling around his mind. At the same instant, he noticed a small pinhole in the roof that allowed a stream of light to trickle in from the lunar landscape beyond.

"I hear you." He said, his voice breaking in colored bubbles.

"Can you see me?"

Ben thought it was an odd question, but as the light from the pinhole began to brighten, a blurry image of Salt's face came into distorted view.

"I see something but..."

"Stay focused." Little by little the face became clearer, the eyes brighter and the details more luminous. Finally, there was no question that it was Salt's face, albeit, disembodied. "Let your thoughts flow free, Ben, you possess a power equal to that of the greatest power in the universe. The creative power within you is the same power that created the entire solar system and all solar systems beyond."

Slowly the face dissolved and Ben was once again left alone in the dark. The silence was pervasive, a deeper silence than he had ever known, so much so, that he could hear the flow of his own blood, the bubbling movement of sweat on his skin, the thumping rhythm of his heart, and almost every other biological aspect of his physical being. The composition of the tank itself had changed, and was breathing as he breathed. It seemed to connect to every molecule in his body. As he continued to watch his breath, the walls of the module expanded and a larger opening in the roof appeared. As more light filtered in, the sides of the tank expanded and then fell away. Suddenly Ben found himself lying on the ground outside, still naked and patched with electrodes. Fear hit the pit of his stomach as he realized he was in airless space without oxygen support. And yet he was still breathing normally. He couldn't explain it, but accepted it as he began to feel air touching his face in the form of colored streaks of light. These forms washed over him like brushes of watercolor that dissolved into his body and impregnated his cells with renewed energy. Getting to his feet, he was better able to make an assessment of the strange lunar world around him. He found himself standing in a field of amber protoplasm that undulated like cool lava between his toes. Streams of metallic light were also flowing up from the ground, passing through the soles of his feet and channeling into every cell in his body. He could feel the sensation of light rush in like a burst of sexual energy that passed through his loins and exploded out the top of his head. As the light streams extended beyond his skull, they curled off into a spray of colorful microdots that drifted back down onto the protoplasm where they formed little platelet's of sizzling flower petals. The air around him had become dusted with a heavy golden mist, luminous, yet breathable. Each time he took a breath and exhaled, a golden amoeba bubbled off his lips and expanded into a purple sun. Within moments there were hundreds of purple suns encircling him, each one bouncing like a dancing ball across a perpetually forming musical score written in the sky. Although his consciousness had been altered, part of him remained aware that he was not unconscious, but residing in a different sector of the mind, a place that he had only glimpsed in brief amorphous moments. The phrase "Je est un autre" split his thoughts like a bullet through glass. It was a famous dictum by the poet Rimbaud, he recalled, that when translated meant "I is another". The intimation reminded him that the subjective self was a construct, and that the other was constitutive. This came to him as an insight, and not as verbal interjection born of philosophy. There was no question that his "I" was definitely another at this point, and that he was functioning on a different plane, a plane beyond the structure of thought itself. In that, he let himself drift into the flow of this mind stream, not trying to fight against the over powering visionary reshaping of his consciousness. Settling into this space, he began to explore the mental/spiritual landscape around him. Several trees stood off to one side, effulgent with colorful orbs of fruit dangling from their sinewy branches. One by one, the orbs broke free and floated toward him like tiny balloons. He touched one with his fingertip, and it burst into a totem of fire and light. He could feel everything around him, sense every sensation, hear every sound, and see inside the life cycle of all that existed. On the crest of a psychic ridge that lay ahead of him, an ethereal figure appeared, juggling something indiscernible in its hands. He was not able to tell if the figure was male or female, but was extremely curious as to why it was there at all. He moved forward, and with each step, music rose from the ground and wrapped his body in a lace of metronomic tones. It was a song of meter and melody such as he'd never heard – a sublime inverted counterpoint played sideways by a triangular band of electrified woodwinds. The sound shifted quickly and reformed into multiple diamond prisms that wafted above him before melting into lullabies that washed over his feet and left traces of musical notes between his toes. This musical juggler danced closer until she was only steps away from touching him. There was no question that she was female, beautiful, naked, and spinning tiny fire orbs between her fingers. Trails of light swirled around her, and diamond dust coated her body like phosphoric dew. With sparkling eyes, her face finally came into focus – a face of extraordinary beauty, and one he instantly recognized.

"Eliana." Her name echoed through his altered consciousness like the lacing of a forbidden stitch. Her body undulated and sent out non-verbal messages. Every movement she made caressed him like a song and drew him closer to her.

"Ben." She whispered, the name wafting into his mind and ricocheting back at her. Psychic threads of light fell upon her breasts and wrapped them in thin rivulets of color. The rivulets grew and curled down between her thighs where they vanished into the darkness of her moist femininity. Ben followed those threads to that same open door, but just as he would enter, someone grabbed him from behind.

"Careful." A voice rang out in a cautionary tone. "Ben glanced back to find Decker at his shoulder. His eyes were black, vacuous pools, and blood was pumping from his chest like a ruptured oil derrick. In that same moment, Ben felt

Eliana's arm reach out and sink into his chest. He could feel her hand clutch his heart and begin to squeeze.

"Stay focused." The voice said again, but it wasn't Decker this time, but Salt. Ben couldn't see him, but he could feel his presence. "You are the shaper of shapes and the former of forms. You have the power to defeat all enemies, all opponents. You are the master of all you see and all that can be seen. Fear nothing and no one. Your mind is the ultimate weapon. Use it."

As the words reverberated through Ben's brain, Eliana continued to squeeze his heart. But at the point where he felt it would literally burst apart, he spun away from her, a bolt of lightning exploding from the center of his forehead. Like a bullet on a death mission, the lightning went through her eyes and set her skull ablaze. She lunged toward him, her arms slithering like serpents and her blackened eye sockets spewing blood. She hurled herself at him with knife thrust precision, but he lunged to one side, her body piercing the tree beside him and withering its branches. A black cloud formed in the hollow of the tree where it had penetrated. Ben leapt over the cloud and onto a tendrilled carpet of rising suns. His body ignited and curled off into a pillar of fire that spun round itself at hypersonic speed. Swirls of flame flickered off of his body and scorched Eliana with incendiary sparks. Within moments, she was completely enflamed and reduced to a puddle of liquefied flesh. Subsequently, the puddle dissolved into the lavic ground and created a black hole of indefinite depth. Looking within, Ben caught a snapshot reflection of himself at its base merging with infinity. The process of life from birth to death unraveled before him in a rapid-fire sequence of images that spun his head off his shoulders and into the ethers. With the detached head spinning above him, darkness engulfed him like a metal shadow. The shadow cracked and a child of luminous ether stepped out. With its feet hovering just above the ground, the child shed its ethereal skin and became a man. Ben felt the warmth of the sun moving through his body, and sensed a radiance emanating from his eyes that shed light upon the entire universe. Everything he touched became a miracle, and every miracle grew into a pyre of power. In that moment, he realized that there was nothing he could not do and that all limitations were only in the mind. Simultaneously, throngs of people appeared and began to gather around him. He could see the thoughts in every one and nothing was withheld.

"Are you still with us, Ben?" Salt's voice came again, softer, almost imperceptible. Ben opened his eyes and saw Salt leaning over him, his face aglow and beaming with what he perceived to be love. It was at that moment that Ben realized he had not moved.

"We're almost ready."

Not only was he still in the module; but everything he had just seen had also come to him in the blink of an eye. The realization that came with that insight was that he was already a master and a supreme mind warrior.

"Almost done." Salt said, his face once again dissolving into the shadows. Ben could not see anything or anyone, but he could feel motion. The motion he felt was not only real, but hyper real. The module was rising and Ben was being lifted from the lunar surface. Spears of flagellic light shot through his mind like rays of spirit. Normal consciousness was breaking through and old mindsets were exiting from his cerebellum. He no longer knew how long he'd been under inducement, or even if he had been under inducement. Everything was impossible to define, and yet clear in its impossibility. Was he a particle, or a wave? "Both" said a voice inside his head. In some ways he felt like he was waking up from an afternoon nap, but in others, it was as if he'd been asleep for an eternity and was at last being rebirthed. But didn't he just hear Salt say they were ready to begin? Begin what, he wondered? For whatever was beginning or ending did not conform to the rules of the real world.

Another moment passed and Ben felt the module settle to ground and all motion stop. The canopy came open and light flooded in like a blast of wind. Ben wiped his eyes and globular sparks jetted up and out into the surrounding room. Simultaneously, Salt's face came into focus.

"Fascinating." He said, almost smiling.

Ben was sitting in front of Salt, not in the module, but in his office. He didn't know how he had gotten there, or how long he'd been there, or even if he was there. His head was spinning and his thoughts were cluttered with the residue of what he perceived had just transpired, but was at a loss to explain. He glanced around the room, everything as he remembered, but with no recollection of coming or going.

"Confusion is a normal component of the psychic journey."

"Am I here?"

"You're here."

"How did I get here?"

"You never left. I know that seems incredible, but when you agreed to undergo the advanced training, you opened your mind to the inner journey. In opening your mind, you allowed the higher powers access. At that point it was just a matter of giving you the proper suggestions."

"Suggestions?"

"Prompts to help you form the hypnogogic dream, the transmogrification of your mind. Normally, you wouldn't be considered a good subject for hypnosis because you're too savvy and your will is too strong. But when you agreed to take the journey as it was proposed, you offered your mind up to suggestion. "

"You hypnotized me?"

"In a manner of speaking."

"And the drugs?"

"You are the drug. You just needed a catalyst. That's my job."

"So there was no illusion, no isolation tank, no Eliana, none of that was real?"

"It was real, but only in the form of a designated state of consciousness – a consciousness that you created, but that I help guide you through. The choices you made there taught you see what you were truly capable of, and that there were no limitations to your power. That state of mind has been patterned into your subconscious and is now a part of who you are."

Ben sat there at momentary loss, still rummaging through the debris of his psychic displacement. He did feel a new sense of power, and an emerging insight into the world of himself, but he wasn't completely comfortable with this change, nor with the fact that he'd been mentally manipulated by Salt. But he had gained knowledge, and one insight of inadvertent but specific value, and that was that Salt was a man of infinite deceptions, even if they were purported to be for his own good.

"I've never been hypnotized before." He said. "And I'm still not sure how you did it?"

"You will know in time....as you continue to evolve."

"And what is the measure of that evolution?"

"For you, there is only one measure - bring me the head of Eliana Ruiz."

CHAPTER ELEVEN

Ben returned to his quarters, and dropped down tiredly into a chair. He stared pensively out the bubble portal onto the vast lunar landscape. The cold blue void outside was a reflection of what he was feeling inside. He couldn't shake the thought that Salt had entered his mind, his most private world, and reshaped it. And even though he had gained certain insights from the experience, he had lost a degree of personal power. It wasn't that he had given himself over to his unconscious that troubled him, but that he had surrendered to Salt in the process. And even though he desperately wanted another chance at Eliana, he didn't want to be Salt's pawn in the game. He knew he was being primed for another mission, but the idea of being controlled by someone else was not only a bitter pill, but an anathema to everything he held sacred. Salt wanted blood, but Ben was not by nature a bloodlettor. Perhaps that was a weakness, but to think it so was to make it so, and that he wouldn't do. He would kill if he had to kill, but only as a last resort. He felt compassion for people, even for the poor souls he outwitted at cards. He would always give a man a fighting chance, a chance to use his brain, before he abjured, or applied mental gymnastics. And he didn't just fleece anybody; he picked the ones he wanted to take, the self-inflated, ego-freaks and testosterone driven braggarts. Sometimes he would beat a simpleton just to teach him a lesson, but he would not send him to the poor house. He wanted money as much as anyone, but he wasn't greedy. He wouldn't take money from a mark if he couldn't afford to lose it. It was the same in matters of the heart. He had plied his craft well and used his gift to charm many a young woman, but not to undermine what he believed were her own set of moral principles. If she was indecisive or too fragile, then he backed away. As for love, he'd been there, but love was a dangerous game with uncertain rules, rules that quickly fell by the wayside at the slightest infraction. Love could turn to hate and heartache in an instant, and he had felt the power of its sting. Nevertheless, he wasn't immune to the desire for it and its intimate bondings. In fact, he wanted love, a deeper and more meaningful love, and hoped that perhaps one day he would find it. It was that specific thought that brought him back once again to Eliana. He had felt something with her, something different, something beyond mere physical attraction. There was a connection between them that went beyond the flesh, and in spite of all that had happened; he still didn't believe those feelings were dishonest. But no matter what her motives were ultimately, he still felt that his own intuitive gut had let him down. In fact all of his recent choices had fallen into this same questionable territory. A trip to the moon, a stash of cash, a romantic adventure, were all lures that he'd taken with little hesitation, and in retrospect, had proven to be Faustian bargains. N-Sight heralded themselves as an elite Force that he should be proud to be a part of, and yet he knew he was still just a cog in the wheel, a mere number in the pecking order to be called upon to do the bidding of the real power players. He hated the Corporate Rulers and had hated them ever since he was old enough to have a social conscience. The irony in that hatred was that he now found himself in the curious position of being one of their lackeys. How could he have let himself be so seduced, and not only seduced, but reduced to being primed as their whipping boy and executioner. These troubling thoughts riddled his mind with doubt, but he knew his strength and that doubt was a passing foible to simply be overcome. He was already building strategies far beyond doubt. But then something caught his eye just beyond the window portal. Someone in a Pressure suit had dropped off the side of the adjacent cubicle and was flying toward him like an oversized bat. The gravity-less flyer soared to a stop just outside the portal and smashed his facemask against it. It took a moment for Ben to recognize the twisted smile on the face within. That smile belonged to none other than Hayden Calder. He was tapping on the portal glass and pointing to an entry tube just off to the right of Ben's cubicle. Ben got the message and pressed the release button to unseal the outer door. Calder entered the pressure tube and a moment later was in Ben's quarters removing his helmet.

"Holy goddamn, Amigo, thought I'd lost you to the blue cha-cha-cha's and was never going to see your ass again."

"What the hell are you talking about?"

"Steppin' in shit and tossin' your balls to the diva devil."

"Could've been worse. I made a few bad steps, but I still got my balls."

"God bless the child that's got his own. I was worried about ya."

"No time for worry, brother, it was just game of cat and mouse that didn't go that well."

"Never does where pussy is involved. I've tripped over more quim in my life than I care to remember. Nothing to be ashamed of."

"I'm not ashamed, but -"

"Yea...there but for fortune. All you can do is lick your wounds, pick your ass up, and get the fuck on with it. I'm just glad you made it back."

"I was lucky."

"And you got fucked too, right?"

"In more ways than one."

"More than I can say about my bitched out mission. They had me crawling on my gut in real shit...right in the bloody asshole of the war zone. Trust me, Ben baby, it ain't no place for a good man to go down. And it was all a bust to begin with. I was there to weed out a traitor who'd been trading secrets for gold, but the fuck was already pushing up dirt before we got to him - shot by one of his own men. So much bullshit."

"It's all bullshit."

"Yea, but some grades have a higher stink factor than others. Anyway, you and me is still packin', and when you count your coins at the end of the match that's all that really matters. What say, let's get a brew and wipe some of this shit off our boots?"

"I'm due for a wipe down, but unfortunately duty calls. They're sending me back out again tonight."

"To where?"

"Back to Junoko to find the bitch that traded me in."

"She must be a serious ho' if they want her that bad? Who is she?"

"Mata Hari on acid. By some accounts, a spy, a witch, a magician, all of the above."

"Sounds like my kind of woman."

"If you're into black widows. She bottle fed me a hot meal of illusion before she killed the two Rangers who were with me."

"Black widows usually kill their lovers too, at least once their done with them."

"Maybe she wasn't done."

****

As part of Salt's enhancement program, Ivory accompanied Ben to the N-Sight Weapons Lab where he introduced and instructed him on the use of a variety of new mind-altering weapons. The first was a Quantum Wave Gun, which Ivory explained would cause the internal organs to expand and the body to blow up from inside out. He illustrated the weapon's power by giving Ben a brief demonstration utilizing a hydroponic pumpkin. Guns weren't specifically Ben's forte, but he was impressed with the mind-bending functionality of the weapon. The second gun was an Acoustical Heterodyning Pistol that used infrasound to fire sonic holograms. These bullet fast holograms carried both visual and audio messages capable of disrupting thoughts and causing confusion in the intended target. Lastly, Ivory demonstrated an RF Counterpoint Gun – a weapon that fired streams of electromagnetic radiation capable of implanting counter thoughts and illusions into an enemy. During the demonstration, Ivory speculated that Eliana might have used something similar to this on Ben.

"These weapons are unique in that they are pre-programmed, but you can also program your own illusions if you prefer."

"How long does the effect last?"

"Minutes, hours, days, depends on the individual and the length of exposure."

"Mind-blowing, needless to say. What about conventional weapons?"

"I have two advance system Walthur automatics for you. But you'll need to remember that a bullet travels six times faster on the moon because of the lack of air interference. So before you pull the trigger, make sure that the target your aiming at is one you want to hit."

Ben and Ivory left the Weapon's lab and went to the Flight Module Base where Chief Warrant Officer Dean Harris joined them. Harris was a hardnosed career soldier with a no nonsense disposition. He had been through three different wars, and had an intimate relationship with death and the infinite games of military engagement. For him, soldiering on the moon, in spite of its high profile locale, was just business as usual. He was old school military, and had little respect for N-Sight, or any other Psy-Ops type unit. He didn't like head games, and didn't buy into what he perceived to be the hocus-pocus auspices that these groups operated under. Nevertheless, he knew his place in the chain of command and performed his duties accordingly.

Ivory made the introductions and touted Harris as being one of the best officers working in the service of Namacal. He and a Squad of his men would back Ben up and support the mission in any way necessary, not to exclude the more extreme measures of violence and death. Harris knew Junoko like the back of his hand and would also serve as a guide.

Ben was introduced to the rest of the Squad who, by appearance, and partly due to the civilian clothes they were assigned to wear, looked more like a ragtag street gang than a highly trained fighting force. But Ben knew appearances could be deceiving, and that these men were trained to kill.

"Harris takes his orders from you," Ivory went on to explain, "but if you're wise, you'll consider his counsel as an asset."

"I'm sure it will be."

"And I'm sure we look like a bunch of fuck heads," Harris grunted, "but don't let this manure couture fool you. We can kick any goddamn ass that comes our way – and joyfully."

"You gotta get your joy where you can find it." Ben said sardonically making note that the men were heavily armed and concealing their weapons from open view.

"But it's bit of overkill, don't you think?"

"There's no such thing as overkill in this man's war." Harris barked back. "But if there was, we'd eat it and spit it back out like rotten buzzard puke."

Ben smiled and took a moment to read the random thoughts of the men, which were mostly expressions of boredom and restlessness. But he also picked up hints of excitement – extractions of simple pleasure like love of the hunt, and the leisurely drool that each felt about going to Junoko. Ben felt some of that same excitement, but kept his emotions closely knit. He noted similar behavior in Harris, who was there to keep everyone alive, and just too old and jaded to give a damn about the frills of any mission. His thoughts came out in thick swirls tinted with cynicism and mockery, none of which were expressed outwardly, but were all too obvious to Ben. Harris was used to dealing with younger, ego driven Commanders and inexperienced Commissioned officers whom he didn't respect personally, but followed as prescribed via the chain of command. In Harris' mind, Ben was no exception, and if he wanted to gain Harris' respect, he would have to earn it.

"You've got forty-eight hours." Ivory continued. "And if you don't find Wonder Woman by then, then she'll have found you. And that won't be pretty."

CHAPTER TWELVE

Ben, Harris, and the squad deboarded their RPC, (Roving Personnel Carrier), at Junoko's LRV Ground Port and entered the colony. They had no specific itinerary to follow, only a goal. All other modes of procedure and directives were left to Ben's discretion. Although he was a natural leader, he didn't relish the position, nor attempt to command with the voice of authority. Any thoughts he wanted conveyed, he relayed to Harris and allowed him to advise the others. This surrogate form of dispensation didn't win any points with the men, who subsequently perceived Ben as weak. The upside was that it added a sense of mystery and intrigue to his persona that kept them curious and wondering just who the hell he was.

They made their way to the Pleasure Sector of the Colony where the hum of revelry and decadence was thick in the air. The young soldiers were eager for action, albeit, not the military variety. The dark days of war had taken its toll on them, and they were hungry for relief of any kind, but specifically the kind that Junoko had on tap. But Harris knew his men well, and did not let them veer far from his guiding hand. Ben also kept a tentatively watchful eye on the men, but was more focused on the mental snippets that he pilfered off the passing parade. Accustom to traveling alone, he felt that the large ensemble drew too much attention, and so broke the squad down into parties of three and sent each group off in a different direction. Ben took Harris with him and they returned to the Lagoon Club where Ben had first encountered Eliana.

No one paid them particular interest, but then again eyes seemed noticeably guarded. Ben read thoughts arbitrarily, but found nothing of obvious suspicion. He ordered drinks from the bartender and casually inquired of Vasquez.

"Not in". The Bartender replied.

"When will he be in?"

"Something I can help you with?"

Reading his thoughts, Ben sensed he was already in covert mode.

"It's a private matter."

"Give me a name, I'll tell him you called."

"I'm not calling; I'm here now."

The bartender gave a nod to two gnarly bouncers standing by the door.

"So you are, but like I said, he's not."

Ben and Harris ignored both the lie and the impasse and took it upon themselves to proceed to the Manager's office. But before they reached the door, the two bouncers intercepted them.

"Afraid we're going to have to ask you boys to leave." The larger of the two said with a mean snarl.

"As soon as we're done." Ben replied.

The Bouncer didn't counter, just reached out to grab Ben, but in the same motion, felt the force of Harris' fist as it smashed his temporal lobe. Ben kicked the second bouncer in the groin and rammed his head into the wall. Circumventing the impedance, they busted open the office door, but found no one inside.

"I tried to tell you, didn't I?" The Bartender cried out as he rushed in behind them.

"Then tell me again. Where the fuck is he?"

"I pour whiskey; I don't babysit."

"Harris grabbed him by the throat and stuck a .45 in his mouth.

"Not babysitting won't save your mangy ass."

But while Harris had him pinned to the wall, Ben read his thoughts again, and deciphered he was telling the truth.

"Let him go; he doesn't know."

Harris didn't see what Ben saw, nor did he agree with the order, but released the man anyway.

"You ain't going to get far by being cuddily cute and kind, Lieutenant."

"I'm not kind, I just know the truth when I see it"

Harris found that argument absurd, but didn't debate it, just kept his mouth shut like the good soldier he was.

****

Ben and Harris proceeded to the Rikko where the Clerk confirmed that a woman had rented the room where Ben had spent the night, but the name on the register was not that of Eliana. And as far as he knew, there had been no reports of foul play, or disturbance of any kind; certainly no blood, or bodies. Ben asked to see the room, but the Clerk refused citing that it was against company policy. Harris countered his refusal by producing an electronic Interpol Badge that indentified him as a Galactic Investigator, and demanded that he reconsider.

The Clerk unlocked the room, which at a glance had not been touched, but this time Ben insisted on doing a more thorough search. With Harris' help, they checked under the bed, dusted the cornices, and ran fingers through the pile of the synthetic carpet. The search provided no specific insights, but while on his hands and knees, something just beneath the leg of the chrome nightstand caught Ben's eye. It was a small stain, almost invisible, but Ben could feel the crusty texture of it between his fingers. Harris knelt down beside him for a closer look.

"I've seen a lot of blood stains in my days, and I can tell you for certain that is definitely blood."
Ben looked back to the Clerk still standing by the door.
"Who cleaned this room?"
"One of the maids; I don't know which one."
"But you can find out?"
"I can check the charts, but..."
"Then do it." Harris said forcefully.
They returned to the lobby where one of the Squad teams had arrived to provide back up. The Clerk checked his computer, but discovered a problem.
"No one is listed to have cleaned that cube."
"Is that company policy?" Harris said with a sneer.
"The Night Manager is responsible for inputting the data."

"Then we'll need to talk with the Night Manager." Ben added.

"He's not on duty yet."

Ben knew he was lying and responded accordingly.

"Then you won't mind if we take a look for ourselves." Harris pushed the Clerk aside and threw the door to the office open. The Manager was at his desk and stood up in protest. Harris shoved him back down.

"Sit tight, asswipe, we'll let you know when we want you to dance."

Ben watched the man's thoughts and sensed everything he was about to say would be a lie.

"Where's Eliana?"

Fear was creeping into the man's eyes, but he was doing his best to hide it.

"Don't know what you're talking about."

"Kill him." Ben said to Harris.

"Whoa, whoa, whoa, wait a minute." The Manager blurted out, fear binding his vocal chords and pinching his words. "What's this all about?"

Harris drew a Walther PPZ high caliber automatic pistol and pressed it to the man's head.

"We want answers, not questions."

"I can't answer what I don't know."

Harris clicked the hammer and --

"I'm telling you the truth. I don't know any Eliana; I swear it."

"Room 222. You don't know anything about that either?" Ben said probingly. At that point, the Manager knew that it was fruitless to try to lie.

"I just got a call to do a clean up job."

"Who put in the call?" Ben said.

"It was a memo from upper management."

"I need a name."

"I...I don't remember."

Ben knew he was lying, but didn't know that he had stepped on a security buzzer beneath the desk. Within seconds, four Armed Security Guards burst into the office. Reacting on impulse, Ben flipped the first Guard over his head directly into the Manager's lap. Harris raked the Walther through the teeth of the next two and set them down howling. But the last Guard was able to get to Harris and pin him to the wall. He pressed a laser pistol to his head, but before he could squeeze the trigger, Ben grabbed him from behind and kicked his feet out from under him. By that time, the first Guard was back up and charging. He came right at Ben, but the two Squad Members who had been in the lobby intercepted him and wrestled him to the floor. Simultaneously, Ben grabbed the Manager and pulled him up into his face.

"I need a name."

The man was shaken, but still holding back.

"Is she worth dying for."

He hesitated a moment longer before finally giving into the pressure.

"Vasquez."

****

Ben, Harris, and the Squad returned to Vasquez's club. Two groups were sent to cover the exits while Ben and Harris lasered through the lock on the rear door. Vasquez was not in his office, but the club had been put on alert and beefed up with additional security. The band that had originally backed Eliana was on stage again, and Ben was anxious to talk with them, but knew security would block that move. But while he was weighing his options, he saw something he didn't expect to see. Vasquez was sitting at the bar alone and in plain sight. A few seconds later, Harris appeared beside him and wedged the Walthur into his rib cage. Ben stepped in with a nudge from the other side.

"Everyone has to die, the question is just when. You make the choice." Ben whispered.

"That's not a choice, that's a ploy. What do you want?" Vasquez asked.

"You know exactly what we want. " Harris spat back at him.

"You've got the wrong man."

"No, the wrong man's got you." Ben said. "The man standing next to you is going to blow your kidney's out your ass in the next twenty seconds."

Harris pressed the gun harder to his ribs, a move that tipped off one of the club's security men. The Security Guard slipped a weapon out from his jacket, but before he could move, he was intercepted by one of the Squad Teams. A scuffle ensued and other Security Guards jumped into the mix. With fist flying and the encounter escalating, Ben and Harris hustled Vasquez out a side door and into an open tube. Shoving him to the wall, Ben fired an electronic stun pulse into his temple. His eyes rolled back and spittle ran out the side of his mouth.

"I don't have to kill you, I can destroy your mind so that you never come back to reality. But it's not you I'm interested in; it's only Eliana."

"If I knew where she was, I'd tell you." Vasquez responded, struggling to get the words out.

"Fuck this lying bastard." Harris blurted, and then butted him in the head hard enough to loosen his teeth. Vasquez could barely mutter at this point, but did so in spite of himself.

"The Rylekev."

Vasquez's statement rang true to Ben, but though he didn't know the reference, Harris did.

"It's a flopper in the Russian Sector. Vodka, vixens, and vermin."

****

Ben and the Squad left the club and made their way to the Russian Sector, an auxiliary block of tubes a short distance away. It was only a small part of the Junoko Complex, but it had a distinctly Russian feel about it. The shops and Sleep Units all had faux bulbous domes and colorful facades mimicking Czarist Russian architecture. To Ben it seemed cheesy, like a crude Disneyland, but then the entire colony of Junoko was a crude Disneyland.

"That's the Rylekev at the end of the tube." Harris said, pointing to the domed Sleeper a half block away. "Used to be a pussy farm but the Federation made'em clean it up. You can still tap a little quim there if you got the rubles. "

"I'll keep that in mind." Ben said. "Send two men in to cover the exits, two to cover the front, and we'll take two with us."

Ben and Harris entered the front foyer where a drunken worker sat on an overstuffed couch and the red-eyed Concierge was draped over the registration desk. Ben approached the Concierge while Harris checked the area for any unexpected surprises. The two other soldiers stayed near the door feigning idle chat. Nerves were tightening as Ben brought up a holographic image of Eliana and projected it for the Concierge. His eyes flickered recognition, but he said nothing.

"I just need the cube number." Ben said sharpening his intensity.

"Cubes are all taken." The Clerk said.

"See that man over there." Ben snapped back, pointing to Harris. "If I don't get a number in the next few seconds, he's going to take your head off."

Harris smiled venomously, and shifted his focus to the adjacent hall where he heard a door crack open. At that same moment, two men entered the lobby behind him. A shot rang out and one of the Squad Team went down. A second pulse hit his partner in the leg and dropped him too. The door Harris had been watching opened and two more armed men charged out. They didn't have a chance to fire, because Harris had already filled their mouths with enough lead to send them to the promise land. The Concierge tried to run; but Ben grabbed him from behind and held him in a death grip. The two Assailants in the lobby were still firing, forcing Ben and Harris to seek cover. But just as the situation was escalating, other members of the Squad Team rushed in from outside and joined in the gunplay. Within seconds, the shooters were dead and a smoky silence swept over the room. Ben yanked the Concierge to his feet, seeing that he'd been hit by a stray bullet. Sirens were going off, and Ben knew that Junoko Security would soon be there to investigate. Taking the

Concierge with them, he and the Squad fled the Sleeper and disappeared into an adjacent tube.

****

The Squad returned to the U.S. Sector, the Concierge bleeding profusely. Harris wanted to finish him off, but Ben resisted.

"We don't kill anyone unless we have to."

"It's a little late for humanitarianism, isn't it?"

"You heard what I said." He leaned into the Concierge close enough to smell his breath.

"You've got internal bleeding that if not stopped will kill you within the hour. The good news is if I let you go you can still make it to the medical facility for help. But first I want to know who tipped you off."

The Concierge was fully aware that he could die, and offered no resistance.

"Amerex's Liaison - Vasquez."

"Fucking Vasquez." Harris muttered.

"And Eliana?" Ben continued.

"He's her shield."

"Where?"

"He has a Cube at the Comstock."

Ben didn't know the Comstock, but Harris did.

"It's where they house most of the Junoko staff."

Ben read the Concierge and felt he was telling the truth. He was ready to set him free when Harris lifted the Walthur and shot him through the head.

"Jesus!" Ben cried out as brain tissue splattered his clothes. "I promised I'd let him go."

"Death is the only promise that has any validity in war. He knew who we were, and would tell Amerex everything."

"But I told you no killing."

"Our life for his. I follow military protocol, Lieutenant, not witchcraft. My job is to protect you and the lives of this squad, and that's what I did."

"But you directly defied my order."

"There was no direct order, what you said was that we would not kill anyone unless we had to. I made a judgment call, that's all."

"Then hear this judgment. Unless we're in an actual combat situation, and unless I give the order, you don't kill anyone. You understand me?"

"If I hadn't killed those men back in that Sleeper, you'd be dead right now."

"You assume too much, Harris, and you're too goddamn arrogant. I felt those men before you ever saw them. I knew what they were thinking, and I know what you're thinking. So let's cut the bullshit, and get the fuck on with it."

****

Entering the Comstock Quarter, Ben positioned the Squad strategically around the suspected Cubicle.

"She's here. I can feel her. If at all possible, I want her alive."

"It was my understanding that this was a search and destroy mission."

"Search first, destroy later."

Harris grumbled beneath his breath, but called up two Squad teams and sent them in to scout the specified area. Each team followed a circular course that would allow them views through the backside portals. As one team moved in for a closer look, a shot rang out and ripped through the eye of the lead soldier. Before his partner could react, he too took a head shot.

"Fuck!" Harris screeched as he heard the explosions. He waited for Ben's order to go in, but Ben didn't give it. He was still trying to pick up mental signals beyond the panic and confusion growing all around him. The signals were weak, but through it all he heard the thoughts of Eliana warning him to back off. It was not a clear voice, but more of a psychic echo. Suddenly, a naked woman appeared at the edge of the building walking toward them in a dream-like saunter. All eyes were suddenly transfixed on her, but Ben was suspicious and Harris cautious.

"Take her out, Lieutenant, we gotta take her out now." Harris barked, but Ben was still trying to read her thoughts. Suddenly another blast of gunfire rang out and another Soldier went down. "Sonofabitch!" Harris screamed and raised his weapon to fire, but by that time the woman was no longer there.

"Ben." A voice called out, but Ben could not place the voice in space. And then another naked woman appeared, another shot rang out, and a bullet ripped through the head of yet another Squad Member.

"Fire." Harris shouted, refusing to wait any longer. The entire Squad sent a barrage of bullets and pulses flying, but the woman again disappeared. Nevertheless, they didn't relent, but kept firing into the suspected cubicle. Doors and windows exploded and dozens of holes appeared in the walls. Ben finally intervened and brought the firing to a halt. No one was moving, but he heard voices and saw mental prisms evaporating in the smoky remains. Suddenly, he spotted two people running from the cubicle toward an exit tube. The Squad opened fire again with even more aggression.

"Hold your fire, hold your fire, Goddamn it."
The firing stopped, but the couple didn't. Ben kept them in his sights as they leapt into a small Inner Colony Pod and accelerated down an exit tube. Ben and Harris followed suit, appropriated another ICP, and took off in pursuit.

The tubes were a circuit of narrow passages that led in, out, and around the Colony like a subway system. The Pod Eliana had taken had reached speeds topping 100 KPH. Given the winding nature of the tube circuit, those speeds would seem foolhardy, but because the magnetic road lock system gripped the titanium tires with such force, the Pods held the turns easily and allowed her to maintain a strong lead. Harris engaged an electronic tracer as Ben exceeded 100 kph. They still had no visual of her, and Ben was beginning to wonder if this might be another illusion. But just as he rounded the next curve in the tube, the ICP came into clear view. Harris engaged a mini-rocket launcher and put her in target lock.

"You're call, Lieutenant."

"Fire."

Harris snapped the trigger and the rocket filled the tube like a ball of fire. It hit the Pod's titanium wheels, lifted its tail, and drove the nose down. The canopy blew off creating a ring of fire that went spiraling back at Ben's ICP. It was only their excessive speed that propelled him past the danger, but debris was still breaking off the other Pod and flying back at them. Suddenly, the bloodied nose of Eliana's Pod hit a transformer connection, ripped through the transmission, and sent her skidding into the wall in a violent bound of ricochets. The Pod flipped upside down and catapulted a hundred yards down the tube before it finally came to a stop. Ben slammed on the air brakes and brought his Pod to a screaming stop just short of the wreckage. He and Harris leapt out and spotted Vasquez outside of the vehicle turning in circles. His clothes were on fire, and though he tried desperately, he was unable to douse the flames. He threw himself into the wall and rolled on the ground, but the fire finally consumed him. Within seconds he was reduced to pile of bubbling flesh. His skin and internal organs could be heard popping and crackling for several minutes afterward.

Vasquez was dead, but they were yet to see Eliana. If she was in the ICP, there was no chance of survival. Although Ben couldn't see anything through the shroud of smoke that surrounded the vehicle, he could feel Eliana's energy and felt sure that she was still alive. Cautiously, he and Harris moved closer until they were able to obtain a partial view of the tube beyond.

"Any way to get to the outside from here?" Ben asked.

"There are maintenance portals every five K or so."

"Where do they go?"

"Nowhere, just to open terrain."

Ben pushed past the burning Pod and a few feet further on found shreds of burnt clothing. It wasn't much, but it was enough of an indication to tell him that she had survived and was not far ahead of them.

They continued to track her for a half kilometer until they found a maintenance unit where a storage locker had been broken into.

"Air pressure suit." Harris said. " They're kept at every station in case of emergency."

Ben checked the adjacent exit portal and could see that the door seal had been broken. Looking out onto the vast grey terrain, there was no sign of Eliana, but there were tracks visible in the lunar soil.

"Radio the men and tell them to bring in the RPC."

****

Images of the burning Pod appeared on a floating monitor orb in Salt's office where Ivory was updating him on the Squad's status.

"As of the last report," Ivory explained, "she's alive and heading into the outback, possibly toward Amerex territory. Our people are in pursuit, but five men have been lost, and Junoko Security is raising immortal hell."

"And the good news?" Salt said sardonically.

"The good news is they've unmasked several operatives and destroyed a portion of their intelligence network."

"Your version sounds pathetic, but better than the previous version."

"What version is that?"

"Junoko claims that our treaty with them was violated and that innocent citizens were killed."

"There's no such thing as an innocent citizen? They're just looking to suck damages out of us."

"And we'll pay them if necessary. I have people on the ground now investigating."

"Who?"

"Calder."

****

Calder was on the tube street outside the club where the shootout had taken place. Four Namacal Rangers had accompanied him and were serving as his backup. People were milling about, talking, gossiping. Midst the vast array of innuendo, Calder picked up whispers of Amerex retaliation. These floating thought forms washed over him like a bad but intoxicating smell. He realized that the door to opportunity was opening and he had a chance to do something special. Ben had been Salt's favorite son, but Calder was now in a position to usurp him. It was an opportunity, he didn't intend to let pass him by."

****

The Squad led by Ben and Harris was in the RPC following the tracks that Eliana had left in the glom.

"She's headed north, somewhat surprising, because that's not Amerex territory." Harris noted."

"Then what's North?"

"Nothing but an Inter-Planetary tracking station about twenty kilometers out. It's small facility, but if she made it there, she could resupply and pick up a vehicle. She's got a good start on us, but not that good. We should be able to intercept her."

****

The terrain was flat and almost featureless save for an occasional crater and rolling mound of regolith. A subtle glow shown from the grey surface that was reminiscent of slow burning charcoal, and made following Eliana's tracks easy. But the vacuousness of the landscape painted the emotions of everyone with a solemn brushstroke of ennui. The oppressive atmosphere of what lay before them did not offer leeway to anyone.

"We need to increase volition." Harris said impatiently. "Right now, we've got the advantage, but if she gets to the station and appropriates transport, she'll be almost impossible to catch."

Ben ordered the Driver to take them to maximum speed, but it was an order the Driver questioned.

"She's close to max now, sir, any more and we'll flip her. Zero G's makes going head over heels an easy transition."

"Do what you can."

The RPC continued to bounce along like a toy truck, but oddly enough the bouncing lightened the mood. The lunarscape was monotonous and offered little diversion, but the amusement park-like ride served a moral uplifting purpose. But just as everyone was beginning to relax, Ben saw something out a side portal that didn't quite compute.

"What the hell is that?"

One quick glance across the plain and Harris had not question as to what it was.

"Solar dust storm."

"But there's no atmosphere."

"It's not a storm born of weather, but of electrically charged particles captured by the moon's gravity and swept along the surface. It's not weather as we know it, but it is wind."

It was difficult to tell just how fast the storm was traveling, but the tracks they were following had already begun to disappear. It was so vast in scope it was impossible to circumvent it, and within a mere matter of minutes it was all around them. The wind force rolled in like a tidal wave, lifted the RPC off the ground, and blew it off course. Simultaneously, the density of the dust blinded them and forced them to drastically reduce speed. The situation continued to digress finally forcing the Driver to bring the vehicle to a stop or risk crashing it. He anchored them to the ground, rocks and dust streaming past with typhoon intensity. So piercing was the sound of the storm, that everyone was forced to cover their ears for protection. The RPC shook so violently that it felt like it would literally break apart. It was an unnerving experience, like being caught in the eye of a hurricane, but fortunately a short lived one. After about ten minutes of unrelenting intensity, the winds began to die down.

When the storm finally passed, the terrain was left as still and silent as it had been before, but the course they were following had been altered. Harris assured Ben that it was only a minor setback, and subsequently engaged the navigation system and set a new course directly for the Inter-planetary station.

"We've lost a lot of time." Ben pointed out.

"True, but if we had to stop, so did she. We can make up for it, she can't."

Soon, they were moving over the terrain at speeds comparable to those before. But the Squad was once again growing restless. They had enjoyed the energy of Junoko, the women, the booze, the unpredictable nature of action, but now they were traveling deeper into the dark of the lunar outback, and its effect upon them was again growing oppressive. Ben heard their thoughts, some of them bad mouthing him for his decisions, but he took no offence. This was war, and for better or worse, someone had to make the decisions. Say what you will, he felt that he had done the right thing by these men, and even though some had been lost, he would not give himself over to guilt.

With the solar wind now behind them, the flat, seamless terrain went by like a blur of grey mist. They were approaching the edge of hill country and were able to see even larger geological formations on the horizon. Suddenly, the Pilot wheeled RPC hard right just missing the edge of a deep crater. It seemed to pop up out of nowhere, but given the shadowy nature of the surface, deep pockets were often hard to see.

No further tracks had been seen since the storm, but Harris calculated they were close to the Tracking Station. Those calculations proved to be accurate as a small outcropping of bubble cubicles soon appeared on the horizon. The Driver reduced speed and the quantum of everyone's alertness intensified.

"It's quiet." Ben said.

"It's always quiet." Harris replied. "But that doesn't mean a damn thing."

"It could mean she changed directions, didn't come this way at all." Ben went on to surmise.

"She could have, but it's a long way from here to nowhere. She needs supplies and transportation. The station is the only store on the block."

"How many personnel?"

"It's usually a three to six man operation."

"Then someone should have seen us by now?"

"That would be my take, unless for some reason they weren't able to see." His words hung in the air with a dark foreboding.

They continued scouring the buildings, but saw no indications of movement. Ben listened for thought waves or mental patterns, but picked up only a sluggish drone that he couldn't identify. The lack of mental energy didn't mean there was no life in the building, but it did mean there were reasons for concern. Using a small bio-resonator with an amplified power system, he scanned the complex for high frequency energies, but still failed to detect even the slightest biorhythm.

"The station is always occupied?"

"Always." Harris assured him.

Off to the right rear of the complex, Ben noted a narrow throughway that trailed off between a small outcropping of rocks and continued into the mountains.

"Is that a road?"

"Roughshod. Most likely Army Engineers."

"Where does it go?"

"Into hell. Ain't nothing beyond the station but frigid cold mountainous terrain, mostly unexplored."

It wasn't the road so much that had caught Ben's interest, but the easily visible the Pod tracks that lay before it.

"I'm going in." He finally said.

"Alone?" Harris snapped back, questioning the decision.

"If she's in there, it's better to risk one life than many."

"I'd still advise backup."

"Then give me a five minute lead and come in after me."

Ben, Harris, and two of the Squad Team snapped on Helmets and exited the RPC. They circled the periphery of the complex approaching it from different angles. Ben entered the Cubicle's main pressure tube weapon ready. As the airtight door sealed shut, a cold chill swept over him and held him at pause. Mental effluvium was in the air, but he was unable to designate its source. He examined the tech panel on the inner door and located the internal entry sequencer. Once engaged, a green light flashed and the door opened.

Ben stepped into the main section of the cubicle and immediately saw Eliana in front of him. He swung his weapon up, but she was no longer there. Realizing that it was only her psychic presence that he had glimpsed, he took a more scrutinous look around. The room was filled with technical equipment, but no human life. He stepped through a second sequence door into the next sector, and froze immediately.

Harris and the two Squad Members had entered the main cubicle behind Ben. They checked out the room, and then following his procedurals, moved into the sector he had entered moments earlier. There they found him leaning against the far wall, his face ashen, his eyes downcast. He was standing in a pool of blood staring blankly at the three bodies at his feet, each with a fatal head shot wound. It was a gruesome scene, but Ben had already detached himself from the horror and was attempting to read the mental residue that remained in the ethers. Diffuse images of Eliana and the struggle that had taken place there were still in the air. He tried to restructure what had happened but could only pick up broken fragments. He heard a gunshot, saw blood spray the walls, and Eliana running toward the exit.

"You okay?" Harris asked as he stepped in next to him. Ben shook off the psychic reverie and brought Harris's face into focus.

"She's taken a vehicle and headed to the mountains."

"How do you know that?"

"I saw her."

"You saw her?"

"Here." He said tapping his head. "She left an energy trail."

Harris heard what he said, but took the comment as pure foolery.

"She left a trail all right, but you don't need to be a psychic to see what happened here."

"What you think happened, may not be what happened."

"What the fuck does that mean?"

"It means it's not as clear cut as it looks."

"It looks like triple murder to me; what the hell else would you call it?"

"Self-defense."

"Are you shitting me?"

"They shot at her first."

"Not on my watch."

"Then your watch may not be on time. I can't see every detail, but I can see enough to know that it wasn't cold blooded murder."

****

The surface layer of regolith spun into huge dust devils as Eliana piloted the stolen Pod over the rugged, lifeless lunar terrain. She was focused on something in front of her, but it wasn't anything external. What she was watching was an internal image of she and Ben on the night they made love. It was a beautiful moment, but as she relived it, a torrent of blood suddenly flooded in and washed the image away. Inklings of thought residue remained, but her mind was stained with blood. Pain shot through her head with migraine force and caused her to wince. Using her mental powers, she tried to erase the bloodstain, but it would not go away. It wasn't guilt that she felt, but a sense of regret that what could have been wasn't. Curiously, she found herself wanting to see Ben again, to feel him, to touch him. But these feelings scared her and made her feel vulnerable, and vulnerability was something she couldn't afford. On the psychic battlefield, vulnerability was a death sentence. She was a master at controlling her thoughts, but emotions were harder to contain. Feelings of tenderness regarding her time with Ben kept coming back to her, but those type feelings were a dangerous indulgement. They undermined everything she had worked for and represented. Pushing those emotions back down, she drew a gun from the lower shelf of her mind and put it to Ben's head. She squeezed the trigger to rid her self of him, but couldn't release it. Lowering the gun, his image faded, but did not leave her.

****

Ben and the Squad returned to the RPC where he sent a digital update to Ivory before they left to follow the tracks into the mountains. As he watched the makeshift road unwind in front of him, Eliana's face kept returning, her voice whispering his name like the melodic drone of a beckoning siren. What was this strange spell she had cast, he kept asking himself. Not love, he thought; one night of lovemaking does not love make. But what he had experienced was an infatuation of such magnitude that he had no words to describe it. Curiously, his desire for revenge was equally fevered, and yet part of him still felt tenderness for her. Every indication told him she was a manipulator with dangerous psychic powers, but she was not void of sensitivity and warmth. It was this strange juxtaposition of emotion that was pulling him forward and backward at the same time. It had become like a tangled dream that he was unable to wake from. The external world, the vast lunar landscape was wrapping around him like frozen cloak, leaving his emotions wildly scattershot. He was beginning to feel like he was going insane.

Harris had been watching him more closely for the last few hours, and though he was meagerly amazed by what he'd seen him do, he was also mistrusting of the type of man who relied so heavily on his intuitions and scorned rational thought. That might be all right for an artist, but not for a military man, and Harris was military through and through. He had faced death many times over and survived because he had learned the art and the pragmatics of war. But Ben and Eliana were not cut from that same cloth; they were freaks who lived by a different credo. He would never say that outwardly, but he thought it. What he didn't know was that Ben had been intercepting his thoughts since the beginning and knew exactly what he was thinking. No that it mattered to either of them, they were men who lived by their own set of rules, not those of the world.

"Amerex territory is southwest, and she's still heading north." Ben noted, but more as a question than a statement."

"She's trying to throw us off track."

"But she's taking herself off track and losing momentum in the process. That could be her undoing."

"Then all the better. The land ahead is colder than Satan's asshole and equally inhospitable. If she makes one mistake, she's dead."

****

Eliana guided her Rover higher into the mountains where the terrain was more difficult to traverse and moon rocks the size of boulders were cluttering the narrow makeshift road. Bits of gravel and rock continually rolled off the hillsides and smashed into the vehicle. Knowing that Amerex would also be looking for her, she put out a coded radio transmission designating her position. She also alerted Command that she was being pursued by a Namacal Military Unit and requested Air Support. The thought of the Calvary arriving helped ease her tensions, but she was far from being out of harms way. Thinking like a psychic chess player, she was already mapping out various moves and escape strategies to apply if necessary. But as she passed through a narrow canyon with cliffs rising high to each side, the vibration of the Rover's engines set off a chain reaction of falling rocks. The rocks were small for the most part, but as they began to build down hill momentum, they set a trio of larger boulders into motion. The first one roared past Eliana's Pod missing it by less than a yard. The second was even closer, but the third broadsided her with such impact that it flipped the Rover onto its side and slammed it against the canyon wall.

Eliana was uninjured, but the Rover was upside down and smashed to silence. She tried to reengage the power thrusters, but the dashboard lights flashed only failure signals. After several more unsuccessful attempts, she put on her helmet and climbed out of the vehicle. The damage appeared minor, and she felt that if she could flip the unit back upright, she might be able to get it started. Assessing what that might take, she climbed up onto the Rover's undercarriage and putting her back to the wall, pushed off with her feet. The vehicle moved a few inches, but not enough to tilt the balance. She needed more thrust to break the angle and shift the weight to the other side. Repositioning herself to allow for more leg and back thrust, she tried once again. The strategy was a thing of beauty, and as hoped for, the Rover tilted to a perpendicular angle, and with one final push, plopped down on its titanium wheels. Pleased with her success, she gave the engine another try, but it still failed to engage. She checked the electrical, and went through computer diagnostics, but nothing worked. She was not a quitter, but with the Squad following so close behind, and time a critical factor, she made the choice to proceed on foot.

****

The Squad reached the high mountain plateau not far from Eliana's last position. The soldiers were weary, impatient, and didn't grasp the importance of pursuing one woman to such extremes. Ben attempted to explain the nature of psychic espionage, and the danger that people like Eliana represented. She'd taken many lives and had cost Namacal untold sums in lost revenue, but because she might have value as an intelligence source, he preferred she be taken alive. That was contrary to what they'd been told earlier, but he clarified that statement by emphasizing that dead or alive, it was imperative she not be allowed to escape. It was a good pep talk, but for the Squad, the thought of heading deeper into unknown territory was making them groan with dread. But Harris, being a less patient man than Ben, threatened to ream each one of them personally if they didn't quit their whining. He had zero tolerance for bitching babies and let them know as much. But as he was soldiering them back into submission, the Driver rounded a curve in the road and slammed on the brakes. A massive mound of boulders blocked the way ahead, half of those on top of the stolen Rover. Murmurs began to spread, hope belching out from the listless Squad that Eliana might be dead.

"Shut the fuck up!" Harris barked. "Keep your mouths shut and your goddamn eyes open." His outburst wasn't about intolerance; it was about the possibility that she had set up an ambush. Ben was also aware because he'd been picking up stronger threads of her psychic energy as they went along.

"She's not here, but she's not far."

"How the hell do you know that?" Harris growled.

"I know."

"She might as well be a hundred goddamn kilometers away for all the good it's going to do us. There's no way in hell we're getting past that rock pile."

"There's more than one way to move a mountain; excuse the cliché." Ben piped back.

"We don't have to move the mountain, sir." The Driver said, "I can take us over the top. These vehicles are made to transition terrain like this."

"Can you do it without killing us?" Ben asked half smiling.

"Just give me the go-ahead."

Ben felt the Driver's confidence and gave the order to proceed. The Driver geared the RPC into a low torque and rolled them up onto the base of the boulders. With the RPC's nose at a near ninety-degree angle, he began to climb the massive rock pile. The shifting under turf and the steepness of the mound made the experience nerve wracking, but the Driver clawed his way up inch by inch until they reached the top and were soon bouncing down the other side. Reaching the bottom and solid ground, Ben and Harris got out, checked the stolen Rover, and verified that it was disabled and not set up as a booby trap. They then searched the surrounding area until they found definite tracks trailing off into the grey glom of the mountains.

"Where the hell is she going?" Ben said thinking out loud.

"Round the goddamn rosies. Not even sure the bitch knows."

"She knows." Ben assured him. "Check your charts again; she didn't come this way for nothing."

Harris plugged in the numbers on the RPC's navigational charts and pinpointed their exact position. Half dozen different maps came up, each one offering an expanded view of everything known about the area.

"There's nothing out here." Harris stated impatiently.

"You mean nothing on these maps." Ben piped back, turning his attention to the surrounding mountains.

"But maybe there's something out there that isn't suppose to be there."

"Yea, and maybe Cat Woman is going to stop by and give us a blow job, but I ain't holding my breath."

As he spoke, Ben caught a glimmer of light reflecting off a smooth surface at the top of a higher ridge.

"You see that?"

Harris located the glimmer he was referring to, and upon closer scrutiny, identified it as a type of metal, most likely man made.

"Could be a shelter or a supply cube." He said, surprised that Ben had eyed it at all. "There were a number of them built in the mountains during early exploration. Most have been abandoned, that's why there's nothing on the maps."

"Could it still have supplies, like food and water?"

"Possibly, but she wouldn't know that?"

"Don't underestimate her. She knew where she was going, and knew we wouldn't know. But we do know, and that's her one mistake."

Ben instructed the Driver to take them higher. The road ahead was clear, but the going remained slow and treacherous, and the anxiety levels high. Everyone knew that it was only a matter of inches separating them from an over the cliff ride to certain death. But they continued to throttle up the roughshod sliver of road for a half kilometer more until Ben heard something that stopped him.

"Quiet."

Talking ceased and ears perked up, but no one heard what he heard.

"She's radioed for help. The transmission frequency is still on the ethers."

"You can hear that?" Harris asked skeptically.

"There's a lot of static, but radio frequencies don't die."

"You must have a helluv a set of ears."

"It's not the ears, it's the mind. The mind can receive signals better than the ears. One just has to know how to listen" But as he spoke, he heard something else, as did everyone else - the sonic boom of a Fighter Craft. Radar signals began to blip simultaneously on the control panel.

"Fighter!" Harris screamed out as he double-checked the instruments. The alert was a call to action, but the narrow mountain road left few choices for escape. Brains went into survival overdrive, but Ben was the first to locate a shallow niche in the rock hillside ahead. It was particularly narrow, but appeared just large enough to shield the RPC from an overhead view. The Driver responded to the sighting and rapidly altered course. The niche was little more than a vertical curvature in the rock, but it did get them out of the open. The Squad's angst intensified as they listened to the Fighter draw closer. If spotted, there would be no reprieve. The seconds ticked off like tiny time bombs, but the Fighter, seemingly guided by the blessings of fate, flew over their position without incident. No one could believe they were that lucky, but just as it appeared they had dodged the bullet, the Fighter veered right and doubled back. It was a heavily armed Space Craft, and carried both laser and sonic weapons, along with pulse rockets and traditional armaments in its stingray wings. On re-approach, the firing vents opened and a sonic boom shattered the airless currents. The rocket pulse ripped through the RPC with the impact of an earthquake. The rock face cracked and a ton of debris exploded outward. The dead air was suddenly full of tiny bits of gravel, rock, and battened metal. The Fighter Pilot shifted his Craft into hover mode and scanned the ground below for evidence of possible survivors. Given that the strike was a dead on money-shot with enough explosive volition to take out an entire unit of vehicles, it left no possibility of life. But what the Pilot didn't know was that Ben and the rest of the Squad had evacuated the RPC seconds before the hit, and taken cover in the surrounding rocks. As the Craft remained hovering, Harris leveled a PR 7 Pulse Rifle and fired a shot head-on into the Fighter's starboard engine. Flames broke out, but were instantly consumed by lack of oxygen. The accuracy of Harris' shot seemed to come to naught, but simultaneously fluids began to spew from the Fighter's ventilation system. The second engine sputtered and the Craft suddenly dropped like a dead weight and crashed to the ground. A series of rapid explosions followed, each one more devastating than the last. When it was all over, there was nothing left of the Fighter, only thin streams of smoke that were quickly gobbled up by the airless void.

Ben and his men broke into wild cheers as they witnessed the result of their actions. Even Harris was grinning from ear to ear, taking pride in the shot he made, and the victory long in coming.

****

Ivory had assembled a Technical Team and they were studying a large laser map of the mountain terrain. They had not heard from Ben in hours, but the lead technician was able to designate the area where his last radio transmission had come from.

"We projected a sonic scan over the entire area and detected several large explosions, each about 14 kilometers from the point of last contact."

"Could they be in a dead zone?" Ivory asked.

"Possible, but unlikely. Our intelligence screeners reported spotting an Amerex Fighter at .00234 degrees outside their zone at about fourteen hundred hours. Given normal flight time, the Fighter could have easily been in the proximity at the time of the explosions."

"Continue scanning the zone and update me with any new findings as soon as possible."

"Yes sir."

Ivory left the recon room and went to directly to Salt's quarters to discuss the details.

"She's still alive and busting balls from here to hell and back."

Salt didn't respond, just stared ahead pensively. Ivory tried to read his thoughts, but unsuccessfully. Although he had known Salt for years, he remained a difficult read.

"And the Squad?" Salt asked, finally breaking his silence.

"Nothing. We can send out a recon craft and -- "

"Don't just send it, go with it." Salt said interrupting him. "I want a first hand account through your eyes."

"We have plenty of eyes just as good as mine, sir."

"But yours are the only eyes I can trust. I want this woman brought to justice whatever it takes. And if it takes putting our best people on the line, then so be it."

****

Following Eliana's tracks and energy trail, Ben led the platoon higher into the mountains. The path was steep and the cold chilling to the bone. There were no sounds save for those of their own boots grinding into the soft grey regolith. Ben couldn't help but be concerned with what he saw and heard outwardly, but inwardly, the sense of Eliana's presence was even more troubling. He could feel her psychic energy, dark in tone, but curiously warm, almost comforting. There was no question in his mind that she was a weaver of illusions, but the question had now become which illusion was real? Ben was experiencing a seesaw of conflicting psychic images that produced and ongoing infirmity in his thoughts. Who was she? The death count spoke for itself, and yet tender feelings still rose up inside of him. Was he mad? Had he fallen into yet another one of her traps? These questions gnawed at him and turned his thoughts inside out. But one thought kept coming back, one that he couldn't escape from, and that was that she had continually spared his life when she could have easily taken it. Again and again, he asked himself why, and again and again, he could not answer definitively. He wanted to believe that she had felt something for him, but the more he entertained that possibility, the more he realized how foolish and dangerous it was to even consider it.

Harris, who had been walking beside him, heard something that was an affont to his ears and suddenly stopped. It was a subtle sound, almost like the cry of an infant. Madness, he thought, but then it came again. This time everyone else heard it too. It could have been the wind, only there was no wind. But then a crying infant was even more of an absolute impossibility. But the cries continued and seemed to be coming from a shallow crater just ahead. Harris moved trepidatiously forward and took a cautious look over the edge. About half way down the crater wall he saw what his mind could not grasp - a woman holding an infant wrapped in a blanket. They were shivering from the intense cold and were as real as the soil under his boots. But how real was that? Harris had seen too many tricks already, and was no longer willing to trust his own senses. The only thing he put any faith in was the power of his weapons. He leveled his Pulser and squeezed the trigger.

"Wait." Ben cried out. "It might be a trap."

"Of course it's a trap; that's why I'm going to blow her goddamn head off."

"No, that's what she wants you do."

"What the fuck are you talking about?"

"The illusion is not the trap, the trap is the illusion."

"What?!"

While they bickered back and forth, one of the Squad Members took his own initiative and fired. The shot rang out and the woman and child broke into fragments of disintegrating light. Ben wheeled round on the Solider angrily, but the damage had already been done. The vibration from the shot was rumbling through the crater and causing the soft soil to shift beneath them. A fast moving rift spread across the lip of the crater and cracked the section they were standing on. A ledge broke away and two of the Squad team went down with it. A rolling landslide swept them up and buried them under a ton of rock and debris.

"Sonofabitch!" Harris shouted. "Who told that idiot to fire?"

Fearful of his anger, no one responded.

"You still don't fucking get it, do you?" Ben said, going after Harris.

"I get it." He growled back. "And I'm going to kill this goddamn satanic whore if it's the last thing I do."

Turning his back on Ben, he laid into the Squad, threatening to strangle the next one who dared act on his own. The men cowered beneath his fury, but Ben knew that Harris would have fired too if the other man had not broken rank. But with each new loss of life, he became more skeptical about who Eliana was, and more determined to stop her. Whatever modicum of feeling he had been entertaining was all but gone. Eliana sensed this too, and was aware of his waning emotions. She had been monitoring their every move from a hidden cavern on the ridge above.

****

Ivory and Calder led a Squad of Spec 4 Rangers driving small LRV's to the crash site of the Amerex fighter. After finding charred pieces of the Pod and RPC scattered around the area, Ivory made a quick assessment of the situation and passed his thoughts on to Calder.

"Here's the picture as I see it. The Pod was stolen from the Monitoring Station, and Ben and his team tracked the woman here. Apparently, she radioed for the Amway boys and the Fighter flew in and took out the RPC. Our boys must have shot it down in the process. Given the lack of dead flesh, it's an educated guess that most of the Squad survived. No question in my mind that Ben is still walking the walk."

"And no question in mine that our Black Widow is too. And given what I've seen so far, I'd say the odds are leaning heavily in her favor that she's not walking, but strutting. "

"She's hard core product all right, but she's not invincible."

"She's doesn't have to be invincible, she just has to be smart. She's already proven she can outwit these po' hard tails. But I'm no easy fix, and I ain't never seen a pussy I couldn't lick."

The Spec 4's laughed at the jibe, but Ivory didn't. He felt Calder was too cocky for his own good, but he also knew that he had an amazing mind and was too valuable an asset to completely dismiss.

"Then you better sharpen that forked tongue of yours to a fine point, because you're about to come face to face with the pussy that ate world."

****

Ben, Harris, and the two remaining Squad Members continued following Eliana's trail. The Soldiers were mumbling, resenting every new step they took. As far as they were concerned, the mission was a blowout, and had been from the start. But the very real possibility of death they were facing had taken what little zeal they had left and squashed it. Harris sensed their dismay, but was not of the same mind. Ever the dutiful soldier, he was dead set, as he put it, on pissing on Eliana's corpse. Ben, on the other hand, felt their unease and tried to address it.

"You've all done a helluv a job, far beyond the call of duty."

"A lot of goddamn good it's done us." Harris snapped back. "The mothers of these boys we lost today won't give a shit about a helluv a job."

"Sadly true, but then that's the cost of war, isn't it? It's all madness, but a madness that's been going on for millennia. We scream patriotism and espouse the virtues of keeping the citizenry safe, but that's all a lie. How much blood has to be shed before people can see the truth. There are no noble warriors, and no noble wars; Harris, all war is a lie. Young men like these have been sacrificed and used by the powerful and greedy since time began. This is not a new scenario here; it's an ancient one."

"Very insightful, but a bit too simplistic. This was not a war mission, it was a mind fuck mission – a mission that cost these boys their lives, but should have never happened. That's the way I see it."

"I know how you see it, and I've known the way you see it from the beginning. I recognized your distain for me, and Psy-ops operations in general. But if there were something you could have done to save these men; then you should have done it. So I don't give a shit what you think about me, or the mission. I don't even give a damn if you continue on. Take your men and walk away if you like – with my blessings. At this point, you're more of a hindrance than a help."

"Well ain't that a sweet little piece of bravado. Even with us here shining your cute little boots, your chances of survival are shit. But without us, you'd be better off just shooting yourself in the fucking head. You're smart, Lieutenant, but not as smart as you think, excuse my impertinence. But let me remind you of one small thing in case you've forgotten; your bitch is smart too, and as lethal as the Grim Fucking Reaper. You trek off up that mountain by yourself and she'll wear your fucking head like a helmet before it's over."

"That's my problem, isn't it?"

"No, it's mine. I didn't ask for this shit for piss mission; you're right about that, but they dropped it in my lap and I intend to see it through. Going back is not an option. If I'm going to die, here is as good a goddamn place as any."

The two Squad Members could easily hear the diatribe, but were hardly as gung-ho as Harris. Ben had, in essence, released them from their duties, so why not seize the opportunity and get the hell out. Harris wasn't a mind reader, but he knew what they were thinking, and quickly snuffed the flame.

"You're fucking warriors." He screamed at them."So don't get your pretty little panties in a wad; we're all going through with this, right to the fucking end, you understand me?" The fierceness in his eyes quelled their protests, but not their desire. They hid their emotions from him, but as they continued up the lunar trail, the grumbling began again.

Their thoughts were mutinous and at the point of breaking when one of the men suddenly heard a strange, high-pitched squeal. It was loud and piercingly oppressive, and yet no one heard it but him. He tried shaking it off, like a man trying to get a bug out of his ear, but it wouldn't go away. His buddy noticed his strange behavior, questioned his antics, but couldn't get anything out of him. In the same breath, he suddenly dropped to his knees babbling incoherently. In the next, blood gushed from his nose and filled his facemask. He tried to unlatch his helmet, but the flowing blood was blinding him. Ben and Harris rushed in to help, but he was jerking and writhing so wildly, no one could keep hold of him. Darting left and right, he stumbled, picked himself up, and then stumbled again. No one knew what was happening to him, but Ben suspected that he had likely been hit by a sonar wave that burst a blood vessel in his brain. Blinded by the blood and riddled with fear, he broke free and ran off as if pursued by demons. With the others chasing after him, he leapt from a rock ledge on the side of the mountain, and tumbled head over heels into a rock-strewn gulley. By the time he reached the bottom, his pressure suit was shredded and his body gnarled into an ugly shape. There was no further movement and no chance that he could have survived. Even if they wanted to, the slope was too steep to even consider a rescue attempt.

"Goddamn it." Ben screamed out, not to the men, but to the mountain above them. "Why are you doing this?" He couldn't see her, but knew she was there.

"Fuck this shit," the lone remaining Squad Member bellowed, "I'm not going another step. I don't care what you do to me."

Harris grabbed him by the shoulders and pulled him up into his face. "Then where the fuck are you going? You're on the moon, fuckhead, in the middle of goddamn nowhere."

"Better nowhere than dead. Why can't we just forget this bitch, Chief, and get the hell out of here?"

"That ain't the way we do business, Soldier."

"Then, I'll take my chances."

"You ain't got no chances, boy. If you try to leave, I'll shoot you right here and now."

"You'd shoot one of your own men?"

"My men don't turn and run."

The Soldier fired Ben a glance, but being out of his mind with fear, he abruptly took off running. Harris wheeled round, and without blinking an eye, shot the fleeing soldier through the back of the head. Ben looked on in stunned disbelief as the man toppled to the ground, blood gushing from the hole in his helmet.

"Are you fucking insane?" Ben screamed at Harris.

"Desertion in war is a serious offence."

"Serious or not, you didn't have to kill him."

"He was dead already, just didn't know it. I actually did the poor fuck a favor."

"A favor?" Ben bellowed incredulously. "You're insane."

"Of course I'm insane; it goes with the territory. If you're not insane, then you shouldn't be here."

****

High on a frozen ridge of one of the tallest peaks in the range stood a lone domed cubicle. It was an older design and had fallen into disrepair, but was still stable enough to provide shelter from the frigid lunar temperatures. Given the absence of moisture, there was no visible evidence of the degree of freezing, but the intense stillness gave time itself an icy distillation.

Eliana finally reached the ash grey ridge that led to the cubicle, showing all the signs of cold and fatigue. She had mapped out the place long before the events of the day, but had no way of knowing what she might find there. She was hoping for food and water, but there were no guarantees. She was dehydrated to the point of nausea, and the lack of good air had taken its toll on her ability to concentrate. The only consolation to her situation was in knowing that Ben and Harris would be suffering the same effects.

Her heart leapt as she heard the sound of the cubicle's pressurized air system. It was a pure mechanical affectation, but it gave her hope and quickened her step. She entered the cube through the pressure gate, and immediately felt the temperature change to something that, although still diabolically cold, was warmer than anything she had felt in over eight hours. Shaking off the chill, she proceeded into the main room where it was warmer yet, and where she felt an immediate sense of comfort and relief. She unlatched her helmet and took a deep breath. The air was musty, but still the sweetest air she could remember. She stood there for a full two minutes just enjoying the simple process of breathing.

With her lungs full, but her belly still empty, she began to search for food and other supplies. The first thing that grabbed her attention was a line of water bottles stacked against a far wall. Like a Bedouin surviving a desert draught, she popped the top on the first container she could reach and shoved it into her mouth. It smelled of old rags and mildew, but tasted, for better purpose, as if it had come from a mountain spring. She emptied the bottle without removing it from her lips and quickly opened another. She took shorter sips this round, each taste of the life giving liquid transforming her into something reasonably more human.

Once she had satisfied her thirst, she found several food packets, C Ration type stores of dried cereals and fruits. It was a meager offering, but for her part, like stepping into a four star restaurant. Some of the stores required cooking, but she had no patience for that, and tore into the packages eating straight from the bag. The food was mostly tasteless, but the nutrients were there, and she had already begun to feel better and think more clearly.

With a bit of food and water in her stomach, she went to the cube's portal to check the mountain slope below. No sign of Ben or Harris, but she knew that they were close. She could feel the energy field of a stranger one hundred yards away, and with people she knew, her perceptions were even better. Not only were her innate psychic skills extraordinary, but in tandem, her abilities with psychic weapons were second to none. From her initial induction into Psy-Ops, she had set out to be the best and felt that she had achieved that. Parties on both sides revered her; and even though she had a reputation for being a heartless warrior, she never saw herself as anything but efficient. What she did, she did to survive. She was fighting a war, a war that she didn't necessarily believe in, but belief wasn't a necessary component of doing the job. She believed in no side and no corporation, it was quite simply financial matters that had forced her to sign on for the tour of duty. Like Ben, she had never envisioned herself as a soldier, but whatever she undertook; she was always determined to be the best. As for the war, she'd heard all the rhetoric, the political and patriotic reasons why they were there, but the sum, in her opinion, was not greater than the parts. The war was about greed, as all wars were, and the common man was ever being seduced into believing that something else was at stake, like freedom, preservation of a way of life, and threats to homeland security. But all these threats were manufactured. They were the golden nuggets of propaganda used to justify the endless competition for dollars and cents. Quite simply, war was a business enterprise, and had been throughout history, but in the 21st Century it was a bigger business than ever. Perpetual war had long ago become commonplace, but war itself was no longer a battle between competing nations; it was now a universal battle between mega conglomerates. The Global Corporations had taken over the job of waging war, essentially because they controlled the wealth and had the most to lose. Nationalistic Governments were passé, and had been reduced to secondary entities that did little more than wave flags and tout their iconic figureheads. Governments had gone the way of Kings and Queens; they were useful tools for propaganda and faux patriotism, but little else. Eliana had no illusions about her plight, and didn't differentiate between the good and bad, or right and wrong of it; she merely wanted to survive. This position had set her apart, and made her something of a woman alone in the world, a world where men controlled everything, and women were still treated like second-class citizens. But now these same men were out to kill her. In that, her choices were simple – kill or be killed. Well trained in mind games, she was able visualize multiple moves in advance, and that's just what she was doing as she stood there at the window staring down the mountainside.

****

Ben and Harris were still climbing, but had suddenly lost sight of any and all tracks. Using a grid technique, they covered the ground ahead for about twenty yards, but came up with nothing.

"You know the thought just came to me that she could have slipped over the edge and all that womanly flesh is now a mush pile at the bottom of a ravine." Harris said wistfully.

"Nice thought, but I still have a strong sense of her living flesh." Ben said.

"I have a strong sense of her too – as a frozen corpse." Harris knelt down and uncovered several faint markings in the soil, marks that indicated an attempt to cover her footsteps. "She's backtracking. Smart, but not that smart. She knows where she's going, and knows we know, so why play the game."

"She's fucking with us."

"To what end?"

"The one we can't see. That's where she seeks her advantage. And that's why we have to look one step ahead of her."

Searching the ground around them, they came on another set of tracks, but these didn't continue up the mountain. Instead they led off toward the edge of a craggy knoll where they abruptly stopped. Ben could feel his thoughts shifting as if by magnetic force. He recognized the energy pull was of a hallucinatory nature and did not give into it. Harris, on the other hand, was more susceptible. His eyes had glazed over and he had already begun to see something beyond the physical.

"Harris." Ben called out, but failed to get his attention because he was watching a storm of golf ball sized meteors spinning toward them.

"Get down." Harris screamed as he dropped to the ground. Ben's eyes were all over the sky, but saw nothing.

"It's a trick." Ben cried out, trying to help Harris break the illusion. But instead of breaking it, Harris pulled Ben down with him, shielding him from the storm of small meteors that were pounding the ground all around them.

"It's not real, Harris, " Ben kept urging, "it's not real." But Harris was unable to accept the explanation, or any alternate view of reality. After a minute of being pelted, Harris suddenly reared up and hit Ben in the face with the butt of his pulser and knocked him cold.

The storm went on for another five minutes before Harris was able to uncover his head and get back to his feet. Ben was still on the ground unconscious. Harris looked down at him dazed, his mind still clouded over what had just happened. But just as the thought hit him that he might have been hallucinating, a huge spider appeared on the inside of his faceplate. Harris bellowed at the sight, unlatched his helmet, and ripped it off. He flipped it upside down, shook it fiercely, and tried to jar the spider free. In the process, the helmet slipped from his hand and rolled on the ground. Simultaneously, he began to gasp for air that wasn't there. He leapt for the helmet, but bumping it with his outstretched hand, nudged it over the edge of the embankment. As he watched it roll into the shallow ravine, he knew he had to retrieve it quickly, or die on the spot. In that same moment, Ben opened his eyes, groggy from the blow, but clear enough to see Harris as he dove over the edge.

"No!" Ben screamed out getting back to his feet, gazing down the short slope where he spotted Harris about sixty yards below. The helmet was in his hand, but there was no movement. His arms and legs appeared to be broken, a matter of little consequence given that his lungs had exploded long before he was able to reach the helmet. Anger washed over Ben with such force that it literally made him throw up. Whatever feelings of compassion he had held for Eliana were finally vanquished and only vengeance was left to fill the darkness that engulfed his mind.

****

Ivory, Calder, and their accompanying Squad, arrived at an overlook about half way up the mountain from where they had discovered the bodies earlier. They checked for tracks in the surrounding regolith and found that only two sets remained.

"I'm no tracker." Calder said. "But it looks to me like the numbers are getting smaller."

"One or one hundred it's all the same." Ivory replied. "One is the only number Ben needs to win."

****

The temperature had dropped to a frigid minus 39 degrees Celsius and Ben was feeling colder and more exhausted than he had ever felt in his life. Even in zero gravity, each step he took was like walking with lead weights tied to his ankles. His will was strong, but the measure of his strength had begun to wane. Twisted images of Eliana whispering sweet nothings kept forming in his mind. With every word she spoke, a dead body appeared beside her. Bodies were circling her like flies and the air was swirling with blood and bits of human flesh. Rage welled up in Ben's throat and a scream blew out of him like a gunshot that hit the mountainside and ricocheted off into the vastness of space. Inadvertently, the force of that scream set a mini-avalanche of rock and lunar scrub into motion. The next thing he knew he was swimming in a sea of regolith and fighting to keep his head above it. The avalanche continued to wash over him, drawing him under its gravely waves until he disappeared completely beneath the deluge.

****

Salt stood up as if stung by an insect. His ears were ringing with the roar of the avalanche as if it had taken place there inside his office. He was over fifty kilometers away, but his senses were finely tuned to Ben's psychic energy field. He knew instantly that something had happened, and acting on intuitive impulse, put out a radio communiqué to Ivory.

When Ivory answered Salt's call, he and Calder were standing over the body of the Soldier that Harris had terminated.

"The shot was at close range." He informed Salt. "A definite execution."

Salt paused to absorb the information, letting the possibilities simmer in his mind.

"And Harris?"

"His status is undetermined, but we're obviously concerned."

"Proceed with caution, Captain, and believe absolutely nothing you see or hear from this point on. If in doubt, kill anyone and everyone who stands in your way.

****

Higher on the mountain where the avalanche had occurred, the silence had once again taken precedent. Nothing of life was evident, only the quiet glow of the sun reflected off the Earth's blue crust gave any indication of living existence. But as that light began to shift, a small stone in the rubble dislodged and rolled free. Timeless seconds passed, and then more stones broke from the pile, until, as if by excavation of the Gods, the earth beneath the stones opened up and a gloved hand appeared. An arm extended, pushing the rubble aside. Ben was alive, but far from safe.

What followed demanded more strength than he thought himself capable of. Putting forth a near supernatural effort, at a handful-by-handful pace, he finally dug free of the debris. He had survived the avalanche, but was at the point of utter exhaustion. And yet to rest, even for a minute, was a luxury he couldn't afford. He had learned things about himself in the last few days, done things that he never thought achievable. And though going on seemed impossible, the drive to find Eliana gave him strength beyond his normal physical capabilities. Bruised and battered, he summoned his will once again and began to climb the last switchback that led to the high mountain ridge.

****

The summit was less than half-kilometer away, and the Cubicle was located just below that. Ben should have been able to sense Eliana's energy at that point, but was curiously drawing blanks. He considered the possibility that she might be dead, but crossed that out, confident that he would have felt some essence of her withdrawal. No, she was alive, but why he wasn't picking up her psychic field, he wasn't sure.

Climbing the last rocky escarpment before the summit, he finally spotted the bubble cube a stone's throw below the peak's pinnacle point. There was no movement and no evidence that anyone had been there in years. But now he could feel her, and the energy was getting stronger.

A direct approach would leave him vulnerable to attack, so he chose to circle the unit and edge in from the rear. His heart was racing and the fear of death was real and raising the hair on the back of his neck. He kept his mind in a defensive mode, guarding against potential hallucinogenic projections, but surprisingly, the area was free of detectable psychic disturbance. But it also occurred to him that he might already be in a hallucination that he wasn't aware of. It was an insane thought, but if she could trick him into feeling secure enough, she could also lure him into a trap. He flashed back to the sleep unit where they had stayed remembering how she had manipulated him into believing a fabricated reality. He was stronger than that now, but was he strong enough to beat her at her own game?

Making his final approach, he remained well hidden in an outcropping of rocks. There were several portal windows on the backside of the structure that allowed him a partial view of the interior, but he was still too far away to see anything clearly. Crawling on hands and knees, he edged closer until he was within a viable viewing distance. In the main room, an air pressure suit and helmet were visible on a utility table. There was no way of knowing whether the pieces belonged to her, but shifting position gave him a better angle and allowed him see the outline of a small convertible bed. He could also see the shape of someone in the bed.

Although he couldn't see her face, the long dark hair that draped onto her shoulders told him unequivocally it was Eliana. At that moment, she looked like a sleeping child, but he questioned whether she was sleeping at all? It seemed a careless and uncharacteristic move for her to fall asleep when she knew she was being hunted. At first, his sense of her seemed muted, but the longer he stared at the back of her head the more he began to pick up REM waves that indicated she was indeed in deep dream sleep. Soft, flowing images drifted toward him, but were fragmented and difficult to read. But the content really wasn't important; all that mattered was that she was dreaming. Seizing the moment, he made his way to the entry tube and slipped inside.

Confident that she was still in dream, he unlatched the secondary door and entered the main room of the cubicle. He stopped to let his eyes adjust to the light, but while standing there in the muted darkness, questions flooded his mind. It was an ongoing quandary that he condensed to one single thought – was this real, or was it illusion? He stood quietly watching her, barely breathing, but finally drew his weapon and took aim. It was an easy shot, one that would suffuse all doubt and bring the ordeal to an end, but he didn't take it. Instead, he kept edging toward her, shifting his position to a point where he was finally able to see her face. She was motionless, almost corpse-like, but she wasn't dead, that he knew. She moved, just slightly, and just enough to make him firm his grip on the trigger. But again he didn't fire; and again he wasn't sure why. He paused to think about all the lives she'd taken and how she had earned her death sentence. Killing her in that sense was like killing a deadly snake and should be easy, but it wasn't. He was, as he'd been from the start, still fighting off doubts and uncertainties. He also found himself wanting to hear her voice again and ultimately what she might have to say. Stupid, he thought, risky, but still he stepped closer, moving so softly that even his own footsteps were silenced. When he was close enough to smell her, he stopped. He liked her smell, the smell of a woman, not perfumey, but a fleshy scent, earthy and warm.

He could see her lips, the same lips that he had kissed and longed for, but also the lips that had delivered so many lies and deceptions. No, he wouldn't let himself be tricked, nor seduced by her beauty, not again, not ever. He put the gun to the back of her head and slowly squeezed the trigger.

But he couldn't do it.

He kept watching her breath, the living energy flowing through her. Finally, he released the trigger, and somewhat tentatively called her name.

"Eliana."

The words left his lips and her eyes opened with them. Alarmed, she sat straight up, started off the bed, but stopped as she met the business end of his weapon.

"Don't move."

She was surprised, not so much to see him, but that she had fallen asleep and left herself vulnerable. She said nothing, as her thoughts unfurled in sleepy tangles and her eyes drifted toward her weapon on a table across the room - too far away to risk going for. Light was reflecting off the faceplate of Ben's helmet making him difficult to identify, but she didn't have to see him to feel him.

"Easy." She said, withdrawing slightly. "I knew you'd come, just didn't know I'd be sleeping when you got here."

"Your mistake."

"We're all entitled to one mistake, aren't we? Actually, I expected you sooner."

"Sorry to have kept you."

Thought prisms were rapidly bouncing back and forth between them. Both were projecting and deflecting constructs that might contain illusionary properties.

"The air is okay here, stale but breathable." She said.

"Just keep your hands where I can see them."

He stepped back from her and removed his helmet. When he ran his fingers through his thick unkempt hair, she couldn't help but smile.

"Are you going to shoot me?"

"Yes."

"I suppose if I have to be shot by someone I couldn't have picked a better someone than you."

"You didn't pick me."

"Didn't I?"

"You played me; you've played me from the beginning."

"Who played who? You were playing me before we even said hello."

"I didn't know who you were before I said hello."

"You came looking for me."

"I was looking for persons of interest, that's all."

"But it wasn't all, was it? That's why we're here today."

"We're here today because you killed two Namacal Soldiers at the sleeper.

"In self defense."

"And the squad that I came out here with. I suppose that was all self defense too?"

"They were hunting me."

"You trapped them."

"They trapped themselves. Just like your buddies at the sleeper."

"They were watching my back, but nobody was watching theirs."

"Did you see what happened? How do you think they got into the room? You think I just opened the door and invited them in for a party? They busted in and I had no choice but to defend myself."

"You're not exactly defenseless. You've been lying since the moment I first saw you."

"And you haven't? You told the first lie. The minute you opened your mouth you were trying to make me think you were someone you weren't, a fucking structural engineer, are you kidding me? I was on to you from the beginning and drew you in like a little puppy begging for a treat. But remember this, I could have killed you at any point from there to here, but I didn't?"

"Don't tell me, you like puppies?"

"Actually I do, but you're not going to believe me no matter what I say, are you?"

"No, but try me anyway."

"Why?

"Let the facts speak for themselves."

"There are no facts, only lies disguised as facts. That's the nature of the game, you know. And I'm not the only one who's been lying to you. That's where you need to begin."

"No, the game began with you, and it will end with you."

"You think you've got it all figured out, but you're still stumbling in the dark. I'm trying to help you...to help you see beyond the lies that have been stapled into your brain by the master liars. I never lied to you, not really. I induced you, yes, fed you a hallucination, but it was built on truth. Think about it. You're here, and everyone that came with you is dead. Is that a coincidence?"

"I've thought about it. I've thought about it every step of the way, over every dead body, but --"

"But you still don't understand it, do you? And what you don't understand is that they were trying to kill me long before you came along. The men I killed were trained to kill. It was them or me."

"So everyone is guilty but you."

"Who came after who? They came after me, didn't they?"

"You drew first blood."

"In self defense."

"You keep saying that, but saying it doesn't make it so."

"Why? Because of what you believe? That's what I'm trying to make you understand. You can't trust what you believe."

"It's the only thing I can trust."

"But where do those beliefs come from? What do you know about me, really? Nothing, only what Salt told you."

"I abide by my own thoughts, not Salt's."

"Then use them. Did I trick you? Yes. Did I lie to you? No. Not about my feelings. There was something about you, something that...I shouldn't have let happen, but I did. I know you don't believe me, but I know you felt it too. Call me what you will; pull that trigger and send me to hell if you choose, but I'm telling you the truth. We shared a moment, brief but real. This is war, Ben, a hateful, bloody, and ridiculous war. I'm a part of it by my own volition, but I'm no monster. And contrary to what you might think, I'm not immune to human emotion."

"Nor blood. You're very articulate, but words are just vessels, they don't make it real, they don't make you real."

"But what I feel is real. And if you can feel that then you'll begin to see the truth. It's like that line from "The Little Prince" that only with the heart does one see truly."

Her thoughts were coming at him in a relentless procession that had begun once again to wear down his resistance.

"No," he cried out, stopping the thought flow and bracing himself against his own emotions. He raised his weapon and once again put it to her head. Anticipating the bullet, the muscles in her face twitched involuntarily, but again he didn't fire. "Damn you, damn you." He shouted and lowered the weapon. He was angry; she could see that, and she wanted to go to him, to touch him, but knew he wasn't ready.

"It's okay." She said, rising to her feet.

"Stay where you are." He warned her, bringing the gun up again.

"I'm not going anywhere."

She gave him a moment to calm before she continued.

"Salt is using you, Ben. He uses everybody."

"And how would you know?"

"Because I use to work for him."

"Another lie."

"It can be checked."

"Then let's assume I've checked it."

"I was a member of N-sight at one time. During that time, he and I had an affair. " She paused to watch the expression on his face change. "Let me put it this way; things haven't been the same sense."

CHAPTER THIRTEEN

Ivory and Calder climbed to the top of the next ridge and were looking down at the mangled body of Warrant Officer Harris. They weren't focused on his physicality, but on the mental effluvia that remained in the dead vacuum of the moon's isolate terrain. The rest of the Squad was waiting for them on the lower ridge.

"This ain't right, brother." Calder said just loud enough for Ivory to hear and not the others. "Something bad wrong with this picture."

"It's not about right or wrong, Calder, it's about whose the strongest."

"Then we must be talking about the fucking Iron Maiden here. Score looks to me to be Bitch: 24, Namacal: 0."

"Don't bother with the score, Calder. She may have the lead right now, but the game's not over yet."

****

Eliana's words struck a chord with Ben; just enough to give him pause. He took a seat across from her, relaxed a little, but kept his weapon firmly gripped. Both were quiet, but not inactive. They were trying to read the other's thoughts while protecting their own. So far, Ben had not received anything from her that violated his own lie detecting senses. But it wasn't the fallibility of his mind that concerned him; it was his emotions. Emotions tended to color perceptions faster than outside manipulation.

"If, as you say, you were working for Salt, how did you end up with Amerex?"

"The Psy Intelligence network is a small community. And in that world, information is as great a commodity as Helium 3. The really good players, as you might expect, are far and few between. Like you, I was originally recruited and trained by Salt. He was not only my mentor, but also a man who ultimately became my lover. You have to realize, I was young and mesmerized by his power. I'd never met anyone like him. I don't think you would disagree that he's quite

143

amazing. For the first few months, our relationship was a thing of beauty, fairytale-like. But after a while, I began to realize that I was disappearing, losing myself in him. I felt I was possessed. And it wasn't that I was being seduced through my heart, but through my mind. He had penetrated my mind and shaped my thoughts to such degree that I literally became his psychic prisoner. When it finally dawned on me what was happening, that even though my feelings seemed real, he had actually tricked me into having them. I felt invaded and manipulated and just wanted to get away. I ask for a transfer, but he wouldn't grant it. I tried to avoid him as best I could; but working under him it was impossible. It didn't take long before he knew what I was thinking and started watching my every move. When I finally refused to see him and threatened to report him to Command, he got angry, extremely angry. It was a threat that didn't go down well, and he threatened me in turn, not in an obvious way, but with the intimation that he could destroy me if he chose. You don't see it on the outside, but Terrence is an extremely violent man. He'll hold you close with one hand, and tear your heart out with the other. About that same time, Amerex had obtained data about our relationship through their psi-network, and seeing an opportunity for advantage, approached me about becoming a double agent. It was a lucrative offer; but believe me it wasn't about money. I just wanted to get away from him. I had no love for Amerex in the least; truth was I hated both sides, so it didn't make any difference who paid my salary. But with Amerex I was a free agent and had some control of my own mind again. So I took the offer and defected. I thought my departure would put an end to the problem, the relationship, but it only made Salt more determined to possess me. If he couldn't have me, no one could. He's not the kind of man you say "no" to. Subsequently, men were sent to find me, but I was good at eluding my pursuers, and that made him even more furious. It wasn't just that I had rejected him, but I'd also broken his power train, something that rarely ever happens. That's when I became a wanted woman, not out of passion, but out of vengeance."

"So what you're saying is he's been using me to get to you."

"I told you, he uses everybody. This war means nothing to him; it's just a playing field for his own private power games. Not to mention the ludicrous amount of profit he's making off of it, but that's another story."

"One I'd like to hear. But staying with this one, wouldn't it have made things easier and less costly in terms of human life just to have told me this in the beginning."

"You can't show your hand before you've seen your own cards; that's not the way the game is played. No matter what I felt for you, or how attracted I was to you; I couldn't trust you, you know that. But you also know, and I think I've proven this by my actions, that I didn't want to hurt you. It wasn't something I planned, but...those feelings came to me as a complete surprise...not something I expected or could have predicted."

Ben stared into her eyes, attempting to read the nuances of the intricate mental and emotional map she'd drawn for him. He had many doubts and concerns that couldn't be disregarded, but he still found himself wanting to believe her. And it wasn't just his gut that was talking to him, but all of his neural receptors where indicating she was telling the truth. But then again, the truth was ever malleable, and he wasn't laying down his weapon just yet.

****

Outside the cubicle a strange glow, reminiscent of sheet lightning, flashed across the dark sky. The moon had no atmosphere, and lightning was essentially impossible, and yet something was creating planks of heavenly fire as vast as the northern lights.

"Everyone in your vehicles now!" Ivory shouted to the Squad. At first no one understood the urgency of his command, but within seconds it all became clear. By the time they had reached their Pods, the sky ignited with a meltdown display of crackling light. Meteor showers were not an unfamiliar sight on lunar terrain, but this one was of a definitively massive scale. The meteors themselves were miniscule, not more than the size of marbles, but were hurtling toward the lunarscape at enormous speeds. Many burned out before they reached ground level, but thousands of others did not. The impact was enough to scorch and dent the metal plating on the Pods, although not intense enough to destroy them. The sound was horrifically loud and the soldiers were nearly deafened by the din. Even Calder grew anxious as the pelting continued for what seemed like an interminable length of time. Ivory, who had experienced these type storms many times, took it all in stride. But what was of greater concern to him was that as the meteors struck the lunar surface, they spirited up towering clouds of dust that spread across the mountains and cloaked the terrain in a shroud of grey. The cloud cover was so thick in fact that nothing could be seen beyond the reach of one's own arm. Although the storm lasted for only a few minutes, the aftermath was complete blindness.

****

Ben and Eliana watched the meteor shower from one of the cubicle's small bubble portals. The pelting was loud, like the sound of a thousand drummers, but the cubicle was built to withstand the elements and suffered no substantial damage. What became a matter of note were the ominous grey dust particles that surrounded them as it ended.

"You're going to be stuck here for a while, you know." She told him, a slight undercurrent of subtexual hope in her tone. He didn't respond to her statement, just stared straight ahead into the clouds.

" At least it's warm here." She continued.

"Not warm enough. But you obviously knew that before you came this far. You knew this place was here."

"Shelter in a storm. It's always good to have an exit strategy."

"And an ultimate destination. Where were you going?"

"Don't you know?"

"How would I know?"

"You see thoughts."

"I see lies."

"Everybody lies. The world is nothing more than a composite of lies."

"We're no longer in the world."

"No, but lies aren't bound by gravity. This is a liar's moon, Ben. And the only truth that exist here or anywhere else, resides in the human heart."

"The human heart is vulnerable and easily deceived."

"But the only meter we have. We still try...don't we?"

"Some do...those that are foolish enough...and then not always by choice."

"But it's really the only choice. Without the heart we're nothing but beasts."

She spoke earnestly as if she were reaching out trying to traverse the emotional abyss that had been created between them. And though she was obviously in a vulnerable position, he didn't feel that her plea was for mercy, but for understanding.

"But when the heart is wounded, it's not that easy to heal." He added.

"Love is the healer...but you have to be able to let love in. It is a matter of blind trust; there's no other way."

He searched her eyes, looking beyond her words into what he perceived to be either illusion, or the depths of her soul.

"You speak well, so beautifully...words that are warm, soothing, alluring even. But we've been here before, haven't we?"

"This is not a game, Ben.'"

"No?"

"Look, I can't make you do what you don't want to do. I can't make you believe in me if you don't want to believe in me. I don't want to die, that's obvious, but I also don't want to lie to you. We've come from a difficult place into a difficult place, but I'm trying to speak from my heart and if that isn't enough, then it isn't enough."

He looked into her mind, as intently as he'd ever looked into anyone's mind in his life. He didn't believe anything he heard, but he believed everything he felt. And that was the conflict. There was an emotional component to all she said that felt genuine. But those emotions only put him at deeper war with himself. Thoughts and feelings were fighting each other on the battlefield of his very soul.

"I don't know what enough is anymore." He told her. "I no longer have a compass for reality. Everything at this point seems like a dream, but not necessarily a good one."

"Then the dream must be transcended. You have to go beyond darkness, beyond your perceptions of good and evil. I can't defend myself any longer; only you can decide what's true. But you have to do it soon. Other men are coming – more of Salt's killers. They are out there - close; I can feel them. And if you don't make a choice, they'll make it for you. Of course that does mean you do have an option."

"The option not to pull the trigger?"

"The option that it doesn't have to be you."

"Maybe I'd prefer it."

"Then that's your choice."

He stood there for a long moment just staring into her eyes.

"What is it that you want me to believe, Eliana, that this was some fairy tale romance that swept us away for a brief moment. And that all the death and deception that followed was just collateral damage that no longer matters?"

"What I want you to believe is that what I said to you at the Rikko was true, and that my feelings were true, and even though we had only just met, and we were caught up in a game we didn't design, there was no way I could hurt you."

"Is that what you told Salt when you were him."

"It wasn't the same."

"Salt obviously doesn't see it that way."

"Salt works in multiples, never directly. He's a chess player. He sees and works in layered strategies all at once. Bottom line is he set you up."

"How? He wasn't looking for you directly, he was looking for information."

"But he knew there was no one working Junoko that knew anything of value except me. And he knew that if you did your job, you'd find me."

"And what was it you were suppose to know?"

"That's a different matter isn't it? We're still on different sides of the board, and that gambit hasn't been put on the table yet."

"Then let's put it on the table and pretend there are no sides."

Ben watched her closely, trying to see not just the tells in her behavior, but any loose thought forms that could offer insight beyond her words. He could sense that she was tightening up, beginning to privatize her thoughts and put up a stronger psychic defense, and she knew he knew it.

"I know you're trying to read me, and you know I'm holding back." She said. "It's not because I'm protective of the intelligence itself, or of you obtaining it, but because I don't want Salt to have it. I don't want to give that sonofabitch anything, particularly anything that will help to make him shine."

"This isn't about Salt, it's about you and me."

"It's military information. That's not you and me."

"It's still you and me. It's about your sincerity and your ability to tell the truth. It might even prove who you really are."

"But what will it prove to me about you and who you really are?"

She watched him closely attempting to read his forthcoming thought.

"The moment I set this weapon down, you'll know where I stand."

His words resonated truthfully and for the first time in a long time there was something ostensibly tender in his eyes. But even though she was still facing the possibility of execution at his hands, she didn't want to be played by him or anyone else. Her heart was pounding and her own indecision was ridiculing her. She walked over to the portal and looked out onto the gulf of grey that surrounded them.

"We're stuck here for at least another hour until those dust clouds lift. But if we can't move, no one else can either. That means we have time...time to talk, to think, to be together...and maybe reach some sort of understanding. If that interest you, then I'll make us a coffee. There's not much here, but there is coffee."

He considered the offer for a moment before responding.

"Coffee would be good."

****

Confined to their Pod because of the Meteor Shower, Ivory and Calder were glaring out impatiently into the dense grey. The storm had left all the vehicles coated from hub to hub in a thick glom of near impenetrable Regolith. Electronic wipers cleared the front portal, but only to the point where they could better see the dark cloud that enshrouded them.

"How long will this shit last?" Calder asked, shifting restlessly in his seat.

"A couple of hours, maybe less."

"Our Black Widow will be long gone by then."

"If she tries to travel in this stuff, she'll end up at the bottom of a ravine. If she doesn't, by the time it clears, we'll be looking up her ass."

****

Ben sat across from Eliana sipping a cup of bitter black coffee. The taste was less than satisfying, but the caffeine was welcome and worth the effort getting it past the taste buds. Ben was more relaxed than he had been, but he kept his weapon close at hand. Thought prisms moved back and forth between he and Eliana like small ephemeral clouds that dissipated with a whisper.

"As you may know the various mining fields and known strike areas for Helium 3 are under the control of both Corporate Factions. Many of the recently explored territories are part of the ongoing dispute as to who owns what and how much."

"This isn't going to be a history lesson, is it?" Ben asked with a hint of impatience.

"These territories represent tremendous revenue sources; that's not history. But what Salt and Namacal don't know...." She paused to consider what she was going to say, careful to choose the right words. But as a result of that carefulness, a blip appeared in her thought pattern, alerting Ben to a potential lie.

"Sorry, I just...you realize that for me to be completely truthful with you means betraying someone else."

"You mean the Corporation. I find that curious because the Corporation doesn't believe in truth, it only believes in profit."

"Yes, and Namacal follows the same dictum."

"But I'm not here on behalf Namacal."

"You're still one of their operatives."

"In name only. In truth, I could give a shit what Amerex is doing. I'm not interested in them specifically, but I am interested in you and the tiny possibility of truth that you may or may not possess."

"Then hear me out. I realize you don't trust me, but you have to realize I've spent a long time not trusting anyone, so this is more difficult than it may seem."

She took a sip of her coffee and gave him a moment to reflect on what she had said.

"The truth, militarily speaking, is that Amerex has continued to do deep terrain testing for Helium 3 in several disputed territories in spite of the war, and against treaties, property rights, and universal law. Namacal stopped exploratory drilling when the war began, but Amerex has continued to do so clandestinely and even expanded their operations. In fact, and what's most significant is that they've found another, larger, and perhaps the richest deposit of Helium 3 ever discovered. Not far from the war zone itself, the supply is estimated to be so large that it could give Amerex superiority in the field and ultimate control of Helium 3 in the future."

"And Namacal knows nothing of this?"

"If they did, it could change the whole complexion of the war."

"And how did you come to be privy to such information; it's not exactly low level intelligence."

"You're right, it's not intelligence that would come to me through normal channels, but then I do have a way of deciphering things hidden beneath the surface. But what's of equal if not greater importance is that the area is not secured yet, militarily, or otherwise. And that makes it open to Namacal intervention. The location is close to controlled lines, too close to be hidden for long. As we speak, troops are being sent in to secure the area. If Namacal knew this, they would attempt to stop it, then all would be lost. Do you see the importance of this?"

Ben had not taken his eyes off of her since she began, nor did he sense anything of a prevaricate nature in what she said. Either she was the most thorough and extraordinary liar he had ever come across, or she had been completely forthright. Still, he could not rid himself completely of doubt, and yet the doubt did not stop him from wanting to believe her, or wanting to be with her. Every signal, every read he picked up from her told him her heart was true. But in spite of his readings, he also realized this was not just a matter of the heart, but one of life and death. And people faced with death would say anything; do anything to stay alive. So once again the question of veracity raised its ugly head. Was she a misunderstood lover with right intentions, or a very clever Black Widow with a venomous bite? To get beyond the question, to have any hope of resolve, he knew he had to take a chance that she was telling the truth; to open himself up to her, ultimately to lay his heart on the line. He sat there for a long time before he made any sign of movement, but finally, and very gently, he set his weapon down and extended his hand. It was more than a gesture of peace; he was taking a leap into the unknown and literally, albeit reticently, putting his head on the chopping block. The instant their fingers touched an electrical charge shot through them, the power of its pulse rendering them speechless. With hands together, they descended into each other's eyes and lost themselves there.

"Thank you." She said softly, grateful for the trust being given.

"Don't thank me, just let me know the truth of you."

"You know that already, you just have to give it a chance. To know a flower takes time."

They moved into each other's arms with a kiss so fragile that it almost broke apart at the touch of their lips. The merger and the energy that it produced rushed through their bodies with the force of an electronic current. They felt the power of that charge to such degree that when the kiss finally ended, they were near breathless. Intermittent doubts continued to bubble up, but were quickly defused as they kissed again. Deeper and deeper they went as if trying to disappear inside of each other. Ben had known passion and its variants, but what he felt in that moment was transcendent and beyond anything he had ever experienced. He knew she felt it too, her body language undeniable in its sensual eloquence. They were both deadly tired, and yet imbued with new life giving energy. Each movement of their bodies was like a sensory incantation that turned the temperature gauge ever higher. To alleviate the escalating fever of desire, they began to shed articles of clothing. Their efforts were clumsy and hurried, like children who had not yet learned how to dress or undress. But with passion guiding their hands, they were soon free, naked before the gods, the glow of the moon luminous on their skin. The next moment found them rolling across the bed in a heated frenzy. They had been lovers before, but this time there was no subterfuge, no games, no head-trips. All they felt and gave to each other was the pure exhilarating joy of ecstatic emotion. So strong was their passion that they had to subdue the urge less they end the moment too quickly.

"Easy, easy." She said, helping him slow the pace. Deflating the pulse of two hearts, their movements became more fluid, not as separate individuals, but as one living organism. Like undulating jellyfish their bodies continued to merge, and when the tension finally rose to an unbearable moment of desire, Eliana opened herself to him completely. The melding of flesh in that moment was so powerful that both cried out. Each nuance of touch rippled through them to explosive effect. Ben had studied tantra in his past, and though he knew how to extend the sexual moment, the current moment was so intense that all control was given over to sensation. Eliana also capitulated to the power of bliss and responded to his every gyration with quickening urgency.

"Easy, baby, easy." He said, this time taking the initiative to remind her not to rush.

She arched her back and tried to break the pulsing rhythm that was driving her, but it was becoming more and more difficult. She felt like a wild animal, hungry for fulfillment, and completely at the mercy of her body. She thrust her pelvis upward with such force that Ben felt he would disappear inside of her. In fact, he was being drawn into her so deeply that all sense of self disappeared and a new organism was born. The wave of their passion kept rising until the apex of their desire rolled over them like thunder. They both caught the wave at its crest and held on as their bodies experienced a series of rapid incendiary convulsions. It was a state of ecstasy that kept repeating in fast breaking seismic waves, flooding the pleasure centers of their minds and hearts with quavering ecstasy. When the last wave finally broke, and they were drained and emptied of all reservoirs, they collapsed gently into each other's arms.

The sweet sweat that dampened the sheets and stuck to their skin helped to cool them down. Soft murmurings bubbled from their lips like tiny prayers of praise and gratitude. Lazy, luscious moments ebbed away and finally returned them to something of a more human status.

"You're amazing." Ben whispered to her.

"Only to your touch." She whispered back.

They remained in each other's arms, saturated in flesh, and comforted by the warmth of their spirits. Finally, the sleep of love set in and they closed their eyes. With the veil of dust just beginning to lift outside, they fell into a deep slumber.

CHAPTER FOURTEEN

The regolith haze had engulfed the lunar terrain for nearly fifty square kilometers, but was finally breaking down into a thin grey fog. Visibility was not one hundred percent, but it was good enough for the Pods to continue up the mountain. The road was narrow and boulders were strewn everywhere. Each switchback maneuvered only led to another more difficult one. Finally, the deterioration reached its limit, and Ivory was forced to stop the caravan short of their destination. He could see the cubicle from their position, and though there were no evident signs of life, he was close enough to sense the human presence within. The point of attack from that point on would need to be executed with extreme caution, a caution that forced him to alter his original plan. He informed Calder and the Squad that he would do the final approach alone. Too much movement would only draw attention to the encroachment and endanger everyone. Calder didn't like the plan and insisted on accompanying him, but Ivory pulled rank and snuffed the notion. Calder was a fierce psychic warrior, that was not a matter of question, but he was also an unpredictable one. Too many men had already been lost, and Ivory didn't want any more surprises.

Arming himself with several smart weapons, he left the Squad and began his ascent to the cubicle. Like Ben, he circumvented the unit, approached it from the rear, and reached the back portal undetected. The light had shifted and left him with a clear view into the main room. There was no visible movement, but the energy within was strong and easily detectable. Keeping his head down, he edged his way to the second portal. The room was darker from this angle, but the view was better. The bed came into focus, along with the two bodies coiled upon it. Ivory made his way to the entry door and quietly stepped into the pressure chamber. Once inside, he checked the air gauges to make sure the air within was breathable, and then removed his helmet.

Cradling a weapon in each arm, he moved ghost lightly into the cubicle, approaching the bed with cat feet lightness. He stopped when he could clearly see the two naked bodies half covered by the still damp sheets. They looked almost like sleeping children, he thought, but was not taken in by the appearance of innocence. With a Jeweler's touch, he took the barrel of his rifle and nudged it against Ben's shoulder. The muscles in Ben's arm twitched, but the nudge didn't wake him. Ivory sensed that they were both in deep dream sleep, and surprised to find them so unguarded. He bumped Ben again, and this time his eyes flicked wide. His body moved faster than his mind, and as he sat up, Ivory's face came clearly into focus.

"Jesus." Ben cried out, the cry stirring Eliana in tandem. She sat up with a start, pulling the covers up over herself.

"Good work, Ben boy." Ivory said, his teeth glistening beneath a shallow smile. Ben didn't respond, but tried to read Ivory's intentions instead. Eliana didn't bother, she had seen through his smile the second her eyes fell upon it.

"Didn't expect to see you here." Ben said.

"Expect the unexpected" Ivory spiked back, his smile narrowing slightly. "You know the rule."

"Never been good with rules. Why are you here?"

"Man says go you go. A lot of dead soldiers out there."

"That's what war is all about isn't it? Filling graveyards?"

"Ask her ladyship; she seems to have a knack for it."

"Knacks aren't always what they seem."

"Sometimes they're more than they seem."

"And sometimes things change. I see things differently than I did before."

"Understandably." Ivory said flashing a glance at Eliana's breasts. "You're obviously seeing double."

"It's not what you think."

"I don't think, I read."

"Every chapter reads differently. Lot of twists and turns in this tale."

"It won't change the ending."

"It already has. And the fact that you're here changes the way we approach it. But you didn't come alone, did you?"

"I've got a few friends back down the hill. They're good boys; they'll come if I need them. But I wanted to make sure you were okay before I opened the door. I wanted to give you a chance to finish up your business."

"My business?"

"Sending this Satan Doll to hell."

"Hell sends its own invitations. I believe she's more valuable alive."

"You can find value in a dead roach if it gives you sustenance, but in her case, it's not your choice to make."

"Things have changed." Ben said as he got up and slipped on his pants.

"You mean to say you've changed...or is it that she's changed you?"

Eliana sat quietly watching both men, reading thoughts, and fully aware they were reading hers.

"She's a manipulator, Ben, a murderer and a mind fucker. And if you see her as anything more than that, then you're fucking yourself."

"I've seen things you haven't seen."

"But have you seen the truth?"

"We all have our own truths, don't we? Look, I'm not saying she's innocent..."

"Then shoot the fuck out of her." He said, shoving his weapon into Ben's face. Eliana pulled the sheet up higher, but remained silent. Ivory watching them both suddenly turned his gun back on her and leveled it. "If you don't, I will."

"No." Ben bellowed.

Ivory was surprised by his reticence and growing increasingly impatient.

"She's cost too many lives, Ben, swayed too many heads."

"But that doesn't alter her value. She knows things, intelligence that could shift the tide of the war."

"What intelligence?"

"Strategic information. I've been interrogating her, and believe that further interrogation will reveal more."

"You're dreaming, can't you see that? She's sucked you into a dream."

Ivory squeezed the trigger, but Ben stepped in front of him. "It's my dream and my reality. I'll take the responsibility."

"But it ain't your head, baby; she's got your head. Step aside."

"I can't do that."

Ivory smashed Ben in the temple with the butt of his gun and brought him to his knees. Eliana lunged for him, but Ivory leveled her with a counter blow. She tried to get back up, but he shoved the gun in her face and pulled the trigger. A shot rang out and the echo of it bounced off the walls. As the sound modulated into a reverberation, Ivory dropped to one knee. The shot had not come from his gun, but from Ben's. Ben lowered the Walthur, watching the blood pump from Ivory's chest. He was glaring at Ben, surprise in his eyes and questions forming at the corners of his mouth. Blood drops bubbled up on his lips as he pushed out a few barely audible words.

"Who...who?" He groaned one last time and then went silent. Ben knelt down, lifted his head, but time had run out.

Eliana touched Ben's shoulder gently. She could feel him trembling and see the pain in his eyes.

"Ben...Ben, I'm sorry."

She knew that he and Ivory had been close, but more profoundly she knew that he had chosen her over him. Trying to give him comfort, she knelt and wrapped her arms around him.

"I know...I know he was a friend." She said softly.

He didn't reply, nor did she say anything further, but tears were in her eyes – not for Ivory, but for Ben's pain.

"You saved my life." She told him."

Finally he let her see his eyes, and the love she saw there touched her deeply. It was a moment that seemed frozen in time, but time, as Ben suddenly remembered, was running out and Ivory had not come alone.

"We've got to get out of here." He told her, but she was aware and already grabbing her things.

"There are two Pods in the auxiliary unit. They'll get us off the mountain."

****

At N-Sight Headquarters, Salt had stopped working, and was staring into the corner of the room as if watching a shadow form. A wisp of cold air swirled up from the floor, the face of a man spiraling within it. Not only could he see the face, but he could also feel the icy glare of its eyes that sent shivers through his body. The shadow vanished as quickly as it came, but left him with a harrowing sense of death. The face hung there in ethereal suspension a moment longer before blurring away. But even after it had faded, it stayed in Salt's mind as a pervading wisp of ghostliness that refused to be diminished - the cold dead face of Ivory Keyes.

****

Calder had grown restless waiting for Ivory, and sensed that something had gone terribly wrong. He was already prepping the Squad for an approach when Salt radioed in and ordered him to lay siege to the cube. Those words were pure music to his ears.

Following Salt's directive, Calder led the men to the high crest just below the cubicle. The storm dust had completely dissipated and a clear, clean view of the small building was available. There were no signs of movement and the degree of the stillness around it was unnerving. Calder directed the men to spread out and approach the cube from different angles. As they forged their way inward, he scanned for energy fields, and though he picked up snippets of mental static, he was unable to identify anything relating to Ivory.

The Squad surrounded the building, and used powerful focal loopers to see inside the portals. The main room was steeped in shadows, but they were still able to make out Ivory's body on the floor.

Upon confirmation of his death, Calder ordered the Squad to open fire on the structure. The sky abruptly ignited with flames as ELF waves blasted through the portals, and a series of rapid implosions followed. The first wave blew the domed roof off the cubicle and sent it spiraling into the sky. With each succeeding shot, the walls came down and flew away like paper shingles. The auxiliary unit was also fired upon, the first implosion destroying the front wall and exposing a rear door. The door was open and Ben and Eliana could be seen escaping on two Monopods down the far side of the mountain.

With Elp waves searing the dead air around them, the couple torqued and throttled the Pods over a forty-foot drop into a rock-strewn ravine. The grade was steep and rugged, but the Pods were built tough and hugged the ground like crampons on wheels.

Calder mounted his Pod and ordered the men to follow. They trailed the duo over the ridge and down the same treacherous mountain route. Bumps, crags, and boulders made up every inch of the slope, but Calder showed no restraint in an aggressive pursuit. The Squad literally bounced their way down the slope, sometimes bounding as high as thirty feet off the ground. They could no longer see Ben or Eliana ahead of them, but the swirling dust that rose up in their wake made them easy to follow.

Calder drove his Pod with mad dog ferocity, hurdling it over the rocky terrain like a tank on steroids. He was far ahead of the others and racing full throttle toward a massive wall of stone. It appeared that there was no way around it, but as he got closer, he spotted a narrow passage at its center. Decreasing speed, he guided the Pod into the opening, the rest of the squad following his lead and motoring in behind him. The canyon pass was short and they were soon on the other side descending into a massive ravine.

The terrain opened up and Calder finally got a bead on the two speeding pods ahead. They were too far away to get a clear shot at, but close enough to hamper. Amping his pursuit, and with no gravity to impede him, he was soon covering extensive amounts of ground in literal leaps and bounds. But Ben and Eliana were also advancing and the distance between them stayed essentially the same. They were actually beginning to gain ground when they heard the voluminous boom of a wave gun behind them. Suddenly ELF pulses were whizzing past like a storm of bees. The shots fell short of the mark, but were too close to ignore. It would only take one lucky hit and the pursuit would be over. But before Calder could fire again, they spotted another canyon pass off to the right and veered their Pods into the craggy opening. Calder fired just as they entered, the shot hitting the overhanging arch and spitting rocks down on top of them. They were pelted by the first wave, but were traveling at such high speeds that they were able to outrun the fallout.

Calder and the Squad dodged the same debris as they followed them through the pass into a long open straight away. They could see ahead for a substantial distance, but quick as a broken breath, there was suddenly no sign of either Ben or Eliana. Calder immediately brought the pursuit to a halt in an effort to evaluate their disappearance. He could still feel their mental energy, but couldn't place it in space. They were there somewhere, but where? He sent one of the men ahead to scout the terrain, but the man had only gone a few meters when his vehicle exploded. A sonic boom followed and wave pulses rattled the canyon walls. With rocks and lavic particles crashing down all around them they geared the Pods back into motion and sped defensively out of harms way.

There was still no evidence of Ben or Eliana, but Calder kept scanning the canyon until he was able to pick up a trail of thought residue that led him to the edge of an oval crater. There he spotted the two descending pods moving down the crater wall toward a narrow ravine on the other side. It could be a trap he thought, but he had to take the chance. The next moment, he and the Squad were bounding down the slope through a blinding dust smog of regolith. The crater was shaped like an oblong bowl, and Ben and Eliana were already nearing the bottom where a tunnel led to the other side of the ravine. Calder knew he couldn't catch them before they got there, but he was not without ideas. He fired an ELF pulse into a rock cleft high on the crater wall, and an out cropping of lavic shale exploded and sent a massive avalanche rushing down into the crater.

Ben and Eliana were still descending, but the power of the avalanche was tremendous. They attempted an evasive route at the last second, but the storm of rock and regolith overtook them and swept them away like toys in a tornado. Eliana's pod was slammed to the ground so hard that it literally disappeared. The cockpit of Ben's vehicle was ripped open and he was thrown thirty feet forward vanishing beneath a mountain of gravel.

As the avalanche rumbled to a stop, Calder and his men brought their vehicles to a halt. A massive mound of rocks and lunar sludge now lay before them. The only sign of life was the tip end of Eliana's pod sticking up from the debris. Calder ordered the Squad to clear the area around it, but to do so with caution and take nothing for granted. Eliana had proven to be a cat with nine lives, and if she were alive, even if injured, she could still be dangerous. Although, she represented the greater threat, he was ultimately more concerned about Ben, not that he had survived, but that he hadn't. Ben was no fool and he would not only know that Calder had fired the shot that started the avalanche, but that he had ultimately betrayed him. Calder didn't see it that way, because in his mind it was Ben who was the real traitor. He had terminated Ivory and helped Eliana escape. Calder had always liked Ben, but he had also been envious of him, and felt jilted that Salt had favored Ben over him. He now had the chance to change that perception, a chance to prove Salt wrong, and to make himself the top dog.

"Try over there." Calder called out, directing the men to a spot where he was picking up strong levels of mental energy. The men began to dig and probe the area and almost immediately heard a muffled voice. Increasing their efforts, they dug down approximately six feet where they got the first glimpse of a patch of pressure suit. Moving rocks and grit aside, a helmet came into view, and with it, the dazed and daunted face of Eliana. Removing more of the rubble that entrapped her, they were finally able to pull her free.

Calder gave her water through a feed tube, which helped revive her, but her breathing remained labored. A digital diagnostic revealed she had a cracked rib and sprained wrist, but nothing life threatening. Ordering three of his men to keep watch on her, he took two others down the hill where Ben's Pod had disappeared. They scoured the area and kicked through the sludge and rock, but found no evidence of either Ben or the Pod. Calder scanned for brain wave patterns, but picked up nothing.

"He's either dead or buried so deep we'll never reach him. Either way, the numbers add up the same."

He didn't express it outwardly, but inside he was rejoicing. He knew there was a remote possibility that Ben was alive, and might be able to dig himself out, but even if he did, he'd never make it back to the base on foot. As far as he was concerned, Ben had dug his own grave. As for Eliana, he thought it might serve him better to keep her alive. She was a true trophy he thought, and putting that prize back into the hands of Salt, could only win him additional favor. With thoughts of glory racing through his mind, he ordered her bound and loaded into one of the Pods. Once she was secured, they made their way back out of the crater and onto flat terrain.

****

After Calder's departure silence fell over the crater with the intensity of a death knell. It was a vacuum of emptiness that seemed to stop the flow of time itself. But slowly and subtly, rocks began to shift and tumble in and around one of the avalanche mounds. A soft hum could also be heard, like that of breath passing through a straw. As the hum grew louder, so did the movement. Pebbles rolled and more rocks shifted in same area that Calder had just left. Gaps began to appear in the mound, and from one of those gaps a boot kicked up and outward. Legs and arms came next, and finally the full form of Ben's torso was exposed. He was desperately short of breath and his face was swollen from the battering he'd taken, but as far as he could tell, nothing was broken. He got to his feet unsteadily and took in his surroundings. There was little evidence to indicate what had happened, but a depression in the mound where Eliana had been removed provided him with a reasonable assessment. Calder had taken her and left him for dead. Because they had been friends, he hated to even entertain the thought, but the evidence spoke for itself. He would deal with Calder later, but there were other problems to address first. He might be able to find his way back, if he went the same way he came, but he was without transport and a long way from anywhere. The odds of survival in that sense were slim. But if he could find the Pod, and if it were still functional, then he might have a chance.

It wasn't necessarily a search for a needle in the haystack, but it was an intensively laborious shot in the dark. Throwing fate to the wind, he started digging in the area that he had dug himself out of, but stopped as he remembered being thrown forward when the Pod crashed. He approximated the distance, and tried again in that area. After digging down several feet, he still felt it wasn't the right spot. But just to his right there was a curvature to the spread of the mound that represented a better possibility. Some of the rocks he had to move were large, and it was a tremendous expenditure of energy, but he stayed with it. Nearly an hour passed uneventfully, but as he reached the point of exhaustion, he uncovered the tip of one of the Pod's wheel rails. It was still attached and that told him the unit was likely in one piece. Tired beyond comprehension, he got down on his knees and scooped away the top layer of regolith with his bare hands.

****

Calder and the Squad arrived back at their RPC with Eliana in tow. Her ribs were tender and sore, but her head was clear and she was once again siphoning mind matter. Calder was an easy read, and his prideful thoughts regarding her capture were obvious. But there was also a strong sexual component in his thinly veiled aura that she readily picked up on, one that he made no attempt to hide. He studied her like a map, letting his eyes roam freely and indiscriminately

165

over her body. There was no question that he wanted her, but not so much because she appealed to him, but more because he saw her as a trophy fuck. He wore his fantasies on his sleeve, and the idea of bedding the Black Widow and surviving her vicious bite flashed before him like a delicious delicacy.

"What happened to Ben?" She asked wryly.

"He had an unfortunate date with darkness."

"And what does that mean?"

"You're the Master Reader, why don't you tell me."

He was toying with her and enjoying it, but he was also inadvertently projecting a thought image of Ben motionless beneath the regolith.

"Did you see his body?"

"I didn't have to; I could feel the droop of his prick as if fell cold."

He was lying, hiding behind his own bravado, but she was picking up every nuance.

"Maybe that was just your own prick you felt drooping, the rotting death that lies inside your own being."

"We're all rotting, just some faster than others."

"And some not fast enough. But Ben was a helluv a lover. It would be a shame to lose him." She said this more to taunt Calder, than to praise Ben.

"If you want to know what a real lover is, talk to me."

"I am talking to you." She said with a hint of challenge in her voice.

"I doubt this is the right time or place."

"Then why did you bring it up?"

"Future reference."

"What future? A lot of people want me dead, you know."

"But you're not dead, and I've got a feeling that Commander Salt will be happier to see you than you expect.

"That's where you're taking me?"

"Where else?"

"You can't trust Salt, you know. Nobody can. If you think there is a reward waiting for you at the end of the rainbow, you're wrong. Salt will take the rewards and the glory. But I'm sure you and I could work something out if we tried."

"It's an appealing offer, but too late. They already know we're coming."

"It's still a long way from here to there. Anything could happen."

"You're right, it could. But unless the Devil steps in and pries you out of my hands like a piece of sticky candy, it won't."

****

After another hour of intensive labor, Ben was finally able to dig the Pod out of the lunar grit. It was badly battered, and the fuel lines were clogged with dirt, but after a quick cleaning and resetting of the computer, he had it upright and running again.

Following the land markings left by Calder's squad, Ben scaled the Crater wall and leveled the Pod back onto flat terrain. The tracks continued in a straight line toward the horizon and were easy to follow. Ben also read the mental terrain, but found it as clear and vacuous as the lunar landscape. The deepening silence made him feel isolated and more alone than ever before. His thoughts kept returning to Eliana, wondering if she was injured, held captive, or worse. Was she thinking of him as he was thinking of her? In the distance, the planet earth was coming into full view. It was beautiful, more so than he'd ever seen it, and offered him a rare perspective on his homeland. It inspired him onward, but also made him feel a bit sad. Before coming to the moon, he had been cynical about the world, its politics, endless wars, racism, disease, and voracious greed, but seeing it from afar after what he'd been through, it appeared as the most beautiful place he'd ever seen, a heavenly orb bristling with abundant life. In that moment, the world for him became a single cell, a living entity containing all other entities. It brought him a feeling of peace and joy, but it also filled him with longing and regret. He had taken his life there for granted, but he swore to himself if he ever got back home again, that would change. The moon was its own adventure, a unique and enthralling experience, but it was also a cold and solemn place not meant for human habitation. He could never love the moon like he loved the earth, even though it had opened him up to a new way of seeing. He had discovered powers within himself that he never knew he had, or was capable of having. But for whatever good had come out of these experiences, the pain had been equally great. Ivory's face kept coming back to him, his smiling eyes; his glorious smile. But as Ben relived the moment, that smile died and the light in his eyes faded. Sadness swept over him and drove him into a state of crushing despondency. He was grieving for all of the loss that he had witnessed. And though grief was a part of living, to give it too much ground was a mistake. With that thought, Calder's face appeared before him again, his eyes wild and laughing. The two friends were racing across the universe on the tails of comets, Calder urging Ben to pursue madness to its fullest extent. Ben loved the adrenalin rush and the thrill of speed, but Calder's words fell shallow and empty. His moral compass had been destroyed long ago, and he wore piety only as it suited him. If the Devil could be conjured, then Calder had made a deal early on. But that reflection brought Ben back to himself and to the question of his own motives. He wasn't perfect by any means, but he did have conscience. And yet, if he were honest, he would have to admit that he too had bartered his soul for money. He had allowed Ivory to sell him a ticket that allowed him to enter the arena of his own lust. He didn't know what was next, or where fate might lead him, but he knew he had to keep going and find a way to transcend his own limitations. And with that thought, yet another face appeared before him, and this time it was the master manipulator himself, Terrence Salt. Salt had been his mentor, something of a father figure to him, but what would he think now knowing that Ben had killed Ivory to save Eliana? There was no way he would be able to reconcile that, Ben thought, but then to his surprise, Salt opened his arms and embraced him like a long lost son. But as the two men held each other,

Ben felt the blade of a knife sink deep into his back. Salt twisted the blade and drove it deeper. With blood gushing from the wound and the world turning a rich and flowing red, Ben dropped limply to the ground. As his body made impact, the image dissolved, but left a disturbing residue behind. Ben felt nauseous and ill at ease. He admired Salt, but knew that he was absolutely ruthless, particularly to those who turned against him. No only had Ben killed Ivory and allowed Eliana to live, but he had also betrayed his mission. And that was a direct betrayal of Salt.

CHAPTER FIFTEEN

The battlefields that lay beyond the Command Post were strewn with bodies and detonated LRV Tanks. The burnt and blackened skeletons of Modulated Air Fighters were scattered over the mountainside. Sonic booms and automatic weapon fire could be heard kilometers away in every direction. The lunar sky was full of multi-colored smoke that created an eerie contrast to the stark blood soaked landscape. This was what Calder and Eliana looked out upon as they were in transit back to the base. Even though the actual the war zone was many kilometers away, its presence was extensive. Everyone was aware that they were subject to attack at any moment, and a palpable angst was evident in all. The shock waves of pulse booms could actually be felt and were endlessly unsettling. Mining operations were still underway in some of the outlying areas, but under constant threat. As a result, most of the production of Helium 3 in the main fields had been halted.

Eliana separated herself from the others, but was under Calder's constant scrutiny. She avoided eye contact with him and kept her inner vision open and perceptive. Calder was reckless, and too full of himself, but not a complete fool. He knew she had been gaming him, but then for him it was all a game. He liked the play, the mind match, the deceptions, and he wanted her to know that, and that he wasn't her pawn. And if she thought he would be her dupe, then she would learn quickly that he was a man to be fucked, not to be fucked with. She read these thoughts as he thought them, and the reading prompted a wry smile in her. Calder was clever, that was evident, but less so than he imagined.

****

The Carrier arrived safely at the Namacal Command Post and Eliana was immediately taken to the infirmary where her injuries were treated. She was lucky to have survived the avalanche, but then she'd always been of the mind that she made her own luck. And even though she was a prisoner at the moment, she knew she could find a way to make that work to her benefit. In fact, it was already working to her benefit even though no one knew that but her.

After being bandaged and cleaned up, she was taken to Salt's quarters in laser handcuffs. As she was brought in, he stopped, looked her over, but gave no indication or clear mental sign as to what he might be thinking. He was for the most part a blank slate, but she could still feel an emotional pulse coming from him that he was unable to hide.

In spite of her recent ordeal, he thought she looked surprisingly fresh. Unadorned of makeup or other womanly affectations, she radiated strength and femininity in a pure and alluring way. But Salt was all too familiar with her allure, and cautious in his approach to her. He scanned her thoughts, but found that she was putting out muted signals in an effort to block him. She was well trained; that was a given, after all, it was he who had trained her. But his ability to read psychically was beyond extraordinary, and in spite of her defenses, he was still able to lift thoughts out of her head. She knew what he was doing, and put up her best shields, but it was still difficult to defend against him. She didn't try to hide the fact that unresolved conflicts existed between them, nor did she make an attempt to subvert the softer emotional intimacies that were also evident. Their relationship had ended badly, but strong emotions still existed between them. She couldn't hide what was there, but she could defy it. This didn't surprise him because it was exactly what he expected from her. Her spirited nature was one of the things that had initially drawn him to her. She had the face and body of a Goddess, but Salt was an admirer of minds, and Eliana had one of the sharpest minds he had ever encountered. Their wordless evaluation of each other continued for several moments before he finally addressed her.

"You've built quite a reputation for yourself."

"I've only done my job."

"Spy, murderess?"

"Cheap jabs by little minds. I'm an intelligence officer; I gather information, and only kill in self-defense."

"If the dead could talk, I'm sure they'd beg to differ."

"If the dead could talk, they'd have a few questions for you also. You took a private matter and made it a public one."

"You give yourself too much credit. This wasn't about you, or us, it was about protecting Namacal's assets and obtaining information which we believed you were privy to."

"If it was information you were after, then why have me terminated?"

"I didn't set out to terminate you; you brought that on yourself."

"So you just wanted me returned to you with a palpitating heart?"

"Do you still have a heart?"

"Do you? Did you ever?"

"My heart is not a matter of contention here."

"Isn't it?"

"I didn't send a hit squad after you, not initially. We knew that Amerex was in the process of a major tactical move, so it only made sense to consider the possibility of a trade."

"I don't trade in information, I obtain it. So if that's the reason you've brought me here, then you're wasting your time.

"It's my time to waste. But let's make this easy. Even a meager amount of cooperation on your part could save you a lot pain and strife. I know you're not dedicated to Amerex, and why should you be, you're not a corporate player; you're a mercenary. So let's cut the bullshit and get down to reality. There's no need to put your self in further jeopardy. I can help you, but only if you let me."

"We tried that before, didn't we?"

"Things change."

"For better or worse? No matter what choice I make, I'll still be serving your purposes, right?"

"I have a job to do, so yes, there is purpose there. But I also try to surround myself with the best people possible. And I consider you, as I always have, to be one of the best. There's no way I can pretend that something didn't exist between us, nor would I try, but outside of our personal relationship, I'd still rather have you working for us than for them. You're not a patriot, and you know I know that; patriotism is for drones. America is no longer a country; it's just a small business living off its old reputation. Namacal is what the United States use to be, but even more powerful. Amerex would like to claim that status, but they're still second tier. We are the most powerful corporation that has ever existed...the biggest, the best, and the richest. And we intend to stay that way. One way to sustain that status is to have the best people possible working for us. This war may go on for some time to come, but in the end we will win, as we always do in whatever we undertake. We pay better, we offer better benefits, better lives; everything is better with Namacal. I know how you feel about the business side of things, but it's all business, always has been. Helium 3 is big business. This war is big business. These aren't new ideas, they're just being activated and played out more openly. The pretense of honest government and patriotism is long over. Now, it's simply about being on the winning side, the best team. And since you're a phenomenal player and we're the best team, it's a perfect marriage, as it always was. That's why you're still alive. So let's be forthright. I can erase your previous actions and betrayals; and no matter what differences you and I have had, it won't stand in the way of me putting you back on our team. Beats a firing squad, wouldn't you say?"

The offer was coldly pragmatic, but still an appeal to her best interests. Not only that, but the attraction between them, as much as she wanted to deny it, was still there. She thought she had put that behind her, but seeing him again face to face, body to body, had brought up a lot of old feelings. She worked hard not show any vulnerability, but he was already finding openings in her psychic defense block, and she didn't know how to stop him.

"Needless to say it's an appealing offer, but I get the feeling you want more than just my acquiescence."

"Everything has its price; the world turns on quid pro quo, but I think the advantages in this case are heavily weighted in your favor. What I'm offering you is something of a gift, a chance to live and to ultimately redeem yourself. But more than redemption, I can put you back on payroll at full salary, and submit a report to Command that you were working for us all along as a double agent gathering intelligence from Amerex. That means, of course, that you must supply me with real intelligence, something worthy of the investment, the loss of lives accredited to you, and my requisition to have you reinstated."

"Reinstatement I understand, but how are you going to explain the body count?"

"There is no hard copy proof that you were the perpetrator of the death log. You were the prime suspect, yes, but you also had an accomplice. Your accomplice will be held accountable. "

"Ben?"

"He was there each step of the way."

"Your men might disagree with that version of the story."

"My men are sworn to silence as is everyone in our division. But that's not a matter for your concern. What I need from you is real information, believable intelligence."

"And if I don't have it?"

"You have it."

He was giving her a get out of jail free card, but the card itself had a price. That was the way he worked, something she could never lose sight of. The question for her was how best to play it.

"Do I need to give you an answer right now?"

"Given your options, do you really need to think about it?"

"Yes."

He was surprised by her response, but knowing her typical thought processes, he granted her latitude.

"You've got twenty four hours."

"You're very generous."

"It's more than generosity."

"I understand. What about Ben?"

"Ben will serve a greater purpose dead than alive. He had all the potential to be one of the best psy-ops ever recruited, but he made several fatal mistakes, and those mistakes ultimately cost him his life. It's a shame really. I saw greatness in him, looked at him like a son. But in the end, he couldn't overcome himself and his romantic view of the world.

"So you have confirmation of his death?"

"I have confirmation on all I need, but why are you so interested? Don't tell me he lit a little flame in that tough girl heart of yours."

"There was no flame, I just saw him as you saw him. He was very gifted player, that's all."

"Unfortunately, not gifted enough."

****

The vast lunar plain had narrowed toward a point in the distance that Ben recognized as the lights of Junoko. His pressure suit was scarred and coated in a fine grain of regolith, but he was still pushing the hobbled Pod toward the lunar settlement. He had no communication equipment with him, or any idea of where he stood with Namacal, but he assumed he had been reported dead, and dead as he saw it, was a favorable position.

Keeping caution high and profile low, he camouflaged the Pod and hid it in a waste dumping area just outside the Colony. He entered the complex through a fire exit door and made his way to the Pleasure Sector. The first order of business was to gather information, on himself, Eliana, and anything regarding the recent series of events. With these things in regard, he entered a small bar on the fringe of the district, ordered a synthetic beer, and tried to act relaxed. But the residual anxieties of his journey were written all over him. He could wipe the dust away, but not the fierceness of his expression. Additionally, his clothes were ripped and dirty, and it was only a matter of time before someone suspected something wrong. With paranoia seeping into his thoughts, he quickly downed the beer and left the bar uncertain where he was going next.

He wandered the tubes aimlessly for a while keeping his head down, but his eyes and ears open. With Ivory dead, and Calder having betrayed him, he no longer had friends to turn to. But there were other possibilities for aid; and the one possibility that stuck foremost in his mind was Amerex. But how to make contact without rousing suspicions? The Lagoon club where he first met Eliana had been destroyed, and the manager was dead, so that connection was also dead. But the Rikko, where he and Eliana had stayed and a cover up had been made, offered a strong potential for finding an Amerex sympathizer.

••••

Ben stopped outside the Rikko and monitored it from across the street. He watched people come and go, but saw no activity nor read any thoughts that would help him. Securing a place in a shadowed doorway, he continued watching the Sleeper for over an hour, but nothing came of his vigil. Finally, aching with weariness, he decided to take a more aggressive action. He started across the tube, but stepped back as he saw the Night Clerk coming out. As a person of definite interest, he followed him into another tube, grabbed him from behind, and pulled him into a waste deposit crib.

"Remember me?" He said, pushing his face in close. The Clerk shook his head feigning memory loss, but Ben tightened his grip and brought him to a painful grimace of recollection. "I'm not interested in you, asshole, I only want information. Understand?"
He nodded his acquiescence and Ben eased up on his grip.

"I know you were working with Eliana, but that's no longer a matter of importance. Right now, I'm trying to help her. She may have been taken prisoner, so all I want to know from you is what you know. And if you lie to me; I'll bleed you out and wash away my sins with your blood."

There was no equivocation in the Clerk's eyes; he knew of Ben's skills and he knew this was no game.

"Word is she was taken prisoner, but that's unconfirmed. I don't know any more than that."

"And me?"

The Clerk paused, not sure how to answer.

"My own people tried to kill me, do you understand?" Ben said, further clarifying his position.

"Haven't heard anything specific...just loose leaks indicating you were a traitor and a dead one at that. Look, I'm not political. I provide services to whoever wants them and is willing to pay."

"Good, then provide me with a service. It's very simple - you never saw me. As far as you're concerned, I am dead. Understand?" The clerk nodded in agreement. " Now get the hell out of here."

CHAPTER SIXTEEN

Eliana was sequestered in her cell alone with her thoughts. The options in front of her were clear, but she was looking beyond the obvious to see how she might use those options to greater advantage. While exploring those possibilities, an image of Ben appeared in her mind, vague and distorted, but with a correspondent sense that he was alive and searching for her. The feeling was undeniably strong, but before she could even consider undertaking a possible action, she first had to deal with Salt. His offer was simple on the surface, but held many layers beneath it. There was no question that he would expect a lot in return for her allegiance, perhaps more than she was willing to give, but her options were such that her choices were limited. But while shaping these thoughts, an electronic key turned in the lock of her door and Salt stepped in.

"Is my twenty four hours up already?" She asked abruptly.

"No, but time moves fast and...I...I was thinking after you left that...I didn't want you to get the wrong impression...that this was just about N-Sight and Namacal." He took a seat beside her, his voice surprisingly soft. "I know we had problems before. I don't blame you for what happened, I hold myself responsible. I was possessive and controlling, but you have to understand you bring that out in a man – any man whose blood still runs flush with life. I tried to suppress you, to make you an adjunct of myself...not intentionally.... it's just...my training. I'm in the habit of being in control, calling the shots, but with you I actually wasn't. I let my emotions get away from me. I knew it then, but couldn't stop myself. I smothered you and..."

"I felt more than smothered, Terry, I felt manipulated."

"I know, but that was never my intention. We had something special, I thought, and I was just afraid of losing it."

"But it was that fear that drove me away. It became possessive. I was overwhelmed by you, your power, your intelligence. I had never met a man as strong and forceful as you, so supremely confident. I fell in love with you, but...I was also intimidated.

"But now you're back...and I want to put that behind us. I've missed you terribly, and I want you to know things will be different this time."

"And you think that's really possible after all that's happened?"

"I think we can make it what we want it to be. It's more than just a job."

"If it was just the job, I wouldn't be here."

Her words came to him as genuine, not just the words, but the thoughts that carried them. He had approached her with sincerity and she had returned it. But as he left the room, she couldn't help but wonder if it was all just a ploy on his part to win her confidence. She read him true, mentally and emotionally, but couldn't forget that he was the most refined and astute liar that she'd ever met. He could bend reality to make it look like something it wasn't. The question she ultimately had to answer was what did he really want? Where did the truth end and the lies begin?

****

Ben continued to keep a low profile while still trying to siphon information throughout the Junoko complex. His efforts were able, but becoming more tenuous, and having been up for over twenty-four hours straight; fatigue was finally getting the best of him.

He checked into a small Sleep Unit outside of the Pleasure Sector where he was sure no one would know him. What he didn't know was that the Clerk from the Rikko had put a call into Namacal and alerted them that he was alive and somewhere in Junoko. Within minutes of that call the intelligence was also on Salt's desk. It was disturbing information that he had not expected. Calder had reported him dead, and yet here he was again, risen from the grave, and even more of a liability than before. He was not happy, not in the least, but since Calder had provided the misleading confirmation of his death, Salt would put the ball back in his court. It would be Calder's mission to now make sure that Ben's coffin was sealed once and for all - no more resurrections.

CHAPTER SEVENTEEN

Calder and a team of Rangers landed at the Junoko Space Port and entered the Colony in lunar civvies. They looked like miners or any other group of workers out for some R & R, but behind their hungry for fun smiles, lay serious intensions. Calder had instructed the men to play the party card as hard as they liked, but not lose their heads. He assured them that if Ben found them before they found him, he would drown them in their own subterfuge. It was good counsel, but Calder was protecting himself more than he was the men. He knew that he was too easily identifiable and would be Ben's primary target. To avoid the possibility of a first strike, he wore a fake moustache and hairpiece, a meager disguise, but enough to throw off any casual stirs of interest. Dividing the team up into pairs, he sent everyone off on different itineraries.

****

Alone in her cell, Eliana found it difficult to rest. Saying yes to Salt would keep her alive, but it was a Faustian bargain at best. Perhaps, she thought, if she played her hand right, the bargain could ultimately shift in her favor. But if the shift went the other way, what awaited her would be far worse than the firing squad. It wasn't dying that she feared, but the manner of death. Traitors to the corporation were often sentenced to fates worse than the simple cessation of life. But why was she even debating the point? She knew the decision she had to make if she wanted to live, and she did want to live. Ironically, she also found herself beginning to warm to Salt. The attraction that had existed between them once upon a time, skewed though it was, still had resonance. There was no question he was a dangerous man, but he was also an appealing one. And part of what made him so appealing was the danger. She could spew hate at him from afar, but when she was close to him, she felt differently. She began to loathe herself for even entertaining these thoughts, but she couldn't deny what her feelings were telling her. Still, she'd been down that road before and wasn't anxious to go again. Signing on with Namacal meant signing on with Salt, a man who up until the last twenty-four hours had issued a death warrant for her. This was not a matter to be simply overlooked as if it had never happened. And then there was Ben. She didn't know for certain if he was alive, but her intuitions were telling her he was. And that presented her with a serious conflict. Something magical had happened between them; and the emotional impact was still there. Salt was an amazing man, but Ben had taken her to a place she'd never been before. These complexities were myriad and not easily reconciled, but be it love or hate, truth or lies, her first priority was to herself and her own survival.

****

Rikert was a young, tough as nails Ranger, who Calder had immediately taking a liking to. Although he had no psychic abilities per se, Calder admired his rough and ready take it to the limit spirit. Together they went from door to door flashing Ben's image and making inquiries. Calder read thoughts while Rikert asked questions, but from the onset, the results of their investigations were nothing more than meager scratchings.

The search went on for hours, but as midnight approached, the teams regrouped to discuss their findings, only there were no findings, Ben remained an invisible man. Everyone was tired, but Calder wanted to give it one more try before calling it a night and sent the teams out for one last round.

One of the teams entered a club called "THE PHASE" where the crowd had thinned, but a handful of dancers were still sweating out the last embers of the night. After some prodding by the Rangers, one of the dancers revealed that she knew Eliana and had heard rumor that Ben had come there earlier asking questions. With their interests peaked, they probed for more details; but were unaware that a man at the far end of the bar was monitoring them. He was inconspicuous other than the dark glasses he wore and the way he kept his head tilted to the side. But behind those glasses his eyes were sharply focused. He didn't have to read minds to know the men he was watching were Rangers. When they finished their drinks, he followed them out of the club.

****

Eliana was once again brought to Salt's office in laser cuffs. He studied her face, scanned her mind, and read her thoughts. She did the same to him, though neither of them let on that than anything inordinate was taking place. Finally, Salt smiled, pressed a remote beneath his desk and disengaged the cuffs that bound her.

"Don't think will be needing these any longer."

"Does that mean I'm no longer a prisoner."

"It means that Command has accepted my terms. It's only a matter now of you doing the same."

"You've always had a way of making the impossible possible. But before we take the next step, I want you to know how grateful I am, but I also want you to understand that we can never go back to where we were, not completely."

He didn't respond, just continued studying her, reading for insincerity. All the signals he got from her appeared to be heartfelt, but he wasn't blind to the obvious. To refuse his offer would be suicide. In that sense, her acquiescence was expected. But what he really wanted to know was where her heart stood. He had exposed himself emotionally to her, something he had not allowed or done in years. He had never given a woman such power, nor made himself so vulnerable. And though it was obviously a risky move, he was willing to take the chance.

"One step at a time, of course."

She sensed his honesty and the sincerity that propelled it, but the intimacy he was suggesting still made her anxious.

"And slowly. Feelings aren't mindsets, Terry. Our work is about mind games, but relationships aren't. They can't be."

"And won't. I've shown you where my heart is, and I've put my reputation on the line for you. Now you have to show me the same. You know where I stand, but Command is more pragmatic. They don't function by intuition, psychic ingestion, or feelings. To reinstate you, I have to take them something real...a piece of intelligence that shows you are what you say you are."

"What I am will speak for itself. What I bring to the table, intelligence regarding Amerex making a new and vital move to control Helium 3, will prove the winning hand for you and I both."

****

Ben followed the two soldiers from the bar back to the Sleep Units where the other Rangers were waiting for them. One of those men was disguised, but Ben saw through the thin weave of that incognito at first glance. Identifying Calder confirmed what he already suspected. He was obviously their prey, but what they didn't know was they were about to be his. The group exchanged thoughts and compared notes for a while longer, and then retired to their rooms for the night.

Cannon and Lacy, two of the younger Rangers, shared a unit together at the end of the second floor hall. They were half drunk and not at all sleep driven, but by the time their heads hit the pillows, they were out. As they drifted off into the world of dreams, the door to their room came open and Ben entered quietly. With one quick palm thrust, he knocked Cannon cold, but the sound of the blow was enough to stir Lacy from the grasp of slumber. But before he was able to pull himself up to full consciousness, Ben had the barrel of a Pulser jammed in his mouth.

"Just do what you're told, or I'll paint this room with your fucking blood. Understand?"

He nodded that he did, and Ben eased back on the Pulser.

"You know who I am?"

Lacy made a feeble effort to lie, but Ben read it instantly.

"This is no game, asshole; you've been flashing my picture all over the colony. Why?"

"You know why; you're designated a traitor and a spy."

"Says who?"

"Says Command."

"Who in Command?"

" I'm not privy to sources, but - "

"Are you privy to Eliana?

"I don't know any Eliana."

Ben read his thoughts and saw the image of Salt in his mind.

"Is she with Salt?"

Ben's perceptiveness surprised him.

"I only work for the man; I'm not his confidant."

"It's a small community. News travels fast."

"It's all rubber necking."

"Then let's neck."

"All I've heard on the chat line was that she was a double agent, working for us, but I don't know if that's real or not."

Lacy was being truthful by Ben's assessment, but was the truth the truth? If Eliana really was a double agent, why hadn't he derived some indication of that before?

"Truth is hard to come by in this old world, so let me give you a bit of truth to chew on. I'm no traitor, but I have been betrayed. I want you to tell Calder I know he's here and I'll be coming for him."

And with that exchange, Ben switched the pulser to stun and shot Lacey in the chest.

****

Salt escorted Eliana to her new quarters, a step up in comfort and welcome change from where she'd been housed since arriving.

"Sweet." She said taking in the niceties of the space.

"And it's going to get sweeter." He added, pulling her into his arms. She didn't resist his embrace, but he could feel her tentativeness. He tried to kiss her, but she turned her cheek aside.

"I'm not ready yet, Terry. You have to give me some time."

Salt couldn't hide his disappointment, something that didn't escape Eliana either. But instead of taking a stance against him, she capitulated and kissed him hard on the mouth.

"Less time than I thought" She said laughing. "Being here with you again…it's almost like we were never apart…reminds me of how powerful we were together…and maybe can be again?"

"Will be. Together we're unstoppable."

****

Calder and Rikert busted open the door to Cannon and Lacey's room and found them awake, but dazed and disoriented.

"What the fuck happened?" Calder screamed at them.

"Sonofabitch was here."

" Denning?"

"We were clocking z's when he came. He didn't stay long enough to cuddle, just asked about Eliana, and told me to give you a message."

"What message."

"The he wasn't a traitor and that he knew you were here. He said to tell you he'd be coming for you."

"Then let the motherfucker come if he thinks he can." Calder shrieked. "I got his goddamn exit papers ready to sign."

****

Ben found a place in the shadows across the street from the Sleeper and was watching as Calder and the Rangers came out. Calder was obviously agitated and that was exactly what he wanted. He knew that anger would dull his mental processes and keep him looking over his shoulder. While he was busy looking back, Ben would be running one step ahead. It wasn't revenge he was after, but he wanted Calder to know that he had the power to apply it when and where he wanted. More than that, he wanted to know what Calder knew about Eliana and her relationship with Salt. Had she lured him in to her web once again, or was it Salt who was being bound in the intricate weave of her stratagems?

CHAPTER EIGHTEEN

Salt and Eliana took a briefing with a group of Namacal Field Commanders to discuss the essentials of her intelligence. During the meeting they evaluated several large three-dimensional topographical maps of lunar terrain. Eliana pointed out specific areas where the Helium 3 was presumed to have been discovered. The territory was familiar to the Commanders because Namacal had claimed sections of that territory over a year ago. It was also part of a larger lunar landmass that was currently under dispute. Eliana explained that a small force had been sent in to secure the area while construction crews built a complex to house workers and equipment. She also stated that the Security force had been kept intentionally small, as any large movement of troops would inevitably draw Namacal's attention. New weaponry was also to be deployed to shield the perimeters, although she had no specifics on the nature or type of these armaments. Once the mining substructure was in place, more troops and weapons would be brought in making it ultimately more difficult, if not impossible to reclaim the territory. But Namacal was not without advantage, she explained, if they could stop the development before it expanded. That's where the intelligence had its greatest value. Amerex was still developing the field and the element of surprise was in Namacal's favor.

It was a thought provoking discussion, and as Salt and Eliana left the meeting they felt satisfied and confident regarding the value of what she'd delivered.

"I'd say they were duly impressed, wouldn't you?" He said.

"Don't know if they were impressed, but they saw the opportunity for advantage."

"Trust me, they were impressed. Your intelligence stops the Amerex move dead in its tracks and allows Namacal to maintain their status as masters of the game. The rewards will come back to us in more ways than one."

"All thanks to you." She said as she took his hand in hers. "If you had told me two days ago that this would be happening today, I would have thought you insane."

"Insanity isn't a bad thing, just a different way of seeing."

"Maybe the best way."

She moved in closer and placed her lips on his. The kiss and the embrace were tenderly offered and without reticence. She could almost feel him quiver in her arms.

"When was the last time you were with a woman?"

"The war doesn't leave much time for romance...or does it?"

"What does that mean?"

"Ben had an obvious affect on you. Otherwise, he wouldn't still be alive."

"I thought he was dead?"

"Would it matter if he weren't?"

She knew that lying would be a mistake, but restructuring the truth was open to interpretation.

"I liked him. He wasn't like the rest, he wasn't just a mercenary; he was...more like an artist cast into a role of something he wasn't really suited for, but played it well nonetheless."

"That's why you didn't kill him, because he was an artist?"

"I didn't kill him because I didn't have to."

"Because he was your lover?"

"I've had many lovers, Terry, but emotional involvement during war time is dangerous."

Her words resonated with truth, but he detected a hint of emotional residue between the lines that troubled him.

"He was helping you escape. Doesn't sound like two people in conflict."

"I needed him."

"Like you need me?"

"Not in the same way."

She moved in and gave him another kiss.

"It was a moment in time, that's all. I'm here with you now, and that's all that matters."

****

The tubes of Junoko were clogged with workers, technicians, and roustabouts. Calder and his men blended in easily as their search for Ben continued. They were no longer relying on an undercover status; their approach had become fully above ground and aggressive. No one liked to be bullied, but profiteers were always about, and eventually someone would talk.

In the OVO Pub, following the lead received from the dancer, hard currency crossed the bar to the red-eyed Barman. He acknowledged seeing Ben the night before and had reason to believe he might be staying at the Aragon, a small sleep unit in the same tube. It wasn't much to go on, but it was enough to shift Calder and his men into high gear.

They proceeded to the suspected unit, and after forcing the Clerk to give them a passkey, entered the room weapons drawn. The room was vacant, but Calder could sense that Ben had been there, and not that long ago. Assuming he might still be in the area, he wasted no time in getting back out into the tubes to continue the search.

Rikkert rushed into a techno repair cube and left two other Rangers standing by outside. As they waited for him to return, one of them heard a scream coming from an alley and went to investigate. The alley was heavily shadowed and he never saw the barrel of the Pulser as it broke the light. The gun fired and brain matter spiraled out the back of his head. As his body dropped, Ben disappeared back into the darkness. Rikkert rushed into the alley a moment later, blood still flowing from the Ranger's head wound.

"Sonofabitch." He groaned as he put in a call to Calder on his radio. "We got a man down and a suspect on the run."

Calder was there within minutes and sent the remaining Squad off to search the surrounding buildings. He could feel that Ben was close, perhaps watching him, taunting him from a hidden niche.

"I know you're there, you motherfucker." Calder screamed out at the top of his lungs. "If you were half a man you'd come down here and meet me face to face."

His voice filled the hollow tube to no response. But high in the portal of a cube across the way, Ben was indeed watching and reading Calder's thoughts. Calder's head was full of curses, but there was also a strong sense of fear in him, and that's exactly what Ben wanted.

****

Calder and the remaining Spec 4's continued their hunt staying to the rear of the cubicles and the darker sides of the tube. They whisked though several shops and tech cubes flashing Ben's picture, but no one had seen him. As they approached the end of another tube, they spotted something that stopped them instantly - a woman, scantily clad and unconscious lying in the middle of the tube. As they moved in for a closer look, her legs jerked backward as if by strong contorionistic muscle reflex.

"Hold your ground." Calder ordered. There was no further motion, but Calder was suspicious and sent Rikert in for confirmation.

Rikert edged in cautiously keeping his weapon raised and ready. When he was close enough to see her face, the shadow of his own frame broke the light falling across her torso – and that allowed him to see right through her. He turned to warn the others, but before he could utter a word, his head exploded. Ben dropped down from the fan housing in the tube roof and fired an auxillary round of pulses into the scattering Rangers. With their hearts bursting and blood blowing out of their chests, Calder clipped off a return sequence of shots, but Ben had already vanished. Calder kept firing even though there was nothing left to fire at. Suddenly, a shot blew the rifle out his hand with stinging force and left him unarmed and vulnerable. He lunged for one of the dead Soldier's rifles, but Ben fired again and the weapon disappeared.

"The next one goes through your baby blues and into your twisted little mind." Ben called out.

At that point, Calder knew he had lost the advantage, and had no choice but await Ben's next move. The move happened quickly as Ben appeared like a phantom beside him, smashing him in the face with the butt of his Pulser.

"That was for the avalanche."

Calder wiped the blood from his lips, but left a sneer in place.

"That was an accident."

" Just like your being here is an accident."

"I was sent to find you, not to kill you."

"You're shit for a liar, Calder, give it up."

"Nothing to give up, man, it's not what you think."

"Don't grovel, it doesn't suit you."

"I'm not your goddamn enemy; I'm trying to help you."

Ben saw an element of sincerity in what he was saying, but knew it was just a projection aimed at saving his own ass.

"Spare me the rhetoric I don't want your confession, I just want information."

"I'm a fountain overflowing, brother."

"Then you can start by telling me why my head is on the chopping block."

"Simple. You killed Ivory. You defied orders, you betrayed Namacal, and the last I heard you were working for Amerex."

"That's a lie."

"I'm not the judge, man, you know that."

"But you judged me out on that mountain, didn't you. You brought it down on my head and left me for dead."

"You were running. Why were you running?"

"Why were you shooting at me? I'm not your enemy, right?"

"She was."

"Was she? Then why did you let her live?"

"Why does the caged bird sing? She was a source, man, a big, wide, gaping source of information."

"Did you know she was a double agent?"

"I didn't know who or what she was, only that Salt wanted her."

"But he wanted her dead."

"A cautionary ploy. He wanted you to think that, but that was a game. The bitch was playing everybody from the beginning, but nobody knew that but Salt. The Amerex thing was a sham too. She was sucking them dry. She and Salt, wow, those motherfuckers are hard core, brother, they live by a different code."

"I'm not your brother."

"You're the closest thing I got man, but these people, they're icebergs. You see their tips, but not all the nasty shit they're carrying just beneath."

Ben listened, but didn't believe anything Calder said. Ironically, he didn't disbelieve it either. Whatever the truth was, it was cloaked in subterfuge and perpetually shifting just out of his reach.

"You can't take it personal, man." Calder continued. "Cunt fooled everybody. Women got that knack; you know. They dizzy you with pussy, and then take you for a ride down the icy slope. But this one, she's got more tricks than a spitting dick in magic show. Let her go, man, she ain't nothing but bad news on a cold day.

"And you're the authority?"

"No, but I'm not the bad guy here either. Like you baby, I may have the head for this thing, but I'm still just following orders. If it wasn't me standing here, they would have sent somebody else."

"But it is you, and that's where we got a problem." Ben lifted his Pulser and pressed it to Calder's head.

"Ben, man, I told you what you wanted to know."

"You told me something, but not necessarily what I wanted to know. But now let me tell you something. You should have killed me when you had the chance. I know who you are, Calder, I've seen the other side of your face."

Calder could hear the sound of Ben's finger pulling the trigger. He was waiting for the explosion to rip through his head, but it didn't come. Instead, Ben raised the Pulser, and with one swift pop, knocked him cold.

CHAPTER NINETEEN

The glow of Earth's billowing light filtered into the bubble portal of Eliana's sleeping quarters. She and Salt were in each other's arms, the flesh of their bodies damp with the heat of growing passion. Hands touched and lips sought delight in the sweetness of a kiss. Eliana, had initially been reluctant to open herself to Salt's advances, but now that she was once again a free agent, she felt she had the freedom to let her self go. The mental games that had been played before were now abandoned and replaced by an expurgated emotional engagement. Both of their defenses were down, and for the first time since their reunion, they allowed themselves to be completely open and vulnerable. But as their passion was allotted latitude, Salt became more assertive, and his touch less agile. He tangled her hair between his fingers in a way that reminded her too much of his aggressive past.

"Easy Terry." She whispered, the softness of her words quieting him, but not the force of his sexual energy, not easily diffused.

"Go slow, baby, slow." She whispered again, her words easing his motions, but also frustrating him. She read his agitation as sure as he had aimed it right at her mind. And he knew the instant she picked it up, but he was too lost in his own desire to fight against it. He wanted her desperately, and like a wild animal, was ready to ravage her, devour her flesh, damn the cost. But as he was about to abandon all control, he remembered that there was more at stake than just satisfying his own libido. Their relationship had only just been reestablished, and he was already using both his physical and psychological force on her, everything that had driven her away the first time. It was a thought that had resonance, so much so that he softened his touch and let her assume the lead. Responding to his shift in sensitivity, she put her hand between his legs and gently stroked him. But just as the give and take sweetened, and the sensual equilibrium became more balanced, his pager went off and blew the air completely out of the moment.

"Shit." The word spewed from his mouth like a fume, and though he tried to ignore the intrusion, the pager just kept buzzing. Finally, he was forced to answer. A bubble hologram came floating out of the unit and stopped in front of him. The image within was of Corporal Ludovic.

"I hope it's important." Salt snapped.

"Calder is back, but the rest of the squad is dead. Evidently there was an encounter with Lieutenant Denning." Salt's eyes froze, an image of Ben crystallizing on his pupils. The image floated upward like an air bubble where Eliana aborted it.

"Where is Calder now?"

"Here with me at the Command Center. "

"I'll be there in fifteen minutes."

He clicked off the hologram, a flood of anger raging inside of him.

"You should have killed that bastard when you had the chance."

"There was no reason to kill him."

"There is now."

****

Salt and Eliana returned to N-Sight Headquarters where Calder and Ludovic were waiting. Calder's face was badly bruised, but it was the psychic bruises that Salt was more interested in. The first thing he noticed was that Calder was subdued, more so than he had ever seen him. His ego had been battered and some of his power chipped away.

"What the fuck happened?" Salt asked.

"He was tracking us from the start, used a telemetric pulser on us, and took the squad out one by one."

"Then why aren't you dead?"

"Because I'm not the one he's after. He wants you to know he can play the game as well as anybody. He feels betrayed and wants vengeance.

"He's delusional."

"But still dangerous."

"He's only one man."

"Right, but I wouldn't under estimate him. I made that mistake. We know he can read like a champ, but he's also snakebite lethal. There's more to this boy than meets the eye."

"Then he hasn't met the right eye yet." Salt shot a glance to Ludovic. "Get him the hell out of here."

Ludovic escorted Calder from the room as Eliana watched and assessed all that had transpired. It wasn't just that Ben had beaten Calder; he had also beaten Salt. Salt prided himself on maintaining control, but the situation with Ben was out of control and had already reached the point of absurdity.

"Your boy has proven himself quite a nuisance." Salt said bitterly.

"He's not my boy, but he is a nuisance, and a threat to all of us."

"Not for long."

CHAPTER TWENTY

Ben monitored the landing pad at the Junoko Spaceport, watching as a Namacal Lunar Craft flew in carrying another squad of Rangers. He didn't need a psychic read to know they weren't in colony for pleasure. Ben recognized the fact that he had no country, no company, and no friend to turn to. He could beat the odds for a while, but eventually the odds would catch up with him. He needed an affiliate and the only affiliate left to turn to at this point was Amerex. But even if he defected, Amerex controlled territories were fifty kilometers away, and the Pod he'd come in on was already on shaky legs. It was not an option he necessarily wanted to employ, but with a fresh squad of Rangers deboarding to search for him, he felt he had no choice but to get out of Junoko.

****

Digging the Pod out of its camouflage at the dump, he geared it back into motion and made his way off into the frozen outback. The terrain was mostly flat, but spotted with periodic craters that blended in with the shadowy landscape and were hard to see until you were on top of them. It was necessary to stay alert, or risk being swallowed up unforwarned. But craters were not the only potential pitfall he faced; there was also the danger of being spotted by Military Spacecraft patrolling the area. Ben's ears were sharp, and he could hear an incoming Craft long before it was near enough to see him. He carried camouflage netting with him, which on a surface level, availed him at least a modicum of invisibility, but there was no guarantee he could escape detection.

****

Back in Junoko, the Spec 4's were questioning people outside the sleep unit where Ben had stayed. Most knew nothing about what had happened or who Ben was, but one woman had seen a man in a pressure suit leaving the complex and walking off toward the dumping ground. The

Rangers immediately returned to their Craft eager to follow the potential lead.

They flew low above the lunar plain, following a rough set of Pod tracks that began at the dumping ground and wound off into the outback. The heat trails left by the Pod were recent and easily identifiable. Given the direction taken, the Pilot speculated that the probable destination was Evon, an Amerex controlled mining colony in the adjacent mountains. Heavy emphasis was placed on catching the Pod before it reached Amerex territory and to lessen the possibility of being shot down by enemy antiaircraft.

****

In the dead lunar vacuum, Ben heard the roar of the approaching Space Craft long before he saw it. Taking evasive action, he guided the Pod over the edge of a shallow crater and anchored it to the crater wall. He quickly draped it with the camouflage blending it with the environment. It wasn't foolproof, but it was a band aide of subtle illusion. The Craft flew over Ben's position, and although it didn't see the Pod on the first pass, it did spot its tracks descending into the crater. Circling back for another pass and dropping to a lower altitude, this time the Pilot spotted the camouflaged Pod and immediately fired a laser rocket. Fiery metal parts shot outward, the flames rapidly extinguished in the airless space. The attack was quick and precise, and all that remained in the aftermath were blackened metal scraps scattered across the crater's embankment. The Spec 4's on board the Craft cheered wildly assuming a definite kill, but the Squad Leader wanted hands on confirmation and ordered the Pilot to land.

On the ground, the team descended into the crater to verify the wreckage. Confirmation on the Pod was easily made, but there were no signs of a body. That prompted doubts in the Squad Leader who sent one of the men off to explore the immediate area. He hadn't gone far, less than thirty yards, when he came upon several foot tracks. He was about to alert the others when the ground beneath the last track shifted. Ben reared up from the glom like a jack in the box and fired a pulse straight through the soldier's chest. The shot set the other Rangers in motion, but Ben kept firing taking out one after the other until no one was left standing. By the time the last man fell, Ben was already ascending the crater wall. The Pilot, still in the cockpit, heard the sounds of gunfire, but had no visual confirmation as to what had happened. Making a cautionary move, he booted the engines and geared the Craft into flight mode. But before he could lift off, Ben reached the rim of the crater and fired a pulse shot straight through the Cockpit's main portal. The craft exploded, sending blood and debris high into the airless round. It was a quick coup, and one that availed Ben the relief of having cheated death once again. But the fight for survival was far from over. He was without transport, still a long way from the Amerex Colony, and facing the possibility of freezing to death. Knowing that the rotation of the moon would soon leave him in total darkness, he had no choice but to strike out toward the mountains on foot.

****

Salt and High Ranking Members of the Namacal Command had gathered in the war room to plot strategy for an attack on Amerex positions. Satellite photos of various mining areas and troop stations were displayed on large holographic orbs that hovered around them like colored clouds. As they discussed the variables at hand, Corporal Ludovic interrupted the conference with an urgent message for Commander Salt. Salt was not happy about the intrusion, but reading Ludovic's thoughts, knew the matter was of a serious nature that demanded his immediate attention. Excusing himself from the room, he stepped outside where Ludovic relayed the information regarding the Ranger team.

"No radio communication of any kind for over three hours. Calls have gone out for the last hour, but nothing has come back."

"Their last position?"

"About twenty kilometers north of Junoko and headed into Amerex territory. Apparently, they were following a suspect seen fleeing the colony. They reported Pod tracks at about seven kilometers out, but nothing after that."

"Maintain your efforts to make contact, but have a Search and Recovery unit prepped and on standby.

"Yes sir."

****

The vast lunar plain stretched out before Ben like a frozen desert. He was moving as quickly as humanly possible, taking advantage of the lack of gravity, and pushing himself to the limits of his physical capacity. But the level of exertion expended was also using up his oxygen and wearing him down faster than he had anticipated. He was no longer sure how far he had gone, how far he had to go, or even if his air supply would last long enough to take him there. But what he did know was that if he didn't reach Amerex territory before darkness fell, he might never find his way. And so he pushed himself harder, beyond the breaking point of all he thought he was capable of. With every arduous step, he was cursing himself for the decisions that had led him to this point. From his first meeting with Ivory, to his acceptance of Salt's training program, to his friendship with Calder, to his trusting of Eliana, every choice he had made had essentially led him to disaster. He ran these scenarios through his head over and over until he was crazy with rage and vowing never to trust anyone again. The chill of the lunar terrain around him was intolerably cold, but the chill he felt inside was of equal measure.

As he entered the lunar foothills, a Search and Rescue Team of Spec 4's landed at the rim of the crater behind him. After sifting through the wreckage and the bodies of their predecessors, they discovered Ben's tracks trailing off into the mountains. Time was of the essence, and they wasted none in leaving the scene to pursue him.

****

Ben was gasping for breath as he climbed the steep, narrow path of one of the tallest peaks in the area. Finally reaching its crest, he fell to his knees in utter exhaustion. He could feel the tissue in his muscles burning to depletion. Checking his oxygen gauges, he determined that he might have enough air for another hour, but beyond that, he was in no man's land. That gave him the impetus he needed to get back to his feet and keep going, but he was moving much slower than before.

On his final descent, a broad vista opened up before him, as bleak and featureless as ever, but to him like a heavenly panacea. He could see all the way across the valley to a small bubble colony on the far side. It had to be Evon, he thought, the very sight of it rekindling his hope. Suddenly reenergized, he began to hurl himself down the narrow path, at times lifting himself off the ground in zero G bounds of twelve feet or more.

After reaching the valley floor, and less than a kilometer away from the colony, he heard the Ranger Craft coming through the mountain pass behind him. The Pilot was aware that they had crossed into Amerex controlled territory and the Craft was now vulnerable to radar detection. The time factor was critical and the window of opportunity for catching Ben was quickly closing. Increasing speed, they crossed the last crest of the mountain and came into full view of the Mining Complex. With the open plateau in front of them, the Pilot easily spotted Ben on the far side a hundred yards short of the colony. There was no question that he could take him out, but he was also now at serious risk of being shot down. The Amerex Security Forces had also spotted Ben, and identified his Namacal uniform. An Armed Rover roared out of a Mountain Cave and bore down on him aggressively. With the Craft closing in from behind, and the Rover in front of him, the question became who would get to him first?

The Pilot had him in target sequence, but if he waited six seconds longer, he could also take out the Rover with the same shot. But the longer he waited, the more the Craft became vulnerable to the Amerex anti-aircraft defenses. Amerex had already picked them up on Radar and were preparing to fire when Ben heard the laser rocket ignite behind him. He dropped to the ground a split second before it zoomed past mere inches above his head. Miraculously, he was safe, but the rocket hit the Rover dead on sending metal sparks and body parts spewing across the sky like bloodied confetti. The impact rattled Ben's bones and set his ears to ringing. With the debris floating down like death flies all around him, he looked back to see the Craft still bearing down on him. There was nowhere left to run, and too little time to do so even if he could. He closed his eyes, not in resolve, but in defying the horror that awaited him. He never saw it, but he heard the whir of the missile as it broke the airless void. The explosion followed a second later. The Craft took the full force of the hit from Amerex Defense and was blown out of the sky. So powerful was the impact, that the remains of the Craft and crew were reduced to dust particles that sprinkled the sky and drifted slowly to the ground like dew. Surprised to find himself still alive, Ben opened his eyes and watched as a rose-colored death mist coated his faceplate. It was an unsettling visual, but one that brought him a momentary sense of relief. But as the moment passed, he spotted another Rover breaking from the cave and speeding toward him. It occurred to him that he could fire on them, but even if he got lucky and crippled the vehicle, more would come. With no acceptable options left to choose from, he threw down his weapon and held his hands up. The Rover screeched to a stop and a half dozen Amerex soldiers jumped out and surrounded him. They scanned him for weapons and other devices, but finding nothing on him, secured his hands behind his back and loaded him into the Rover to return to base.

CHAPTER TWENTY-ONE

Calder had returned to his quarters and was nursing a synthetic whiskey, staring pensively into the bottom of the glass. He was mentally kicking himself for blowing the recent mission and letting Ben out-psych him. But he was also visualizing Ben's death and the various ways that he might revenge his defeat. The thought of revenge gave him great pleasure, but did not end the self-loathing that had been growing inside of him. He went to the med cabinet to peruse the buffet of various drugs he had on hand. The possibilities covered the spectrum from up, down, to all around and then some. Ultimately he chose a black skull shaped opiate that he knew would take him on a trip to dreamland. He popped the top on the bottle, poured two capsules into his hand, but stopped as two N-Sight Rangers appeared behind him.

"We have orders to take you to Commander Salt."

"I was just there." Calder said.

"He wants to see you again."

Calder read their thoughts for any mental mischief or clandestine motivations, but saw that they were clearly just following orders. He took a long hungry look at the pills, but the moment of need had already passed, so he tossed them in the sink and joined the Rangers.

****

Calder entered Salt's office with apprehension in his eyes, and thoughts on his sleeves. Salt missed none of this, but neither did he take a hard line on him. Instead, he spoke like an understanding father would to a son.

"You look anxious."

"Just pissed off."

"That's natural."

"Not for me. I fucked up, and don't like fucking up."

"We all make mistakes, but that's how we learn and grow. Unfortunately, in war, mistakes aren't just errors in judgment, they're too often death sentences. If you want to stay alive, you can't afford to make mistakes. You have to calculate every move and be able to see ten moves in advance. And when in doubt, there's only one rule to follow - kill. You don't wait, you don't hesitate; you pull the trigger."

"My finger was on the trigger the whole time I was in Junoko, and it's still on the trigger. I want to go back after Denning, and this time I won't..."

"No." Salt said, stopping him in mid-sentence. "I'll take care of Denning, but I have a more important job for you... something that will lift you above your self and give the Corporation a boot up in this conflict. This is an important mission with you in the starring role. In war you rarely get a second chance, but this is not only a second chance, it's a supreme opportunity."

"I appreciate your confidence, sir, but I'd rather..."

"This isn't about what you'd rather do, Calder, this is about winning a war. We've recently received intelligence that Amerex has discovered a large and valuable territorial deposit of Helium 3 in neutral territory. They're in the process of securing that location and establishing a new mining operation. Their success in this endeavor could feasibly change the complexion of our conflict. Needless to say, we can't allow that to happen. The Chiefs of Staff and I have developed a psy-ops strategy for combating the effort, and I've recommended you to lead the assault. At base level, it is a military mission, but one that demands psy-op job skills. A large military approach would draw too much attention and put our forces in jeopardy, but a small stealth unit with psy-sonic weaponry could move in by cover of darkness and destroy Amerex Security forces before they knew what hit them. We have a narrow window of approach and the element of surprise is our one ace in the hole."

"I...I'm not sure what to say, I...."

"Say, yes sir, I'd be honored."

"I am honored, but..."

"Then say no more."

"No more than a thank you...thank you for giving me the opportunity. You won't regret it."

"I don't live by regrets, Mr. Calder, only by actions. Corporal Ludovic will apprise you of all the particulars, so put your head in gear and ready yourself for engagement."

"I'm always ready, sir."

Salt stepped forward and embraced him, his eyes sinking deep into Calder's.

"Don't disappoint me, son."

"Never, sir. Never."

CHAPTER TWENTY-TWO

Ben, bound in laser cuffs and leg lacings, was brought into the Quarters of Captain Victor Brancusi, an Amerex Security Field Officer. He took a long, hard look at Ben, studying him as if he'd just discovered a new biological species. In turn, Ben sifted through Brancusi's thoughts, most of which consisted of questions regarding how he came to arrive on their doorstep. This evaluation went on for several moments before the Officer finally broke the silence.

"A Namacal Soldier on foot, alone, and miles from his home base is not an every day occurrence here in our little corner of the moon. Nor is it common for a Namacal Fighter Craft to enter our territory just to attack one of our Security vehicles. Even more curious is that they also appeared to be firing at you."

"They were firing at me."

"Then I'm sure you'd like to explain why."

"I was branded a traitor by my Commanders because I shot one of our officers who was threatening the life of an Amerex operative. I was put on a kill list and forced to go on the run. Going back to Namacal was/is not an option. By shooting that Fighter down you saved my life. But I didn't come here just for sanctuary, nor did I come empty handed. I'm an Intelligence officer with intelligence I believe could help Amerex."

"Interesting story, but why would you want to help us at all?"

"I've come to believe that Namacal is the most dangerous and destructive Corporation in the world. Before there can be any hope of peace and prosperity, they have to be defeated. That's my personal view, philosophically speaking, but I'm not here to wax philosophical, I'm here because...I already work for Amerex. I'm an undercover operative who was able to infiltrate a Namacal Psy-Ops unit."

"If true, I presume you can verify that?"

"Major John Ronson. He's a high-ranking member of Amerex Intelligence. He's my contact. He knows my background."

"Then we obviously need to talk to Major Ronson."

****

Eliana looked out the portal window of her quarters to where two personnel Carriers were being loaded with equipment and weapons. It appeared to be a small- scale operation but by the fact that Ranking Officers were milling about on the airfield, she sensed it was an important one. She also noticed someone there she had not expected to see. Calder was on the tarmac consulting with the Officers and giving orders to a detail of men loading the Carriers. That's when it hit her that the mission being organized was the one that she had set up, the push to stop the new Amerex mining development. As that thought crystallized, it became evident that Calder had been put in charge in place of her. She had reported the operation and was under the impression that she would lead the mission. So why was she being excluded? Seeking answers to those questions, she immediately left her quarters for Salt's office.

****

Eliana's emotions were flaring out of control as she arrived at N-Sight Headquarters. Ludovic, noting her demeanor, hesitated to let her go further.

"I'm Okay; I'm not going to kill anybody. This is a matter of grave importance that the Commander needs to be apprised of." She told him.

He resisted her assurances as his guard dog duties dictated, but after additional inveigling and calming; she finally got him to allow her entry. Stepping through the door, she saluted Salt in a formal manner, something she had not done since her return.

"Good morning, Lieutenant." He said, sensing her irritation.

"Excuse the interruption, Colonel, but can we speak freely."

"Don't we always."

"No."

Her answer was pert, but not divisive. She walked over to the window where she indicated the field where the troops and equipment were still loading.

"You're making a move on the Mining Operation."

"You knew we would."

"I was under the impression that I would be part of that mission."

"You are a part of it, the most important part "

"Calder was on the field spouting orders."

"He's one of the best Psy-Ops officers we have. An excellent choice for the mission."

"But not the best choice."

"And that would have been you, is that what you're suggesting?

"Who knew more? Who's more qualified?"

"We both know the answer to that, but you're too valuable to squander on a mission like this. The dangers are formidable and the military aspects far beyond the mental playing field."

"I live in a world of danger, Terry, and have experienced combat in many forms."

"All true, but we've just welcomed you home again, and I'm not willing to lose you so quickly."

"You promised me I'd be involved…that I would be an integral part of the push forward."

"And you are part of it. But you didn't expect me to put you on the front line. That would be a frivolous move. Calder may not be the best, but he's expendable, you're not."

"I'm not looking for special treatment."

"You're treated according to your value, and your value goes far beyond my own personal interests. It may seem like I'm selfishly protecting you, but I'm actually protecting a company asset."

There was truth in what he said, but she still felt manipulated. This was exactly what she'd had trouble with before, a soft form of control, but control just the same. "

"I appreciate what you're trying to do, but it's not what I want."

"I understand your feelings, but you have to understand mine. You feel that I'm trying to control you; but the bottom line is this is a military decision. And militarily speaking, I needed to put Calder back on the ground before he lost more confidence in himself. All things considered, that's a job decision. Making those type decisions is why we're still the best Psy-Ops force in the world."

"And I feel fortunate to be a part of that, but not if I can't be my own person and fight my own battles. I don't need a protector, Terry."

"War offers no guarantees for anybody, but I'd like to keep you alive. You serve no one, not even yourself, if you're dead."

"But if you hold me too closely, too tightly, lock me away in your protective prison, then I'm dead already."

Even before she spoke, he heard and felt her words. This was a discussion they'd had before. And as much as he wanted to keep her under his wing, he knew he couldn't.

"Whatever you need, I..."

"You know what I need, just allow me the space to have it."

She said nothing more, just saluted him again and left the room. She stopped outside the door and fell back against the wall as if she had suddenly ran short of breath. Her mind was spinning with thoughts, but her emotions were subdued. She saw a Security Guard approaching from the far end of the hall, and not wanting to be questioned, hurried back to her quarters.

****

Ben was being held in a holding cell with a bed, a toilet and no creature comforts. Comfort came in terms of his thoughts, which were mostly on Eliana - her eyes, her laugh, the touch of her skin. The good moments they had shared together kept coming back to him and filled him with longing. But there were still reservations. His feelings and psychic emissions told him she had been telling him the truth, but her actions and the actions of her associates made it all seem a lie. Had he been so blind that he couldn't see that? These were hard notions for him to accept and he wouldn't accept them until he could gain more insight into her connections with Salt and Namacal. But while he was pondering these thoughts, the cell door opened and Brancusi stepped in.

"We have a problem. We've been unable to locate your Major Ronson. He is listed on roster, but his current station is unknown. We'll continue trying to find him, but in the meantime you should know that the Operative you proposed to be helping turned out to be an undercover Agent working for Namacal."

"I find that hard to believe, unless of course, that's what they want you to believe."

"What I believe doesn't matter, but the evidence, as you can clearly see, doesn't help your case."

"My case?"

"Until we can prove otherwise, you're still regarded as an enemy combatant."

"There is no case if you simply talk to Ronson. He can clear everything up."

"As I said, we're trying to locate him. What type of work were you doing for him?"

"Generally referred to as psychic espionage."

"You're a psychic?"

"Let's just say I have different way of seeing."

"Do you always see truly?"

"There is no always in anything. But I was working with Namacal's N-Sight division, and I can provide intelligence to Amerex that would prove extremely beneficial."

"What type of intelligence?"

"Classified intelligence. I report to Ronson, and no one else."

****

Calder and the Namacal Company he was leading boarded the Carrier and were on their way across the great lunar plains. Seventy kilometers of rugged terrain would have to be traversed before they would reach their destination. Most of the Soldiers spent their time playing cards and in idle ramblings, but Calder avoided any interplay with the men. He was more serious in his intentions and determined to make the mission a success. He gazed abstractly at the dark terrain, but his inner vision was filled with images of future glory. He envisioned himself the conquering hero, a master player in the game of war. Satellite surveillance photos of the strike zone flashed in his mind and fueled him with feral excitement. He saw troop movement and gunfire, and perceived that a great destiny awaited him. He sensed an opportunity for a quick and decisive victory, a victory that would also wipe the memory of Ben from Salt's mind and raise Calder to a position of power and respect. This was his chance to shine, and shine he would. It was perfect, the perfect moment and the perfect time. Like Ben, he was a lover of games, but the game of war was in its own special idiom. In this game life and death were at stake, and those stakes pumped his adrenalin up into a wild frenzy. He kept imaging himself as the master soldier, an indefatigable Alexander the Great, God-like Warrior who would blaze a trail of glory all the way to Valhalla.

"To Valhalla." He shouted, drawing the attention of his men who found his behavior odd and had no idea what he was shouting about.

****

The door to Ben's cell opened and three Guards rushed in, laser cuffed him, and removed him from the room. He asked where they were taking him, but they gave no reply. As they passed through several corridors, he tried to read their thoughts; but found only inconsequential ramblings. But one disturbing image kept breaking through that didn't belong to either of the men, one that he was unable to ignore, and that was an image of death bubbling out of an evaporating skull.

The Guards took him to a tube resembling an old time retro bowling alley. He assumed it was probably a mineshaft, but had no way of knowing. The Guards placed him against a wall and stepped away. A moment later, Brancusi appeared out of the shadows.

"There's been no response from Ronson, and no additional information as to his whereabouts. For all intent and purpose, he seems to have disappeared. As for you, our intelligence remains the same and strongly suggests that you were, are, and remain a Namacal Agent."

"I explained that to you already. But think about this; if I'm working for Namacal, then why are they trying to kill me?"

"Perhaps because it paints a convincing picture, although not necessarily a believable one."

The three Guards stepped back into the light, this time cradling rifles. No orders were given, but as if following an unwritten script, they placed the rifles on their shoulders and silently took aim. Ben suddenly felt extremely vulnerable. He had risked his life many times since he had been on lunar turf, and not once did he believe he was actually going to die. But this time was different; this time he could feel the cold chill of death creeping up around him.

"And who am I trying to convince? I have everything to lose, and Amerex everything to gain."

"Gain or lose, is not my decision; I have orders."

"You're a man, not an order. You have a mind of your own. Orders are only guidelines, not empirical facts."

"You're not hearing me. We can't locate Ronson, we can't substantiate your story, and you haven't given us anything of value to make us think otherwise."

"Value? I can give you endless details about the inner workings of N-Sight. I know what Eliana knew, and that if she is working for Namacal then Amerex is at serious risk."

"And what risk would that be?"

"The risk of losing the new Helium 3 operation. I know that those lands are disputed and that territorial security has to be set up or that resource will be at risk of falling into enemy hands. If Eliana turned that intelligence over, which I believe she did, then they will surely execute a strike. But there's still time to stop them, if you adhere to what I say and act now."

Brancusi said nothing, but looked to the Riflemen who were waiting for his signal. The moments ticked away with the pounding of Ben's heart growing to maximum intensity. Finally, after what seemed like eternity wrapped in a pulse beat, Brancusi nodded. The indication was for the men to lower their weapons, but they didn't. And as Ben heard the sound of their clips engage, he felt that his heart would burst from his chest at any moment. He knew the next sound he heard would be that of gunfire, followed by silence and the sleep of death. But that sound never came. Instead, Brancusi stepped in next to him and unlatched the cuffs on Ben's wrists.

"Command recognizes the value you represent. But we had to be sure that what you were offering had validity. Major Ronson was wounded in battle, but is expected to recover. We have a Craft waiting to take you to our Main Post for further questioning."

****

Calder and Company landed in a narrow valley deep in the mountains, twenty kilometers from the target area. Before de-boarding, the men were briefed on more specifics of the mission and how their planned advance would be to enter the strike zone on foot. An air approach would be quicker, Calder explained, but would rob them of the element of surprise. And given that surprise was imperative, the intention was to march across the mountain and be at the location by the break of dawn.

****

Ben arrived at the Amerex Base and was immediately taken to a Military Intelligence Room to meet with Major Ronson. Ronson had been wounded, and was on crutches, but easily recognizable as the Crew Cut Man who had been monitoring Ben the night Ivory recruited him. The two men shook hands, both happy to see that the other was still alive, albeit, not untouched by the wages of war.

"Nice sticks." Ben said noting the crutches.

"Sniper's pulse shot ripped through our carrier's fuselage right after landing. Shattered the femur, but the laser surgery seared it back together nicely. It's coming back around."

"You're lucky."

"We make our luck, don't we?"

"Not always successfully."

"You seemed to have made it through in one piece."

"There were some close calls."

"From us or them?"

"Both."

"Were you exposed?"

"Not outright. They don't know about our mission, or that I was working undercover, but I had to inadvertently kill one of their officers. So essentially, I'm dead in the water, and so is the mission. They've labeled me a traitor and put out a kill order on me. I don't see anyway to reverse that."

"Then maybe you should look further. You've made a helluv a lot of progress; it'd be a shame to let it go to waste. We went to great lengths to get you inside."

"You're not hearing me. I'm a traitor; they want me dead."

"But what if we could make them think you weren't a traitor?"

"That would be a real magic trick. They already know I'm here, and they'll know I didn't just stop by for a cup of coffee."

"Maybe a cup of tea. Look, all they know is you were on the run, and you ran here. At the end of the day, there aren't a lot of places to run."

"What are you saing? Are you suggesting I go back?"

"I'm suggesting it's a possibility we should explore."

"They'd shoot me on sight."

"Not if you bring them intelligence more compelling than what you brought us."

"What intelligence would that be?"

"We could provide you with something of poignancy. Hypothetically, you're our prisoner, right. But what if we

213

arranged for you to escape, put out an alert for you, and made sure they intercepted that alert. Running from us, you would be perceived in a new and different light. And if they thought you had intelligence, which we'd make sure they did think, then you could play right into their hands. You'd be an escaped prisoner in flight. Once you're picked up, you can bet the high end of a straight they'll want the intelligence that you'd be perceived to have, and that would leave you in a position to make a deal with them."

"You mean if they didn't kill me first."

"They won't kill you if they think you have something to offer."

Ben considered the plan, and felt it was far too risky, but didn't express his dissent outwardly.

"So what is the compelling intelligence that I would be bargaining with?"

"Are you accepting the mission?"

"Do I have a choice?"

"I wouldn't send you back into the lion's den, if I thought the mission would fail. You're too valuable an asset to lose." Ronson was articulate and convincing, but Ben knew he had the ability to lie with great sincerity and that his priorities ultimately lay with the corporation and not Ben's personal safety.

"Sounds absolutely insane...but if the intelligence is strong enough, then we might have a chance."

"Trust me on this, it will be strong enough."

****

A hazy darkness engulfed the N-Sight complex forming shadows that resembled blood veins in the curved arches of the structures. The Personnel Quarters were also cast in deep shadow and pin drop quiet. But inside Cubicle 23 tactile activity was underway. Ben and Eliana were bedded down, devouring each other with hungry caresses that went deeper than the flesh. They had abandoned all psychic games, and only the purity of hearts and minds merging one into the other remained. Any misgivings had been wiped away, and they, like newborn children, were freely responsive to the flow of the sensations that pulsed through their bodies. When their passion reached its pinnacle and ultimate consummation, they lay in each other's arms, breath slowing and sweat drying into the cool resonance of love. As if waking from a dream, Eliana slowly opened her eyes and looked at Ben who was still lost within his own crucible savoring the remnants of their sensual engagement. She didn't disturb him, but glanced out the portal onto the dark lunar landscape. Suddenly, she saw Ben's reflection in the bubble glass. He was standing over her, extending his hand to touch her. But before she even heard the shot, she felt the bullet go through her brain. It shattered her skull and sent bone fragments splintering the air. She could feel the piercing lead passing through the soft neural tissue and exiting the back of her head. A section of her skull broke away like a shingle blowing off a rooftop. Bits of brain matter splattered the wall in a strange mosaic pattern. Blood was spewing out of her in rhythmic pulses, and she knew instantaneously that she would soon be dead. As her breathing diminished, the room darkened, but she could still see Ben as he lowered the gun. He was watching her with a curious and chilling gleam in his eyes. She tried to speak, but the words failed to form. As she drew her final breath, her eyes suddenly flicked wide open.

The room was dark, quiet, and motionless. Ben was not there, nor had he been there. There was no gunshot, there was no head wound; there was no lovemaking; it had all been a dream, a nightmare so real that it left Eliana shaken to the core. On the surface the dream was unsettling, and yet she was reminded in the strongest possible way that the connection between them remained ineffably strong. But had he turned on her again, she wondered. What was he thinking, feeling, and was it she who had underestimated him? Doubts clouded her thoughts and fogged her countenance. Maybe he was more sly and treacherous than she assumed. Maybe it was all only a game, a game in which he had duped her into thinking she had duped him. The dream was just a dream, but perhaps it was also a warning, a reminder that the layers of deception ran deep. Maybe she had played her hand too well, been too convincing. The truth was so skewed at this point; even she began to lose sight of it. But to entertain these thoughts, sans confirmation, was fruitless mental masturbation. She sat there alone in her bed, cursing the war, it's corporate armies, and all the Military Bureaucrats that gave birth to these mind states. Yes, she had signed on to play the game, to partake in the conflict, to spy and lie, but when all the subterfuge and calculations were wiped away, she hated it. And if there was anything she could do to stop it, then she would. But it seemed so futile to even consider such a thing, much less to believe that she could actually make a difference in what had already been accepted as normal by the world at large. War was commonplace and rarely even questioned by the masses. What chance did one woman have of stopping the lie, the insanity, and the madness that had poisoned the minds of human kind for thousands of years? What chance? What chance?

****

Calder and his men crossed over the last mountain ridge as light was beginning to break in the dark lunar sky. They kept themselves concealed in the mountain shadows and approached the strike zone with sustained stealth. Calder charted their forward motion via micro-topographic laser maps and pin pointed the site of the mine to exactness. Using a teletransportive lens built into the faceplate of his helmet, he scanned the area in close up from horizon to horizon. There were obvious signs of human intrusion, but no evidence of machinery, excavation, or any form of security force. In fact there was nothing there to indicate activity of any kind, specifically that which would warrant a military assault.

Calder adjusted the high intensity sound monitoring spurs on his telemetric equipment and listened closely to the amplified ambiance of the outside world. Everyone in the unit had been ordered to remain quiet to the point of withholding breath, but the lunar canyon remained void of any sound. Something was wrong, Calder thought, but he continued to move forward, scanning every inch of the mountainside. Angst among the men grew more intense, not because of the potential for engagement, but for the lack of it. This was not what they expected to find, nor could they explain it. They were too close to risk radio contact with command for fear of any communication being intercepted, so they just kept forging their way deeper into the valley. Calder's psychic senses were sharply focused, but he was receiving virtually nothing, only the dead drone of the vacuous landscape. As they reached the rear of the canyon, the troops spread out, but stayed close to the surrounding walls so as not to be seen from above. A series of caves lined the perimeter, and Calder surmised that they could easily hide men and equipment, but he needed direct confirmation. He sent two men out to scout the caves before the rest of the unit moved any closer.

The Scouts stayed low and approached the area with careful vigilance. The entry to the first cave was large enough for a vehicle to pass through, but there were no tracks or evidence to suggest that anyone, not even a single soldier had been there. The two Scouts moved inside, shining the beams of their gun lights down the length of the cavern. The darkness was too deep to penetrate all the way to the end, but for all intent and purpose, they saw nothing. They returned to the entry, signaled Calder as to their findings, and then proceeded to the second cave. The mouth of the cave lay only a few yards away, but as they started in to investigate they heard a distinctive metallic click. Before they could react, sonar pulses cut the darkness and struck the two men imploding them on the spot. Their bodies disintegrated into instantaneous flesh particles too small to distinguish.

"Fucking hell." Calder cried out as he and the rest of his men hit the dirt. More pulses and bullet fire followed, but the shots were not coming from the canyon floor, they were coming from above, high on the canyon walls.

Two more men went down in an incendiary rush of sonar pulses. The Company scattered bolting for any form of cover, and though they were able to find some shielding behind low-lying mounds of regolith, for the most part they were left exposed to the relentless attack. Calder engaged a telemetric Sonic Culler and fired a blast high into the canyon wall. A dozen Amerex troops blew out of the rock their bodies coming apart like balls of bone confetti. It was a good beginning to a counter attack, but Calder estimated that there were as many as one hundred Amerex soldiers hidden in the canyon's cliffs, and that would not be a disadvantage easily overcome. With each passing second, another Namacal troop went down. Calder fired another sonic blast into wall, but to less fatal results. Two bodies fell, but there was so much fire coming back at him that he couldn't raise his head even for a second. Drawing a Microwave Emitter from his pack, he fired a sonic emission in a circular pattern that literally coiled itself around the upper canyon wall. The wire-like current of microwaves caused instant epileptic-like seizures in dozens of Amerex troops, and subsequently, they began to topple from their perches like wounded birds. Calder was both resourceful and aggressive, but the odds were still heavily stacked against him. The Amerex numbers were going down, but the Namacal death count was logging faster, much faster. More than a quarter of the company had already been wiped out, and there was no place to hide except in the caves that had already proven to be potential death traps. But for Calder, staying in the open offered even less hope, so making a difficult choice, he led the remainder of his men into the second cave.

Safely inside, he fired a Microwave blast down the length of the cavern, the light from its wave giving him a clear view of what lay ahead. There was no sign of an Amerex insurgence or any immediate danger, but he knew that wouldn't last. Their backs were to the wall and there was no viable exit from the cave. Using the laser teleprojector on his rifle, he bounced a laser beam off the cave wall, the curved line of its beam providing him with a vertical telescopic view to the outside world. Through the hollow laser he could see the Amerex troops leaving their perches and descending to the canyon floor.

Calder had used every trick at his disposal, but had not yet stemmed the tide of the attack. He put out a Mayday Call alerting Command that there was no mine, nor security force, and that the company had been ambushed by Amerex Forces. Command responded, telling him to hold his position, air support was on the way. It was news worthy of celebration, but Calder knew it would still take at least 30 minutes for support to reach their position. Whether they could hold out that long was questionable. Nevertheless, they continued to fight shelling the area to the front of the cave with an assortment of sonic and conventional weapons fire. They were able to pick off a handful of the descending troops, but overall there were far too many to contend with. Not only were the numbers a problem, but ground forces were already setting up a S2-Phantom Pantheon Gun on the other side of the canyon. The gun had long been a myth in the making, but this was one was real and capable of hitting multiple targets simultaneously while disintegrating everything in its path. With no avenue of escape and certain death waiting just outside, Calder led the Unit deeper into the cave, hoping against hope for any sign of light.

As they moved through the darkness, they had no idea how far into the mountain the cave went, or if there might be another way out, but being trapped inside was its own nightmare. But no matter what lay ahead of them, going back was not an option. The hard, cold fact, as it appeared, was that there were no options whatsoever.

At about eighty meters deeper into the abyss, Calder fired another curving tubular laser beam back to the front of the Cave. Through the beam he could see that the Amerex troops had finished setting up the Phantom and were preparing to fire. With certain death only seconds away, he lit the cavern ahead and saw that it dropped off into what could best be described as a bottomless pit, one that offered little, if any, hope of survival. Taking one last look at the terrified faces of his men, he let the deathly silence speak for him. They read his expression, but too late to act in unison. The prelude to death had begun and he cave walls began to rumble. Calder said nothing, just turned and leapt into the pit. As he disappeared from sight the S2 fired, and with the shocking resonance of a sound breaking boom, vaporized everything in its path. The men had no chance at all. The cavern collapsed and the mountain came down on top of them. A powerful after shock shook the entire canyon for several minutes before the violent rumbling finally stopped.

Once the violence had ceased, the Amerex troops rushed in and sifted through the debris. It was nothing more than painting by the numbers because they already knew that no one could have survived.

With the taste of victory on their lips, they began to disassemble the S2 and celebrate. But while they were busy savoring the moment, a shallow mound of rock at the bottom of the pit where Calder had disappeared began to shift every so slightly. None of the Amerex troops saw, nor heard anything, but as the moments passed, more rocks shifted. The Amerex Soldiers were so busy bragging amongst themselves that they never heard the sonic pulse that shattered the dead air and hit the S2 head on. The massive weapon exploded on impact and blew everyone within a hundred meters of it into tiny bits of bone and flesh.

With debris still raining down on the canyon floor, Calder dug himself all the way out of the rock crust still cradling the Pulser in his arms. Dismembered body parts were everywhere, but somehow a handful of Amerex troops had managed to survive the blast, and were trying to get to their feet. Calder opened fire, spraying the area with a roundhouse of pulses that took out the remaining soldiers in one broad sweep. When no one was left standing, he moved through the field of bodies firing additional shots at those who showed any potential for life. He went about his task tirelessly and when he was finally done, the faceplate of his helmet was splotched with blood, and his eyes were wild and madly vibrant. He was panting, not from fatigue, but from the pure rush of adrenalin pumping through his veins. Not only was everyone dead, but he, the Master Warrior, had outwitted the entire Amerex task force and managed to survive. He felt such exhilaration that he began to laugh, to cackle uncontrollably. He was badly bruised and his skin had been shaved away to the blood layer, but he was alive, a walking miracle. In that moment, he felt ecstatically supernatural, as if he had transcended death and entered the realm of the Gods. And that made him laugh even harder, a mad laugh that echoed through the canyon with a ghostly resonance. But suddenly, in the middle of his insane laughter, his helmet exploded and his head came off his shoulders. As it rolled to the ground, shock filled his eyes and a horrible glare froze on his face. The Amerex solider who fired the shot fired again, and two more times after that. The Soldier had been badly wounded, and was holding his own intestines in one hand while firing with the other. He was about to fire a fifth time when his lungs collapsed and he dropped to the ground dead. A dirge-like silence abruptly rushed through the canyon and consumed everything in its path, even the memory of life itself. But the silence did not last and was soon broken by the sound of a Fighter Craft on approach. No one was left to hear the sound save for the spirits of the dead, but Namacal Air Support had finally arrived.

CHAPTER TWENTY-THREE

Dust spirals of regolith flared up in flurries as Ben geared an Amerex Monopod into Namacal territory. He was not only posing as an escaped prisoner, but also divesting himself of his attachments to Amerex. To play the part of the puppet on a string was not an idea he embraced. He knew once Namacal security picked him up on their scanners, his life would be up for grabs. Amerex had attached monitoring devices to his vehicle, but in his mind, this had reduced him to nothing more than bait. He was caught in the middle between the two opposing forces with death seeming to be the only certain outlet. Determined not to let that happen, he brought the Pod to a stop and sat listening to the space around him. The subtle sounds heard in the moon's vacuum told him what he needed to do.

A Namacal Fighter zeroed in on his position, but all they found was an unoccupied burning Pod. They circled the area for survivors, but saw no evidence of life. Meanwhile, the Amerex Monitors were trying to figure out why they had lost the Pod's signal. Ronson was informed of the situation and assumed it to be technical failure, but that view changed when he was shown the last incoming image from the Pod's monitoring system. That image was one of someone covering the lens of the monitor just before it went dead. Ben's body monitors and had also ceased to transmit data, and Ronson knew this was no malfunction.

****

Having outwitted his monitors, Ben had come out of hiding and distanced himself from the destroyed Pod. He stopped at the rim of a lunar crater that lay just beyond the Namacal Base and evaluated the situation ahead. Radar and Proton detection systems were always active, and though air attacks were frequent in the area around the base, ground assaults were almost unheard of. Ben felt confident that he could enter the complex undetected.

It took him another hour to reach the facility on foot, but once there, he was able to gain entry through a maintenance portal; and dressed in a Namacal uniform, he quickly blended in with the other soldiers.

****

By the time Ben had reached Namacal, Major Ronson was fully aware that he had broken off communication and failed to comply with the MO of the mission. Angered by this betrayal, he ordered intelligence to be leaked to Namacal that indicated Ben was alive and working as an undercover agent for Amerex. Ben didn't know the specifics of what was taking place behind his back, but he assumed nothing and trusted no one. What he did know was that he was a marked man, an anathema to either side, and that every move he made from here on out had to be carefully calculated.

He waited clandestinely in a tube near the N-Sight Sector until he spotted Salt's Attaché', Ludovic. Knowing he would be a good source of information, he followed him to his quarters. As Ludovic opened the door, Ben slipped in behind him, placed him in a strangle hold, and shoved him inside.

"What the fuck do you want?" Ludovic blurted as Ben pressed him to the wall without responding. "You're a dead man, you know that?"

"Shut up."

"You won't get away with this."

"I already have. I need information, understand? Simple, factual information."

"Then you've come to the wrong place."

"Have I?"

Ludovic lunged for a desk drawer and the concealed weapon within, but Ben busted the attempt, and shoved a Walthur Super 45 up his nose.

"Try that again, and I'll splatter your tiny brain all over these walls."

Ben removed the weapon from the drawer and emptied the chamber.

"Psy-ops brought in a prisoner recently; I think you know who she is."

"And?"

"Where is she; what's her status?"

"You're the psychic, you tell me."

"Do you reaally want to die? I'm not asking for corporate secrets, just simple information."

"You're a traitor; I don't give information to traitors."

As he spoke Ben read his thoughts and picked up prism images of Eliana and Salt strongly indicating their relationship and her role as a double agent.

"So she's not a prisoner?"

"I'm not telling you a fucking thing."

"You already have."

He pinched a pressure point nerve in Ludovic's neck and rendered him unconscious.

****

The Air Support Craft that Calder called in had landed in the canyon and the Crew was out surveying the destruction. They could only speculate as to what had transpired, but Calder's headless body was still warm indicating that he was one of the last to die. They loaded his remains into their Craft and prepared to return to base.

CHAPTER TWENTY-FOUR

Salt was summoned to the Military Morgue to confirm the identity of Calder's body. He stood over his corpse absorbing the wounds and sensing the aura of death that surrounded him. A replay of Calder's SOS played over the intercom. General Ashworth, Commander in Chief of Lunar Forces for Namacal, was also in the room.

"We lose good soldiers everyday," The General said. "It's the nature of war. But I have one big problem with the situation here, Commander. Contrary to your intelligence, there was no mine, no camp, no equipment, and no security force. Only an Amerex Squadron lying in wait. Approximate number of dead, one hundred. Considering that this was a pre-planned surprise attack, our men gave an amazing performance. Nevertheless, the so-called new Helium 3 discovery was no discovery at all, but a lie that was used to bait us. I believe we know where that lie came from."

"Obviously, we know its source, but not its origin." Salt said. "It could have been a lie before it reached the source. If you will, General, allow me to investigate this further before we make any knee-jerk decisions."

"Investigate as you will, Colonel, but I need something legitimate, and not a malleable invention created by an astute manipulator. Excuse the metaphor, but we must all be reminded that when handling serpents, no matter how beautiful they may be, they remain ever unpredictable, and that at any moment one is subject to be bitten. You have forty eight hours to get back to me."

Salt left the morgue and went hastily to Eliana's quarters. He rang the entry buzzer, but to no response. Unable to get past the security code, he called in a technician to open it electronically. Inside, he found nothing out of order, or specifically unusual. The bed had been made, clothes were neatly hung in the closet, but Eliana wasn't there. Salt stood in the doorway silently trying to pick up any mental residue that might give him insight into her state of mind, but the reading only produced a flat line return.

"Put out an immediate all points alert for Lieutenant Vasquez and have her brought to my quarters the moment she's found."

CHAPTER TWENTY-FIVE

Ben left Ludovic's quarters and entered the greater base complex. As he was making his way to the N-Sight Sector, an alert for Eliana was broadcast over the Intercom system. There was no indication as to why she was wanted, only that it was urgent and she was to report to N-Sight Headquarters immediately. As Ben was listening to the message, he spotted a Military Police Unit just ahead of him. They didn't appear to be interested in him, but he opted to avoid them nevertheless. He slipped into a coffee cube, and nonchalantly ordered a quick espresso. While sipping the coffee and watching the door, he overheard two Soldiers talking about the death of Calder. It was mostly just a meandering rap about the bravery of the unit, but there was mention of the bad intelligence that Eliana had provided which led to their deaths. This didn't come as a complete surprise to Ben, but it threw more questions into the mix, and added another twist to the drama in his own mind. Who the hell was she, and whose side was she really on? He had flip flopped back and forth so many times at this point that he no longer knew what to think.

"I knew Calder." He said, interrupting the soldier's conversation. "He was a good man. What about the woman; have they charged her?"

"Far as I know, she hasn't been charged." One of the soldiers replied. "It's good to have friends in high places."

"You mean Salt?"

"Do the numbers. She's got a death list wrapped around her longer than a snake's tail. Somehow that got conveniently overlooked."

"But not if she was a double agent."

"Yea, and the moon is made of nano quarks. But what the fuck do I know? In a world of lies, what's one more lie."

"Nothing at all, unless it's the truth."

Ben left the cube juggling the mental balls of uncertainty, lies, and reality. He no longer knew the truth, but he knew who did.

****

Keeping a low profile, Ben made his way to the N-Sight Complex. Guards were stationed at the entry to the main tube, and without proper ID it would be difficult to get past them, but he had a ploy.

He approached the Guards, identified himself by false name and rank, and then proceeded to tell them that he may have seen Eliana only moments before. The Guards put in a call to Command who in turn ask for Ben to be brought to the Operations Offices for questioning.

One of the Guards escorted Ben, but before they reached their destination, Ben knocked him cold and pulled him into a storage bin. He took his weapons and Security Badge and cuffed him with his own cuffs to a supply cabinet.

Ben didn't go to Operations, but to the N-Sight's Personnel Vector instead. Showing his security badge at the entry tube, he was able to get inside without intervention. But knowing that the Guard would soon be missed, timing was of the essence. Moving through an exchange of tubes, he scanned for mental residue, specifically anything relating to Eliana. And though his psychic senses were acute, he found nothing that would alert him to her presence or whereabouts. He continued searching the area until he spotted a Guard stationed at one of the sleep units and knew that was not normal procedure. He walked up to the Guard and displayed his badge.

"Anything?" He said probingly.

"Anything?" The Guard replied not understanding the question. Ben didn't answer, just slammed his head into the door, and kicked his feet out from under him. He threw the door open and dragged the Guard inside.

He scanned the room quickly, but it was obvious the room was unoccupied. And yet he had a strong sense that Eliana had been there and not that long ago. He walked over to the main Portal where he saw a group Security Guards in the opposite tube running toward the sector he was now in. Alerted to the obvious possibility that they were coming for him, he left the unit immediately.

Fleeing the area, he confronted a Maintenance Technician and forced him into a custodial cube. There he bound and gagged him with cleaning rags, took his maintenance suit and work cart, then immediately went back into the tubes.

Working his way toward the outer sectors, he kept his head down, but his senses alert. His mind was filtering through the mental data around him, but he was still coming up with little of value. But then he came upon something that struck him as odd, an immediate and powerful sense of Eliana's presence. There was no physical sighting of her, but the mental energy he was reading told him she had to be close. Unfortunately, so were two MP's who suddenly appeared at the end of the tube before him. Avoiding a possible confrontation, he backed the cart up and returned to the custodial cube. With only one door leading in and out of the room, his choices were less than oppurtunistic. Taking the safest measure available, he dove down a laundry shoot that emptied out into an underground wash facility. The MP's showed up only moments later and found the Maintenance Man bound on the floor, but no sign of Ben.

****

Salt was at his desk fielding reports of a possible break in security and an intruder in the N-Sight Sector. One of those reports specified an attack on a Security Guard at Eliana's quarters. A digital sketch of the perpetrator provided by the Guard appeared on Salt's holograph, and offered a clear picture that the culprit was highly likely to be Ben. But as Salt was studying the image, the door to his office swung open and Eliana stepped in. His rage upon seeing her came fast and furious.

"Where the fuck have you been? What the fuck are you trying to do to me?"

"I'm not trying to do anything to you. I was under the impression I was on my own time."

"You're time is my time. You're on twenty four/seven call; you know that."

"I went to the library to do some research. I was only linked in for an hour...when I came back out I heard my name over the P.A. and came here immediately."

He didn't respond, just kept sifting through her thoughts looking for the suspected lie. What he found in turn were mostly perplexed questions as to why he was so upset.

"You're over reacting, Terry, what's going on?" She asked maintaining a steady sense of equilibrium.

"Calder is dead. And everyone in his unit is dead. Ambushed. There was no mine, no camp, no security force, nothing but an Amerex Squadron hidden in the canyon walls. We're talking about a slaughter that was initiated and fed by bad intelligence."

Her eyes sank into his, sifting through the undercurrents of his agitated thoughts. Beyond that he offered little, only the hard glance of accusation.

"If that intelligence was bad, then I was the first one to be fooled. The first protocol was to protect Amerex and the new Helium 3 Mine. The only reason I was brought into the loop was to make sure that Namacal had no knowledge of it."

"You're a very perceptive woman, Eliana. You're telling me you didn't see the deception before hand."

"There was no deception to see. I had no plan, no MO other than to gather pertinent information. That information came to me as truth and not something I was obliged to reveal. I was captured and brought here against my will. I didn't offer up the intelligence gratuitously, you forced my hand."

"Force isn't the word I would choose. But the pieces to the scenario that you presented still don't fit. If there was no new Helium 3 discovery, then there was no reason for Amerex to bring you into the loop because there was nothing in the loop to protect. The only reason would be for that false intelligence to be leaked, which is exactly what happened."

"But they couldn't have known that I would be captured ahead of time. They couldn't have known what would happen between point A and point B."

"Unless those points were predesignated."

"You're assuming a lot."

"Just looking at the facts. Color it as you will, the facts remain. They gave you the intelligence and the intelligence leaked. Whether you knew or didn't know, remains a matter of question, but either way it puts us both in a very bad and precarious light. Bottom line is, if you weren't sure of the intelligence you should have never offered it up. Command is asking for your head, and I have serious doubts if there's anything I can do that will change that."

She went to him and put her arms around him in gentle supplication. He remained aloof to her, but it was an aloofness that strongly conflicted with other emotions.

"I didn't lie to you, and I didn't set those men up. If I had known it was a set up would I have asked you to send me? It was my mission, not Calder's."

"Yes, but a mission in which you could have conveniently disappeared."

"That's a big leap of "if, and, and maybe". You still don't believe anything I say do you? You told me you wanted a new beginning, a fresh start, but we're going right back to the same old place. You were always suspicious of me, and still are. But it's not just about me, is it? No one can tell you the truth and no one can get close to you, because no matter what anyone says, you won't let them in. For you, everything is a lie. No wonder I withdrew from you before, I don't know what I was thinking when I agreed to try this again."

"I know what you were thinking; you were thinking about how to save your pretty little ass. But things don't always go as planned, do they. It's the un-plan we have to plan for. But this is not just about you; it's about what Command is going to think and want from you. You don't have to convince me of anything, but you do have to convince them. And after all that has gone down, no matter what you say, or how convincing you are, I'm not sure they'll buy it."

"I'm not selling anything, the only thing I have to offer them is the truth."

"That may not be enough."

****

Dozens of Security and Military Police filled the base tubes searching for any sign of the man they believed to be Ben. Both Ludovic and the Maintenance Man had been found and confirmed Ben's identity. An APB was put out and blasted to every sector of the Namacal Base. But even as the search intensified, Ben remained an invisible man.

The laundry facility was quiet, undisturbed, and had not been searched. Ben, knowing he had to make a move, slipped out of the industrial hamper where he had hidden himself and exited the room through a secondary maintenance door. Entering the open corridor, he spotted a food cart left from one of the mess halls. Seeing it as a potential tool, he confiscated the cart and used it to make his way to an adjacent tube.

More people were in the area, but using the cart as a diversion, he had his eyes and ears tuned to everything around him. He knew he was being sought, and that it was imperative to get out of the sector as soon as possible. Spotting a Military Police unit ahead, he shoved the cart into a narrow alcove and knelt down as if he were adjusting one of its wheels. A glance back revealed the MP's still coming toward him - six of them, all well armed. They were only a few feet away when something suddenly stopped them. At a glance it appeared to be a glob of larvae oozing out from beneath a doorway. Its shape kept fluctuating from the abstract to the form of what, at a glance, appeared to be a writhing woman. A piercing sound erupted from the walls and spears of razor light crisscrossed the tube in front of her. Some of the MP's froze in place; others held their ears trying shut out the sound. The lights kept flashing on and off and the larvae were now oozing from the woman's pores. One MP, suspicious of a telemetric projection, began firing into the dark of the open hall. Other personnel in the vicinity heard the gunshots and stopped to see what the shooting was all about. But what the observers saw was nothing- no larvae, no woman, no flashing lights. Neither did they see Ben in the alcove with a telemetric pulser emitting these hallucinations. The MP's were under siege, but didn't know from where or how. They began to collapse, their bodies knotting with grotesque muscle spasms. As they were contorting into twisted epileptic shapes, Ben hurried past them and disappeared into the dark of the tube.

****

Eliana paced back and forth across the holding tank where she was being held. She'd been lucky to date, and fortunate to be able to call her own shots, but like a cat with nine lives, she sensed her luck might be running out. Namacal command would not go as easy on her, certainly not as easy as Salt. They had a bottom line that they strictly adhered to. Even if she could talk them into believing her story, she had burned too many bridges and left too long a blood trail behind her to garner their sympathy. The chances for receiving a pass were meager at best. Ultimately, she knew that her tenure on lunar terrain had expired, and that if she didn't find a way out, she was a dead woman. Getting off the moon would not be easy; even with trustworthy friends it would be difficult, but she had no trustworthy friends. Still, there was Ben, and at least a remote possibility that their relationship had a viable life that could possibly be resurrected. But she had no idea where he was, how to find him, or what would happen if she did find him. Nevertheless, she had a solid sense that he was still alive, and within that perception there was an element of hope.

****

Looking for a way out of the sector, Ben avoided the flow of traffic and the eyes of the Searchers. He was trying to reach the motor pool where he might be able to confiscate a vehicle, but even at best it was a hit and miss venture. Spotting two Security Police coming in from another tube, he darted into small PX store and concealed himself at the back of the room. As he waited for the Guards to pass, images of Eliana returned to him. As always with her, it was a Devil or

Angel dilemma that he was yet to reconcile. But just as he was entertaining these thoughts, the two Security Police entered the store.

****

The Guards outside the holding tank where Eliana was being held were able to monitor her via an in room camera system. The space was small with only one door and no windows making observation easy. But during a routine check, the Guards were suddenly unable to find her. They rotated the camera from side to side, but came up with nothing. Responding to this development, they entered the room for a first hand look. At a glance, it appeared that she had vanished into thin air, but after a brief search, they discovered the body of a nude woman beneath the bed. There was also an odd hum in the room that they were unable to identify. Suddenly the cell twisted to one side and blurred into a strange pattern of heat waves. As the waves washed over them they began to mutter incoherently. They looked back at the woman only to find that she was up and walking toward them. Her face was distorted and misshapen, making her impossible to indentify. One of the Guards tried to call out on his radio, but the woman kicked the unit out of his hand. Another spiraling kick leveled the second Guard and before either of them could defend themselves both were unconscious. As darkness engulfed their thoughts, the hallucination evaporated like dew in sunlight. Eliana dropped down from the corrugated ceiling where she'd been hiding, procured their weapons and quickly fled the room.

****

The Security Police searched the store, but Ben had already slipped out a side door. The Clerk had noted his exit and alerted the Guards. They pursued him into an open tube, but while attempting to apprehend him, they were hit by two rapid-fire sonar pulses that knocked them both unconscious. Ben left them face down in the tube and took an exit ramp to an LRV Maintenance Garage. He used his Security Badge to gain entrance to the Motor Pool, and once inside saw a number of vehicles being repaired and prepped for the war zone. A Mono Pod, similar to the one he had used earlier looked to be a good choice. A technician was tweaking the Pod's computer system, but its engines were running smoothly.

No one seemed to pay Ben any mind as he went to the locker area where pressure suits were stored. He suited up, grabbed a helmet, and returned to the Pod where he briskly overtook the Technician. He retrieved the computer codes from him, but as he was climbing into the cockpit, the two Security Cops entered the garage. They spotted the Technician on the ground, and identified Ben in the same breath. They ordered him to surrender, but he ignored their call and engaged the Pod's engines. With the thrusters thundering, he fired the hand accelerator and drove the Pod straight at them. They had ample time to shoot, but didn't for fear of inadvertently hitting someone or igniting a fuel explosion. Instead, they dove to one side and Ben sped past them and entered the pressurized exit tube. Gearing the Pod to high velocity, he blasted through the safety door and out into the outer atmosphere.

Soldiers on the ground scattered as Ben zoomed past them. The way to freedom was wide open, but he didn't take it. Instead, he amped his speed with fevered insistency, and coursed the Pod toward the N-Sight Sector at the far end of the landing field. Speeding through a maze of winding tubes and bubble cubicles, passing under bridges and around massive lots of equipment, the route was circuitous, but exactly the way he wanted to go. With sirens going off and Military Police in pursuit, he had only a small window of opportunity in which to execute his plan.

Salt was in his office meeting with two Psy-Op officers when the first alarms went off. Hearing the disruption, he fired a glance out the window and spotted the Pod racing across the open field toward his bubble. An image of Ben burned through his mind and told him exactly what was about to happen.

"Run." He bellowed at the two officers, the sound of alarm in his voice strong enough to put everyone in motion.

Salt looked back again just in time to see the Pod speeding up an LRV loading ramp outside his Portal. Reaching maximum RPM's, Ben hit overdrive and catapulted the Pod off the ramp into the zero G sky. The thrust carried the Pod forward like a slow moving missile and straight through the portal into Salt's office. The window exploded on impact, and the internal Oxygen was sucked out in one gigantic swoosh. Salt sealed the inner door in time to keep from being pulled out with the air. The Pod crashed to a stop in the middle of the room, debris spinning around it like the winds of a tornado. Aware that Salt had escaped, Ben shifted focus to the sealed door that led to the outer office. He pumped the accelerator, blasted forward, and crashed the Pod into the door. The impact was hard, but not hard enough to break the seal. What it did do was crack the adjoining wall, which in turn prompted an air leak. Ben backed the Pod up and rammed it into the wall again. This time, the wall split wide open and the blast sucked the air from the outer room instantaneously. Corporal Ludovic, working at his desk, was pulled out with it. His body flew past Ben and into the open lunar vacuum.

As the Pod stalled again, Ben saw that Salt had already escaped into the exit tube. He tried to engage the engine, but the gear system failed to move. He quickly grabbed his weapons, exited the Pod, and tried to unseal the door to the outer area. But as designed, the locking systems on all doors in controlled air space automatically shut down in emergency situations. Pressurized air was the life force of all lunar facilities and vitally well protected. Ben knew this, but having come this far, he wasn't about to be deterred by a sealed door. He fired several close range pulses into the door, the third shot finally breaking the seal.

With emergency alarms going off all around the compromised area, Salt and other N-Sight Personnel evacuated the sector, sealing the tube doors behind as they went. This was standard protocol when under attack or in other emergency situations. But Ben, still in his pressure suit, kept moving forward in determined pursuit. He was less than a tube length away when he spotted a flank of troops on an overhead monitor moving on his position. Another overhead monitor revealed Salt fleeing into an emergency evac tube that led to a Security Bunker. Ben knew that area and that it would be difficult to access if Salt was able to make it there.

****

Eliana was in the tubes when the alarms went off, and she too was watching the monitors and gathering information on the attack in the Psy-Ops wing. As she learned that the assault had been carried out by a single individual, she immediately knew it was Ben.

Hundreds of Namacal personnel were evacuating the Psy-Ops Sector, but Ben moved through the tubes virtually unimpeded. He was hoping to reach the Bunkers ahead of Salt, but kept running into resistance in the form of heavily armed Security Units. They had already closed off most of the connecting tubes and were in the process of pinning him in when he found a maintenance sector door that led to an auxiliary tube. The move helped him evade the MP's, but it took him further away from Salt. He had no idea where Eliana was, but suddenly and quite surprisingly, he had a strong sense of her psychic presence. It was a fleeting sensation, but he recognized the force of her energy as it passed through him. He wanted to search the area more thoroughly, but found himself confronted by a dozen armed Spec 4's. They immediately opened fire and left him no choice but to retreat.

He backtracked through the tubes, finally returning to the outer office where he had left the crippled Pod. With the MP's moving in behind him, and other avenues of escape rapidly closing, he withdrew into the inner office as a last resort. While he was busy trying to fend off the approaching MP's, a second squad came through the ruptured Portal to his rear. He engaged his telemetric, but the signal jammed. Caught in crossfire between the two factions his only remaining option was to flee into an adjacent file room. Once inside, he kicked a hole in the damaged wall that allowed him to see the Soldiers in the outer room. He only had a split second to act, but he took that second and sent a pulse blazing into the Pod's Fuel tank. The fuselage exploded and took out every Soldier within its peremiter and half the building in tandem. The impact was so powerful that it blew Ben backward all the way through the wall into the adjacent tube. He was stunned by the explosion, but managed to get back to his feet and limp away.

As the search for Ben went on, Eliana arrived outside the ruptured portal where she was able to see the full extent of destruction that he had caused. The flames had died out via lack of oxygen, but body parts and miscellaneous structural debris were still floating in the air. A decapitated head wafted down, brushed against her shoulder, and startled her. She had no idea if Salt or Ben had survived, but neither did she feel any sense of their deaths. She was surrounded by chaos, but it had at least given her the opportunity to move about freely without being noticed. Ben didn't know it, she thought smiling to herself, but his actions had inadvertently given her the means to escape.

****

Eliana took a tram to the Namacal PX sector, a small Rec facility at the far end of the base. It was a less flamboyant micro-version of Junoko, consisting of several service men's bars, cafes, and party rooms. Eliana had a friend, Lourdess, who was a cook in one of the café's, and who was one of the few people she still felt she could trust. Lourdess was on the Namacal payroll, but was not political and had only come to the moon for the paycheck and to indulge her passion for cooking in new and innovative ways. The lack of fresh fruits and vegetables hampered her ability to create truly great cuisine, but she was nevertheless inventive and adventurous enough to come up with tasty dishes. Eliana was drawn to her because she was smart, open-minded, and creative, but when she showed up at her kitchen door, Lourdess was nothing less than dumbfounded. She had heard many rumors about Eliana in recent days, and though she considered her a good friend, she wasn't sure what to believe as to her shifting part in the lunar war. Although the truth was illusive, she knew one thing was certain, and that was the simple fact that if she were caught harboring a traitor, then she would put herself at risk of severe punishment. Even so, Lourdess was not one to turn her back on a friend and she agreed to give Eliana the laser key that would allow her entry to her quarters.

Later that night when Lourdess came back from her shift, she and Eliana had a long talk about the circumstances that had led to Eliana's return. Lourdess knew of her affair with Salt and why she had defected to Amerex, but she was having a hard time understanding why she was back. Eliana sensed her tentativeness and tried to ease her concerns by assuring her that she had worked for Namacal all along, and that the blow up with Salt was just a performance to add a reality base to her defection. She explained that she couldn't tell Lourdess or anyone else at the time because of the covert nature of her mission. Lourdess accepted this version of the story, but it didn't make the situation any less problematic. Eliana was extremely clever, and had amazing powers of perception, but when all was said and done, the truth remained apocryphal. If she was truly an undercover operative, why were they searching for her and calling her a traitor? She embraced her friend, loved her charm, beauty, and generosity of spirit, but there was always an indeterminate element in Eliana that she could never quite put her finger on. In other words, she was just too good at what she did to give her complete trust. Lourdess never expressed this outwardly, but she always felt it.

They talked late into the night until both were exhausted and desperate for sleep. But even though Eliana was dead tired, she was unable to rest. She sensed Lourdess had doubts about her, but she had doubts about Lourdess too.

****

As night wrapped its cloak around the lunar Base, Ben escaped the main sector and fled into the darkness. He was traveling on foot toward a pre-plotted destination, a small monitoring station on the outskirts of Namacal territory.

The Station was a "first alert" facility equipped with a radar and proton sensory system for detecting incoming spacecraft and war jets. It was approximately two kilometers from the base and occupied by alternating Technicians, who were on duty twenty- four hours a day.

Arriving at the station, he monitored the cubicle for a good half hour before making his approach. Attacks on the Namacal base were infrequent, but the alert systems were monitored constantly. While one of the Technicians tended to the more mundane affairs of the station, the other kept vigil on the radar and various other scanning devices. Alarms were attached to every piece of equipment, so anything entering the upper atmosphere from any direction would be easily detected. The readiness factor was impressive, although most of the time the Technicians went about their duties mechanically and in a state of quiet disinterest. But this particular evening was different. The Chief Technician began to hear a slight, but very discernable hum. It seemed to be coming from one of the scanners, but he saw no indication of unusual activity on any of the control boards. Still, the hum kept getting louder, loud enough to alert the Second Technician, who was working on the opposite side of the cube, to the problem.

"What the hell is that? " He asked, walking over to the tech panel to see what was going on.

"Nothing is registering on any of the LED's." His partner replied, but no more had the words left his lips than a face suddenly appeared on one of the sensory devices. Given that the device did not offer pictorial depictions, something was obviously wrong.

The two men watched with fascination as the face began to morph into other faces, those of unknown men and women. Suddenly one of the faces popped off the screen and appeared in front of them in the full physical form of a woman. The men recoiled and grabbed their weapons. The woman said something, but her words came out garbled. She started toward them, but with each step she grew paler and more ethereal. Whatever she was, she was not human. They fired two shots through her chest, but drew no blood. The hum had reached a degree of decibels so extreme that it was bulging veins in their foreheads. They covered their ears attempting to block out the sound, but nothing would make it go away. They were caught in an auditory hallucination and unable to escape from it. Suddenly, the door from the pressurized entry tube burst open and Ben lunged into the room. He fired two stun pulses into the men, quickly incapacitating them. He withdrew the telemetric signal, dissolving the hallucination, and using a length of electrical cord, bound their hands and feet.

****

Eliana had finally drifted off to sleep, but her dreams were filled with images of unknown assailants pursuing her. The dreams were generic and abstruse, but so unsettling that she fought against them with her psychic will until she was able to break their binds and wake herself up. The moment she reached consciousness, she heard voices, just whispers at first, but whispers that were drawing closer. As she became more alert, she realized that Lourdess was no longer in bed, nor was she anywhere in the room. And then she heard footsteps in the hall, and counting the pattern of the steps, knew she'd been betrayed.

The door swung open and a half dozen MP's swarmed the room. The flash of guns and lasers crisscrossed the bed, but Eliana was no longer there. The bathroom portal was open and Eliana was spotted running toward an exit tube. The MP's fired on her, but she turned the corner in time to elude their assault.

As they pursued her into the adjoining tube, the MP's were calling ahead for all adjacent tubes to be sealed off. With exits closing left and right, Eliana veered into the last alternate tube, but suddenly found herself face to face with two Security Police. They drew down on her, but she kicked the guns out of their hands and leveled them both with short order power punches. Escaping from additional pursuit, she blew the seal on an emergency door and fled into a Prime 1 evac tube. She looped back into a storage area where supplies were brought in, and overwhelming a dockworker, stole his light keys. Using the keys, she was able to access a secondary tube where she suited up and quickly exited the cubicle. Once outside, she appropriated a LRV Supply Vehicle and headed out into the lunar maria.

CHAPTER TWENTY-SIX

After the attack, Salt was taken to an undesignated security bunker. Unable to rest, he stayed busy evaluating data regarding the activities and whereabouts of both Ben and Eliana. According to available intelligence, Ben was unaccounted for, but search parties had been sent into the surrounding lunar outback following possible leads as to his suspected whereabouts. The data on Eliana was more concrete as reports were coming in stating that she had hijacked an LRV for a destination not yet known. Salt was furious beyond measure at the advent of this news. It was bad enough that Ben had attacked his private offices and then escaped an entire brigade of armed forces, but that Eliana had betrayed him yet again was a turn of events he found unbearable. The long-term feelings he had held for her were poisoned and beyond repair. And yet, he still maintained a slim thread of hope that the reports were wrong, and that there was an acceptable explanation for her actions. As for Ben, there was no longer any question of reprieve. Ben had betrayed him in the most abominable manner thinkable, and he would use the full extent of his power to see that he was not only reprimanded and punished, but terminated with extreme prejudice.

****

Eliana headed back into Amerex territory, believing her chances were better there than with Namacal. Even if she could win Salt over once again, Namacal Command was not likely to accept anything she had to say. Ultimately, her only legitimate hope of survival was to get off the moon, but that possibility was essentially unfeasible. Nevertheless, Salt had taught her well, and she was, as always, thinking ahead and plotting multiple strategies. She altered the direction she was taking and veered away from Amerex. She traveled a short distance, and then altered direction again. She kept repeating this action in an effort to confuse any would-be pursuers. It was a good plan, but it didn't take into account tracking by air. With the Pod creating dust trails that billowed up behind her, it wasn't long before she heard the sound of an approaching Fighter Craft. The vast lunar plain offered little cover, which made her an easy target from above. She readied her weapons, but the Fighter zeroed in on her with such swiftness that any attempt to fire on it would have been suicide. But as the Fighter passed over, it didn't fire, but instead dropped an optic laser net over her. The electronic beams laced round the Pod's wheels, entangled the axel, and brought it to a bouncing halt. The net was tightly knitted and prohibited any possibility of escape. With further options reduced to zero viability, the only choice she had left was to drop her weapon and raise her hands in surrender.

****

The two Monitoring Station Technicians had regained consciousness, only to find themselves bound and gagged. They watched helplessly as Ben went through their gear, gathering up weapons, a GPS system, and nibbling their left over food.

"This food is shit." He told them as he spat out a mouthful of freeze-dried hash. "You should complain." Checking their monitors one last time, he made sure everything was clear and ready for his departure. But before he could exit the cubicle, he heard a radio dispatch coming in from Command. It was a normal call with no urgency or reference to him, but he knew that if the message were ignored, Command would interpret that as a problem. Rather than risk using the Technicians, he opted to answer the call himself.

"Glasdown here, come back."

"Glasdown, an All Points Alert has been sent out from N-Sight to all Monitoring stations to be on the watch for any personnel or parties not associated with you or your directives. A rogue Amerex operative is thought to be in the area and could approach. Follow all normal cautionary procedures, but be prepared to use extreme force if necessary. The suspected agent has been designated as armed and dangerous and should not be engaged with anything other than extreme caution. Repeat; engage only with extreme caution. Do you copy?"

"We copy, Command." Ben replied in an altered tone of voice. There was a long pause before dispatch responded.

"Please provide your security code, Glasdown."

Ben didn't know the security code, but quickly responded back.

"One Second Command, we're experiencing a technical glitch."

He rushed to one of the Technicians and ripped the gag from his mouth.

"Code." He spat the word out forcefully. "This is not about you and not worth dying for." But despite the potential threat, the Technician was defiant. Ben didn't bother to argue, just raised his fist and smacked him in the head. The force of the blow left him stunned, and Ben ripped the gag from the mouth of the second technician with the same aggression. "Your choice." As he waited for a reply, Command came back on the radio.

"Glasdown, we need to know your status now."

Ben knew that Dispatch would start asking more probing questions any second, and unwilling to wait for the Technician, he grabbed a chair and slammed it into the control console. The radio message began again, but Ben kept attacking the console and battering it with the chair until it was finally silenced. At that point, he went back to the Technician and pressed a gun to his head. He knew that the men would not be able to call for help, but he also knew Command, failing to get a response, would send someone to investigate.

"You're lucky I'm a compassionate soul. Someone will come to free you soon, so stay warm." On those words he retreated out the rear door and boarded their ARV. A moment later, he was soaring off toward the distant mountains.

****

Two Guards escorted a laser cuffed Eliana into Salt's Security Bunker. Dismissing the Guards, he went to her, and without saying a word, slapped her across the face.

"You stupid fucking bitch."

The slap surprised her, but she was defiant in the same breath. He was trying to read her inner dialogue, but she was putting up such defensive measures that all her thoughts came out scrambled.

"Why did you run?"

"Why wouldn't I run? I was tried and convicted without a day in court. You were suppose to help me, but ----"

"I've always helped you, always been there for you, so don't try to make me the scapegoat. You've got a real gift for making matters worse."

"I do what I have to do. If I didn't, I'd already be dead."

"FUCK!!!!" He screamed at her. "I could have gotten you out of this before, but you blew it. So if you have any bigger magic in your bag of tricks you better pull it out now."

"I don't have a bag of tricks; I've told the truth, that's all I have to give."

He was locked on her face and reading her every thought, all expressed with unshielded sincerity. But she had enraged him to such degree that he was forced to turn away from her before losing his cool again. As he stood facing the outer portal, she stepped in next to him, looked straight into his eyes, and kissed him.

"I'm sorry, Terry. I understand your feelings, your doubts...all justifiable. But if there's any possibility of understanding between us, then understand this. What I feel for you is real. I'm not asking for a miracle, I just want you know how I feel, and for you to see me for what I am."

She spoke so gently and earnestly that he was moved in spite of his reticence. He searched her eyes, looking both into her mind and heart. There was nothing there in conflict with what she was saying, but he was not oblivious to the fact that she was still the best of the best, a mind game player of the highest order. So even though he wanted to believe her, he could no longer afford to give himself over to her emotionally. But then, as impromptu as the flutter of a butterfly, she kissed him again - harder, deeper, wrenching his soul and warming his flesh with a simple touch. Finally, she broke the kiss, leaving him weakened, but not weak enough to keep him from bucking against her charms.

"I'll do what I can, but I can't guarantee anything. In the meantime, you'll have to be put in maximum security until I can work this out. But be well advised, Eliana, one wrong move, one more mind game, one more escape attempt, anything to raise the suspicion of this corporation, and you're a dead woman. Understand?"

"I'll do whatever you need me to do."

"Start by keeping your mouth shut. Don't talk to anyone without talking to me first."

****

While Eliana was taken away to a padded, security cell, Ben was in route to Junoko. The shadowed form of earth loomed before him like a giant scrying mirror that reflected the inner turmoil of his own thoughts. He was nearing the main Space Port, and knew that the flight controllers would soon ask for his approach data. He was able provide that, but given that he was in a stolen ARV, the risk of being shot down was extremely high. Not wanting to take the chance, he veered off to find a landing spot somewhere short of the airfield. As he was searching for a safe piece of turf, he suddenly picked up a Namacal Fighter Craft on his radar. He shoved the flight stick forward and shifted the ARV into an abrupt nosedive. With the Craft descending toward the lunar surface, he pushed the ejection seat release and popped open the cockpit. The Fighter fired simultaneously and easily blew the Craft out of the sky. A huge explosion spread flames and fiery debris into the surrounding vacuum. Smoke clouds were thick and obscured Ben as he drifted down onto the glomy hillside. The veil of smoke had prevented the Fighter Pilot from seeing him, but he still flew over the area several times for routine coverage. There was no evidence of a body, but the Pilot suddenly spotted part of the ejection seat sunk in the regolith. Although the seat was empty, the likelihood of a survivor was strong. Engaging his landing gear, he set the Craft down on the lunar surface. But as he was exiting the Craft for a closer look, the ejection seat toppled to one side, and like a diver emerging from a sea of sand, Ben's helmet popped up. His pulse rifle came with it and a series of rapid shots followed. The Pilot heard the pulses a split second before his body came apart. The Fighter exploded simultaneously, pieces of flying debris shooting high into the lunar sky. Cubes of flesh rained down like red hail creating an eerie pattern of death on the dark surface. Ben got to his feet, dusted the glom from his pressure suit, and surveyed the scene. A few feet in front of him, two fingers and part of a foot drifted slowly to the ground. Blood drops and burnt ash coated his faceplate and partially obscured his vision. Wiping the plate clear with the back of his glove, he scanned the area for any other possible trackers, but saw no one. He no longer had transport, but a simple calculation told him that Junoko was less than five kilometers away.

****

Eliana paced restlessly back and forth across her solitary cell. There were no creature comforts of any kind, only a bed and a toilet. There was no question that her situation had become desperate, and desperate measures would have to be taken if she were to survive. Even with Salt's power and influence, the possibility of execution loomed large. Corporate Armies had zero tolerance for traitors and death sentences were a common deterrent. Given that she was a high profile prisoner, she feared that no matter what testimony she offered, or how convincing the case she presented, they would use her as an example, someone they could hold accountable for the slaughter at the mining field. Salt might try to defend her, but he wouldn't take the fall for her. Essentially, her choices had been narrowed down to one - escape. But being in a maximum-security cell presented a formidable set of problems. And so she began studying the sink and toilet in an abstract, yet creative way. The piping could feasibly be used as a weapon she thought, but how to detach it without tools. Another possibility was the padding on the walls and what might lie behind that padding? She circled the cell, pulling at the heavy fabric until she found one section that was slightly looser than the rest. Tugging at it did little if anything, but she could feel the slightest give in the folds and knew that if she persisted she might be able to eventually peal a portion of it back. But even if she succeeded, she would still be looking at a blank wall – or perhaps not. Extrapolating the thought, she remembered that every cubicle she'd been in had at least one portal window facing the outside, so why not this one? With that in mind, she circled the room again, beating on the walls in a grid like pattern noting the differences in sound. All she heard was the dull thud of her fist against the thick cushioned fabric, but one spot gave a little more and had a slightly spongier feel to it than the rest. It was the only place in the room where she could detect any difference whatsoever. But even if there was portal behind it, she still faced the problem of breathable air. Without a pressure suit, she could only survive for a matter of minutes in the airless space. But then again, a matter of minutes might be all she needed.

****

Salt continued to execute command from the sequestered security bunker. He was on the horn speaking with one of the Generals, when the alert came in that a fighter craft had been shot down just north of the Junoko Colony. The last communication received from the Pilot was that the stolen ARV had been destroyed, although sans confirmation of a body. Salt translated that to mean that Ben was still alive and once again the culprit of an act against the corporation. From their very first meeting, he felt Ben to be special, but now he had come to believe that even with that high regard he had under estimated him. Ben had not only defied capture and death, but was taking the offensive and proving to be a very dangerous man. Salt had always been the hunter, but now he had become the hunted. And the more he thought about this reversal of fortune, the more it enraged him. He snatched a bookend off the desk and hurled it into the wall so forcefully that it left an imprint in the metal alloy.

"Goddamn it!" He bellowed as he rang for an assistant.

"Get me a carrier craft and a platoon of rangers ready with full armaments. Prep my gear and weapons and have everything set to go within the hour."

****

Ben entered the Junoko facility through a maintenance area door posing as one of the many technicians who work in the hangars. He slipped into the locker area and quickly changed out of his military uniform into a jump suit.

Leaving the area disguised as a Junoko worker, he easily blended in with the crowd, watching, listening, and reading tells. He was primarily interested in information about the Namacal Attack and the downed fighter, but was only able to pick up a few meager threads of inconsequential gossip.

Like a thief returning to the scene of a crime, he took a unit at the Rikko, figuring that no one would expect him to go back to such an obvious place. As he entered the room, a flood of memories washed over him, mostly reflections of the lovemaking that he and Eliana had shared. He could still feel her presence almost as if she were there in the room with him. Maybe it was his own emotional network emitting vibrations into the atmosphere, emotions that he was picking up on the rebound. These vibrations were like a visual echo circling from his heart back into his head. But darkness was also in the room; a darkness that felt like the cold whisper of death. The faces of Decker and Blalock floated up from the floor and hovered in front of him like grotesque piñatas. He closed his eyes in an effort to shut them out, but when he opened them again, they were still there. Their deaths had been an ongoing source of pain and they continued to haunt him. He walked over to the portal that looked out onto the spaceport where he could see a Namacal Carrier Craft on approach. This was not an uncommon sight as Carrier's were always shuttling personnel back and forth, but in this instance, the sight of it gave him a very distinct chill. He interpreted the chill to mean that N-Sight was now tracking him specifically. With that thought, a thick amorphous fog seemed to settle around him. Out of that fog he saw Salt walking toward him, eyes ablaze. He was firing an automatic weapon with relentless aggression. With the sound of the shrapnel exploding in his ears, a knock came at the door and broke the image apart. Ben drew his weapon and pressed himself to the wall.

"Yea?"

"Maid service."

"I don't need maid service, I just arrived."

"Sorry sir, I must have the wrong unit."

He listened to her walk away, counting her steps until he was sure that she had reached the end of the tube. He opened the door, looked out, and saw that she was exactly where he thought she'd be. With her back to him, he was unable to see her face, but there was something about the way she moved that felt familiar. As she turned the corner, he stepped back into the room and locked the door.

The Maid went to the front desk where she spoke to the Clerk in an inaudible whisper. As they talked, soft light fell gently across her face, but it was not the face of a maid. Her movements were also not those of a maid, but those of a performer, more specifically, those of the singer, Donna Carrado.

****

Eliana had managed to pull a small section of padding far enough from the wall to see that there was a portal behind it. It had been plated over, but the metal plates were loosely applied and not difficult to pry off. The portal itself was made of strong safety glass and would be difficult to break with just her hands, but she was not without ideas. She went back to the pipes and noted that one protruded out just far enough from the wall to get her boot on it. With that as an incentive, she jumped on the pipe with all her weight, but there was little give. It seemed an impossible endeavor, but unwilling to accept defeat; she stayed with it. With the pipe she'd at least be able to break the safety glass, but what then? The air in the cell would quickly dissipate, and unless she could make it to an entry tube she would be dead within minutes? It was pure madness she thought, but it got down to the simple question of madness or death. And in this case, madness seemed the preferable of the two.

The process of trying to break the pipe was painful and exhausting, but little by little it began to give way. It took her an hour of sweated effort, but finally it snapped. A small amount of excess water spilled out, but not enough to create a problem. With her makeshift tool now in hand, she tried prying the metal seals off the portal frame, but that proved fruitless. The only other option was to use the pipe like a battering ram to crack the glass. But even if that worked the portal was so small, she questioned whether she would even be able to squeeze through it. Getting stuck was not an option, and once the glass was broken, all the air in the cell would evaporate and she would be forced to hold her breath. She gauged that she would need three to four minutes, five at the most to get through the portal and across the outer sector to the closest entry approximately five hundred yards away. Her calculations told her it would take every second of that allotted time and maybe more.

She began pounding on the glass, lightly at first as not to alert the Guards, but quickly realized that lightly wasn't going to work. The glass had a strength factor equivalent to that of steel. And even when cracked, it remained bonded. There was no assurance of success, but there was no success without trying. And so she continued crashing the pipe into the portal until little by little, small hairline cracks appeared. Inspired by her progress, she kept at it, thrusting the pipe even harder until the cracks began to spread and open wider. The sucking sound of air going out was immediately evident. Time became crucial at that point and she worked frantically to break through the remaining section of glass. The moment that happened, every molecule of air in the room gushed out with a cyclonic swoosh. Taking one last breath, she forced her body through the narrow opening and out into the lunar vacuum.

The portal window was two stories up, but she floated to ground safely and was bounding toward the entry tube the second she touched down. Holding her breath, the distance seemed longer than estimated, and by the time she reached the door and decoded it, she had already begun to asphyxiate. She had been without air for over four minutes, and though decoding the door was simple, it was also maddening. She hit wrong key after wrong key, and it took her a full thirty seconds more before the door finally opened. She lunged inside the sealed tube and collapsed on the floor. By the time air refilled the tube, she was over the six-minute mark, and her lungs were ready to explode. Dizzy and gasping, she could actually hear the flow of air rushing into her body. She lay there for several minutes taking long deep breaths until her consciousness finally returned to normal. Even then, she didn't feel like moving, but knew that having violated the door's entry code someone would soon come to check the breech. Tired and depleted of energy, she managed to get to her feet and flee into the tube.

****

Salt and a team of Rangers had landed in Junoko and were making their way toward the Pleasure Sector. After a short briefing on the specs of their mission, each Ranger was dispatched individually. Salt took one man with him and went directly to the Majog Club. It wasn't a place he was known to frequent, but the Bartender appeared to recognize him and gave him a nod. Salt nodded back but said nothing.

****

The Maid returned to Ben's room, knocked several times, but received no answer. Using her passkey, she opened the door and stepped inside.

"Maid service." She called out to make sure no one was there. She then went to the beverage-bar and removed several water bottles. Opening each one, she used an electronic eyedropper to season them with an unknown substance. But as she was dosing the last bottle, Ben stepped in behind her and punched her in the face. It was solid blow that dropped her on impact. The next thing she knew, he was on top of her, hands round her throat, pressing her windpipe.

She was at the point of blacking out before he finally eased off.

"Who the fuck are you?" He growled.

"Just the maid."

"Like hell."

He wrenched the eyedropper from her hand and sniffed it. It had an obvious chemical smell, one he couldn't identify. He put the dropper to her lips and threatened to squeeze a pinch into her mouth.

"No, no." She cried out.

"No?"

"It's acid."

He hurled the dropper across the room, and slammed her head to the floor.

"Why?"

She didn't respond, so he slammed her head down again, so hard this time it sent shockwaves through her body. The room went black for a moment, but slowly his face came back into focus. He was watching the fear come off of her in bubble prisms, her lips trembling and her mind resonating the word Amerex.

"Amerex." He said, echoing her thought.

"I...I..."

"Quit lying."

She was trying to block the reading, but he was psychically stronger and got through to her in spite of her efforts.

"You murdered Eliana."

"What?"

"She's dead because of you."

"When?"

"Today."

"I haven't seen her today, haven't seen her in days."

"But it was you who put her in jeopardy. She was killed while trying to escape from lock up."

"You know that for sure?"

"I know enough."

"Then you should know I didn't kill her."

"You may not have pulled the trigger, but you killed her just the same."

Her accusation meant nothing to him, but that Eliana might have been killed did. Contrary to what she was telling him, he still had no sense of her death. And on the psychic plain, he knew he would have felt something. But ironically, he was now feeling a strong sense of Salt's presence. He could feel his psychic energy and that wasn't a matter of question. He picked the woman up off the floor and shoved her against the wall.

"Tell me one good reason I should let you live."

"This is war; it's not personal."

"It's personal. Who gave you the order?"

She refused to speak.

"I need a name."

"They don't give me names, just orders."

He placed his fingers on one of her eyes and pressed hard enough to pop the pupil.

"Maybe this will help you to see things differently."

"Ronson." She cried out and with knee jerk quickness.

"Ronson never communicates directly, he always uses a liaison. You have another contact?"

She hesitated, but as he moved his hand back to her eye, she broke.

"Front desk."

He fired a stun pulse into her chest and rendered her unconscious. He exited the room, but hearing voices in the hall, retreated out a rear door. Looping around the Cubicle, he returned to the front desk to question the clerk, but discovered that someone had gotten to him first. His body was crumpled on the floor, a hole in his head the size of a baseball. A reading of the residual psychic residue revealed Salt's presence once again. With more unanswered questions forming, he went back to the sleep unit where he left Donna Carrado. She was still on the bed when he got there, but in his brief absence someone had also put a bullet through her head. It was a surprising find, but there was no doubt in his mind who had pulled the trigger.

****

A small LRV with Eliana at the controls crossed the lunar Maria at a thunderous rate of speed. She had defeated the odds, pulled off the impossible, and was now on her way to Junoko. She was still a few kilometers out, but the colony had long ago been visible on the flat lunar plain. What fate awaited her she didn't know, but with Salt and Ben both there and in search of each other, her destiny, for better or worse, lay on the horizon.

CHAPTER TWENTY-SEVEN

Ben monitored the Majog club from a shadowed doorway at the end of the tube. Patrons came and went, but he had no sense of the presence of Namacal operatives. He could feel Salt's energy with every move he made, but the fact that he had not seen him yet made him wonder if those sensations might be hallucinations. If so, who was projecting them? Shifting his thoughts into a defensive mode, he noticed a man exit the club and stop on the street to check for messages on a thumb nail monitor. Nothing unusual in that, but Ben noticed that his haircut was too long, and his shoes army issue. He quickly read his thoughts, which were simply about his desires over woman he'd just met inside. But through those patterns he picked up several brief interjections that told Ben the man was part of a mission – a mission led by Salt.

The Soldier clicked off the monitor, looked up, and noticed a woman smiling at him from a doorway across the tube. It was an entreating smile that all too obviously beckoned him closer. Male ego in tact, and curious to see how lucky he was, he accepted the entreaty. But by the time he reached the doorway, she had mysteriously vanished. It was a phantom move that he failed to completely grasp, but as he looked back over his shoulder, Ben slammed him into thewall. The impact shattered the hallucination, and by the time he realized what had happened, Ben had a gun to his head.

"Death is close at hand, so let's make this easy. I'm not interested in you, only in Salt."

"He just wants to talk with you."

"I'm sure he does. How many people in your unit?"

The word eight came out of his head before it came out of his mouth. Ben said nothing, just took his weapon and radio from him.

"Deliver a message to Mr. Salt for me. Tell him that the lie is not a lie and that I'll be seeing him soon to deliver the truth."

Ben stunned him with a pulse and lowered him to the ground. Leaving him unconscious, he disappeared through the doorway and came out into a different tube. He stopped, opened a channel on the Radio, and sent a call straight through to Salt.

"I left your man in the street, Commander." He said, his voice obvious to Salt's ear. "With a message of what's to come."

"So now you're a fortune teller?"

"You tell me. But if you are truly interested in the future, meet me at the Vapor in thirty minutes – but just you. If I see anyone else around you, I'll kill them."

****

Eliana hid the Rover in the scrub near the rear of Junoko and entered the complex through a delivery dock where supplies were unloaded. She was able to distract security and make her way into the tubes unimpeded. Once inside, she continued to the Majog where she slipped in the back door to meet with Lola, a bar maid she was friendly with. Lola told her that Namacal had been in asking questions about Ben, and her description of one of the man leading that group fit Salt to a tee.

****

The Vapor was a stained metal lunar eatery that offered synth beer, along with bar staples, and various other pleasures on the side. Salt monitored the comings and goings of its patrons from an adjacent tube. He was also reading random thoughts, shuffling innuendo, but picking up nothing that would aide him. As he moved forward, his eyes shifted like radar beams weaving through endless nuances of psychic energy. Windows in the surrounding buildings popped with living images, but they were only vaporous interpretations of shadows that faded in and out of his mind. Suddenly, something stopped him – a woman entered an adjacent cubicle, and at glance, she was a dead ringer for

Eliana. He could see her clearly, but didn't feel her. He slipped his hand inside his jacket, fingered his weapon, but didn't draw it. In spite of what he was seeing, he was immediately suspicious of his own mind and the tricks that might be underway. He scanned the tube expecting to see Ben break through the hallucination at any second, but it didn't happen. The woman suddenly appeared again, but this time in a different spot. He locked eyes with her, but was still unable to get a psychic reading. He rarely got nervous, but today his nerves were on edge. He was not prone to fear, but he was all too aware that he was in a cat and mouse game with people who were extremely competent. He felt challenged, but liked challenge, and firmly believed that he was the best player in the game and could not be defeated. He was already plotting multiple moves to respond to any encounter that came his way, real or illusionary. With these thoughts furrowing new tracks through his mind, the woman stepped out of the doorway and started toward him. He could feel the pull of her psychic will attempting to bend his own. She was still walking toward him, but he was hesitant to make a move, fearing that, even if she wasn't real, a ruse might still lay behind her smile. He waited for a moment more, feeling the strength of her presence, and then without prompt, drew his weapon and shot her through the head.

The instant the gun went off every eye in the tube turned. Salt had not moved and was still holding his weapon, but the woman was nothing more than a vapor. The gunshot was an echo, but an echo that had no resonance in reality. Salt had destroyed the hallucination with his mind, and all that remained was a blip on the surface of the hard copy world. As that blip dissolved, his eyes drifted up and down the real tube again. A lot of conflicting psychic energy was in the air, and though he had no true sense of Eliana, he was feeling the force of Ben's presence. He knew he was watching and wanted him to know he knew. To make that even more obvious, he strolled out into the middle of the tube and stood there spreading his arms wide and making hand gestures as if to say, "I'm alone and ready to talk." It was a clear visual message, but if Ben could see him, he didn't respond. Salt didn't like being manipulated and was tired of playing Ben's game. He started to walk away, but someone called his name – not out loud, but within his mind. His eyes shifted, and with that shift, the world turned abruptly upside down and presented him with an inversion of double realities. Momentarily disoriented, he wasn't sure what had happened, but from that skewed perspective, he saw Ben standing in the portal window of a cubicle next to the Vapor. His presence was indelibly strong and Salt felt certain this was the real Ben and not an illusion. His eyes shifted again and the world turned back upright. Curiously, it didn't break what he thought was an illusion. Ben was still in the window, signaling for him to come up.

Salt remained adverse to the game, but knew he had to play it out. He entered the building from the front and took the lift to the upper cube where Ben had been standing. He pushed the door open, but Ben was no longer there. He went to the same portal and looked out to the street. Ben was standing exactly where Salt had been a moment before – and was now holding a gun to the head of one of Salt's Rangers who had been hiding in the shadows.

"I told you to come alone." Ben called out over the tube noise. Salt felt even more manipulated than before and was about to voice his anger when Ben shot the Ranger point blank. At first Salt thought it was a hallucination, but as people on the street panicked and blood spewed from the man's head, he knew it was real and the game was no game. He drew his weapon, but Ben had already disappeared into the crowd.

By the time Salt reached the street, other Rangers were standing over the body. They were angry, and glared at Salt with condemning eyes. Their emotional directives couldn't have been more brittle if Salt had pulled the trigger himself.

****

Eliana returned to the Rikko where she saw Paramedics removing the bodies of the Clerk and Donna

Carrado. Seeing the body of her dead friend struck a hard emotional chord within her, and an even greater sense of disbelief. A small crowd had gathered, and wanting to know more about the events at hand, she eavesdropped on arbitrary thoughts and conversations. Although these reads suggested that Ben was the prime suspect, she found that difficult to accept. Ben might want vengeance, but he wasn't a capricious killer. Salt, on the other hand, could justify killing anybody, and intuitively, she sensed that it was he who had been involved. But why would he kill Donna, she wondered unless it was some diabolical plan to steal intelligence and frame Ben for the murder. The label of traitor and murderer would certainly seal Ben's fate. And that was typical of Salt's thinking. But as she was digesting these possibilities, one of Salt's Rangers stepped out of the crowd coming toward her. She didn't see him at first, but as he was about to grab her, she lunged to one side, and using a bystander as a temporary shield, was able to elude him. Gaining a second of momentum, she broke into a run, but he tackled her from behind and brought her to the ground. He rolled her over with a doubled fist, but discovered that it wasn't Eliana at all, but a woman dressed in similar clothes.

"Fuck." He bellowed, spitting the word out as he got to his feet. With eyes shifting, he spotted her again, hurrying into the turn of an alternate tube. He followed her round that corner, but there met the butt end of her pulser head-on. The next thing he knew he was on his back and she was on top of him.

"Where is Salt?"

"We're not looking for you."

"That's not what I asked."

"I don't know where he is."

She pulled the radio out of his pocket and shoved it in his face.

"Call him. Tell him where you are and that you have me in custody."

When he hesitated, she jammed the radio into his mouth bloodying his lips.

"This ain't no game, baby." She pressed down harder, squeezed a grunt of compliance out of him, then withdrew the radio and handed it to him. He tapped in the numbers on the keypad, but as the call was going through, he rolled to one side and kicked her feet out from under her. Suddenly he was on top of her, pounding her with punches. She tried to fight him off, but he was physically stronger and equally as willful. He stripped the pulser away from her, but as he did, it melted in his hand like a stick of butter. The sight of the melting gun stopped him and threw his mind a curve ball that he didn't see coming. He reeled backward trying to retrieve his consciousness, but she grabbed his wrist and twisted the gun back on him. The trigger went down and his head came off. The severed head rolled across the alley, eyes glaring up blankly. Eliana got to her feet, nose bleeding, and nursing a set of bruised ribs. Voices were approaching and alarms were ringing. She grabbed the radio and without missing a beat disappeared into the darkness at the end of the tube.

****

Salt and his men were in and out of every club, tech unit, and virtual cubbyhole in their ongoing search for Ben. The Rangers had been cautioned to be on the guard for strange sights or occurrences that might be hallucinations. The Pleasure Sector with its carnivalesque atmosphere offered plenty of visual oddities, so it was tricky terrain for anyone to be subjected to mind games. Some of the men were armed with telemetric weapons, also capable of creating hallucinations, but no situation had arisen that warranted their use. Salt observed everyone with suspicion, and though his neuro-scanners were up and well attuned to Ben's particular psychic vibe, he had yet to detect any impression of him.

After hours of searching, and with the men growing tired and agitated, Salt agreed to check the team into a Sleep Unit for a few hours of rest. A head count was taken that revealed one man missing. Salt tried to reach him via radio, but got no response. He went ahead, against his own internal directives, and dismissed the men, but kept trying to make radio contact on his own.

"Where the hell are you?" He spat into the receiver.

"Close." The voice on the other end suddenly came back. But it wasn't a male voice, or the voice he expected, but that of Eliana.

"Are you insane?"

"Of course, but you already knew that."

"Where is my Ranger?"

"Unfortunately dead."

"You are insane."

"I have to see you."

"There's nothing I can do for you."

"But there may be something I can do for you. You are still looking for Ben, aren't you?"

"Ben is a dead man."

"Sometimes the dead are known to rise. You're an expert player, Terry, but he may be better at this game than you gave him credit for."

"I gave him too much credit, and you the same."

"Then let me give something back. I can help you trap him."

"Why?"

"He wants me dead, just like he wants you dead. But you don't have any bargaining power, I do."

"Where are you?"

"Where are you?"

"Don't play games with me."

"There's no game. Bacaran Sleeper, unit 333."

"I'll be there."

****

Across the street from the sleeper, a woman stood in the shadows of an upper tier bubble cube. Her face was hazy and difficult to detail, but the silhouette of her body was strong and muscular. Her eyes were opaque, illusive, and focused directly on the Sleep Unit. She blinked once to the sound of a subtle telemetric click and then vanished. In that exact frame of time, Ben appeared in her place. His eyes were locked on that same room, the only room with any visible movement. A man was on the floor at Ben's feet, gagged and bound.

"Sorry for the inconvenience." Ben told him never taking his eyes from the portal. It was past midnight and everything was quite, but glancing down the tube, he saw someone scurry into an open doorway. He only got a glimpse, but the glimpse was enough to suggest that it was Eliana. Following his instincts, he hurried to that same doorway, but found only an empty cube. Even though no one was there, Eliana's psychic presence was strong and undeniable.

****

On the third tier of the Sleep Unit, all was quiet. Food trays had been left out in the hall, the only signs that the rooms were occupied. A utility Person came through pushing a service cart and stopped outside cube 333. She rang the electronic call buzzer, but no one responded.

"Cube Service." She said in a subdued voice. When no one answered, she tried the door and found it unlocked. Cautiously, she eased it open, immediately seeing signs of a struggle.

"Terry." She said tentatively, the voice clearly that of Eliana. She didn't advance, but made note of an overturned table and lamp. Pieces of broken glass were also scattered over the carpet. She drew her weapon and closed the door, but something immediately stopped her. On the other side of the bed, she spotted a body in a pool of blood. The eyes had been blown out of the sockets and the shattered pupils were glaring up at her. As horrific as it was, her suspicions told her it wasn't real. There was no sense of death in the room, nor did she feel the dissipating energy of the human spirit that would normally be evident. What she sensed instead was a living presence, a very strong and powerful sensation of life. Using the force of her psychic will, she broke through the illusion and the body on the floor disappeared. But by that time, Salt had already placed a gun to her head.

"Death comes to us all, but fortunately, it's not my time."

He carefully removed her concealed weapons and tossed them aside.

"I'm relieved."

"Of course you are. That's why you brought these with you."

"Tools of the trade; I'm just trying to stay alive."

"And you've done amazingly well. But you've only so many lives to bargain with, Eliana, and it appears you've used the last one."

"Didn't realize you'd been counting."

"Then you should have."

"Are you my judge and jury, Terry?"

"I don't make judgments; you did this to yourself.

"I've only done what I've had to do."

"Please Eliana, I can see right through you."

"And what do you see, black?"

" Not all black, but dark, very dark."

He didn't bother to elaborate, just slowly squeezed the trigger. As the cylinder turned, a strange hush swept through the room. Gunshots suddenly shattered the silence, but they came from the hall and not Salt's weapon. He turned toward the door, and in that brief break in his concentration; Eliana dove through the window to the tube below. She hit hard, but sprang back to her feet on the run. Salt tried to get off a shot at her, but more gunfire exploded behind him. He dropped to a defensive position, but in actuality there was no one there. The sequence of events had been nothing but a snap shot illusion. He fired another glance out the portal, but Eliana was already gone.

In the hall, he found the bodies of two of his men. Other members of his unit were in the stairwell engaged in a gun battle. Salt joined them just in time to see Ben fleeing at the foot of the stairs.

The Squad descended the stairwell in pursuit, but as they reached the tube, they suddenly felt themselves sink into an amorphous vortex. The tube spun sideways, disappeared, and left them free falling through a bottomless darkness. They clawed at the black emptiness trying to stop their fall, but no action worked as a preemptive. Gruesome, serpentine apparitions came at them like leaves swept up in a storm. Salt knew instantly that he'd been drawn into a hallucination, and igniting his will flipped the psychic switch. The telemetric manipulation dissolved, and he abruptly found himself back in the tube at the foot of the stairway. He was all right, but the rest of his men were on their backs writhing in epileptic-like seizures. Two of them weren't moving at all. One had taken a bullet to the head; the other suffered a gut wound. Salt grabbed the two remaining Rangers and shook them psychically from the stupor of their hallucination. Leaving them to peal back the cobwebs of illusion, he ran up and down the tube raging at every door and portal. Both Ben and Eliana were the source of that rage and he wanted them as desperately as he'd ever wanted anything in his life. But dead soldiers were lying in the tube street and it was only a matter of time before Junoko Security would show up asking questions, and he had no desire to explain himself. Sending the two Rangers off in one direction, he took an opposing route. But as he entered the tube that led back to the Pleasure Sector, he noticed that it was darker than usual. The overhead lamps were blinking on and off and that made him instantly suspicious that the world was askew. The strobe-like radiance of the lights was short-circuiting his mind and drawing him into a trance. Conjuring his psychic forces, he defied the draw and willfully stopped the blinking.

"Salt." A voice rang out.

He recognized the voice, but was unable to place it in space.

"Salt." The name came again, and this time he was certain that it was the voice of Eliana. That certainty was soon confirmed as he spotted her in a portal on the far side of the tube. She was staring directly at him, and the look was of such intensity that he could feel his head begin to swim. He closed his eyes, and made a concerted effort to break the mental delusion she was attempting to weave. As psychic cracks began to appear, he opened his eyes again, but she had vanished like a vapor. He went to the portal where she'd been, and there within a slender penumbra of light, he saw Ben telemetrically projecting her image. Salt fired, but Ben was gone even before the shot rang out. In his place were footsteps trailing off into the darkness.

Salt pursued those footsteps down a dark hall that led into another tube. But as he entered the new sector, he found one of the last of his men there on the ground, blood oozing from a head wound. Ben was watching his reaction from a shadowed niche just a few feet away. Salt couldn't see him, but knew he was there. He stepped to one side and the dead Solider rose up and flew toward the niche like a rabid vulture. The flying corpse burst through the hollow shadow and slashed at Ben with laser talons. Ben stumbled backward and fell, the Dead Soldier circling above him, hand talons extended, posed for the kill. But Ben saw through the image all the way into Salt's eyes where the projection was coming from. He snapped the illusion, rolled to the side, and lunged into an open doorway. The walls within were made of glucose, and people with fish heads were swimming there in thick, green effluvia. The rest of the room was splotched in timbres of aquamarine and the feeling was one of being inside of an aquarium. Ben tried to push through the glucose ethers, but his movements were strained and sluggish as if wading through syrup. Off to one side, he saw an inverted hammerhead shark with a spiked tail and spider eyes swimming toward him. But just as the jaws opened and were ready to snap, his training kicked in and he mentally broke through the hallucination. But Salt was still firing illusions one after the other. They were exploding like paint balls as they moved in and out of Ben's mind. To escape the assault, he dove through a side portal, but drug two of the illusions with him. They expanded on contact and stitched his mind with dozens of images that stretched the fabric of reality like ethereal taffy. More Hammerheads appeared along with horrific alien lunar bodies that shifted perpetually and had no stable definition. This strange world was rapidly wrapping around him and tightening its hold. But before he was completely submerged in this illusionary quicksand, he fired a counter projection back at Salt. Two serpents hit Salt in the face and wound their way down his throat. Four more circled his feet, tangled his step, and brought him to the knees. As he rolled across the floor, the illusions flew off him like a dog shaking water off its coat. Pieces of hallucinations splattered bystanders in the tube like illusionary slaps in the face. By the time Salt had fought off the thrust of these distortions, Ben had once again disappeared, or made himself invisible to the seeing eye of reality. Too many people were now in the tube, and Junoko Security was rushing in to investigate. Salt got back to his feet, and fleeing the onrush, made his way to an adjacent tube. There he stopped to catch his breath and center his mind. The engagement had been psychically brutal, and he was wary of more tricks, but he wasn't about to let Ben slip through his fingers. He continued down the tube firing arbitrary illusions left and right, but something suddenly made him stop and look back. The one surviving Ranger who had accompanied him was standing behind him motionless like a statue. There was a strange look on his face that Salt couldn't at first define. But then he saw it. A bullet hole was widening in the center of his forehead. And then his body folded like a paper napkin and dropped to the ground. Salt took a defensive stance and threw his scan out in a wide circle. There was no longer any sign of Ben, nor any sensation of his presence. That should have been a relief, but in that one split second, Salt felt so completely alone and vulnerable that it gripped the very fiber of his being. It was a moment of supreme weakness, but he refused to let it hold him. Junoko Security was rushing down the tube toward him, and for the immediate moment the danger had passed.

****

Salt returned to the Junoko Spaceport and the Craft that he and his men had flown in on. He was livid with anger over what had taken place in Junoko and anxious to return to the Namacal Base to regroup. But as he was crossing the tarmac to board the Craft, it burst into flames. Salt dove to the ground, pieces of debris shooting past him like bullets. When it was safe enough to raise his head again, he saw that the Craft was still in one piece and no explosion had occurred. Obviously another hallucination, and yet he felt no sense of Ben's presence near or far. He got back to his feet and started for the Craft, only to have it explode again. The force of the impact blew him backwards and set his ears to ringing. Once more he picked himself up, but reality rapidly shifted and remained an ongoing question mark. He had prepared a strong psychic defense before arriving at the Spaceport, and was surprised that Ben could have broken through it, but the events spoke for themselves. He waited for the hallucination to dissolve, but as metal fragments continued to rain down around him and chaos spread across the landing field, he realized that this time the attack was real.

Salt was stunned by the audacity of Ben's actions, but not alone in his staggering bewilderment. Eliana had witnessed the attack from the portal window of an observation tube just off the field. Ben, as she realized now, was much bolder than what she had believed him to be. He was much more than a psychic spy with a romantic bent; he was a hardcore warrior. And even though at the moment he seemed dead set on destroying Salt, she hadn't lost sight of the fact that their situation remained unresolved and he would be coming for her next.

****

With no flights leaving the Junoko Spaceport for hours, Salt opted to take a Land Tram back to the Namacal Base. It wasn't an ideal mode of travel, but it was safer than staying in Junoko without backup. The Tram consisted of three passenger cars that were rarely full. Most of the passengers were working personnel and enlisted men on leave from the front. Two MP's accompanied Salt and sat with him in the Officer's section of the first car.

As the Tram departed the Colony, he tried to rest, but was haunted by ongoing visions of death. He had always felt in control of his world, but the events of recent days had shaken his confidence and undermined his power. He held Ben accountable as the source of all his problems, and no matter how long it took or how far he had to push himself, he was determined to see him dead.

As the flat lunar Maria stretched out before him, he forced his mind into a more tranquil state and closed his eyes. But no more had he begun to let the strains of slumber wash over him than he felt a gun press against the back of his head. His eyes flicked open and the gun disappeared, but the MP's were no longer seated beside him. They were sprawled on the floor in pools of blood. As the blood streamed down the aisle, he expected to see Ben there with a smoking gun, but found Eliana instead.

"Jesus." He cried out, blinking his eyes and shaking off the illusion. No one was in the car but the MP's and there had been no shooting. Still, the image flash was so disturbing that he had to get up and pace to rid himself of the paranoia that it induced. It wasn't so much the illusion in and of itself that troubled him; but that his own thoughts were becoming more fear driven by the ongoing psychic attacks. He had never been one to succumb to fear, and was not about to let this be the exception, but he was fighting hard to stop an overwhelming feeling of weakness and doubt that kept creeping into his mind. The MP's watched him pacing, but respectfully said nothing. But then the lights in the car went out, and the MP's bounded to their feet. Salt wasn't sure what was happening, but even in the dim light, he could see them coming toward him, weapons cocked, ready to fire. But he fired first, and with zealous precision, shot both men dead. But as blood popped in ghastly splatters and their bodies toppled to the floor, the lights suddenly came back on. Pools of blood had formed into curdling waves, but Salt's mind was trailing far behind. Confusion blasted through his brain cells and left him questioning what he had just done. He had been under such relentless psychic attack that his perception of the MP's may have been yet another mental manipulation. But if so, that meant that someone had to be on the tram creating those illusions. Salt rushed to the connecting door of the second car and gauged it open. The expression on his face was indescribable as he discovered that there were no other tramcars behind him, only the open maria. He took one step back, trying to dislodge the image from his mind, and forcing his thoughts back to a reality base. The cars abruptly returned and the illusion vanished, but that did not ease the razor tensions that were clawing at the very fabric of his being. Instead of going on to the next car, he resealed the door and screamed out in rage.

"Goddamn you, goddamn you, goddamn you!"

With his voice reverberating, he suddenly felt a dark, foreboding presence. Ben's face flashed in front of him followed by that of Eliana. As their faces continued shifting from one to the other, Salt slammed his fist into the wall of the car and snapped the pattern from his mind. At that same moment, he felt a sudden chill wash over him. Looking down, he saw that he was standing in the blood of the men he'd just killed. Mixed feelings welled up inside of him, rage, confusion, and uncertainty, but he refused to submit to them. He wasn't about to play the role of victim for Ben, Eliana, or anyone. He rushed back to the door of the second car, yanked it open, and this time stepped inside.

Several passengers were there, all asleep, but for one young Soldier with a bad hangover. Salt quickly read his thoughts, which were essentially mindless.

"You lost?" The Soldier barked as he looked up and saw Salt watching him.

"No, but you will be if I hear another fucking word out of your mouth."

Seeing the viciousness in Salt's eyes, the Soldier sank back down in his seat.

Salt went on to the next car where he found only two passengers, both wrapped in blankets, heads tucked down between pillows. Although he couldn't see their faces, the obvious shapes of their bodies identified them as women. He tapped the first one on the shoulder, but as she lifted her eyes, she shoved a laser knife hilt deep into his stomach. The blade came out through his kidneys and shot a spray of blood across the aisle. He tried to grab her arm, but she rolled to one side and the other woman sprang up in her place. Salt drew his pulser, but before he could fire, both women were back asleep and he was still standing where he had been a moment earlier. There was no blood and no stomach wound. Furious at being tricked yet again, he backed away from the women and continued to the last car of the tram. Surprisingly, the car was completely empty, which caused him only more puzzlement. The hallucinogenic attacks were real, and the culprit had to be somewhere on the tram, but where? He remembered that there was a storage compartment on top of the tram, but it was not pressurized. There was also a small LRV attached to the tram roof that served as an emergency vehicle in case of a break down, but it too was not activated.

Unable to reconcile these events to satisfaction, he returned to the lead car. But this time he found that the two MP's he had left on the floor were now very much alive. There was no blood, no damage, and no aftermath to what he thought had happened. This twisted his psyche and spun his mind into overdrive. In the past, he had been able to beat back projected hallucinations, but now he was falling victim to them ever more frequently. Reality was getting exceedingly difficult to grasp, much less to adhere to. He was standing in the aisle staring at the MP"S, but no longer sure if they were real or not. They were staring at him too, but he was unable to place their expressions into a category of any logical form.

"You alright, Commander?" One of them asked.

"I have to get off this tram." He said, paranoia rising in his voice.

"Excuse me."

He didn't bother to explain himself, just busted the safety glass out of the security panel and pressed the emergency stop lever. The tram's brakes grabbed, hurled everyone forward, but by the time they came to a complete stop, Salt was already on his way out.

"Stay with the tram; reset the controls." He barked at the MP's. "I'm taking the LRV and going ahead."

"What's the problem, sir?"

"It's an emergency. I'll see you back at Namacal."
Without further account, he opened the roof hatch and crawled into the fin shaped upper compartment that held the LRV. He resealed the hatch leaving the MP's completely baffled as what had prompted such a sudden and unexpected exit.

****

Salt climbed into LRV's cockpit and prepared for engagement. It was a larger vehicle than the normal monopods, and capable of transporting a dozen people in an emergency. Checking the instruments and computer data to insure everything was in order, he fired the engines, and accelerated off the roof down to ground level.

Crossing the Maria at a clip just above cruising speed, he knew it would only take an hour at most to reach the base and he was already feeling better just to be off the tram. He was still troubled by the fact that he'd been so thoroughly out maneuvered, but now that he was alone in the LRV, he was once again beginning to feel some sense of control. But that moment of ease was short lived as the main engine began to skip. Warning lights flashed and fuel suddenly blasted out from the vent pipes.

"Fuck." He cried out. "Fuck?"
The mere idea of facing yet another obstacle was beginning to break him. Maybe it was nothing, and the engine would readjust, but it didn't. Instead, it began to limp and lose compression. He attempted to lower the torque to add more thrust, but nothing seemed to work.

"Goddamn it!!" he screamed, growing more flustered by the second. He continued to apply technical band aides, but the LRV simply wasn't responding. As the vehicle finally coasted to a stop, he got on the radio to report the malfunction and give his GPS to the base. But the radio also failed to respond, and produced no sound more than a thin line of static. He slammed his fist into the console in utter frustration.

"Fuck!"

As he continued trying to finesse the set into operational mode, a feeling came over him that he was not alone. His senses were always tuned to energy fields and this moment in time was no exception. Ben was standing behind him cradling an M77 Pulser.

"I fixed the radio before you boarded."

"How thoughtful of you."

"Knew you'd appreciate it."

"I appreciate excellence, and in that, you're no exception."

"Should we hug and kiss."

"This doesn't have to be this way, you know."

"You should have thought of that before you put out a kill order on me."

"It goes with being a traitor. And you didn't just betray me, you betrayed Namacal and your own country."

"Namacal is not my country. It was my country that sent me here."

"Amerex?"

"Corporations aren't countries, Salt, they aren't people, and they never will be."

"Semantics. Countries are passé'. We're on the universal plan now, and Namacal is the country of the future...something you obviously haven't been able to accept. You're very talented, but you've made some grave errors, and have ultimately put yourself in no mans land with little hope of redemption. But because I know who you are and the value that you represent, I could still create a place for you in our organization. I have the power."

"All my sins forgiven, and the slate washed clean. Sounds like a bargain. Only you're no longer in a position to bargain." But as Ben spoke the LRV was suddenly hit from behind, impacted forward, and rolled on its side. The next moment Ben found himself on the ceiling looking up at the floor. Salt was hanging onto to the arm of a cockpit seat, but losing his grip, dropped on top of him. Recovering the breath that had been knocked out of him, Ben found himself not upside down, but looking straight ahead into the business end of his own pulser. The illusion he'd just broken out of was brief, but effective, and Salt had once again regained the power position.

"You should have taken my offer when you had the chance. You've failed to see the bigger picture all the way down the line. It doesn't matter which side your on, Ben, as long as it's the winning side." Salt eased back on the trigger, but before it could engage, something hit the LRV again. This time the impact was much harder and sent everything into a spin. The Pulser came out of Salt's hand and slid across the floor. The LRV turned upside down, then toppled over a ledge into a shallow crater. Eliana brought her Pod to a skidding stop at crater's edge where she had just made impact.

She climbed down to the smashed vehicle and found the two men dazed, but not badly injured. She blew the cockpit door open, and greeted them with trigger ready pulsers in each hand. She didn't wait to exchange niceties, just pulled both triggers simultaneously. The explosions shattered the dead atmosphere, and the illusion at the same time. Ben and Salt were standing across from each other just as they had been; only now Eliana was beside them. She hadn't shot them, but she had slipped on board the instant they started to hallucinate. There was no crater and no wreckage, but the Pod she rammed them with was real and still parked behind them.

"You're no longer the dealmaker here, Terry, nor you either, Ben. I made you both the deal of all deals early on - be honest, be lovers, be true. And yet you both tried to kill me."

"That's bullshit." Salt bellowed.

"Shut up, Terry. I know what's real and what's not. I've had my fill of your manipulations. I may never make it off this cold slab of lunar rock alive, but neither will you."

"You're looking at this the wrong way; you can make it off alive." He fired back. "But you can't do it without me."

"Everything I've done to date of any merit, I've done without you."

"But I've always stood behind you. Who do you have behind you now? You've burned your last bridge. If you destroy me, you destroy yourself."

Ben said nothing, just watched and read between the lines of their interchange. They were difficult reads as they had always been, but now their thoughts were going back and forth like bullets flying through the air.

"You underestimate me, you always have."

But while her focus was sharply set on Salt, Ben slipped a laser knife from his pocket, and with a quick thrust, stabbed her dead in eye. She screamed in horror as the pupil popped, splattered eye tissue, and sent everyone into motion. But the motion was cut in half as the hallucination shut down as quickly as it came. Eliana found her eye untouched, but the dynamic between them had changed again. It was Ben who was now holding the gun on she and Salt.

"Sorry to break up the party, but I have something I need to say. You're the most amazing woman I've ever met...but also the most amazing liar. You shifted gears so many times you had my head spinning, and yet I still wanted to believe you. But not this time."

"Don't be stupid, Ben, this is not about us. It's only about stopping Salt and Namacal. That's all it was ever about."

"If you believe that crock of shit; you're a fool, Denning. She's double-crossed everybody she's ever come in contact with."

"Double-cross is double jeopardy and Namacal's philosophical credo, but not mine. I've only had one agenda from the beginning, and that was to uncover the truth behind this dirty war. Yes, I used you, Ben, but only to get to Salt. I knew that if you thought I'd betrayed you, you'd come after me. So in that sense I set you up, but I set myself up at the same time. I set myself up to be captured and brought back to Namacal. It was the only way to make Salt believe in me again, to trust me. Once I was back in the fold I knew he would want intelligence, but the intelligence I gave him was also a set up; you know that. But that wasn't my only directive; the more important action was to steal intelligence from him."

"She's working you, Denning, can't you see that? She's been working for us all along, and she's still working for us. You were and have always been only a pawn in the game – a pawn in the wrong place at the wrong time. I tried to help you, tried to open your mind to the truth, but she had her web so tightly wound around you that you couldn't see the nose on your own face."

"I'm not immune to truth, Salt." Ben barked back. "And I was never just your pawn, nor did I ever trust either one of you. But I knew I had to make it appear that way. And as long as you both thought you could control me, you gave me the upper hand."

"I wasn't trying to control you, Ben, then or now." Eliana said. "And you don't have to trust me or believe anything I say, but you do need to know the truth."

"And what truth is that?"

"The truth behind this war. What Salt and Namacal have been hiding since it all began."

"Another gambit, Denning."

"Shut up." He shouted at Salt, then glared back at Eliana. "You have a funny way of talking about truth, Eliana. New versions keep appearing all the time. Is this the latest version?"

"There is no latest version, but there is a different kind of truth, the only one that really matters. Lies have lives of their own, but what I told you, my feelings for you, those weren't lies. I lied about other things, yes, but they were necessary lies. I had to get close to Salt to get what I needed. There was no other way. The lies surrounding this war are sumptuous, but there is one lie greater than all the others, one that's been hidden, and for the sake of our future, needs to be revealed."

"She's playing you again, Denning, pitting us against each other, don't you see that?" Salt spouted.

"She doesn't have to pit us against each other, we are against each other. I'm pitted against you, everyone like you, and everything you stand for" He blurted, then turned his attention back to Eliana once again. "And the lie."

"The lie is the justification that puts all the wheels in spin - not territorial boundaries, not the fight for lunar terrain, not the battle to control Helium 3, but the essential lie, the greatest lie - the fact that there is no more Helium 3 on lunar terrain." She paused on that word, the revelation dropping hard and with resounding silence. "The foundation fields for Helium 3 have been depleted for nearly a decade. I have source code hard copy on that now, lifted and transcripted from the brain patterns of Salt and Namacal Command. The idea that these two corporations are fighting over territorial rights is a scam of the highest order, and has been used only to justify the war itself. Given that Namacal is the largest weapons manufacturer in the world, it only makes sense. They sell to everyone, including themselves and their archenemy, Amerex. The war is just a pretext, a theatre piece performed for the global public. Blood for gold; it's an age old game."

But just as she was about to continue, the gun flew out of her hand, hit the ceiling, and blew a hole through the roof. Simultaneously, Salt punched her in the face and knocked her to the floor. Ben grabbed him, pulled him off, only to find a sonic grenade hair triggered in the palm of his hand. Salt released the pin and the grenade exploded. The Rover blew apart, pieces of it flying off in a dozen different directions. The cockpit canopy crashed to the ground and blew open Ben's eyes -- he was on the floor of the Rover, Eliana standing over him with a gun to his head.

"Nothing is what it seems, Ben, you should have learned that a long time ago."

Salt was on the floor beside him, a bullet hole through his temple. Ben watched the blood flowing from the wound, trying desperately to grasp any thread of reality. Different images and scenarios kept shuttling through his mind, but finally he stopped the illusionary reel, and realized that the blood flowing from Salt's temple wasn't his blood at all, but a trickle that was running from the side of Eliana's mouth. It was she who was beside him, dazed from a blow to the face. As for Salt, he was nowhere. But from nowhere they heard the sound of an engine engaging. Ben and Eliana got to their feet, and rushed to the portal where they saw Salt in her Pod speeding off across the Maria.

"We have to stop him." Eliana cried out as she shook off the last vestiges of the illusion. But Ben was already moving and had dropped into the pilot's seat to engage the Rover's engines. Seconds later, they were in full throttled pursuit.

Salt pushed the Pod to full power, but Ben was gaining on him. Closing in from behind, he amped the speed to overdrive and rolled over the smaller Pod crushing it beneath the Rover's huge titanium wheels. Shards of glass and metal spewed out from beneath them like a spray of hard water as they brought the pursuit to a sputtering, splintering halt.

Jumping down from the Rover, they circled the crushed Pod searching for Salt, but found no sign of a body dead or alive. The lunar plain from horizon to horizon was also void of any life, which left them in a state of undefined puzzlement. Was it possible they were still trapped within an illusion? Even if Salt were dead, he could have projected a hallucination before his last breath. The possibilities were there, mental manipulations tickled their synapses, but no, the reality before them was real, and yet it still didn't account for the fact that they had not found a body.

Perplexed, but driven to siphon out the truth, they crawled beneath the Rover and examined the undercarriage. There was nothing obvious to the eye, but what Ben discovered after a needle and thread unstitching of the elements at hand appeared to be strands of bloody flesh and sinew wrapped around the transmission. He inched in closer, but as he reached out to touch one of the strands, he saw it move and drew his hand back. At that exact same moment, he heard the sound of an approaching Space Craft.

"It's a Namacal fighter." Eliana exclaimed, alarmed by its sudden appearance over the Maria. "A radio transmission must've gotten through."

With the Fighter on searing approach, and the Rover an easy target, they were already up and moving. There was nothing on the vast plain to offer them cover other than a small outcropping of rocks a quarter kilometer away. But time was slipping out from under them quicker than they could run. A second later, a laser rocket ripped through the Rover and blew it to pieces. A thousand metal fragments speckled the sky and coated the ground in a dew of black metal dust. As the smoke cleared, the Fighter looped back around and circled the area several times. Given that there were no signs of survivors, no signs of life, the Fighter finally soared away into the thin atmosphere beyond. But as soon as the Craft was out of view, Ben and Eliana emerged from the rocks. They were safe and uninjured, but the Rover and Pod had both been completely destroyed.

"If we can get back to Junoko, I have people there who can help us." Ben said.

She looked at him quizzically, not quite grasping who the people were he was referring to. "The International Peace Task Force...they're the ones who organized my mission."

At that moment it became clear to her who Ben had been working for all along. And though it didn't come as a complete surprise, it was a revelation that she hadn't read before hand. And that made her smile.

With darkness settling in and the temperatures steadily dropping, they started off on foot to make their way back to Junoko. But before they were even out of sight of the destroyed Pod, the regolith beneath it shifted and formed a slight indentation. Something was there, moving, emerging.

CHAPTER TWENTY-EIGHT

In a Junoko Conference room, the Peace Delegation led by Chancellor Soledad was meeting with Junoko Officials to discuss the various options for bringing an end to the war. The discussions had come to an impasse, as was common in any effort to reach an agreement on peace. But as the particulars of the stalemate continued to be discussed a Delegate came in with a message for Soledad. The indication in his eyes was obvious that something important had occurred. Soledad excused himself and went outside for privacy.

The transcripted message was that a Namacal Communication had been intercepted regarding the attack on an LRV traveling on the lunar Maria. Soledad had received an earlier report regarding the confrontation between Ben and Salt, so this appeared to be a connecting piece to that encounter. He immediately requested that the Junoko Council send out a Rescue Craft to search for survivors.

****

The Rescue Craft, given a GPS location, was flying low over the designated area in a grid pattern. The flat and lifeless nature of the terrain provided excellent visibility and it wasn't long before Soledad and the Pilot spotted two people crossing the plain on foot. Bringing the Craft to ground, Soledad jumped out and ran to greet the two itinerants. He had never met Eliana, but he obviously knew Ben well. The two men embraced like old friends.

"We have them." Ben said with a weary smile.

CHAPTER TWENTY-NINE

Soledad arranged passage for Ben and Eliana on a Shuttle leaving from the Junoko Space Port back to Earth. They waited in the bubble domed passengers lounge as loading preparations were being completed.

"And I thought I was the slippery one." Eliana said to Ben. "I don't even know how you did it. I read you inside and out, and still never saw through your disguise."

"Because it was no disguise, I tricked my own mind via self-hypnosis to disbelieve what I wanted hidden. I formed a mental block around the mission and stored it in a neural basement room for which only I had the key. Even if you found the room, you couldn't get inside. I'd given myself various triggers to help me find the way back. One would lead to the other, but in the interim I was almost ninety per cent self induced amnesiac, and that was the best defense I could have created."

"It worked, but I'm still surprised Salt didn't sniff it out. He was so unbelievably good at that kind of thing."

"He did sniff it out, but he thought it applied to Amerex, and never went far enough to discover there was another door beyond the one that he had opened."

"And you seduced Amerex into the same game."

"It was a necessary gambit in order to hide the real mission and keep both sides off balance. Amerex thought I was theirs all along, but they never had a clue."

****

The Shuttle blasted off from the Junoko Space Port for its sojourn back to Earth. Ben and Eliana were safely on board, happy to at last be leaving the moon. The great blue orb of Earth lay directly ahead, and it had never looked more beautiful. A look into Eliana's eyes left Ben savoring that same sense of ethereal beauty in her.

"It's been an amazing journey."

"Even more amazing that I'm off that rock and still alive." She said. "I'm an eternal optimist, but truthfully, I never thought I'd make it out alive."

"But you did it."

"We did it."

Soledad stepped in and sat down beside them.

"And you both did it well. But we still have work to do. We may have won the battle, but we've not yet won the war. Namacal is now claiming they have found new fields of Helium 3 on earth – fields that are conveniently located in disputed territory. Sound familiar?"

"Business as usual." Ben said.

"Salt believed that perpetual war was the way of the future." Eliana interposed. "And the profits gained from those endeavors would be beyond anything ever imagined. Given his psychic skills, he had become a very powerful man in that network. He knew every secret behind Namacal Policy, but he forgot one important thing - when he opened his mind to me, his secrets came with it."

"No secret policy can last forever. But revealing their secrets won't stop them from creating new policy. Our job now is to increase public awareness." Soledad added.

"Easier said than done. The truth is not something the public readily wants to embrace. If it was, Corporations like Namacal would have never risen to power in the first place."

****

The Shuttle returned to earth landing at the International Space Port in the California desert. Ben and Eliana deboarded and crossed the airfield to the Re-Entry Facility. As they were approaching the first Security Check Point, Ben noticed a maintenance crew working on a disabled Fighter in an adjacent hangar. There was nothing unusual in what he saw, but intuitively he picked up a rogue pattern of broken thought. Eliana sensed the same current at the exact moment, but before either of them could react, automatic weapons fire broke out. Ben took a shot in the shoulder and went down. One of the maintenance crew had appropriated a fueling truck and was firing at them as he raced across the tarmac. Eliana dropped beside Ben, bullets pinging all around her. Ben had only one good hand, but was still able to draw his Pulser and clip off a shot. The shot hit the truck's gas tank and ignited it. The Assailant lost control of the truck and crashed into a Fighter Jet off to one side of the runway. Both the Fighter and the truck exploded on impact.

Ben and Eliana got back to their feet, the sky full of fire and sirens going off all around them. They knew from the first shot that the attack was not random and that they had been the intended targets. Someone had obviously ordered the hit, and there was little doubt in their minds who that someone might be.

CHAPTER THIRTY

Ben was taken to International Infirmary where he was treated for the gunshot wound. Eliana and Soledad joined him at bedside and two Guards were stationed outside for protective measures.

"The shooter was a Namacal Operative who had infiltrated the motor pool some weeks back." Soledad said. "They knew exactly who you were and when you were coming in. Our intelligence sources tell us a price has been set and a large bounty placed on both of your heads."

"Lovely. But once we go public with our report, they'll have to back off." Eliana said with a degree of confidence. "Our profile we'll be too high to risk outright assassination."

"I don't think they'll give a damn about our profile." Ben argued. "Given that most of the media is controlled by Namacal, and there's no way to get our story out on the broader scale, at least as nothing more than conspiracy theory; you can be sure they'll attempt to bury it in whatever way they can."

"They can slow it down, they can diffuse it, but ultimately they can't stop it." Soledad added. "The truth can only be hidden for so long."

"But how long?" Ben said pensively.

Out the window of the infirmary, the moon was just beginning to rise in the evening sky. It was in its fullest phase and seemed to be glowing more brightly than ever. But the perspective was quite different as seen from a different window some distance away. There, dark clouds shaded the moon and gave it an eerie glow. Salt was standing at that window taking it in, feeling the subtle pull of its magnetic force. And though it held a definite fascination for him, his thoughts weren't on the moon, but on Ben and Eliana. They had betrayed him and left him for dead, but he was far from dead, and soon they would know the true power of his wrath. And contrary to popular belief, and the waxing and waning of truth and lies, the war wasn't ending; it was actually just beginning.

ABOUT THE AUTHOR

D.J. Wallace, (AKA Doug Wallace), has been a writer in Hollywood, working in both Film and Television, for many years. He began his career writing for the TV Shows "Monsters" and "Tales from the Dark Side". He went on to write the feature film "Sensation" which premiered on HBO and is currently distributed by Sony Entertainment. After optioning several screen properties to independent producers, he sold the feature film "Sevens" to Warner Brothers, "Gargoyles" to Paramount, and wrote a Sci-Fi feature for Summit Entertainment. Early in his career he worked as a Story Analyst for NBC, Showtime, Imagine, and Turner Entertainment among others. He was also a contributor to "Ask the Pros", a book on screenwriting. He has written two novels to date, the Sci-Fi Thriller, "Phase Out – The Liar's Moon", and Book One of the Fantasy Trilogy, "A Force of Will". He is currently working on his third novel.